To my ...

Enjoy the show.

DEATH TROUPE

Vincent H. O'Neil

www.vincenthoneil.com

Also by Vincent H. O'Neil

The Frank Cole Mystery Series:

Murder in Exile

Reduced Circumstances

Exile Trust

Contest of Wills

This book is dedicated to the graduates of the

Fletcher School of Law and Diplomacy

at Tufts University

past, present, and future

but especially the classes I knew

1995-1998

Pax et Lux

Acknowledgments

In 2009 I took part in a play at the Sleuthfest mystery convention in Deerfield Beach, Florida. The courtroom comedy-drama was developed by the talented (and undiscovered) writer Victoria Landis, and I was deeply impressed by the story's twists and turns. Many other gifted people participated, including Vicki's partner-in-crime (and undiscovered writer) Ann Meier. Although *Death Troupe* bears no resemblance to that play, it did give me a nudge toward writing a mystery theater-themed novel.

In addition, I want to thank the friends and relatives who read this book in essentially draft form. I would especially like to mention three of my West Point classmates who helped out: Michael McGurk, who was assigned to the American embassy in Paris at the time, John Surdu, who read the book while deployed in Iraq, and Meg Roosma, who brought a lifetime of stage experience to the project. Many thanks.

As for the murder mystery play in 2009, I won't reveal who the true culprit was—other than to say that my character got away with murder.

Chapter One

Counting the man in the casket, the troupe was all assembled. It could have been a curtain call at one of their annual performances, with the cast arrayed on stage, taking their bows to what was always explosive applause.

They were not on stage, of course, and that day's costuming— variations on the shade of black—bespoke a different venue altogether. The Jerome Barron Players stood on a gently sloping hillside in a snow-covered Maine cemetery, surrounded by grave markers that in some cases dated back centuries. A carpet of fake grass had been laid around the casket, an ostentatious piece of furniture whose brass handles and rich wood gleamed in spite of the overcast. A gray-haired minister in vestments was speaking to the crowd, but the man observing the scene was much too far away to hear any of it.

But not too far away to identify the players. Partially hidden by a large stone cross, the man could make out the gray beard of Jerome Barron—director, manager, and God of all Gods for the actors, designers, and minions informally known as Death Troupe. The Director was bundled up in a long coat, wide-brimmed black hat, and a scarlet scarf which probably rested on one of his trademark turtleneck shirts. Barron occupied center stage as usual, with the dead man's only living relative—a sister who had heartily disapproved of the troupe—standing to his left.

The position to his right was taken up by the company's leading lady and the crown jewel of the Barron Players, none other than Allison Green. Her famous blonde locks hung straight down from a fur-trimmed hat, framing the oval face which had enthralled audiences all over the globe. There was no smile today, and the man watching the ceremony pondered which role Allison might have selected for the occasion. Earth Mother Allison. Grieving Paramour Allison. Unfaithful Girlfriend Allison.

Despite the mockery of his thoughts, the man was still drawn to her. Allison's eyes were her greatest feature, depthless emeralds that seemed to pull in all the light around her. He remembered the first time he'd seen her in the flesh, and then the first time he'd seen her naked, and allowed himself to wonder if he'd ever see that again. Maybe.

He took a moment to look around him, making sure that he was indeed alone in this section of the graveyard. It would not do to be recognized, hovering there, watching. The cold, white scenery stretched out all around him, crowded with marble and granite testimonies to the inescapable march of time.

Alone. Outside the group. As always.

Looking across the rolling landscape, he noticed how the more distant headstones, black against the snow, resembled the stumps of a recently cleared forest. All of this had been woodland once, and he marveled that living things could be cut down to make way for dead ones. A chill wind slid over the frozen whiteness, migrating across the border from Canada in much the same way as the dead man's forebears. The Betancourts had made a fortune in Maine timber and, although none of them now lived in the area, most of them chose to be buried there.

His gaze returned to the black-clad assembly, noting which eyes were being daubed and which were not, before he reminded himself that the actors were not the only players in the group. They were all part of the same con game, the annual stage production which pitted the wits of an entire town against the collective wiles of Jerome Barron and his company of deceivers. The rumors about the Barron Players were legion: Death Troupe actors could switch the play's ending on a mere hand signal from the Director, who often designated the production's murderer in mid-performance. The troupe's design team, a twisted gang of special effects wizards, lived for the chance to divert the attention of an entire audience already primed to resist such chicanery. The play itself, an original work penned by a writer residing in that year's host town, contained so many alternate endings that the script looked like a telephone book.

8

The chameleon-like transformation of the troupe's playwright had always fascinated the man watching the funeral. The writer—or writers; at one point there had been two—would begin his residence as an outright celebrity, wined, dined, and spied upon by many of the locals. As the months went by, however, he would become such a fixture in the host town, scribbling in a notebook here or tapping on a laptop there, that he would virtually disappear. Although he created the play's blueprint right under the audience members' noses, by the time the troupe got there the playwright would be almost completely overlooked.

As always.

Except maybe not today, the man mused. Today one of the troupe's writers had managed to seize center stage in the most final curtain call of them all. He might be taking his bows from inside the casket, but even that fit the theme: There was always a corpse when Death Troupe came to town.

Part One

The Players

Chapter Two

Jack Glynn took a deep breath before pushing on the hotel's frosted revolving door. It had been two years (two performances in Jerome Barron-time) since he'd seen any of the others, and he was unsure of his welcome. He wore a maroon sweater over a black collared shirt, khaki trousers, and snow-dusted hiking boots. He'd left his coat in the rental car despite the night's coldness, knowing that a good entrance meant something to this particular crowd.

Ryan Betancourt, his old writing partner and the subject of the evening's reception, had had a saying about this: Actors are all about entrances, but writers are all about exits.

Ryan had been full of pronouncements like that, but Jack agreed with this one. Theater actors sought to hold the attention of live viewers, and knew that an entrance was usually the best opportunity to create that interest. Writers, on the other hand, shaped everything from entire acts to single lines so that they built toward a particular result. Some of these exploded in jaw-dropping climaxes, while others merely set up whatever followed.

Once warmed to the subject, Ryan had usually gone on to compare writers to the best pool hustlers, the ones who sink the ball while arranging their next shot so that it all looks like an accident. When no actors were present, he would conclude by saying that the entrance-obsessed thespians were more like pool parlor rubes—a loud break and very little else.

Having worked so hard on his entrance, Jack was a little disappointed to see that the hotel's bright lobby contained no one he recognized. The members of Death Troupe were nomadic by nature, and it was unusual not to find one or two of them simply wandering around. Their absence reminded Jack that he had no idea what part of the hotel had been selected for the troupe's remembrance of their deceased writer. He looked around for guidance, half expecting to see a sign directing the hotel's guests to the Smith Wedding Party or, in this case, the Ryan Betancourt Funeral Reception.

He didn't have to look for very long, as a brief burst of laughter rumbled from somewhere to his right. The hotel was spread across two large wings with its back to a mountain, and its lobby seemed designed to contrast with the dark and cold outside. All caramels and greens and potted tropical plants, it was tastefully lit up with hidden track lighting and two massive chandeliers. Jack passed beneath these as he headed toward the noise that had to be Death Troupe. Even in mourning, they were loud.

Jack was thirty-two, not tall and not short, and the most remarkable thing about his appearance that day was the deep tan under his closely-cut black hair. His eyes were an observant brown, and they roamed over the lobby's many sofas and chairs as he walked. He felt it odd that none of the Troupe's members or hangers-on were seated there, knowing how quickly the band broke into smaller groups that drifted around the main party like ice floes surrounding an Arctic island.

He passed through an open glass door and found himself on a small landing looking down into the hotel bar. The carpet was green, the walls were caramel, and hourglass-shaped wall sconces bathed the room in a warm wintertime glow. To his left a gang of locals was watching a hockey game on a widescreen television, but the real show was in front of him.

The bar narrowed after the television area, and the bottleneck was crammed with people. Jack finally saw a few faces from the old days, but was dismayed to note just how many of the attendees were strangers. He told himself they must be relatives or friends, unwilling to think that the troupe had changed so radically in his absence. As he stepped down into the well, Jack pondered the idea that some of the new faces might be replacements instead of additions, and calculated who else might be missing from the group he remembered.

In addition to their playwright, of course.

"Jack Glynn!" A man with graying black hair and a merry smile grabbed him with one arm, artfully managing not to spill the drink in his opposite hand. "I was wondering when you'd show up."

He returned the hug sincerely, liking this actor more than most of the others. His stage name was Anson Addersley, but within the group he was known as Puff. Celebrated on two continents while still in his twenties, Addersley was one of the troupe's few real stars of the stage. He loved the Barron Players, and it was rumored that the contracts for all his other appearances gave Death Troupe total precedence. He enjoyed mysteries of all kinds, and believed that Barron's brainchild was the only true innovation to come out of theater in the last two decades.

"Anson." Jack took a step back from the older man, but still stayed close. It was hard not to, as they were now inside the bottleneck created by the crowded bar off to the left. Jack craned his neck to get a better look around, noting that much of the group still wore outfits befitting the funeral which he had missed. Many of the others, presumably staying at the hotel for the night, had taken the opportunity to change into more comfortable and less somber clothes.

As if changing costumes between acts, the burial now dismissed as a scene that had already been played.

"Sorry I didn't make it in time. My flight got hung up at O'Hare, and then I got turned around on the road . . . how did it go?"

Addersley raised his free hand, palm up, while shrugging both shoulders of his gray suit. "Considering the circum-stances, not bad. It was a graveside ceremony—you probably knew Ryan wasn't religious—and then we came back here. His sister was at the cemetery, but she left for the airport right after that." He smiled at the nearby throng, like a tolerant uncle supervising a teenage barbecue. "Can't say I blame her; our little bunch never could stay subdued for long."

Jack had just picked out a few more familiar faces when a pair of younger men emerged from the crush like dark matter ejected from the sun. Although their eyes were fixed on him he knew he'd never met them before, as they were a type which he'd trained himself to notice and avoid. Their hair was too well-managed, their clothes were the latest style, and he'd learned to steer clear of people like them during his brief trips to Hollywood. They were clearly headed straight for him.

"Jack Glynn? Are you Jack Glynn?" They both spoke at once, smiling, but their raised voices sounded almost accusatorial. One had light brown hair cut like a monk's tonsure, and the other's was cropped so short that it was hard to tell if it was light or dark. Their too-smooth complexions and insanely fashionable boots put the tally over the top for Jack, who decided then and there that he didn't like them.

"It's Jack Glynn indeed, straight from his Hollywood bun-ga-low!" Puff bellowed this at the interlopers while giving Jack's left elbow a gentle squeeze from behind. The pressure gave him a moment of genuine warmth, as this was an old Death Troupe signal, a warning that they were in the presence of overly interested outsiders.

He found a bland smile slipping onto his face, his practiced response from the old days. "Arizona, actually. I don't spend much time in LA."

"And why would you?" Puff didn't let the two newcomers launch into their act just yet. "You took the place by storm, so why stick around?"

Jack found the bland smile slipping, and fought off the blush of embarrassment that threatened to replace it. "I just got lucky, that's all."

Puff turned an open palm at him, as if inviting the other two to have a look. "Listen to him! Pens the script for the biggest war movie in decades, and he calls it luck."

"*Beaten Ground* the biggest war movie in decades? It hasn't even started *filming* yet." The monk-haired one said this, his eyes squinting as if he were in pain. Whatever had brought these two over, Jack guessed that they were somehow connected in Hollywood—or wanted to be.

"And who cares if they never make it at all?" Puff was enjoying himself, having lured the two men off the path that lead to whatever they'd meant to discuss. "How much did they pay you for the script, Jack?"

"Oh, let's not talk about money, shall we?" Jack adopted Puff's buoyant manner, hoping to move the conversation away from his recent coup. "To answer your first question, I am Jack Glynn. Former writer for this gang of gypsies. And who might you be?"

"I'm Mickey Parsons, and this is Todd Lambert. We work for a good friend of yours." The monk said this, and the burr-cut picked up the next line as if they'd practiced it.

"The head gypsy, to be specific—"

Jack cut him off, already guessing that they worked for Allison. "Oh, so Barron finally got some extra helpers? That's great! Berni always did have too much on her plate."

"Poor, overworked Berni." Puff shook his head minutely, his lips pressing together while his eyes sought the carpet. Jack tried hard not to laugh at this, as the Director's diminutive assistant Bernice could turn out more work than the rest of the troupe combined. She seldom seemed to sleep, was maniacally devoted to Barron, and wouldn't have allowed these two knuckleheads anywhere near her turf.

"I meant Allison Green." hissed the short-haired Todd, his eyes burning holes in the top of Puff's head.

"Oh, Allison! I get it, the head gypsy. Sure." Jack lowered his voice, remembering why he was there. "How's she taking this?"

"Very well . . . considering how close she and Ryan were." Mickey threw that one in, his head bobbing as if suggesting agreement while Jack darkly considered how anyone could refer to lovers as being 'close'.

Puff touched Jack's arm in an effort to disengage him. "Drink, sailor?"

"Yeah, that would be great." Jack moved a shoe in Puff's direction. "It was very nice meeting you—"

"Actually, we wanted to ask you a question." Mickey turned an expectant face toward Puff, who returned it. A second passed, and then another. "He won't be a minute."

Puff kept it up for a moment longer before letting the mask dissolve into a laugh. "See you at the bar, Jack." He turned a shoulder and passed through the crowd like a ghost.

Jack put the bland smile back in place, feeling his heart starting to beat just a bit faster inside his sweater. A question. From Allison?

Both Mickey and Todd moved in a little closer and Jack inclined his head, for the first time wanting to hear what they had to say.

"Is it true that you walked away from Barron? Just up and quit?"

As big questions go, it was a disappointment. Particularly when he had harbored some small hope that Allison had dispatched her minions to find him.

"I didn't quit. Barron asked me to oversee the film version of *The Wind in the Palms*."

"Oh, right. Which one was that? The troupe's third show?"

"Fourth." The wildly successful *Wind in the Palms* performance had put Death Troupe on the map, and it had been optioned for a movie deal a year later. As it was the last play he'd written for the troupe all by himself, Jack had agreed to adapt it for the big screen. When resigning a year after that, he'd gone along with the cover story that he'd be shepherding the script through the valley of death which sometimes leads to the big screen.

"Well whatever the number, it's stuck in Development Hell. Lucky you had another script handy." Development Hell: Wannabe-speak for a film project lost somewhere between a good idea and actual production, usually for lack of funding. Not that it mattered to Jack; he'd never believed that the play's appeal would transfer to the

17

cinema anyway. His sham management of the project had yielded an unexpected opportunity, however: A chance introduction had put Jack's now-famous *Beaten Ground* script in the hands of people who could actually make a movie. They'd paid handsomely for that right, even if they didn't know the age of the script which they had called fresh and innovative.

"That's right—lucky me. Listen, is Allison actually here? I'd like to speak to her."

Mickey and Todd didn't miss a beat, trading off on their prepared lines. "Oh sure, sure. She's upstairs, taking a break."

"Exactly. As you can imagine, this whole thing has been rough on her."

"Losing Ryan like that . . ."

"So tell us: Are you really finished with the troupe? That big check for *Beaten Ground* got your feet planted out west?"

There. That was it. Jack finally saw why Allison's servants were talking to him, and decided to have some fun with it. He furrowed his brow before asking in a low, concerned voice: "Is Allison thinking about leaving the troupe?"

Though he caught them off guard with that one, they didn't seem to mind. Mickey answered first. "Oh, don't we wish! Don't get me wrong; Allison owes so much to this . . . experience. It's just that the success she's had with the last two movies . . ."

"Exactly. Did you know she *just missed* a Best Supporting Actress nomination?"

"I heard something like that." Jack had heard no such thing, but he'd read the raves about Allison's last role. The critics had loved it, and more than one of them had suggested it was high time for Allison Green to leave the stage for good.

I wonder what the Barron thinks of that idea.
Maybe I should ask him.

It took almost an hour to work his way through the jam, but Jack didn't mind. Five minutes after leaving Mickey and Todd he was honestly questioning why he'd been concerned about reuniting with the old gang. Although he supposed his two-year absence might have made some hearts grow fonder, he didn't remember being this popular when he'd been writing the words that the troupe presented on stage.

The next face he recognized was Robert Hale, the troupe's Leading Man actor. Jack had come to regard each of the players in terms of their most common assignments, and Hale was almost always cast as the lead male, in roles ranging from the unjustly accused to the crusader seeking the true murderer. Aged thirty, with thick brown hair and matinee idol good looks, he was a game if limited performer. Jack remembered him as a hard worker who quickly learned every version of the play and also seemed at ease with Barron's demanding style.

"Jack of Arabia! Or is it Arizona?" Hale gave him a hug, dragging him into the center of an admiring circle. Jack didn't know any of them, but Hale quickly cleared that up. "Gang, this is the troupe's first writer, the guy who put us on the map before he ran off to the desert and started writing for real money. I give you the wordsmith himself, Jack Glynn."

Hale was wearing a black tie and a white shirt over a pair of black trousers, but he'd presumably exchanged his suit coat for the blood-red v-necked sweater that now made him look like a college kid. That fit the look of his little clutch, all under twenty-five and mostly female. Their dress was even less somber than Hale's, and Jack tucked them into the category of local celebrity hounds. He answered the obligatory questions about *Beaten Ground*, waited until they lost interest in him, and pushed on.

The next segment of the throng was composed entirely of familiar faces, and he managed to get through it without revealing that he didn't recall many of their names. Jack felt bad about that, as they were the troupe's costume designers and had what he considered the toughest job of all. In most productions the arrangement of the set and the design of the costumes were decided early on, but not so with the Barron Troupe. The whole secret to fooling audience after audience lay in keeping as many options open as long as possible, and the Director was infamous for last-minute changes to costumes and props. The set designers received only slightly more lead time, and of course the writer went through a similar wringer, but the costume people were the ones who truly bore the brunt of Barron's manic intellect.

Strangely, they were also the group within the group that seemed to mind it the least. Jack respected them because they always responded with an easy calm, no matter what Barron sprung on them —in marked contrast to some of the actors. Over time he had come to suspect that they viewed Barron as a kind of emotional cripple, a clumsy member of the herd that had to be protected and understood. Jack didn't stay with the costume folks long, even though one of the men brought him a rum and coke (his second) before he moved on to the next bunch of familiar faces.

He now passed the flight of carpeted stairs that led up to the high landing that was the bar's main entrance. The doors at the top were propped open, and through them he could see part of a mezzanine, complete with sofas and armchairs. Looking up the stairs, he finally found one of the satellite parties that he'd expected to encounter in the lobby. It was a younger group, and he recognized its central character.

Kirk Tremaine, the twenty year-old actor who normally played firebrand roles ranging from misunderstood teenager to budding journalist, was orating to anyone who would listen. Sally Newsome, his blonde counterpart in age, looked up at him from one of the sofas with an expression that combined affection and concern. Tremaine's dark bangs slid down across his booth-tanned forehead as he spoke, and he impatiently combed it back without missing a beat.

Impatient. That was Tremaine in a word. Sally knew how to balance him, though, and could usually keep the young actor from seriously locking horns with Barron. At least that was how it had worked when Jack had been with the troupe; he'd often written them both into the same scenes to preserve that equilibrium.

Standing at the foot of the stairs, he now saw that the lounge was formed in an L-shape, and that the main entrance was where the two legs came together. Jack had worked his way through the long leg of the L, and finally found the Director when he turned to look down the shorter axis. The bar ended in a small alcove, which resolved into a large leather booth as Jack approached. Had he known of this spot, he could have guessed Barron's location without ever leaving Arizona because the booth was the only seat in the room that resembled a throne.

At sixty years of age, Jerome Barron would have looked much younger were it not for the steel gray hair which covered his head and lower face. He wore one of his famous long-sleeved turtleneck shirts, this one a rust color. Though seated, it was obvious that Barron was a tall man; both of his long arms stretched along the back of the booth. His shoes rested on the square table in front of him, almost touching an earnest young woman seated across from him who was jotting something down in a small flip-top notebook.

Jack might have mistaken the girl for Berni, Barron's assistant, except that Berni had a photographic memory and seldom wrote anything down. She was also present, seated to Barron's left and keeping a close eye on the lady with the notebook. Both women were small in stature, both wore jacket-and-skirt business outfits, and they both had dark hair pulled back and pinned behind their heads. The earnest young woman wore a pair of circular glasses, and Berni was regarding her without any ocular assistance.

"Of course Ryan is a big loss to the troupe, not just because he was a brilliant playwright but because he was such a mainstay of the whole performance. He was the complete package, and he understood theater in a way that I quite frankly have seldom found in a writer." Barron's deep, deliberate voice easily floated over the nearby people that Jack didn't seem to notice anymore. It was always like that. Barron commanded attention even when he was talking to someone else.

Jack stopped just short of the alcove, waiting for the interview to end and sensing that Barron had tossed in the compliment of Ryan's ability solely for his benefit. The Director had told him many times that writers knew even less about theater than actors did—and that actors knew almost nothing at all. Standing there with the bland smile back on his face, Jack wondered just what Barron had meant to say before noting his approach. After altering the endings of so many murder mysteries while the play was in progress, it was no chore for Barron to do the same thing in mid-sentence.

The girl with the glasses started asking another question, but Berni rose with an air of finality and told her that it was time for the Director to spend some time with his fellow mourners. The reporter gave Jack a slight glance as she passed, and he caught himself feeling disappointed that she hadn't recognized him.

Since when does anybody recognize the playwright? And what *mourning?*

He kissed Berni on the cheek before leaning across the table to shake Barron's hand, offered from the sitting position. He cracked a grin at the older man as he sat down. "I had no idea you liked Ryan so much."

Barron pressed his lips together and tilted his head to one side for just a moment, his patented expression of disagreement. "He was a gigantic pain in the ass. Thank God you're here, Jack; I've wanted to say that to *somebody* for the last week."

"So why say it to me?" Jack felt himself sinking into the oversized seat cushion. "Because we wrote together and I knew him best?"

"Nah. It's because no one listens to you. You could repeat it a thousand times and it would never come back to me."

"As if you'd care, even if it did." Jack laughed as he said this, inured to Barron's insults.

Barron studied him for a moment or two. "So look at that tan. Been writing all those golden scripts outdoors?"

For the second time that night Jack's smile almost slipped, and for the same reason. *Does he know? How could he? No one knows except me.*

He willed the smile back into place. "Writing? Haven't you heard the news? I hit the jackpot. I'll never write another word."

"Then the old saying's true: 'tis an ill wind indeed that doesn't blow some good."

Jack shook his head slowly, for once unwilling to let Barron control the discussion. "So why'd he do it?"

Berni silently came to a standing position and left the alcove, but Jack sensed her presence just a few feet behind him. Keeping everyone else out of earshot.

"Who knows? Why do writers do any of the crazy things they do?" Seeing that his answer wasn't going to be enough, Barron lowered his arms to his thighs. "Come on, Jack. People kill themselves all the time without the slightest warning. And you've been writing murder long enough to know they don't always leave a note."

"I heard he was on his boat, out at sea."

"That's right. He always greeted the New Year alone on the ocean. Except this time he decided to ring it in with a shotgun."

Jack winced, even though he already knew how Ryan Betancourt had ended his life. Barron took his silence as an indication to continue.

"He was supposed to call his sister on New Year's Day, so she got worried when he didn't. She got in touch with whatever amounts to the Coast Guard in Bermuda and they found the boat. As I said, no warning, no note."

"They sure he did it?"

"His sister identified the shotgun as one of his. She said he'd never carried one of those on the boat before, and nothing of value was missing." Barron looked down for a moment. "Apparently the doctor confirmed it was self-inflicted."

Jack took a long pull from his glass. "My God."

"Right." Barron's eyes came back up. "You haven't asked about Allison."

"Sure I did. I met two of her lackeys just after I got here. They wanted to hear all about striking it rich in Hollywood."

"So why'd they ask you?"

Jack handled the barb better that time, but the same question came back into his head: *Does he know?*

"Beats me. How did Allison handle it?"

"You know her. It's hard to tell when she's performing and when she's not."

Boy, do I.

Barron was studying him closely, and when he took a deep breath Jack knew what he was going to say. "Jack, we're in a bit of a bind here and could use some help. We have less than five months before the next performance—"

"Five months? Your last one was November! How come so soon?"

"That's hardly the question. The fact is we've got a new show coming up, Ryan had only just begun his brainstorming, and I simply don't have the time to catch and tame a new writer." Barron stopped himself there, having let a touch of heat enter his voice. "Look at it this way: If you come back, just for this one show, it'll all be over five months from now. Then you can go back to Tombstone and write more slam-bang action flicks."

"*Beaten Ground*'s not an action flick. It's a serious war picture."

"You can't be surprised that I'm asking. There are maybe six, seven writers in the world that can do what you and Ryan did. And all those other guys already said no."

"You're making it easy for me to join them. And I still can't believe you've got two shows so close together."

"That's what I love about writers—they're such lousy actors. Don't pretend you haven't been following the troupe in the news."

"I've been busy."

Barron slid around the cushions until he could put a hand on his shoulder. "Come on, Jack . . . you could write for Allison again."

Berni gave the gentlest of coughs behind him, and Barron looked over Jack's shoulder toward the staircase. Seeing something that pleased him, he slowly raised a finger and pointed, but in a way that couldn't be seen beyond the booth.

Allison stood on the landing at the top of the stairs, the two lackeys on either side of her. She wore a sleeveless black dress, and even though she was talking to a star-struck local two steps below her, Jack told himself she'd been looking his way just a moment before.

This crowd really does love their entrances.

But nobody makes an entrance like Allison Green.

Barron leaned in even closer, his hand still on Jack's shoulder. "Honestly, I always thought you two were a much better couple."

Jack didn't get to his room before one in the morning. Berni had been dispatched to get him checked in, and had taken his car keys in order to have his things brought inside. Somewhere in the middle of the ensuing party she'd given them back, along with a small envelope containing the key to his room for the night.

Of course he'd already spoken to Allison by then, but they hadn't said much. After all, they were surrounded by prying eyes and had just buried the man who had been her boyfriend and his old writing partner. Jack had sealed the deal with Barron before leaving the alcove and after getting some more detail on the next performance. Towns competed fiercely for Death Troupe, and so he already knew that the next location was a small place in the Adirondacks called Schuyler Mills. He'd solemnly shaken hands with Barron before climbing out of the throne room and approaching Allison.

As he'd slowly eased his way through the throng, trying to imitate Puff's wraithlike ability to navigate such human shoals, Jack had reflected that he'd almost never seen Allison alone in public. Not even when they'd taken that long driving vacation through the Florida Keys, just after Death Troupe's third engagement. Whenever they stopped, at roadside stands or gas station variety stores, she would always end up with someone talking to her—and this was long before she became famous. Watching the sun set in Key West their first night there, Jack had looked around at the other viewers, local and tourist alike, enthralled as the shrinking orb turned the sky red and the water pink. Allison got the same kind of rapt attention from total strangers, and Jack had enjoyed the idea until the writer in him had remarked that car accidents draw a crowd too.

Allison had sensed his approach, or perhaps one of her lackeys had alerted her, because she'd turned just as he was about to reach out and touch her shoulder. All thoughts of the car accident metaphor had left his mind as her mildly attentive expression blossomed into a smile of both joy and relief.

"Jack!" She'd almost moaned, her bare arms coming up and around his neck. "Oh, Ja-ack."

He'd slipped his arms around her, noting that she was just a little thinner than he remembered and trying not to hug too tightly. Somewhere in his mind a tiny clock was counting down to the moment when she would end the embrace, rendering it meaningless and snuffing out the flickering ember in his heart. The moment had come and gone several times before he realized that she was not going to release him, holding him there in silent display while everyone watched. It was then that he'd returned the hug with all his strength.

They'd swayed together for a few more moments, and when she released his neck it was only with one hand, which she then placed on his chest before murmuring, "Nobody hugs like you, Jack." She'd given him a brief kiss before stepping back, and it had felt like every event, every action around them had been stopped in mid-motion. Jack could have sworn that there hadn't been a single sound in the last minute, and a quick glance showed that he was partially correct. Everyone in the immediate vicinity had stopped to stare, and now that Allison had let go of him they seemed released as well.

Allison had stayed by his side for almost an hour, deftly redirecting the group's conversation to his wild success in Hollywood whenever it slipped too close to her. She'd slowly sipped a martini brought by one of the lackeys, and Jack had unconsciously eased his own consumption in response. Puff had joined the group at one point, mispronouncing Schenectady as 'splenectomy' when someone had asked the name of the city closest to Schuyler Mills. He'd gotten away with it, too, until Jack had corrected him with the proper name and the observation that Schenectady was not that close to their next venue.

"Ah, you know the Broadway crowd, Jack!" Puff had replied airily, his free hand indicating the people closest to Allison. "Everything north of Harlem is 'upstate'!"

That had gotten a laugh, but Jack hadn't really heard it because Allison had used the distraction to take his hand and give it a brief squeeze. He'd turned his head just far enough to see her, and to catch the slight nod. Allison had excused herself shortly after that, saying she'd seen someone she absolutely had to greet, and then disappeared into the crowd with Mickey and Todd.

Jack had caught sight of her several more times after that, using the vision to stoke the glowing coal of that hand squeeze and its accompanying signal. He'd switched to water by then, no matter how many drinks were offered by old friends in the group, and after a time this had allowed him to see just why Ryan Betancourt's funeral reception had so quickly devolved into a party. It couldn't have been more obvious if it had been written across the bar's long mirror in red paint.

They don't miss him.

This surprising deduction had come with the clarity of unexpected intuition, and Jack turned it over in his head several times. Barron had added the second writer just after the success of *Wind in the Palms*, having recruited him straight from Broadway. Although Ryan and the Director had bickered frequently during the two years that Jack had remained with them, that was expected.

Everyone but the costume team knocked heads with Barron at one time or another.

What made it surprising was that the Ryan Betancourt Jack had left as the troupe's sole writer had been a very popular guy, and for good reason. It didn't all stem from the fact that he was tall, rich, humorous, and good-looking, or that he knew big names in New York theater. It wasn't even that he could write great soaring scenes in a way that had always escaped their original writer, Jack Glynn.

It was more than that: Ryan had a touch of Allison's charisma, and he worked at fitting in with the others. He deferred to Puff, commiserated with Kirk, and treated Berni like a queen. Jack himself had been pleased to find writing with Ryan to be quite fun, and had counted him as a friend right up until the awful night when he'd learned the truth. He'd been too stunned to make a scene, and had quietly resigned just after the performance a few days later. As an unintended result, most of the troupe didn't know that the subsequent pairing of Ryan and Allison had been born of betrayal.

And yet something had obviously changed in the two years Jack had been gone. He could feel it in every hand wringing his own and every welcome back once the word got out that he'd signed on for the upcoming show. Looking around at the many smiling faces, he half-expected to see a new, companion revelation written on the mirror as well:

They're glad he's gone.

Now in his hotel room, Jack finally gave up on trying to deduce just how Ryan had so alienated the troupe in the two years since he'd quit. He would be meeting with the outfit's advance man, Wade Parker, before traveling to Schuyler Mills, and made a mental note to ask the Director's spy just what had happened.

Thoughts of the advance man and his talent for digging up skeletons brought back a darker question, one from earlier that evening, when he'd been talking with the Director.

Had Barron been signaling that he knew the truth about Beaten Ground? *And how could he have found out?*

It was almost impossible for the Director to know that Jack had penned the script for *Beaten Ground* years before, when he was still in college. Not that it made any difference in the long run; he was the script's author, and it had stood on its own two feet when the producers had started passing it around. They'd loved the thing, paid him a small fortune for it, and certainly hadn't allowed it to descend into Development Hell.

Even so, the question still irked him: How could Barron know? Jack was sure he'd never mentioned the script to anyone in the troupe, in fact having forgotten all about it until the day of the chance meeting with the smiling mogul who had asked the most hackneyed of Hollywood questions: What else have you got? He'd frozen for a second or two, unprepared for the inquiry and knowing that the rotten adaptation of *Wind in the Palms* was the only screenplay he'd written in years. Then, out of the blue, he'd remembered his old World War Two script, sitting in a closet in Arizona. He'd blurted out an impromptu pitch, the mogul had asked to see it, and now the deal was done.

So why did it bother him that Barron, or anyone for that matter, might know?

Because you didn't deliver on the job that sent you to Hollywood in the first place.

Was that it? Was he hiding the screenplay's provenance because he'd failed to translate *Wind in the Palms* into an effective film piece? There were numerous possible reasons why the newer script was dead in the water, but that didn't remove Jack's nagging doubt that what he'd written had somehow failed to pass muster. About the only thing he knew for certain regarding *Wind in the Palms* was that he'd given it everything he had.

He'd tried every trick he knew to translate the stage script into a film. He'd focused on the play's visual elements, the seen instead of the heard, and had then written such a meaningless hodgepodge that he'd actually burned the first draft in his backyard barbecue. He'd taken all the instances where the stage had restricted the action and re-set them to ape the limitless space offered in a movie, only to end up putting them right back where they'd been originally. The adaptation which he'd finally submitted had been the third complete re-write, and if he'd been asked what he thought of it he would have pronounced it mediocre at best.

Sitting there on the edge of the bed, he finally realized just why he feared someone might discover that he'd written *Beaten Ground* as a college kid. It was because the war movie he'd written years before had been awfully good, and the recent adaptation he'd made of a highly successful play (which he had also written) was not.

Staring at the carpet, Jack then considered that he might have mistaken Barron's jibes for something different, but still related: Perhaps Barron hadn't been prodding at anything as specific as a single script. Maybe the Director had simply been hinting at something Jack had been asking himself for most of the last year: Have you still got it?

The question seemed to hang there, as if someone had spoken it out loud, and Jack was still mulling it over when the soft knocking

27

came at the door. He knew who it was, had known ever since Allison had nodded at him in the middle of Puff's joke. Even so, he practically ran to the door.

She was framed in the light from the hallway, and for a moment all he could see was the fineness of her hair and the slimness of her waist. He slipped an arm around her without a word, and guided her into the room as if rescuing her from a blizzard.

She didn't say anything either, taking him into her embrace instead, and he returned it in the same silence. It was a resumption of their old habit of abiding quiet, and it overwhelmed him with the feeling that she had never really left. All thoughts of plays and scripts fled, but he did manage to take note of a new notion before giving himself over to the moment he had wanted for so long. In his mind, Jack Glynn finally allowed himself to admit that he was in agreement with the rest of the troupe.

I'm glad he's gone.

Chapter Three

It was early evening when Jack pulled into Utica, New York. He'd flown back to Arizona the day after Ryan's funeral, made arrangements for an extended absence, and driven off in his tan pickup a day later. He frequently took the truck on camping trips in the desert and so the vehicle's bed, shielded by a modest cap, was full of his camping gear and the items he would need in Schuyler Mills. The clock was already running on Death Troupe's next performance, but he wanted his own things with him for the months he'd be writing the play.

Utica was just short of the enormous Adirondack region, an expanse of forests, lakes, and mountains bounded roughly by Lake Champlain to the east, Canada to the north, and I-90 to the south. Perhaps best known for Lake Placid, the site of two Winter Olympics, it was home to numerous small towns like Schuyler Mills.

As far as Jack could see, the whole state of New York was covered in snow. He'd crossed the Mississippi at St. Louis and then begun a northeasterly climb that had taken him through Cleveland and Buffalo. Although he'd been on main highways the whole trip and only hit a few snow showers along the way, it had been a long time since he'd driven in the cold and he was thankful for the pickup's four wheel drive.

He would spend the night in a hotel in Utica before heading into Schuyler Mills, still two hours' drive away, the next morning. He wanted the last quiet evening for himself and would also be meeting the troupe's advance man, Wade Parker, for a briefing.

29

In a replay of his arrival at the hotel in Maine, he left everything in the vehicle and headed straight into the building. Crossing the largely featureless lobby, he walked into the dimly-lit lounge and spotted Wade at the far end of the bar. The place was nearly empty, but that wasn't surprising; the advance man preferred places like that.

Wade Parker was one of the plainest-looking men Jack had ever met. Somewhere in his late forties, losing his hair, and always dressed in a jacket and tie but never a suit, he seemed to melt into whatever scenery surrounded him. Parker turned on his barstool to minutely wave a hand at him, and seeing him in profile reminded Jack that Barron's spy was immensely fit. This wasn't surprising, as his job kept him busy.

Wade was semi-retired from the insurance fraud business, where he'd made a small fortune recovering assets worth millions. He was connected all across the country, and his previous life as a private investigator sometimes called him away from his duties with the Barron Players. In addition to covertly observing potential Death Troupe venues, Parker was responsible for everything from the anti-hacking software on the writers' laptops to the physical security of the theater once the actors had come to town.

But that wouldn't be for months, and it would be up in Schuyler Mills. Tonight Jack was glad to see him, liking Wade despite the investigator's mocking attitude toward everything theatrical.

"Hello, Jack." Wade took his hand, his voice a low murmur without a trace of an accent. "You know, when Barron told me you were signing on for this gig I didn't believe him at first."

"Come on. You must have known he was going to ask."

"Sure I did . . . I just didn't think you'd be dumb enough to say yes."

Jack swung a leg over a barstool and ordered a rum and coke when the bartender approached. Wade was drinking his usual Jim Beam, neat, but Jack knew better than to offer to buy him a refill. Although there was little more than a finger of the brown liquid left in his glass, the advance man usually nursed a single drink for hours.

"So . . . a little bird told me you're back with Allison."

"Don't start."

"What? Warning you, like I've done so many times, that she's not right for you?" Wade took a sip of the bourbon. "Or anybody, for that matter."

"Now that's a new one. What's it mean?"

"It is a new one. It came to me during your hiatus. Did you know she had Ryan on the same date schedule as you? Saw him once in a blue moon, always heading off to some distant engagement while he slaved away at his keyboard, writing great scenes for his lady fair."

"That's not the same as me at all. I never wrote great scenes for her." They both chuckled at that, but Jack noticed Parker was studying his face, as if choosing whether or not to continue. He decided to help him. "Give it to me straight, Doc. I can take it."

"Oh, it's not like that. Allison was monogamous with Ryan, same as with you and probably every boyfriend before you. It's just that I finally realized something that most of the men in America haven't: Allison Green's always going to go back to her first love, and that's the stage."

"She did make a movie or two."

"And her assistants want her to do more. They want her to quit the troupe and concentrate on making them rich."

"Did they tell you that?"

"No. They were talking to each other at the time."

"So how'd you overhear it? Listening device of some kind?"

"Why would I want to listen in on two low-level nitwits? I was standing near them, that's all."

"Convenient."

"How many times do I have to tell you this? Keep your mouth shut and your eyes and ears open, and eventually you'll know everything."

Parker looked down at his glass, which still held the finger of bourbon. He seemed to be weighing something, and Jack wondered if the relationship advice was going to continue. He hoped not, as memories of the recent night with Allison had buoyed him across America.

"You hungry?" Parker slung a heavy canvas briefcase over one shoulder, picked up his drink, and stood. "I can brief you over dinner."

"Here. Guard this with your life." Parker handed him the canvas bag once they were seated in a booth on the far side of the hotel's more brightly lit restaurant. "Everything you need to know about the town is on the laptop, under the Background folder. Nothing special to this one. Just another out-of-the-way place trying to drum up some publicity."

"Publicity? In country like that? They must be up to their armpits in skiers during the winter and campers during the summer. Why would they need publicity?"

"Actually, Schuyler Mills is a little too far away from the ski slopes—other towns get that business—but you're right about the fishing and camping crowd. They're a discriminating bunch up there in your new home. They like the outdoorsy types, but don't seem to miss the ski bums."

"Can't say I blame them. The ski crowd at my college was a bunch of rich snobs."

"Sounds like somebody we both used to know." As with everything else he'd turned his hand to, Ryan Betancourt had been an excellent skier.

"That's not what I was talking about."

The waitress came and took their order, and Parker waited until she was gone before sliding a little closer in the booth. This was usually a sign that he was going to divulge some useful dirt on a location, so Jack gave him his full attention.

"Jack, did you ever get the impression that Ryan was suicidal?"

This was unexpected. Wade had never liked Ryan very much, although Jack believed he was the only one who'd detected that. The advance man had joined the troupe two years after its inception, and he and Jack had become friends right away. Wade's duties frequently kept him on the road, so his closest contacts had been Barron and the writers. He'd been noticeably more reserved in the two years when Jack had been writing with Ryan.

"Suicidal? Him? Not at all. He had everything to live for, and he was one of the most confident guys I've ever known. Even before he started dating Allison." Jack took a swig of his drink. "But then again I hadn't been in touch with him since I left. So how about you? You notice anything, Mr. Open Eyes and Ears?"

"No. He seemed to miss Allison a lot more in the last town, the one up in northern California."

"Red Bend."

Wade grinned at him, as if enjoying a private joke. "So you *were* keeping tabs on us."

"Hard not to. Death Troupe's been getting a lot of ink since I left."

"And we both know why."

"Yes we do. And I still say I'm right." A severe disagreement had brewed up between Jack and Barron in the years before he left the group. Barron had wanted to inject more local lore into the plays, believing this would increase the bond with the audience, and Jack had disagreed. His earlier mysteries had been largely generic tales, using only the host town setting and avoiding the gossip and legends so eagerly pushed on him by the townsfolk. Jack had feared they would eventually hurt someone's feelings, or unknowingly get pulled into a small-town feud, by using such story lines. Ryan had embraced the Director's preference wholeheartedly, and the troupe's success since then seemed to have proved Jack wrong.

"Turns out you were right." Wade fixed him with a dull, almost sorrowful expression. "We stepped on a family's reputation in Red Bend, and I think it might have contributed to Ryan's suicide."

"Barron didn't tell me any of this."

"Probably didn't want to hear you say, 'I told you so.'"

"No one else mentioned it, either." Not even Allison.

"I don't believe they know. We pulled out of there the same as always, not a lot of hanging around and everybody going to the four winds. Something happened about a week after we left, and Barron and I jumped on it as fast and as hard as we could. It looks like we succeeded in stamping it out."

"What happened?"

"You know Red Bend is up in the wine country. Lots of money, even in some of the smaller towns. Anyway, there was this local scandal from thirty years back involving one of the old money families. Swear to God, we believed they'd all died out—and we were almost right. Anyway, one of the locals told Ryan about this big, juicy scandal and he wrote it into the play. It went over well. The crowd related to it nicely, and the whole thing was a great success."

"Until a week later."

"Yeah. A reporter wrote a follow-up piece laying out the facts of the old scandal, and unfortunately there actually was a member of that family still alive. He was in a retirement home a couple towns over, from all reports so senile that he didn't know what day it was. But somehow he got a copy of the newspaper, and the next thing they knew he'd jumped off the fire escape."

"Dead?"

"Four stories. You bet."

"Wow. That's horrible." Jack settled back against the booth's leather, looking at the table for an instant. "And you think Ryan felt responsible for this?"

"Oh, I know he did. He was absolutely crushed when I told him. I wish you'd been there. He said, 'We should have listened to Jack' a half dozen times." A tiny sip of bourbon. "Anyway, the Barron and I went back to Red Bend and met with the mayor right away. You shoulda seen old Jerry in action: He sounded all mournful and conciliatory, but he controlled that meeting from start to finish. He didn't mention the word lawsuit even once, but when he was done talking that poor mayor knew that any connection between the fatality and the troupe was going to bring a storm of litigation. He walked us to the door swearing that there wasn't any way we could have known, and that he considered the matter closed."

"The Barron's a persuasive guy when he needs to be."

"Oh, yeah. I've always thought he'd've made a great con man. He's an expert in body language, subtle manipulation, individual motivation—all the things that make him a great director."

"So you think Ryan killed himself because he felt guilty?" Jack fought the question which followed right behind that one, but it forced itself on him anyway: *Then why didn't he kill himself when he stole my girl?*

"Maybe . . . and maybe not." Wade lowered his voice even more. "Ryan was a vain guy, but they say he used a shotgun on himself. That strike you as odd?"

"Yes it did. In fact, that was my first thought when I found out. I asked the Barron if there was a chance this was a murder, and he said the authorities didn't see it that way."

"Exactly." Wade whispered the word as if Jack had offered the clue that solved the whole mystery. "*Which* authorities?"

"I think he said it was some kind of Bermudan Coast Guard. Why?"

"Because I can't determine who went out and got that boat. Or who inspected the scene. Or even who pronounced Ryan dead."

"His sister Emily would know. Did you ask her?"

"No. The Barron told me to drop the whole thing when I mentioned it."

"Why?"

"He said Emily stiff-armed him when he called to offer his condolences. The Betancourts are heavy players in that part of the world, and if they want to keep the details of a family tragedy secret, that's what's going to happen. Besides, after being forced to quash that other thing in Red Bend, I wonder if the Barron wasn't content to let this one go. As much as he could, of course; Ryan's death was in the papers and Jerry had to explain that to the folks in Schuyler Mills. Maybe he didn't need me digging up more bad publicity."

"Whew." Jack placed his hands on the table, as if to steady himself while assimilating the spate of information. "Wait a second. You said Emily was the one keeping the details under wraps?"

"Yes."

"Jerry told me she was the one who alerted the authorities— whoever that was—when she didn't hear from Ryan. That's why they went out looking for his boat." Jack inhaled slowly. "You don't think . . . ?"

Wade smiled while shaking his head slightly. "No I don't. She had half the family fortune already, which is plenty, and near as I could tell she got along fine with Ryan. Right?"

"Yeah, they were pretty close. She didn't like the troupe, though. She thought Ryan was wasting his talent with us."

"Not exactly a reason to kill him, then." He shook his head again. "Be careful with the free association, Jack. You're out of your league. This isn't one of your plays."

"So what are you saying?"

"That there's a lot of coincidence here, most of which required an action by Ryan himself. First, he had to be alone. Sure, everyone knew he spent the New Year all by himself out at sea, but that put him in a nice jurisdictional black hole, where the family money could write the story anyway they wanted. I already mentioned that I can't find out who pronounced him, or who reeled in the boat. And that's where I come back to the shotgun: It guaranteed that Ryan would be buried closed-casket. So we have no police or navy report, no death certificate . . . and maybe even no body."

Jack raised his eyebrows at the advance man. "So you're not saying he was murdered. You're saying he's still alive."

"I'm saying I'm keeping an open mind. Ryan may have done himself in, for his own reasons, and maybe that's all there is. Or maybe that old man in Red Bend tipped him over the edge, far enough to blow Taps on a shotgun barrel. But there were other things . . . strange things . . . during that engagement that really rattled him. He was well and truly spooked when the troupe finally got to town, and the old man's suicide might have convinced him to drop out of sight for awhile."

"What kind of 'things' are we talking about?"

"The troupe's always had its fair share of crazy fans." Wade briefly pointed a finger at Jack. "As you well know."

"Cut it out. It was one time, and I admitted it was a mistake . . . besides, she'd been following us for years. It's not like we were strangers. I thought I actually knew her."

"That was your biggest mistake of all. But let's forget about your little fling for the moment. You might not know this, but after you left and the troupe got popular, more and more of the crazies began showing up. Worse than the usual groupies, too. One guy, some total outsider, came into Red Bend pretending to be part of the act." The build-up to a Death Troupe performance included the unannounced appearance of various players, in character and dispensing clues, in popular parts of the town. The locals would already have been given an introduction to the mystery by then, and

35

so the itinerant actors appearing in their midst would be largely recognizable. "Jerry thought it was a good sign, that we were attracting that kind of attention, but this guy was different. He seemed to *know* things, like he was in on the plot."

"Really?" Jack's heart began moving at a faster rate. He'd always been leery of the people who were too enamored of Death Troupe, fearing the combination of an unbalanced mind and the ubiquitous theme of murder. As the group's sole representative in a given town—at least until the actors arrived—he'd always felt distressingly vulnerable to these faceless devotees.

"Yeah. That bothered Ryan a lot, because this guy seemed to have guessed a curve ball that he hadn't even put in the story yet. We never did figure out who he was, or what he was up to."

"You sure the Barron wasn't playing games? Trying out something new?" The Director met with his writer frequently during the months leading up to the show, and would have known every plot in development.

"Oh, you can bet I asked him. He denied any involvement, and he brought it up again himself when the old man jumped off that roof." Wade fixed him with the examining look again. "I know you don't like to talk about her, but have you been in contact with Pauline since you left?"

Pauline Scott was a fan who had followed Death Troupe for three years before the fateful night when Jack had learned Allison was dumping him for Ryan. Devastated, he'd gotten knee-walking drunk and then compounded the mistake by bedding the sultry Pauline. It was the only time he'd done anything like that, and he'd regretted it the very next morning. Not the sex, of course; Pauline was in her mid-twenties and had proven herself quite skilled, but it had been a mistake all the same. She'd accepted his apologies with a disarming calm, and had dropped the group just after that year's show —just as Jack had.

"No I haven't. Has she shown up since I left?"

"No, and I was on the lookout, too. So if you haven't been in touch with her and I haven't seen her, she's probably found somebody else to follow around. But we still don't know who that guy was in Red Bend, so keep on your toes up there in Schuyler Mills." He tapped the canvas bag on the seat between them. "There's a new cell phone in there, and I want you to carry it on you at all times. It's secure, long-range, and it can really hold a charge. Best of all it's got a tracking device in it that I can trace without having to go to the phone company.

"I'm going to be in touch with you frequently during this one, Jack. I want you to call me if you see anything strange. Anything at all. Even if you don't *see* anything but *feel* that something's wrong. Promise me you'll do that."

"Count on it. You're actually starting to scare me here."

"Good." Wade finished the last of his drink. "For the first time since I joined this outfit, I don't know what's going on. I don't like it, and you can bet I'm going to figure it out."

"How are you gonna do that?"

"By doing what I should have done in the first place. Going back to Red Bend and finding out what really happened when that poor old man went off that building."

Chapter Four

Jack ate a leisurely breakfast the next morning before getting back on the highway. Wade was already checked out and gone, so it was too late for the question he'd forgotten to ask the night before. The riddle of just why the troupe had seemed relieved by Ryan Betancourt's passing seemed trivial by comparison to the events in Red Bend, so he decided to put the question to Barron next time they met.

He loaded his luggage into the pickup and rolled out of Utica in weather that promised a bright, cold day. The ascent into the Adirondacks began almost immediately, and he soon found himself on a curving highway that ran between snow-covered hills, frozen lakes, and a steadily decreasing number of towns.

The trip across America had slowly reintroduced him to winter in the north, but his little house in Arizona had contained enough cold weather gear to keep him from freezing on the way. Driving down a road flanked by high banks of plowed snow, he could tell that he was headed into a land fully in the grip of Old Man Winter. The evergreens looked like they'd been draped in white bunting while most of the other trees, stripped of their leaves and adorned with frozen snow, resembled the masts of wooden ships with their sails securely tied down.

Jack had researched the Adirondack area during the trip, but he was still amazed by the number of lakes he encountered. Viewing them over the snow piles lining the highway, his writer's eye compared them to a floor made of gray-blue marble. The lakes had obviously frozen solid by that point, as every now and then he spotted an ice fishing party clustered around an opening in the surface. Their motionless vigil made him feel as if he'd stumbled across an ancient ritual, some sort of dowsing cult using fishing rods to locate and propitiate the creatures beneath the barrier.

He hadn't forgotten Wade's ominous words from the night before, but they were now pushed into the background by an emotion that bordered on euphoria. Jack had always approached a new writing idea with this same sense of expectation, no matter how many times the resulting work had fallen short of the piece envisioned. He would be essentially marooned in Schuyler Mills for the next three months, like a resupply cache awaiting a gang of Arctic explorers, but he was used to isolation and looked forward to the new experience.

The last few months in the desert had been a time of frustration, and the only thing he had to show for it was the deep tan earned while trekking or running in the scrubland surrounding his tiny home. Of course he'd been sustained by the steady train of accolades over *Beaten Ground*, but even that trickle of refreshment had carried its own brackish taste. It was disheartening to know that he'd written *Beaten Ground* while in college and hadn't penned anything as good, not even *Wind in the Palms* (the play) since then.

He'd somehow expected this to change once he'd quit the troupe and returned to his roots in the desert. He hadn't been terribly surprised when *Wind in the Palms* resisted adaptation to the screen, and hadn't blamed himself when it stalled out in Hollywood. He'd been casting about for a fresh idea when *Beaten Ground* caught fire with the producers, and had spent a dizzying week in Los Angeles hammering out the deal which followed. Feeling vindicated by this success and liberated by its large remuneration, he'd headed back to Arizona with the sense that he would now be free to create something even better.

That hadn't happened, and one afternoon he'd felt the slow crawl of doubt coming up his sweat-drenched spine. He'd been jogging across the open, letting the sun purify him, when the disturbing thought had first reared its noisome head: What if *Beaten Ground* was it? What if that was where he topped out? Would he now become one of those writers who penned a big hit early in life, and then spent their remaining years proving it had been a fluke?

Although the traffic was light, he still found himself behind a slow-moving truck on the winding Adirondack road. Black ice lay in wait where the many hills blocked the highway from the sun, and he didn't feel comfortable trying to push the pickup past the eighteen-wheeler in front of him. He coasted in its wake for several minutes,

39

content to roll along in the woodland scenery, until a small car with a stack of skis on its roof suddenly swept by him.

The car's occupants, in their late teens or early twenties, had apparently grown impatient waiting for him to pass the truck. One of them let him inspect her longest finger as the car surged past, and the driver gave him a double-honk on the horn in reprimand. Jack watched in fascination as the car, too light to grip the slick well, took a dangerously long time to get past the longer vehicle. Just as they disappeared from the oncoming lane, another truck came around the next curve. Apparently its driver had not found the incident remarkable, as he flashed by on Jack's left without comment.

Having committed his first regional faux pas, Jack decided to drop back so that the next hothead could pass him easily before attempting to leapfrog the truck. It made him dawdle along at a ludicrous pace, but he was in no particular hurry and was drawing inspiration from the wintry panorama. He started to detect a backwoods theme in some of the isolated stores and businesses he passed. Some of them were actual log cabins, and much of their signage would have been more fitting at a frontier trading post instead of a convenience store.

The truck finally took a fork in the highway, and he was freed to accelerate just a little. Ice crystals danced across the gray tarmac, and he had no intention of testing the road's friction. He soon hit a level stretch flanked on both sides by frozen water, and saw yet another ice fisherman. This one was alone, sitting on an overturned bucket, and he looked as if he might have frozen there. Jack watched him in the rearview mirror, sitting there bundled up against the cold, and the man never moved a muscle.

The exotic scenery and newness of the trip had stirred Jack's dormant imagination, and he soon began free-associating as if in the first stages of brainstorming. He found he preferred the single fisherman to the group he'd passed earlier, comparing the man's lonely watch to his own experience as a writer. Like the man on the lake, he too maintained a solitary vigil, laboring on one side of an opaque barrier in the hope of summoning something magical from the void.

The similarity continued in his mind, and he found that he liked it enough to consider putting ice fishermen in the play that he was to write. Death Troupe mysteries were supposed to include details specific to the locale, and he couldn't very well write a scene where a snowmobile drove across the stage. The troupe's special effects people were good, but they weren't gods.

Coming back to the lone supplicant on the lake, Jack allowed his mind to ponder the extended periods of time when his work required him to be alone. This too was strange, as he liked people and had secretly enjoyed the attention he'd received as Death Troupe's sole representative in a host town. Almost in spite of that sociability, however, there was always a point where the story assumed a life of its own and demanded that he find a quiet place to nurture it.

His friends and family had never understood that this was why his long-distance relationship with Allison had worked so well . . . that is, until Ryan had come along. Just as Allison's career forced her out on the road, performing onstage for months, his writing also required their separation. It was a pattern he'd identified with most of the girlfriends who had preceded her: If they lived anywhere near him one or the other, the girlfriend or the work, would eventually suffer from neglect.

That was one reason why Jack had initially been so disappointed that his quiet little homestead in the desert had failed to yield even a modest literary crop. After the soil of his imagination had been proved barren by numerous attempts that had ended up in his barbecue, he had finally begun to question his total isolation as a bit of overkill. His celebrated screenplay, after all, had been written in a noisy college dormitory. He'd done some marvelous writing for the Barron troupe amid a whirlwind of demands enforced by the vagaries of its Director, the interpretation of its actors, and the wiles of its audience. He'd even collaborated successfully with an overbearing rich kid who'd ended up stealing the love of his life.

Perhaps the answer lay somewhere between the two extremes, then. Maybe Death Troupe's approach was the way to go, with the writer ensconced in the town and surrounded by prying eyes, but creating scenes and plots meant to deceive those very observers. It was an amazing paradox, really: Although he lived as a minor celebrity in a small locality awash with people, the need for secrecy meant that the troupe's writer was still very much alone. No matter how much he might be taken into the locals' collective bosom—it had happened before—his job made him as much an outsider in the town as it made him with the troupe.

Jack reminded himself that he'd been writing good, solid stuff right up until he'd resigned. It therefore made sense to use Death Troupe's next engagement to help jump start his imagination once more. Just this once. And after that, Allison or no Allison, he would drop the murder circuit for good and go back to writing on his own.

He hoped.

As was often the case, the prospect of a new project quickly took precedence over everything else on Jack's mind. In the last miles toward Schuyler Mills, he found that his powers of observation had assumed the enhanced level which he associated with the first flutterings of an idea trying to burst the eggshell which enclosed it.

Now deep in the Adirondacks, he'd started getting used to the many miles of road and woodland which separated the tiny patches of civilization. If not for the highway itself, he could have envisioned his surroundings as they were when the first men had walked the region. Though deep in its wintry coma, the land was still awe-inspiring with its rolling hills, sprawling lakes, and plummeting ravines. So attuned to the seeming emptiness of the Arizona desert, Jack couldn't stop marveling at the huge stands of trees which bearded so much of the land.

With his imagination finally challenged, he found his mind flashing all around him, taking everything in as if his brain were a camera. His eyes captured ice-faced cliffs which loomed over the highway, bridges both old and new, and lonely observation towers spotted on sun-dazzled peaks, and he tucked them all away for later use. As much as he tried to hold the net of his musings wide, it was impossible to keep from associating the vistas with the troupe's theme of dark deeds and deadly deceit. Despite the sun and the faded blue sky, he noted how quickly the forest darkened beyond the tree line's edge, and imagined that the effect would be multiplied by the summer's foliage. Bends in the road suddenly became their own little worlds when hemmed in by the battlements of the hills and the tree-choked ravines. He wondered if the set designers would be interested in playing with that, using their special effects magic to recreate the lonely and disquieting scene.

It was almost with regret that he began encountering scattered homes and road signs indicating that Schuyler Mills was just a few miles up ahead. Telephone poles, their age-splintered trunks glistening with runnels of ice, soon took up a position on one side of the road. They seemed to accompany him as he sighted the outskirts of the town.

From Wade's detailed assessment, he knew that Schuyler Mills was spread out in roughly two pieces along many miles of a main east-west road. The town center was the first segment he would encounter coming from this direction, sitting on one of the highest plateaus in the Adirondacks. Not that it was flat; Schuyler Mills was flanked by rolling hills as it stretched east in the general direction of Vermont.

To his right, a large lake sat in frozen stillness between the road and a distant ridgeline which ran as far as his eyes could see. Off to his left a simple road sign announced that this was indeed Schuyler Mills while another sign below it gave the distance to Highway 87, many miles to the east, as if in suggestion.

The first store he encountered backed up against the lake, and it didn't appear to be open. Up close it turned into an elongated warehouse on stilts, and proclaimed itself the one-stop shop for all his boating, canoeing, and kayaking needs. The longhouse was fronted by a desolate parking lot forested with metal racks that presumably served to display various boats during the warmer months.

The next structure along the lakefront was a two-story building that could have been mistaken for a ski lodge. Snow frosted its eaves, and red-painted shutters stood open on either side of the upstairs windows. A carved sign over its double front doors announced in big letters that this was the Visitor's Center, and underneath that was a smaller sign which identified the place as the location of the town offices. Jack knew this already because he was supposed to meet the mayor of Schuyler Mills there, but without that forewarning he probably would have driven straight past.

The Visitor's Center had a large parking area, and the town square started just after that. Jack pulled into the mostly vacant lot, speculating that it was probably chock-full during the summer, while looking down the street at the business district. He found this sight encouraging, as several two- and three-story buildings surrounded a huge rectangular town common flanked on its long axis by a double row of trees and park benches. The empty park's center was occupied by a stone monument topped by the image of a man in a uniform from the Civil War. Looking around the center, Jack noted the marquee of a small movie theater, two restaurants, and even a four-story affair that looked like a hotel. Although Schuyler Mills derived the main part of its annual revenue from summertime tourists, Wade's précis had indicated that most of the town's businesses were year-round.

Sliding out of the pickup, Jack was surprised by the stern cold of the higher altitude. He was only two hours' drive north of Utica (which he had considered glacial) and yet here in Schuyler Mills he found himself hurriedly reaching for the tan parka he'd purchased at a factory outlet store in Buffalo. Despite the midday sun, he feverishly searched the unfamiliar coat's pockets for a blue woolen watch cap and ski gloves, also bought in Buffalo.

Shutting the truck's door and locking it, he quickly shuffled across the parking lot toward the wooden ramp which led up to the town office's front door. After getting about three steps he hit a thin patch of dark ice and almost went down, slightly wrenching a muscle in his leg when he fought the sudden slide.

"Easy, Jack, easy. You're gonna be here a long time." He muttered to himself as he walked up the ramp and reached for the door handle.

Its rustic exterior notwithstanding, the Schuyler Mills Visitor's Center was bright and welcoming. The front foyer was two stories high, lit by a wagon-wheel chandelier and the second-story windows he'd noticed earlier. The wood-paneled wall facing him sported a huge aerial photograph of the town in summer, hanging above and behind an empty reception desk.

The walls to his left and right were painted a soothing beige, and each hosted similar aerial photos, these showing the entire region. The one to his left was taken in winter, and he recognized the long lake he'd passed as he entered the town limits. The one on his right was taken in the summer, and he was struck by the beauty of the lush woodland and blue water. Directly beneath this photo was a billiard table-sized diorama of the same scene, complete with tiny houses and a set of power lines which crossed the forested northeastern corner like a troop of giants.

"Oh, you must be the writer!" exclaimed a female voice from behind him, and Jack turned in surprise to see an elderly lady approaching him with a raised fireplace poker. He hadn't noticed that the foyer took a right turn just after the front door, but now he saw the brick-faced fireplace where the woman had obviously been stirring up the logs. She was dressed in a multicolored sweater and long pants which disappeared into a set of smart black leather boots.

"Why, yes, yes I am." he stammered, extending his hand. "Jack Glynn. I just got here."

The woman almost hit him with the poker as she tried to shake hands, letting out a little peep and taking an alarmed step backward when she saw how close she'd come to braining him.

"Oh, my goodness, I'm sorry . . . it's just that we're all so excited to finally meet you!" She turned and walked back toward the fire, speaking without turning her head. "I almost hit you with this thing! Wouldn't that have caused a stir? It would have been right out of that board game, you know, the mystery game? Melanie Archer, in the lobby, with the fireplace poker!"

"Well don't do *that*, Mel! At least not until he's written our play!" a male voice called out from behind Jack, and he turned to see a tall man standing in the entrance to the back part of the center. He already knew that this was Marv Tillman, the town mayor. Barron had specifically warned him to be on his toes around Tillman, but at the moment he couldn't see why. The mayor was dressed in a dark blue checked shirt and a blood red tie, with a faded set of jeans that almost covered a worn set of black boots. Nearly bald and a little paunchy, he wore a set of thick-lensed glasses and a broad smile.

Jack's face broke into an answering grin, pleased at the reception so far. Although most towns threw themselves into the process wholeheartedly, some did not, and every now and then there was a hardcore element that actually resented Death Troupe. From the sound of things, Schuyler Mills was going to be all right.

"Jack Glynn. It's nice to meet you, Mr. Mayor." They shook hands, and Jack noted that Tillman looked him over from head to toe, literally sizing him up. Barron believed that Tillman was a lot sharper than he acted, and Jack was reminded of their parting conversation in Maine.

"Watch this guy, Jack. He seems all right, but every now and then I get the feeling that he's one of those 'who-cares-if-we-identify-the-murderer-we're-just-having-a-good-time' types who changes on the night of the performance. You know what I'm talking about: All smiles and laughs and then WHAM-O, suddenly the whole audience is bringing their ballots to him for a 'yea or nay' just like some old-time political boss."

"But that's almost exactly what you *do."*

"That doesn't mean it's okay for him *to do it!"* Barron had chuckled, shaking his head. *"You know, Jack, sometimes you say things that are just . . . plain . . . crazy."*

"Marv Tillman. And I'm more of a Town Manager than anything else."

"Town shrink is more like it." Melanie Archer, minus the lethal weapon, approached and shook Jack's hand before taking his coat. "Marv's just like one of those nice youngsters who come up here every summer to be camp counselors. Dealing with everything from stubbed toes to teen break-ups. By the end of the summer I swear half of them are qualified to hang out a shingle as headshrinkers, just like Marv here."

"You'd be my best customer." They both laughed at this, obvious friends, while Melanie shook out Jack's overcoat and hung it on a peg next to the semi-circular receptionist desk. Tillman took Jack's arm and led him down the hallway, presumably toward his office. As soon as they were out of earshot he spoke in a low voice. "We're very sorry to hear about your other writer, Jack. I didn't get to meet him, but from everything I've heard he sounded like a talented guy."

"He was. He really was." The words popped out easily, and Jack wasn't surprised that he meant them.

"You two were close?"

Barron's warning came back into his head before Jack answered. "We wrote together for two years. I moved on to another project after that, and he was on his own for the last two performances. They did very well, so I think things worked out."

The hallway was a short one, and they approached a sunlit room at the end that had to be the mayor's office. Just as they entered, Jack caught a look from Tillman that was a mix of judgment and confirmation. Barron was right; the man was taking his measure and knew that Jack hadn't answered his question.

Tillman was speaking when they entered the small office. "I believe you two have already met."

He pointed a finger sideways toward a young woman seated in front of his desk. The walls of the office were painted white, and they reflected the sun off the frozen water outside the windows. Even so, Jack recognized the young reporter who had been interviewing Barron at the reception in Maine. An expression of confusion slipped onto his face, but he swept it off just as fast. Why hadn't Barron told him the girl was from Schuyler Mills?

"Hi Mr. Glynn. I'm Kelly Sykes. I handle publicity for the town." She rose from her chair and politely extended her hand. Jack took the opportunity to study her, kicking himself for dismissing her so quickly at the reception. She had a pretty face beneath dark brown hair that was still pulled back on top of her head the way it had been in Maine. The big glasses were gone, though, as was the business suit. Now she wore a ribbed brown sweater over a tartan skirt that barely covered her knees. Dark nylons took up where the skirt ended and then disappeared into a set of black boots topped with beige fur. In a male reflex action, he noted that she wasn't wearing a ring.

"Is that what you were doing at the funeral, when you were talking to Mr. Barron?"

"Mr. Barron? He let me call him Jerome."

"Really? He lets me call him Jerry. I thought you were some kind of local reporter."

"Oh no . . . although we do have a small newspaper here. I was gathering background so that I could respond to any questions about what happened to . . . the other writer."

"You can say his name. Ryan Betancourt. I wrote with him for two years. He was a great writer." Again he noticed the honesty of the words. "But you could have got all that over the phone. Why go to Maine for a press release?"

"And miss seeing the troupe together? Not a chance."

"That's funny. I was at the party pretty late and I didn't notice you."

"Now there's something every girl likes to hear." Kelly had been wearing a hard look throughout this exchange, but she abruptly dropped it. "Well haven't we gotten off on the wrong foot! I'm going to be your liaison here, so let me apologize. I thought Jerome would have told you who I was."

"Once you get to know him, you'll find that 'Jerome' marches to the beat of whatever's drumming around in his head. It's generally not a good idea to assume he'll do anything." Jack stuck his hand out, letting his tone soften to match hers. "Let's start over. Jack Glynn, current writer for the Jerome Barron Players."

"Kelly Sykes, Chamber of Commerce Liaison to Death Troupe —or don't you call it that?"

"Most of us do. Barron's not partial to it, but who cares about him anyway?" He turned to face Tillman, who had settled into a large leather chair behind the desk. "Did you condemn this poor young lady to babysitter duty?"

"Guilty as charged. But Kelly's much too busy to be a full-time sitter, so you'll be on your own as much as you want. Which brings up one of my questions: How much do you *want* to be on your own?" Jack noted the newest indication that Tillman had the town wrapped up, at least enough to regulate his interaction with the locals.

"Not much, at first. I like to rub elbows with the people in the town as much as possible. It helps me to get a feel for the location. In the past it's actually been part of the contract that the writer makes himself available. Is that still the case?"

"It is, but we're not going to stifle your creativity just to make some lawyers happy. The truth is everybody's very excited about the whole project, and especially the notion that we're going to have an actual play written about our town. It's caused quite a sensation."

"It's funny you should say that, because it's one of the things that convinced me to sign on with Barron years ago. You should have heard him selling it to me—" Jack roughened his voice so that it became an almost perfect imitation of the Director—"'Part of the attraction is that this play is *theirs*. It's written in their midst, and it's about *them*. It's guaranteed to be original, too, not a warmed-over version of *Streetcar*.'"

Tillman straightened up, glancing at Kelly before speaking. "Wow. You sound just like him. You sure you're not one of the players? Maybe sneaking a clue in right under our noses on the very first day?"

"No, although I wouldn't put it past us. I once thought I had the acting bug, but it turned out to be more like the twenty-four hour flu. Wait until you see the real ones in action. It's quite a thing."

"And when will that be? Your boss wouldn't even ball-park when the first actors would be making their appearances. He said that was more your area."

Damn you, Barron. As if the writer decides anything in this circus.

"Well, he's right that we can't start programming the clue distribution and the introduction of the characters until the play's almost completely written, but believe me—" he gave each of them a promissory smile "—you'll know it when the clues start to drop."

"I still say that's the best part about this." Tillman was fairly gushing now, and Jack had to remind himself that the mayor might be pumping him for information. "Even with our theater, which is top-notch, we can't get more than 300 people to the actual show. But by having your players showing up unexpectedly, dropping clues, we get the whole town involved."

"I'd say they get involved when their tax dollars are used." Kelly inserted drily. "Wouldn't you, Jack?"

Tillman shied a dismissing hand at her. "Don't worry about that. We're gonna be the first town to identify the killer, and then we'll get the show for free. Isn't that right, Jack?"

"Well, you'll have already paid for a lot of it." Jack had never been comfortable with Barron's famous wager with the host towns. If a majority of the show's audience identified the culprit in a vote taken just before the final act, the town didn't have to pay the rest of the troupe's fee. He felt it cheapened the whole process, and lent itself to accusations that Barron had changed the ending to ensure that the wager wasn't lost.

"Paid for what? A few meals and airfare?" Tillman said this to Kelly, causing Jack to consider that the Chamber of Commerce Liaison might not fully support the chosen use of the town's funds. "When you tally up everything that's being donated, like Jack's food and lodging for the next few months, we're practically getting them for free."

"Actually, I'll be paying for all my meals myself. I know that I'm not supposed to, but that part of the arrangement dates back to the troupe's early days, when there was a real chance that the writer would starve. It's not really necessary now." *And this way, if I want a steak, I order a steak.* "I've come into some money recently, so please tell your local eating places to bring the check to me."

"Oh, that's right! You made a big score out in Hollywood, didn't you? Kelly was telling me all about it. A war picture, right?"

Now it was Jack's turn to give Kelly the long look. "Barron tell you that, or have you been doing some extra research?"

She didn't get a chance to answer, as Tillman cut in like a proud parent. "Extra research? I'll say! She probably knows more about your troupe than they know about themselves."

Jack doubted that strongly, and Kelly seemed to doubt it too. "If I'm going to be your point-of-contact, it makes sense for me to know how you operate. But the Web's been my only source, apart from that interview with Jerome, so I'll probably have lots of questions for you as we go along."

"Feel free to ask me anything. That's the true deal here, and I want you both to know I hold up my end. I'm a friendly guy, I like people, and until I get my ideas finalized I'll be hanging around all the public places here, happy to meet anyone at all. Let your people know they can come right on up, even if I look like I'm writing. Seriously, it helps me get the lay of the land—and it's your party."

"Well then let's get the party started," Tillman looked at his watch. "Why don't we all head over to the diner for lunch? We've got a little welcoming get-together tonight, but this'll help you ease your way in." He rose and reached for a red-and-black hunting jacket on a stand in the corner. "And no, Jack, you're not paying for lunch or dinner today. You can start buying your meals tomorrow."

Tillman invited Melanie to join them as they passed the reception desk, and they had to wait while she checked on the fire before locking up. This was yet another aspect of small-town life that Jack had forgotten during his hiatus; closing up shop to go to lunch was often a commonplace. Locking the door was probably the only unusual part, but Jack took the opportunity to step out to his truck.

Kelly went with him, having donned a full-length olive-drab parka that looked like it was made from a comforter. Jack must have pulled some kind a face when he saw it, for she chided him brightly as she pushed past him at the door: "Don't laugh. It's warm!"

She followed him to the pickup, nodding in appreciation at his choice of vehicle and inspecting the tires while he opened the back. In a comical frenzy, he whipped off his gloves and overcoat before snatching up a gray tweed suit jacket and donning all three articles in reverse order at top speed.

"I don't think you have to worry about getting dressed up around here, Jack. We're a pretty casual crowd."

"That's not the reason for the jacket; there's a notebook and pen in the pocket. I like to have those handy as soon as I arrive. It's amazing the kind of ideas you can get from the locals."

"From observing them, or from listening to them?"

"It's really a bit of both, but I've gotten my best suggestions from people who've just walked right up and given them to me. I need to write it all down because I've got a lousy memory."

She gave him a slight smile, as if he'd just passed some sort of test administered to outsiders. He returned it while buttoning his parka all the way up to his chin. The wind had picked up, coming across the powdered surface of the lake behind them and trying to fly up under his coat.

He'd only spoken a half-truth just then, but that was all part of the game. It was true that the townspeople usually gave him good ideas. They were tuned in to the local lore and Jack felt that legends served as excellent background to a story. He tried to record everything that was said to him, often finding pleasant surprises in the items he'd forgotten. He usually avoided gossip and feuds, and wished that Barron had done the same, but the notebooks served another purpose as well.

Wade Parker had introduced him to the concept of disinformation years before, and he'd found it useful in confusing those citizens who wanted to solve the troupe's murder mystery by looking over his shoulder. Jack liked to camp out in public places when on site, and made no effort to hide what he was writing because he essentially assumed the role of a vacuum cleaner, sucking up and recording everything around him. He had his own code system for marking the passages that he considered important, and the truth was that he never wrote any part of the play itself out in the open.

"I told you that tie would give him the wrong idea, Marv." Kelly sang out suddenly, just before Jack heard the crunching on the ice that said Tillman and Mel were approaching. "You made him practically change clothes out here!"

"Well don't do *that!*" Tillman responded cheerfully, and Jack noted that this was the second time the mayor had used the phrase. If it was something he said often, it could be worked into the play as one more touchstone for the audience. "After tonight you won't see me wearing one of these silly things except at church."

"And on opening night, of course."

"Hell no! We're going whole hog on the big evening. Tuxedos, gowns, the works. I've already alerted the shops in Glens Falls and

50

Saranac Lake to be expecting us in May." He motioned for them to start walking toward the town center. "Wouldn't want the prom crowd to get all the good outfits."

"Like any of the men around here are going to fit into a high-schooler's tuxedo!" Mel, dressed in a quilted coat similar to Kelly's, snorted at Tillman.

"Well I dunno about that . . . look at Jack here. Sportin' a tan in mid-winter and probably fifteen percent body fat at most . . . he might start a fitness craze all by himself."

Mel called out to Jack as they walked across the common on a pathway of dead grass that had been uncovered by a snowblower. "Don't listen to him, Jack! Be careful you don't do what we do—pack on so many pounds under all this extra clothing that you want to kill yourself come swimsuit season!"

The concept of wearing a swimsuit in this region seemed ludicrous to Jack, and he looked up and down the wintry square as they approached the street on the opposite side. It was one of the things that bothered him as a storyteller: While he could easily describe this same ground as drenched in sun, with waving grass and trees made top-heavy with leaves, somehow his imaginings never seemed real to him. Of course he knew that the inescapable change of the seasons would bring the sun, the greenness, and the tourists, but just then, standing on the edge of an empty field buried under two feet of snow, it seemed patently impossible.

Kelly led the way across the street toward a single-story restaurant with an electric sign in one of its wide front windows identifying it as the Schuyler Mills Diner. The first letters of the town's name were larger than the others, and Kelly pointed at it as they approached.

"The S&M Diner. I think that says it all."

From the outside the S&M looked like a railroad car, with a flat roof and rectangular windows laid lengthwise. Whatever its nickname, it was clearly one of the town's more popular lunch destinations, as Jack could already make out several faces inside. They passed through a glass door straight into the dining area, and Jack imitated the others when they hung their heavy jackets on the many pegs which protruded from the nearest wall.

"Well this must be the Word Doctor!" a happy voice cried out, and Jack saw a large, red-faced man wearing an apron coming toward them. The rattle of dishes and the smell of cooking food rose from a window behind the long counter, and it was easy to guess that the greeter had just come from the kitchen. The man's hair had once been blonde, but what was left of it was mostly gray. He wiped his palms on a full-body apron as he approached, and took Jack's hand in both of his own. "Hiya, Doc! Welcome to Schuyler Mills!"

The Mayor tried to make introductions. "This is "Maddy" Madden, owner of the diner as well as the next place over—"

"Maddy's Place! You'll be spending a lot of time there; it's the best watering hole in the whole town!" Madden dropped Jack's hand abruptly, turning his head so that only one of his eyes was visible. "You do drink, right?"

"What writer doesn't?" Jack responded with a grin, becoming aware of the many faces from the booths to his right and the tables just past them.

"Wonderful! I know we're putting on a little shindig for you this evening, but everybody ends up at my place after those things, so I'll see you there!" Madden looked over his shoulder toward the kitchen, sniffing in alarm. "Gotta run! Sit anywhere!"

He was gone a moment later, and a woman roughly the same size came up from Jack's right, shaking her head. "He's a handful, isn't he? You should try living with him. I'm Tamara Madden, please call me Tammy." She took Jack's arm and started walking him past the window side booths, the others following obediently. "I just can't tell you what it means to us to have your troupe, Mr. Glynn. You should have been here—well, over at Maddy's anyway—when we got the word that Schuyler Mills had been selected for this year's performance. I thought the yelling was going to raise the roof. There was more than one hangover in town the next day, I can tell you."

She almost managed to deposit him in the last booth, but Jack's old instincts were kicking in and he was surprised that none of the people at the counter or window seats had tried to say hello. A mix of genders, ages, and dress, they'd offered a series of big smiles but no one had tried to say anything. That kind of timidity was infectious, so Jack let the others slide into the booth before clearing his voice and speaking so that the whole place could hear him.

"Hi everybody, I'm Jack Glynn, and as you know I'll be in town until the performance in May." This got a smattering of applause, but it was the upturned faces that told him to continue. "There's a little get-together on for tonight, I'm assuming you're all invited . . ." he stopped and looked down at Tillman, who was seated facing the crowd. "Am I right? Are they all invited?"

Tillman didn't miss a beat. "They are *now*, Jack."

That got a big laugh, and he stood there grinning until it ended. "Great. So I'll be seeing you all there. I just want to say that this is your play, written for your town, and that I'll be all over the place. So please feel free to come up and talk to me wherever you see me."

A man in a plaid work shirt, obviously one of the town's wiseacres, called out, "Even if it's in the john?"

That brought on more laughter, and Jack joined in while his face reddened. This was going to be all right. "Why not? Seriously, I want to meet you and get your ideas, so don't be shy. And remember one thing: If the director doesn't like my first draft I'm gonna blame it on you anyway, so you might as well step up and be heard."

After lunch the quartet walked back to the parking lot outside the Visitor's Center. Tillman stepped up to Jack's truck and peered inside the cap.

"Okay, this'll work just fine. You have to be careful at this time of year, Jack; you're gonna get stuck in the snow at some point and you have to be ready. I've asked Kelly to help you put together an emergency kit with the stuff that most of us carry in our vehicles. Is that a sleeping bag I see in there? Excellent. Keep it in your truck at all times. That way if you get stuck so bad that you can't get out, at least you'll be warm."

He turned to Kelly, having clearly passed into some kind of Town Father mode. "Make sure he gets a good shovel, a bucket of sand, a few energy bars, and a flashlight."

Kelly replied in a high-pitched voice that Jack usually associated with bubble-headed blondes in the movies. "Thanks for telling me all this, Mr. Mayor! I'm new in town myself."

Tillman smirked in response, the tip of his tongue sticking out between taught lips for a moment. "I know you know what to do. It's just that I don't want anything getting in the way of Jack's work. He hasn't got a lot of time, and I don't want to see him catching pneumonia traipsing back to town one night." This reminded him of something else, and he turned back to the writer. "Speaking of that, I see you've got a good hat and gloves. Keep them on you at all times, and pick up some spares as well. Keep those in the truck—they won't do you any good sitting in a bedroom drawer."

He looked Jack up and down, as if considering whether or not to hire him for a job requiring manual labor. "I like the jacket. Kelly, make sure he has a scarf . . . or better yet, take him over to Bib's and have him get one of those neck gaiters that he can pull up over his nose if he has to. While you're there, have him pick up a set of insulated boots, too."

Jack was slightly taken aback, having walked his hiking boots over many desert miles and priding himself on how broken-in they were. "What's wrong with them?"

"Oh, nothing. Keep 'em around for springtime and I'm sure they'll come in real handy. What you need is a set of boots that'll keep your feet warm and dry, and those aren't going to do it. You go walking in the snow in those . . . which reminds me, until you've been here a few days don't go walking away from habitation. You're obviously some kind of outdoorsy guy like the rest of us, but the woods around here are really tricky. Some of the trails are marked—"

"But most of those are snowmobile trails." Mel interrupted with a scowl on her face. "Stay off of anything that's marked with a snowmobile silhouette, Jack. Amazing how seemingly normal people just lose their minds when they get on those things. You're likely to get run over if you're not careful."

"It's not that bad." Tillman reached out and tapped Jack's upper sleeve, as if to reassure him. "We love our winter around here, and there are all sorts of fun things to do. Skating, snowmobiling, skiing . . . do you ski, Jack?"

"Not downhill, no."

"Good man. Just an opportunity to break a leg. How about cross-country?"

"I saw it on TV once. It looked like fun, and a good way to check out the scenery."

"Exactly. Kelly, let's see if anybody's got an extra set of cross-country stuff that'll fit Jack. We'll take you out and show you how . . . it's really easy and you'll be surprised at how much ground you can cover."

A muffled beeping stopped him, and he reached into his coat pocket after pulling off one of his gloves. He flipped his phone open, saw the message, and made a face like a child who's been told it's time to come in and wash up. "Sorry, Jack. Gotta run. Tooth extraction."

Jack was surprised by this sudden announcement, having failed to notice any discomfort on the mayor's part when they'd been eating. "Sorry to hear that. I hope it turns out all right."

"It's not me, Jack. I'm the town dentist. Mayor's only my part-time job." Seeing the newcomer's reaction, he laughed and slapped his arm again. "We're a little out of the way, sure, but you haven't fallen off the map! We've got a town doctor, our own clinic, and for anything serious we can whistle up a chopper—" The beeping sounded from his coat again, and he raised both hands as if in supplication. "Okay, that's it. See you tonight! Kelly, make sure he gets moved in all right. Mel, I'll be over at my office . . ." whatever he said after that was obscured by the wind as he hustled across the lot to a large SUV.

A moment later he was gone, leaving Jack with the two smiling women.

"The way he goes on, you'd think we were all born last night." Mel shook her head, but the words were spoken with obvious affection. She raised a gloved hand in farewell before starting toward the Visitor's Center. "See you tonight, Jack."

"Okay, let's get you over to the hotel and move you in." They both climbed into Jack's pickup, and he started to take a left-hand turn in the direction in which he'd arrived that morning.

"Right! Right turn!" Kelly hissed sternly, and when he gave her a questioning look she explained, "It's a one-way street."

Jack, his foot firmly on the brake, took a long moment to look left and then another to look right. The street circumscribing the town common was completely empty, and the Schuyler Mills Hotel was directly across the common from where they sat.

"You're kidding me, right?"

"No I'm not. You should see this place when summer gets here. The street's not wide enough for two-way traffic once it's parked up, and . . . can't you read?" She pointed at the one-way arrow affixed to one of the lamp posts surrounding the square.

"All right, all right." Jack turned the wheel and started up the long side of the town square. "Wouldn't want to get arrested my first day . . ."

"By whom? There's no police here. Heck, even our Fire Department is volunteer."

"And where is that?" Jack craned his neck as if searching an empty vista, trying to hide a smile while he drove. To his right he saw a long, two-story stone building that was marked as the town library and then a short block of stores that included the aforementioned "Bib's Outfitters". The main road continued east, where Jack saw several houses just before he turned left to go down the short side of the common.

"Main Street forks a little further out. If you take the left fork you'll go by the fire station, and if you keep going you'll end up at Round Pond. That's where the Playhouse is, along with a campground that the summer theater programs use."

Coming down the other side of the square, they passed the small marquee for the Schuyler Mills Moviehouse and then another block of stores. A wide, empty veranda came up after that, and it didn't take much imagination to see that it was the outdoor seating area for Maddy's Place, a two-story building with gabled windows, old-fashioned shutters, and a sign in Old English script.

"Theater seems to be big here. Those summer programs of yours do some pretty ambitious stuff."

"It's a really good combination of art and camping, and it gets the city kids out in the fresh air too. You'd be surprised at how good some of the productions are. Turn in here." They had already passed the diner, and Jack took a right just after the four-story wood-and-stucco front of the Schuyler Mills Hotel. It wasn't a big place as hotels go, but the parking lot was enormous. The ground behind the building was level for a long way before rising toward the largest of the hills near the town. Numerous houses stood between him and the base of the tree-studded slope, but Jack's eye was drawn to the top.

"What is that? A fire tower?" He pointed up at a spike that stood out in girders and zigzagging steps against the slowly clouding sky.

"That's right. Campion Hill is the highest point for miles, so that's where they put the tower. I'll take you up there once you've had a chance to look the town over. It's quite a view."

"It's open? I mean, just anybody can go up there?"

"Well sure—it's not as if somebody's going to steal it."

"I was more concerned with accidents. People falling off the thing, the town getting sued."

"Oh, wait until you've been here a while, Jack. After the snowmobiling, the drinking, and the hunting, the fire tower's probably the last thing we worry about." She gave that a thought, and continued. "There is a boom across the one road leading up there, and we do lock that every night in the good weather. Right now it's open most of the time."

Kelly carried two of his bags with ease, and counting the two he was hauling it was close to everything he had with him. They passed through a back entrance into a dark central hallway with numbered doors on either side that shortly opened up into a main lobby that was only a little brighter. The floor was covered with a rug, but the planks beneath that groaned as Jack crossed it. A support post of some kind stood in the center of the room behind several overstuffed chairs that faced a widescreen television set suspended in the corner near an unlit fireplace.

The unmanned hotel desk stood off to the side facing the main door, and it looked like a cyclone had hit it. Random papers and tourist brochures were scattered across the counter, and the wall behind that was even more haphazardly arranged. A set of moose antlers stuck out over a matrix of small cubbyholes, most of which held small brass keys in addition to an eclectic collection of figurines, tiny stuffed animals, and sports-related knickknacks. Kelly went behind the counter after dropping Jack's suitcases, selected a key from the overloaded rack, and came back around as if this was the most natural thing in the world.

"Um, shouldn't I sign in or something?" He asked stupidly, still holding two bags of his own.

"You're not paying for it, are you?" she asked in reply while picking up his luggage and motioning toward a stairway that disappeared around a carpeted corner. "The hotel's only got two or three other guests right now, and I already checked you in this morning. They're a little short-staffed in the winter, so we pretty much help ourselves."

They climbed four flights of creaking stairs before emerging on the top floor, which was well lit by a series of rectangular skylights in the roof. Even frosted over and outlined with snow, they gave the narrow hallway a welcome, and even festive, feel. Jack followed her to the very end, which he guessed was a corner room facing the common while she worked the old key into the door's tarnished lock.

Jack found that he'd guessed correctly, and was pleased to see that he not only occupied a corner room with all its light-giving windows, but that it was actually a small suite. They entered a sitting room of sorts, with a television, a refrigerator, a desk, an empty bookcase, and a wing-backed reading chair. The room itself was paneled in light brown wood up to waist height, where it changed over to white plaster that stretched all the way up and across the ceiling. A framed watercolor of a tiny man fly fishing in a snowstorm hung near the desk, and a lacquered fish of some kind was nailed over the doorway leading into the bedroom.

The décor continued in the same fashion, with a four-drawer bureau-and-mirror, a closet, and a double bed covered by an earth-tone comforter displaying various woodland scenes. A door led off into a full bathroom, and Jack found himself liking the place immediately.

"How long can I have this for?" he asked as he dropped his bags and swung his laptop onto the bed where it jumped in the air with a satisfying bounce. As his lodgings were donated, he already knew he'd be moving around a little in the next few months.

"You like it?" Kelly asked from the sitting room in a distracted voice. "Right now we've got you scheduled to be here 'til at least the end of January, but if you want to stay longer . . . it shouldn't be a problem."

Puzzled by the change in tone, he stepped back into the connecting doorway and saw what had caught his guide's attention. Kelly kept talking, her eyes fixed on an item which sat on the desk. "We figured you might want some privacy once you started your writing . . . so we've got a quieter place at the motel outside of town pegged out as well."

Jack joined her at the desk, getting a good look at the flower arrangement which he'd completely missed upon entering the suite. It wasn't big, but it should have caught his eye. Standing in a low plastic vase that resembled a wooden bucket, the display consisted of six short black roses, a background of tangled straw, and two small plastic skulls on wooden sticks stuck in the dirt. A pitchfork-looking cardholder held up a printed note that said, "Welcome to Schuyler Mills" in a bleeding red script.

"Wow." Kelly looked up at him, for the first time seeming to be at a loss for words. "Those weren't here when I checked the room this morning. Seems you've already got an admirer."

"Yeah." Jack responded in a quiet exhalation. "Or maybe somebody's started the show a little early."

Chapter Five

Just before six o'clock, Jack inspected himself in front of the bureau's large mirror. Kelly would be there to pick him up in a few minutes, and he wanted to be ready. Unsure of the local dress code, he'd opted for something that wouldn't be mistaken for big-city opulence but still showed respect for the arena where Death Troupe would eventually perform. The guy looking back at him had too deep a tan, but otherwise he was dressed in an open-necked collared shirt, a gray sweater, and khaki trousers. Jack had opted for a set of brown dress shoes, but intended to notice how many people at the reception were wearing boots. He suspected that was the standard footwear during the winter months, regardless of the occasion.

The hotel's cable television offering was extensive, and he could have watched anything while waiting for his ride, but Jack tuned into a local news broadcast mostly composed of school sports and the weather. It was important to begin the immersion process right away, given the compressed timeframe caused by his sudden call-up. That thought reminded him of Ryan's unexpected passing and, without knowing why, he turned and looked at the strange welcoming present which still sat on his desk.

He'd laughed the flowers off as some sort of prank, unsure of just how much Kelly knew about Ryan's death and the troupe's last performance. Wade believed that he and Barron had severed any link to the unfortunate event in Red Bend, but Kelly still might have heard something at Ryan's funeral. She'd interviewed Barron and then circulated through the crowd of mourners while the liquor had been flowing, so it was possible she might have gained an inkling.

Jack had watched her reaction to his joking dismissal of the gift and, believing she hadn't completely bought it, decided to take another track. He'd been surprised, even as he spoke, to see how easily he fell back into the deceptive practices of Death Troupe. Kelly was obviously intelligent, and Tillman had said she knew everything about the act, so maybe it was time to try a little verbal sleight-of-hand. He'd suggested that the gift was from one of the third parties who sometimes showed up at Death Troupe engagements, and she'd known what he was talking about.

That wasn't surprising, as Barron had practically incorporated these uninvited players into the act long before. He liked the unscripted interference because it kept everyone guessing and forced people to check the troupe website. Once an invalid rumor or clue had circulated long enough, Barron killed it officially in a part of the site labeled 'Rumor Control'. Every valid clue was eventually listed there as well, allowing everyone to keep up, but Barron had a bad habit of taking his time updating the information stream.

Kelly had ended the conversation with the hope that nothing was going to interfere with the play's smooth operation, making Jack wonder if the confident Chamber of Commerce gal might have a touch of the control freak in her. Barron liked to know the idiosyncrasies of anyone who might help shape the vote on the night of the performance, and in the past Jack had passed items of that nature on to Wade. For no reason at all, he decided to keep this one to himself.

He did think about calling Wade, though. The flowers were just eerie enough to raise a qualm, and there were no stickers or markings anywhere on the arrangement to help identify its origin. Wade was probably back in Red Bend by then, surreptitiously looking into the tragedy at the old folks' home, but he'd urged Jack to call if anything bothered him. Two people connected to the troupe had recently died, and here was a floral arrangement that could easily be taken as a macabre threat.

Jack shook his head as if to clear it, uttering a slight laugh. He hadn't been there even twenty-four hours, and yet he was already reaching for the phone. He was reminded of Melanie Archer's comment about the teenaged summer camp counselors. Maybe he needed one of those adolescent stalwarts to buck him up, suggesting that he give his new environment a try before calling mommy and begging to be taken home. Standing there in the cozy room, getting ready for what was likely to be a fun night out, Jack made himself admire the jet-black roses for their beauty, and the plastic skulls for their kitsch.

"It's a *murder* mystery, dumbass." He said aloud, using a finger to test the moisture in the arrangement. Dissatisfied with the result, he went into the bathroom and got a tumbler of water. Pouring it in, he wondered if there might not be a way to use this in the play. Nothing as obvious as a floral delivery with a note, of course, but there had to be special meanings for various flowers like the black roses he had received, and he decided to investigate those when he returned.

There was a loud knock on the door just then, and even though it was almost certainly Kelly come to pick him up, he almost dropped the glass.

The Schuyler Mills Playhouse was a modern theater two miles outside of the town center on the banks of Round Pond. The road to Round Pond was two lanes and mostly woodland, although Jack did get to see the town firehouse and elementary school enroute. His jogger's eye took in the surroundings with pleasure, but the early darkness and the hard-packed snow told him he wouldn't be making this loop in running shoes anytime soon.

The theater itself was impressively large, and the number of cars and trucks parked next to it could be described the same way. From the front the Playhouse almost resembled a church, with a roof that sloped off diagonally on both sides from an open cupola which could have easily accommodated a half dozen people. The entire building was lit up, and its digital marquee kept morphing between a personalized message welcoming him to Schuyler Mills and the animated logo of Death Troupe.

The Jerome Barron Players had two insignias, one that was fixed and one that moved. The stationary logo took the symbolic Janus masks of the theater, one happy and one sad, and superimposed black eye-and-nose masks on top of their own natural disguises. The active insignia, which opened the troupe's homepage, introduced the Janus faces one at a time against a pitch black screen. The smiling mask faded in first, and a twin then materialized so that they were smiling at each other. The first face then received its ovular black mask, and the second one shifted to its more traditional frown. Only then did the sad face receive its redundant mask, and a grinning skull materialized out of the darkness between them. The orange-and-black lights of the marquee performed the dance admirably before announcing that the Jerome Barron Players would be there the first weekend in May.

Climbing out of Kelly's car, Jack noted a long, thin pennant flapping in the breeze at the top of the cupola. It was mostly black, but he could just make out the three-headed logo of Death Troupe in white. He pointed up at it.

"Wow. This is quite a welcome. I didn't know we had a pennant like that."

"You don't." Kelly was bundled up in her comforter again, but Jack had seen her without it back at the hotel and knew she wore a smart black business suit-and-skirt combination over nylons. "The ladies of our sewing club started work on that months ago. Every time there's a play here, they fly some kind of flag—"

"Just like the Globe Theater."

"Exactly. It's a local tradition. Now let's get inside before we follow another local tradition and freeze to death."

The church theme reasserted itself as they crunched across the parking lot. Above the marquee, which sat on a porch-like roof covering the entire front of the building, were three windows. The tallest was in the middle, directly beneath the apex of the roof, while the two on either side were shorter by a third. The windows were latticed as if made of stained glass, but instead of that they transmitted a warm butterscotch color from the bright lights inside.

Climbing the wide set of stairs, Jack saw that two long ramps ran from either side of what amounted to the theater's front porch. Looking down one of them, he noticed several indistinct objects out in the darkness near the lake and stopped to see if they would resolve into something he recognized.

"Those are the cabins the campers use during the summer, the ones who are here for theater camp." Kelly didn't let him stand there long, obviously keen on getting inside. They each took hold of a door handle and stepped through.

The foyer of the Schuyler Mills Playhouse was a thing of beauty. The main doors leading to the auditorium itself stood open one hundred feet in front of him, but Jack was too busy admiring the lobby. A rust-colored carpet covered the floor, reaching across to a long counter which did triple duty as the ticket office, concessions stand, and gift shop. A bar was set up off to the left, a buffet dinner was arranged to their right, and cream-colored walls rose above them. A banistered walkway ran all the way around the room overhead, and Jack could just make out the tops of the doors leading to the balcony.

Two wagon-wheel chandeliers provided much of the light, and Jack quickly made out a few of the faces from the S&M Diner in the crowd. He and Kelly ducked into the unmanned coatroom to ditch their winter wear, but they'd already been spotted by the time they came out.

"Jack! Whaddya think?" Marv Tillman, wearing a suede sport coat over his checked shirt and red tie, approached with his palms held out and raised toward the ceiling. A blonde woman in a festive sweater and brown skirt followed in his wake, and Jack assumed he was about to meet the mayor's better half.

Jack shook his head as if speechless, pressing his lips together while turning the ends up. "I saw pictures of it on the website, but I have to admit it's even better in person. How did you manage to put this together?"

"It wasn't easy—even with the grant money we still had to float a bond to make it happen. That was ten years ago, and even though it took us until last year to pay it off, I'd do it all again. You have to see this place during the summer, all jammed with kids, acting their hearts out."

"Let's not forget the local talent, dear." Intoned the blonde woman who had moved up next to the mayor.

"Speaking of local talent, this is my wife Kate." Tillman said with a smirk, even as Kate Tillman elbowed him in the ribs when he went to put his arm around her.

"It's very nice to meet you, Mr. Glynn." Kate gave Jack a smile as she extended her hand. "You've made quite an impression already. I wish you could have heard Marv after he came home from the office. He was simply gushing about how friendly and approachable you are!"

"Well, it *is* in the contract." Jack replied, and the four of them enjoyed a quiet laugh.

"Now to get back to what I was saying when my husband decided to get funny. We really do have quite a talented theater group right here in town. It's not like this place gets boarded up once the last camper goes home."

"I've heard that. In fact, Mr. Barron commented on how much he was looking forward to working with your players." That wasn't exactly true, but it was close. Right from the earliest days of the troupe, the Director had known that his brainchild contained a potentially fatal flaw. By descending on a small town for exactly one performance, Death Troupe could have engendered the hostility of the area's amateur theater group, and Barron had taken steps to avoid that.

Instead of shutting out the local talent, he'd adopted them right from the start. In a bold stroke that ended up using everyone in the local troupe (including its director) Barron had instructed Jack to write a small prologue segment into the script, something that would set the stage for the mystery to follow. That segment would be arranged, designed, and rehearsed by the local group and then performed at the beginning of the show. It neutralized the potential animus of the indigenous thespians without bringing them too close to the actual play, and Barron usually enjoyed the experience of checking their progress.

"Well I know he's going to be pleased when he starts working with our people," Kate continued, her smile growing wider. "Of course some of them are just doing this for fun, but wait until you see Glenda Riley on stage! She's simply an angel."

Mrs. Tillman turned to look through the meandering crowd, quickly finding what she was seeking. "There she is right there, the redhead standing next to the main entrance."

Jack obediently looked across toward the double doors leading into the auditorium. Every town had its overlooked star, but in this case he had to admit that this one certainly had the looks. Tall and slim, Glenda Riley looked to be about twenty-five. She wore a multicolored dress that showed off her figure, and was the center of attention in a group conversation that was suddenly interrupted by the arrival of a small child. The youngster, just old enough to run and sporting a wild tangle of red curls, came racing out of the forest of legs and ran straight into the redhead's leg, wrapping his arms around the woman who was clearly his mother.

Jack liked the local groups, having been recruited to the Barron Players from a murder mystery dinner show that had been only a notch or two above amateur level. He'd been their writer for only a few months, telling himself it was just to make ends meet while he worked on screenplays, when Barron had attended one of their events. Although no one had been aware of the famous stage director's presence, something in the performance had caused Barron to give Jack his card with instructions to call him the next day.

Before he could ask Kate about Glenda's background, a giant of a man stepped out of the crowd. The party's attendees varied in dress, but this man had to be the most casual of the lot. He wore a blue blazer over a set of bib overalls, a checked shirt, and heavy snow boots. He sported a full head of ginger-colored hair and a walrus moustache of the same color.

"Mr. Jack Glynn!" he took his hand in one massive paw, giving it a good solid squeeze but letting go just before it hurt. "I'm Frank Hatton, but everybody calls me Bib. As in Bib's Outfitters on the edge of the town center." He looked down at the denim pocket in the center of his chest before muttering, "Not sure why everybody calls me Bib."

Jack took up the gauntlet. "I'll try and find that out for you, Bib. I am, after all, a mystery playwright."

"Well thank Gawd you're here, then! Otherwise I was gonna have to contact the FBI! Say, Mr. Playwright, you don't seem to have anything in your hands. Wanna drink?"

"You bet. Which way's the bar?" Jack let Bib steer him across the lobby, detaching him from Kelly and the Tillmans. It was important to start mingling without his babysitter, and also to be seen with different people. Small town feuds run deep, and hanging around with the same group, no matter how much he might like them, could taint the whole engagement. When the players arrived they were so great in number that no one noticed who they spent their time with, but as the outfit's sole representative Jack had to be careful.

He and Bib had barely placed their orders—a rum and coke and a Canadian beer—when a fortyish couple approached. Bib saw them coming and tapped Jack on the shoulder to make him turn. "Look out, Jack, here's your competition. This is Dennis and Patrice Lawton, the only smart people in the whole town. They run our theater group."

Jack shook hands with the newcomers, a man and woman who resembled each other to an extent that was almost painful. Tall and thin, they both sported wire-rimmed glasses and dark hair that was either pulled back in a bun or cut short. Luckily they were both smiling.

"Don't listen to Bib, Mr. Glynn. He's just trying to get you to let down your guard by making you think the town's a pushover." This from Patrice, who inclined her head as if taking him into a special confidence.

"Besides, it would be better for you if we *were* the smartest people in town. As part of the performance, we certainly couldn't betray a confidence." Dennis Lawton said this with a face drenched in sincerity, and it took Jack a moment to remember that Lawton was the director of the local troupe and not one of its actors.

"Oh, you can betray anything you like." Jack shied a hand at them. "With the three-ring circus that we put on, half the actors don't know who the killer is anyway. But Barron's certainly looking forward to working with you and your players."

Although Barron always shepherded the host town's actors through their preparation, in Schuyler Mills he'd be spending a lot more time with them than normal. The town was hosting a Mystery Weekend in March, complete with a film festival and symposia conducted by Death Troupe's director and playwright. The event would attract devotees of every description, and Barron planned to make the Lawtons and their actors an integral part of his class.

"We're just thrilled to be included in this, Mr. Glynn, and we can't wait to start."

"Please call me Jack." He sipped his drink and looked over his newest acquaintances. The Lawtons' words were loose and accommodating, but everything else about them was pretty stiff and he decided to test them. Lowering the glass, he took on a bright expression and spoke as if telling the punch line of a joke. "And that way, the next time one of your actors says 'You don't know Jack!'. . . you can tell them you actually do."

This outburst was followed by a long stare from both Lawtons, and silence from Bib. A split second before he was about to start apologizing, Patrice Lawton let loose a high, tittering noise which slowly built into a full-throated laugh. Dennis Lawton's confused expression turned out to be just that, as he too began to giggle a moment later. "That's very good! Very good! Took me a minute, but . . . that's very good!"

Jack turned his head just enough to see Bib, who gave him a quick roll of his eyes before joining in on the general merriment.

Patrice continued after the laughter subsided. "Mr. Barron already asked us to prepare some things for his Mystery Week classes, and we were hoping to pick your brain if it's not too much trouble."

"Oh, I'm not sure how much help I'd be. The Director and I usually don't think along the same lines, and I'd be concerned about steering you wrong." As much as Jack hoped he'd deflected the invitation, he couldn't resist asking the question. "What's he asked you to look at?"

"Shakespeare's Scottish play." Dennis replied, avoiding the bad luck that many stage people associated with uttering the title of *Macbeth*.

"My goodness." That simply slipped out, and Jack moved quickly to counter it. "I mean, that's one ambitious piece . . . did he ask you to focus on a specific part?"

"Yes, two scenes: Where Lady Macbeth convinces her husband to murder the king, and the killing of Lady MacDuff and her son. I imagine he'll add some others as time goes by; those scenes don't really show off half the talent in our little troupe."

Jack nodded, unsure of Barron's intentions but reasonably certain that showcasing the skills of the local theater group wasn't among them. As a play, *Macbeth* was so well-known that the Director might be relying on that familiarity to save time on the day of the class. Even so, Jack couldn't see the connection between the two scenes Barron had requested—as usual, the workings of the Director's mind were beyond him.

He was about to ask if the Lawtons had received any specific guidance with the request, but Bib cut him off. "Watch out, Jack, here comes real trouble."

Before he could turn, Death Troupe's new writer found himself swamped by a collection of townies who barely got their names out before they began throwing bits of local lore at him. They were mostly middle-aged and older, both genders, and more than half in the bag. The Lawtons were quickly swept aside.

"I hear you like to use the local history in your plays!" shouted one woman who had elbowed her way past the others. "Did you know that Dutch Schultz *and* Legs Diamond were up in Saranac Lake during Prohibition?"

"Prohibition? I remember that!" called out an older man with mock seriousness. Even so, he tugged at Jack's arm and ended up practically yelling into his ear. "Forget the gangsters, that was just a fad! This is mining country. My father was a miner, and his father before him . . ."

A disembodied voice came at Jack from behind, but he was so closely hemmed in that he couldn't turn to see who it was. "You *have* to include our theater group . . . that Glenda Riley is *so* talented . . ."

" . . . I bet he doesn't even know that the silent picture industry was *all* Adirondack in the early years . . ."

"Did anyone tell you we have a ghost town not an hour north of here?"

"At the end of a dead-end road. Why would he want to go there?"

"Of course it's a dead end! It's a ghost town!"

An hour and a half later, Jack was seated on the railing in the theater's balcony. Bib had rescued him from the first mob by offering to buy a round, and Jack had then begun to work the crowd in earnest. He'd listened intently to the bits and pieces of local history being offered, already liking the items about Prohibition and the silent film era, but knowing he would never be able to remember them all the first time around. The important thing was to give everyone there the excuse to approach him later, and now they had the icebreaker of being able to say that he'd met them at the first reception.

There was a drawback to shaking so many hands in so short a time in such a setting, however; by the time he got inside the auditorium itself he'd already consumed three rum and cokes. He'd managed to turn down one or two others, largely because he'd been holding a fresh one at the time, but it was clear that power drinking was one of the winter sports in Schuyler Mills.

Sitting on the rail which ran the length of the balcony's front, he looked out onto the forest of seats below. The stage curtain was closed, and even though several small children were racing each other up and down the aisles it appeared that no one was allowed to mount the rostrum. The curtain was a subdued red, but a bank of colored lights dressed it up by roaming across its crenellated face in a preset sequence. All Death Troupe venues had to have state of the art systems, including light and sound, because Barron wanted every option when he staged a play. While some of his contemporaries on Broadway objected to almost everything technological, Barron refused to limit his presentation in the name of someone else's concept of purism.

There were, of course, practical reasons for this. No matter how many clues Death Troupe might have managed to disseminate in the run-up to the performance, they had only three acts in which to utterly bamboozle their audience. That was why Barron had slowly moved in the direction of shooting what amounted to a short film, something that would set the stage, which he often used as a brief introduction to the evening's mystery. To do that, he had to have access to the latest digital broadcast media, a suitable background, and a film team that was up to the job.

Over time, the Barron Players' film arm had risen to high prominence in the troupe. Years before, while directing one local theater group through the filming of its introductory short, Barron had experienced an epiphany regarding the use of backgrounds. Instead of static stand-up or drop scenery, he'd challenged the film team to create panoramic shots of well-known locations around the host town. At first these had been the digital equivalent of a painted canvas hung behind the players, but in time they'd become a dynamic, almost living part of the story.

The moving background had reached its most complex usage in a theater-in-the-round performance the year after *Wind in the Palms*. This had been quite ambitious, as the circular stage was completely surrounded by the audience and ran the risk that the digital scenery would block the players from view. The set designers had avoided this by ringing the stage with an ingenious selection of retractable half-screens which slid down to just above the actors' heads or popped up to just below their waists as required. The sky had swept across the top panels while the ground had flowed on the lower ones in a shifting dance that was an art form all by itself. The effect had been downright mesmerizing, but that wasn't the high point.

The film crew had noted the resemblance between the round stage and a carousel, and so Jack had been asked to re-write the scene of the murder to include that image. The effects people had broadcast a flickering light show across all of the panels high and low while a tinny soundtrack had played a carney version of 'Listen to the Mockingbird'. Even without the actors, the stage had appeared to be rotating in the darkened theater.

He could still see Allison, her hair blown back by a concealed fan, laughing with abandon while bobbing up and down as she and the other players aped the ride on the carousel. A series of gunshots had roared out just as the light show had climaxed in a strobe effect, and the players had fled through the crowd as if running from actual bullets. The lights had then come up, showing the *corpus delecti* sprawled face-down on the empty (and motionless) stage. The crowd had loved it, reviewers had deemed it an entirely new brand of theater, and Barron had received all the egging he would ever need to try and top it.

Of course that had greatly added to Jack's workload. As tough as it was to convince Barron to accept one of his storylines without changing it, Jack now had to worry about even crazier ideas from the film team. They shot promiscuously, and brought every pixel to the Director for consideration. This frequently left Jack doing rewrites to incorporate scenery like the view from atop the town hall, or to place the action on a tour boat cruising the local river at night. Looking out at the dancing lights here in the Schuyler Mills Playhouse, he shuddered at what the film people would do to him with the enormity of the Adirondacks.

"Watcha thinkin' about, stranger?"

He turned abruptly, and felt a woman's hand grip his upper arm with surprising strength. It was Kelly, and she clearly feared she'd almost tipped him over the rail.

"Wow—that's the second time someone's tried to kill me today!" he laughed before giving her hand a gentle pat, refusing to climb down from his perch. "First Mel almost brained me with a fireplace poker, and now you almost pushed me off into the cheap seats."

"I didn't push you, I saved you!" she protested with an answering laugh. "You heard the Mayor today. It's one of my jobs to make sure nothing happens to you."

"Well if something happens to me in a theater, you can honestly say it was my fault. I've spent enough time in these places to know my way around." He turned and looked at the stage again. It was a standard proscenium type, with the audience facing it from the front.

"Did you know we did a show in Florida that was theater-in-the-round?"

He could tell the alcohol was taking hold now, because if Kelly was as familiar with the troupe as Tillman had said, she'd certainly know about the acclaimed Florida show. It was impossible to tell, as she slid up onto the rail next to him with a look of true interest. "That was the one after *The Wind in the Palms*, wasn't it?"

"Good memory. *Wind in the Palms* was such a success that we were all feeling pretty cocky. Did you see the tape?"

"I did. The murder on the carousel looked very cool. I wish I'd seen it live."

"Theater-in-the-round's tough. You can end up with important players having their backs to one part of the audience for too long, so the dialogue has to jump around or the actors themselves have to keep shifting positions. Or at least that's what Barron says."

"You learned a lot from him, didn't you?"

"Yes . . . yes I guess I did. I was writing for a murder mystery dinner theater outfit when we met. It was strictly a part-time gig for me, but most of those actors really put in the effort and I respected them for it. Anyway, I didn't know my ass from a hole in the ground when it came to real theater, so Barron had to give me a crash course. Several, in fact." He took a sip from his latest drink, afraid that he'd start talking and not stop for an hour.

"He recognized your talent in dinner theater?" The question might have sounded snobbish or obsequious if he hadn't been able to see her face. She genuinely wanted to know, and for a boozy moment he wondered why.

"Oh, I don't think that's what happened." The Director had been romantically interested in the troupe's leading lady, and that was the only reason he'd been in attendance. "I think he got some kind of Archimedes-in-the-bathtub inspiration midway through the show, and I was the closest writer to hand. He gave me his card and told me to call him the next day. I was so ignorant of the theater world that I had to look him up online to find out who he was."

"You're kidding me."

"Not at all. I was a couple years out of college, and as far as I was concerned I was headed for Hollywood. I was gonna write screenplays and make millions. Lord knows what I'd be doing right now if Barron hadn't spotted me that night."

"Judging from recent events, I'd guess you'd be writing screenplays for Hollywood."

He smiled weakly, hoping it would be taken for modesty. "Maybe so. But what about you? You a local girl?"

"In a way. I'm from Binghamton. It's a city pretty far south of here, close to the Pennsylvania state line. My family always went to the Adirondacks for summer vacation, so when I finished college I started looking for a job that would let me have it year-round." The words flowed smoothly, a tad too rehearsed. Jack wondered if it was just the standard defense against the modern age, where anyone seeking a job off the beaten track was sometimes viewed as an oddball. He didn't get to ponder it for long. "So you were the only writer for the troupe's early years, then you wrote with Ryan Betancourt, and now you're writing alone again. Is it hard to switch back and forth?"

Not when you're so mad at your partner that you'd like to kill him.

"I think so. Luckily I've been on my own for a couple years now, so it's not such a big change. I'll tell you what was hard: Learning to write with Ryan and then having Barron change everything we'd come up with. When it's just two scribblers bouncing ideas off of each other it's pretty easy to come to some kind of agreement, but when a third party comes in and starts spit-balling after that . . . it can be tough."

"So it's probably better that you're doing this one on your own, huh?"

Jack tried not to show his concern at the strange tack of their conversation. Why was she so interested in all this stuff? "I guess so. It's easier to make the changes 'suggested' by the director when it's only one writer."

"Think you'll stay with the troupe when this engagement is over, or are you headed back to Hollywood?"

"I live in Arizona, actually. And as far as the troupe is concerned—"

"Don't jump, Jack! You have everything to live for!" a loud male voice sailed up from the seats below, and Jack and Kelly both looked down at the upturned face of Bib Hatton. He'd donned a blue parka with a fur-lined hood, obviously preparing to leave, and was surrounded by several of the faces from the earlier ambush. "The Mayor's tryin' to close up shop here, so we're headin' over to Maddy's! You wanna lift?"

Jack turned a questioning look at Kelly, who raised both hands and shook her head. "Oh, there won't be any Maddy's for me tonight. I'm helping clean up here."

"But you're my ride."

Kelly hopped off of the rail, pointing over her shoulder as she headed for the exit. "Your ride's calling you from downstairs."

Jack stood at the corner window of his suite, looking out into the darkness. It was just after midnight, and he was mildly drunk. He'd gone back to Maddy's with Bib and the others, where the group quickly showed they were ready for a long drinking session. He'd kept himself on the move, making small talk and trying to avoid anyone who was doing shots, but in the end he'd consumed much more than usual.

His new friends had been loud in their protest when he'd announced that it was past his bedtime, but Tammy Madden had saved him by reminding the partygoers that Jack probably had some writing to do. He'd hustled out into the cold with his coat in his hand, fearful that the grace period bought by Mrs. Madden might expire while he was still bundling up.

The wind had died down considerably while he'd been inside, and so he took his time walking the short distance to the hotel. The town square was deserted at that time of night, and he'd enjoyed the cool air on his face. Now he stood looking out onto the snow-covered common, a large glass of water in his hand, sorting through the information he'd gleaned during the evening. He intended to fire up his laptop in a few minutes, to jot down what he'd learned and to check his mail, but first he needed to rehydrate.

The lamp poles on either side of the common threw a surprising amount of light, and he tried to imagine how the square must have appeared just weeks before, covered in Christmas decorations. The scene he imagined had an almost fairy-tale, snow-village quality to it, and he could envision holiday ice skaters spinning around on the shimmering expanse even though it wasn't a skating rink.

The lamplight didn't penetrate the alleyways and side streets, and so he was startled out of his reverie when a figure on cross-country skis emerged from the shadows on the other side of the field and began sliding down the snow-packed road. It was hard to tell much from that distance, but the lone skier knew what he or she was doing. The movements were all fluid, as if the traveler's muscles had gone slack and the equipment was doing all the work. The poles seemed to reach ahead on their own, one following the other, and the stranger's legs, alternately bending and straightening, followed the long thin skis as if pulled by them instead of propelling them.

Jack noted just how anonymous the hat and goggles made the figure, and decided to try and work that into the act. He'd had a similar thought earlier, watching Bib zip up his fur-lined hood so that it completely obscured his face. *In this part of the world at this time of year, someone who wanted to remain anonymous could move around in broad daylight without ever being recognized.* He watched the skier disappear up the road, light reflecting off the figure's safety vest, before turning away from the window.

He went into the bedroom and knelt to open the small, rectangular safe which was home to his laptop when he was out. He'd secured it to an exposed pipe behind the bedroom door using a locking cable, and saw with satisfaction that it had not been disturbed. Although it would be child's play to cut the restraint and steal the entire safe, the intent was to make it difficult for someone to mess with the laptop without his knowledge.

Carrying the machine back to the desk, he gently pushed the arrangement of black roses off to the side and set it down. He plugged into the wall socket and the room's Internet connection before heading into the bedroom for more water while the laptop awoke. When he came back it was still cycling through Wade's security software, but in another minute the screen told him that no unauthorized user had accessed it and that no one was trying to do that now.

He had two messages when he opened up his email, one from Barron and one from Allison. He opted for Allison's first, and wasn't surprised that it was a terse wish to break a leg. She would be in Vancouver for the next few weeks, and had warned him in Maine that the shooting schedule of this particular film would be eating up a lot of her time. Jack wasn't surprised by that, knowing that Allison threw herself into every role she ever played. She'd never been big on correspondence or even phone calls anyway, but he wondered why that bothered him now when it never had in the past.

Saving the message, he moved on to the one from the Director. It contained a surprise, in that Ryan's sister Emily had located the notebook in which the writer had been scribbling his ideas before he killed himself. A courier would hand deliver the item to Jack the next day, and he was advised to keep his cell phone nearby to receive the call.

The revelation about the missing notebook tweaked Jack's curiosity, and he clicked on the folder containing Ryan's initial thoughts for the Schuyler Mills play. It was just a few notes, but it described a modern-day mystery tale with roots in the Great Depression. Ryan had been noodling around with the idea of an Adirondack stock broker who had lost the life savings of an entire town in the Great Crash. The fictitious broker had supposedly killed himself in shame, but there was speculation that the town's money had been stolen instead of lost. Ryan had listed several possible culprits, from a crooked assistant to a romantic competitor, who

73

might have taken the money and then faked the suicide to cover the crime.

The description ended in a switch to modern times, when a descendant of the disgraced financier comes to town hoping to clear his ancestor's name. The investigator is of the opinion that the real truth, in the form of a confession from one of the culprits, was discovered long ago and then hidden somewhere in the town. Needless to say, he is hell bent on finding it.

Jack sat back, admiring the last green shoot to sprout from the fertile mind of his old writing partner. Although it represented the very beginning of a brainstorming session that was supposed to have lasted weeks, it was a solid storyline with a main character that could be played as anything from a knight in shining armor to a near-lunatic obsessed with the past. Ryan's genius for laying the foundation of big, meaty scenes was evident even in this merest outline, but something twitched uneasily in the back of Jack's alcohol-lubricated mind all the same. Marveling at Ryan's handiwork, he had almost overlooked the obviously dangerous elements of a family's disgrace and a town's dark secret.

"Did you write this even after what happened in Red Bend?" Jack asked aloud, reaching out and absently plucking one of the plastic skulls from the floral arrangement to his left. He twisted the small death's head back and forth on its tiny wooden pike, imagining different ways of making Ryan's idea more palatable. He glanced down at the grinning effigy and, after a moment, smiled affectionately in return. "Alas, poor Ryan. I knew him, Horatio: a fellow of infinite talent."

He put the skull back in the soil and began to type.

Chapter Six

". . . the meaning of the black rose is a source of endless debate. For some it is an expression of hatred or even the declaration of a vendetta, while for others it is merely symbolic of death. In some cultures a black rose was presented when the giver was about to embark on a trip or mission from which return was unlikely, while in others it represented rebirth or the acquisition of transformative knowledge . . . "

Jack sipped a steaming mug of coffee while reading the laptop's screen. He was seated at a rectangular table in the coffee shop portion of Wicked Wanda's, an arts and crafts store on the Schuyler Mills town common that he'd discovered while out walking that morning. He'd slept in, and had been pleasantly surprised to wake with only a mild hangover. Shaving and showering quickly, he'd set off to explore the businesses around the common and get some air.

Completing his circuit, Jack had then dropped into the S&M Diner for breakfast. He'd received some good-natured ribbing from Maddy, who had assisted in the S&M's pre-dawn opening despite having stayed late at the bar the night before. Seeing Jack through the window, Kelly had popped in to tell him he was on his own for the day while she handled some unspecified town business. Jack hadn't seen Tillman anywhere, but he was far from alone; several strangers dropped into his booth claiming to have met him the night before. It was past noon when he asked for the check, and several pages of his flip notebook were filled with comments and suggestions gleaned from his visitors.

His cell phone had rung obligingly as he was going out the door, and he'd accepted delivery of Ryan's notebook in the lobby of the hotel. Returning to his room, he'd decided to pack up his laptop and take advantage of the remote Internet access advertised in the window of Wicked Wanda's. The arts and crafts shop was an old brick building with a well-trafficked wood floor and two entrances. The left-most door led into the workshop, where Jack had seen several students of varying ages employed at everything from painting to sculpture before being politely directed back outside to try the other entrance. That one led into the store, where racks of supplies stood next to shelves loaded with a wild assortment of items for sale which had presumably been created in the next room. The exposed bricks of the store's walls had turned tan or gray with age, and Jack had decided that Wicked Wanda's was going to be one of his hangouts.

His computer's security software had given the thumb's up once he'd logged on in the small coffee area, and he'd diligently transcribed his notes from that morning's interviews into a growing research file.

With that chore complete, he'd bought a mug of coffee from Lynnie, the young girl working the counter. An enticing selection of rolls, cookies, and cupcakes beckoned from the counter's transparent display, but he'd just eaten and only wanted the caffeine. Returning to the laptop, he'd started searching the web for the meaning ascribed to various flowers like the black roses he'd received the day before. Although much of the available information was confusing and even contradictory, it held his attention to the extent that he was unaware of Lynnie's approach when she cleared one of the tables behind him.

"Black roses? You looking to put a hex on somebody, Jack?" The voice could have been a teenager's, but Jack had made small talk with Lynnie while she'd prepared his coffee and guessed she was in her early twenties.

Though behind him, the girl was far enough away that she could not have read the words without meaning to do so. Jack was on the verge of saying something smart about her outstanding eyesight when he noticed that the background of the article he was reading was made up of black roses. Mentally slapping himself, he put on a pleasant face before turning to reply. "It's a little research, actually. Somebody left me some black roses . . . once . . . and I wanted to see if I could work that into the play somehow. Not necessarily black roses, but any flower that has a meaning."

"So what did you find out?" Lynnie approached slowly, wiping her hands on the towel she'd been using to wipe off the tables. She was average height and pretty, with blonde hair parted in the middle that flowed in a perfect arc to just below her jaw line on either side. She wore a tight-fitting brown top that showed just a little cleavage, and the white apron below that bulged in a promising way. Jack noted the black polish on her nails and guessed that the top's long sleeves concealed more than one tattoo.

"Looks like I might not be able to use it after all. There's lots of stuff here, loads of different meanings for various flowers and even for their colors, but I'm not sure how many people in the audience would know them."

"Would that make a difference?" Lynnie came close enough to read the words, and Jack saw for the first time that she wore a tight set of black jeans over a ratty pair of red sneakers. He also noted that she was just a little on the plump side, which he normally didn't consider a negative, but given her age it didn't bode well for the future.

"Well it could." Jack took a moment to get his argument together, simultaneously considering how he might include this topic in his class during the Mystery Weekend in March. "It's okay to use something like that, provided you work in an explanation so that you don't leave the audience behind."

"What if most of them would know the meaning?"

"That's even worse, in my opinion. Imagine what it would feel like to be one of the people who don't see the significance, but clearly just about everybody else does?"

"Oh I don't have to imagine it; that's how I feel most of the time. But I don't think you should dumb things down, either. If I don't understand something, I get off my ass and crack a book or ask somebody about it." She smiled to take the heat out of the words. "I mean, unless it's something I really don't care about, and then it wouldn't bother me that everybody knows something I don't."

Jack laughed helplessly, recognizing some of the attitude from his own not-too-distant youth. "I'm the same way myself, but it doesn't fly in theater."

"Really? What about all those old plays, like Shakespeare, where you practically have to speak a different language to get half the jokes? They perform those all the time."

Jack gave her a look of mock suspicion. "Have I been ambushed by some kind of theater major here? Out to stump the starving writer who's just trying to earn a living?"

She slapped his shoulder with the towel before heading back toward the counter where a new customer waited. "Not a chance. This girl's school days are all done."

Jack smiled as he watched her go, questioning his earlier impulse to include the issue in his Mystery Week presentation. If he got tied up in knots by a school-hating coffeehouse server, what would a serious theater student do to him? He caught himself just then, recognizing a bias against small towns that he'd once associated with Ryan Betancourt.

Ryan had displayed a dismissive, big-city attitude when they'd first started writing together, but he'd dropped it before the end of that engagement. Jack had privately taken credit for the improvement, along with one other: Though an outstanding playwright, Ryan had initially lacked the practicality required in a mystery play. Logic errors could be forgiven or overlooked in the more dramatic work he'd done on Broadway, but a mystery audience was actively trying to solve the murder as it unfolded before their eyes. The viewers of a Death Troupe performance had to buy the explanation when the show was over—particularly when they'd just lost a sizeable wager to the players who controlled the entire story. Ryan hadn't attained any great skill at this before Jack's departure, but he'd seemed to accept its importance.

The random memories of Ryan sent him into the laptop's carry bag, reaching for the dead man's notebook. While Jack preferred flip-top pads for his paper ruminations, Ryan used a bound leather journal as if intending to preserve his notions for posterity. He'd concealed his brainstorming by surrounding it with little asides that ranged from arguments with Barron to the local weather, and the end result was practically a history of the engagement itself. Jack remembered that Ryan started a fresh notebook with every new assignment, and so he didn't expect this one to contain much more than the scanty outline he'd already seen.

It was with a fair amount of surprise, then, that he saw that most of the pages in the inch-thick journal had been used. He recognized Ryan's handwriting and his impressively artistic sketches, and quickly came to understand that he was holding the other writer's observations from the engagement in Red Bend. Flipping to the back, he saw that his former partner had used the last few pages to jot down his initial thoughts about the Schuyler Mills performance, including his ideas about a Depression-era back-story.

Jack was sure that Barron had forwarded the book because of its final entries, but he felt a cold sensation all the same. Within the pages of the journal he was holding lay the genesis of the play which

Wade believed had caused an old man to kill himself. Jack suddenly became very aware of his surroundings, especially the large frost-bordered windows over his shoulder. The latest customer at the counter was a hulking delivery man ordering a small coffee, and he heard Lynnie's playful voice hustling the man to buy a more expensive drink.

"That's kinda small, for a big guy like you . . ."

The man took the bait willingly. "Well what would you suggest, sweetheart? I'd probably do whatever a pretty girl like you told me . . ."

Slowly reading backward, Jack saw that the pages concerning the performance week in Red Bend contained only final editing notes and nothing about Barron, the weather, or anything else. He wasn't surprised to see that many pages had been razored out in the rest of the volume, knowing that Ryan censored his journal at the end of a show.

Scanning the pages one after another in reverse, Jack finally saw a passage that he'd hoped wasn't in there. In Ryan's neat, tightly written script, he read a line that chilled him as if the nearby window were wide open.

Last night some lunatic came into the town center, howling about the impending arrival of one of the characters. He wasn't with the troupe (I checked with the D right away) but he picked the right name all the same. How did he know which suspect was the killer? Wish to Christ someone had called the police on him . . .

Jack finished reading Ryan's journal late that night, after retreating to his room and begging off two dinner invitations. Sorting through the entire volume of stream-of-consciousness notation had been anything but easy. Wade had trained Ryan in the art of disinformation the same way he'd taught Jack, and the result was a mishmash of ideas that would make no sense to any outsider who managed to steal a peek—or even the journal itself.

Though familiar with Ryan's coded markings, Jack still had to apply a fair amount of intuition to follow the evolution of the Red Bend play. It helped that he knew what the final performance had looked like, but even then he could see that Ryan and the Director had gone round and round on this one.

The origin of the local scandal that had allegedly caused the old man's suicide was not listed in the journal; it gradually appeared alongside Ryan's research and could be presumed to have been provided by one of the locals. Tracking the germination of Ryan's ideas, Jack felt he could tell where his former partner had dropped certain scenarios in favor of others, and he was surprised to see that Ryan had come away from the scandal story more than once. He only seemed to return to it after meetings with Barron, when his normally neat script took on a hurried sketchiness or an angry tint.

Noting this pattern, Jack sagged back in his chair and picked up the mug of cold tea that he'd prepared in the room's microwave much earlier. The journal raised more questions than it answered, and he found himself particularly puzzled by the conflict between the writer and the Director over the inclusion of the scandal tale. Hadn't they both favored using such devices when he'd worked with them? Why had Ryan shied away from this, then? And why had Barron insisted on keeping it?

Lacking an answer for any of those questions, he'd read on and soon discovered that the stranger who'd appeared in Red Bend, yelling in the streets, had not been the only thing which had upset Ryan's equilibrium. Wade had alluded to a string of strange events that had occurred in the wine country, and now Jack felt he knew what they were.

Ryan's notes had taken a bizarre twist for a couple of pages early in the engagement, and Jack had wondered if the writer had been drunk when he'd penned them. Ryan himself had explained the incoherent lines the next day, complaining of a monstrous hangover and the suspicion that someone had slipped something into his drink the night before.

Jack read that passage twice, shivering even though it was warm in the hotel room. He genuinely feared an attack of that sort, believing it would be all too easy for a deranged fan to drug him and spirit him off so that he would never be found. Knowing Ryan's thrill-seeking side, he'd probably laughed the whole thing off or hoped that he'd been ravaged by a female townie too shy to simply proposition him. It was hard to tell just how Ryan had felt about that episode, and Jack's only question after reviewing that segment was why Ryan hadn't later cut it out as he had with so many other pages.

The Red Bend performance had taken place the previous November, and Ryan had experienced another unsettling event around Halloween. The town had welcomed the newly arrived Jerome Barron Players with a massive party at a local ballroom, and attendees had demonstrated great flair in their choice of costumes. Relieved by the completion of the script and the arrival of his friends, Ryan had let his guard down and imbibed heavily. He'd felt safe in the crowd, right up until a tall, masked stranger had spooked him badly.

The alcohol had been flowing freely and Ryan had joined most of the partygoers in a frenetic dance which involved a fair amount of wriggling on the floor. At the point where the wrigglers were supposed to pop up into a standing position (a move more capably performed by college students than the older crowd at the party) he'd suddenly felt an arm wrap around his windpipe from behind. He'd thought it was an over-exuberant member of Death Troupe until a deep male voice had whispered the same phrases in his ear that had been yelled by the stranger in the town streets weeks before.

Struggling free, Ryan had turned to see that his tormentor was a man roughly the same size as himself wearing a dark suit and one of the ovular eye-and-nose masks from the Death Troupe logo. Completely flummoxed, he'd only been able to stand and stare at the apparition before him. Even wearing the mask, the stranger could have been his double. The impostor had simply stood there laughing for a moment before disappearing into the boisterous crowd as it jumped up and down with the climax of the song.

In an uncharacteristic admission of fear, Ryan finished that segment with the observation that he'd slept inside the Red Bend Theater that night, the building guarded by Wade and his security people.

No one had ever determined just who the stranger was, although it seemed likely that the masked man at the party and the voice crying out in the street had been the same individual. No doubt Wade considered the stranger a prime suspect in the death of the old man which had followed a few weeks later, at least as the provider of the newspaper which had almost literally pushed the old man over the edge.

Judging from Ryan's reaction to this sneering doppelganger, Jack had to wonder if the stranger hadn't managed to push his old partner over the edge too.

Chapter Seven

"Glide! Work the glide!"

Kelly's voice rang out in the cold afternoon air, and Jack tried to obey. They were in the middle of the snow-covered town common, and Kelly was trying to teach him the fundamentals of cross-country skiing. They'd spent the morning picking up the cold weather items which Tillman had suggested, and after lunch they'd driven out to Bib's Outfitters so Jack could buy a set of skis, boots, ankle gaiters, and poles.

For all his comedy in other settings, Bib was dead serious when it came to outdoor sports. He obviously knew a lot about every piece of equipment in his store, and had taken great pains to make sure everything was the right size. He drew the line at actually giving instruction, though, so it was fortunate that Kelly had her own skis and could spend the time teaching him the basics.

Jack had done a little downhill skiing in college, so he was surprised to discover how light, narrow, and springy the cross-country skis were. "Think of them like the arch of your foot. When you put your weight on one foot it flattens out, but when you take the weight off it bounces right back into a curve. Once you get the rhythm, you'll start placing most of your weight on the forward ski while taking it off the trail one. The scales on the bottom of the ski will bite into the snow, and you'll get a nice lift as the ski springs back into a curve."

That had proved to be more easily said than done, and just a few circuits around the common had left Jack feeling like he'd run up several flights of stairs. He had particular trouble synchronizing the poles and the skis, finding that he naturally tried to extend the pole on the same side as the forward-most ski when it was supposed to be the exact opposite.

"It's like walking, Jack! You don't swing your left arm with your left foot, do you?" Kelly laughed as she easily slid along next to him, looking very cool and fashionable in a waist-length pink jacket and light ski pants. She'd warned him against bundling up, particularly once he graduated to actual trails in the woods, explaining that trapped heat caused perspiration which could quickly chill him if he stopped for more than a few minutes.

"I don't usually use a set of poles when I'm walking, thank you." Jack replied between breaths, trying to figure out how he was supposed to wipe his brow when both his hands were wrapped around the poles' rubber grips. The long rods ended in a flexible plastic circle that reminded him of a sand dollar, and a hard metal point which caused him to mentally label the pole a pigsticker.

Kelly smirked at him from underneath a purple knit cap ringed with red hearts and a set of yellow ski goggles. Without a word of warning, she hopped in the air and swung her hips so that they collided. Caught with the wrong pigsticker extended, Jack toppled over sideways in a spray of snow that somehow found an opening where his ski pants met his shirt.

"See? You alternate the poles so you can keep your balance!" Kelly deftly transferred one of her pigstickers to the other hand before offering him a lift up. "Okay, that was a cheap shot, so I'll let you tip me over a little later . . . if you can catch me."

Jack looked down at the two long, narrow skis attached to the toes of his boots. This was something else that was different about cross-country: His heels had to be able to lift off the ski, so the only attachment was a staple-like metal bar affixed to the boot's toe. This clipped into a fastener that kept the toe on the ski but allowed the heel to rise and fall as the skier slid one leg forward while pushing off with the other.

"A man shouldn't have to wait *that* long for revenge." Jack reached up with his left hand and took hold of the offered glove while grabbing up a handful of snow with his right. He was just about to fling it upward when his arm was restrained as if tethered to the ground. Looking down, he saw that the thong from his ski pole was still around his wrist and that Kelly had had the sense to step on the shaft where it lay half-buried in the snow.

"Gee . . . I thought you mystery writers were supposed to be tricky!" She laughed brightly, plucking her hand from his and gracefully hopping back out of range.

Jack struggled back onto his skis, noting that it was much easier to do this in cross-country than downhill, and brushed himself off. When he looked up, Kelly was halfway across the common, her legs sliding so smoothly that she could have been on ice skates. She wore a set of red gaiters that covered her legs from just below the knee to the top of the ankle-high boots, and the color maddened him like a bull.

She turned when she reached the base of the Civil War statue, a high stone pedestal and statue of a Yankee soldier holding a rifle diagonally across his chest. The sky overhead was a light, bleached-out blue, but the sun seemed to beat down on Jack with particular force as he chased after her. He saw the white of her teeth as he got closer, and was surprised when she didn't move away. Instead, she reached up, pigstickers dangling, and raised her goggles onto the purple hat before cupping her hands to imitate a bullhorn.

"Don't look now, Jack, but you're actually doing it! Now that's what I call a glide!"

He looked down into the whiteness at his feet and was astounded to see that he was leaning on his left leg with his right pole thrust forward, the ski sliding along the snow just before his right shot forward and took its place. His weight shifted onto his right foot, his left arm swung the opposite pigsticker into the snow, and he glided forward as if riding on ice.

By the time he reached Kelly, he'd completely forgotten his original plan to knock her on her ass. She'd stuck her own poles into the snow pile at the foot of the statue and was gently applauding, clapping the heavy snow gloves in a way that made almost no sound. He pulled up in front of her, and she pointed a thick finger in the direction from which they'd come.

"Look at that. See that big kicked-up spot? That's where you fell over. And when you started doing it right, look how fast you covered all that distance."

Working to control his labored breath, Jack slowly turned his body as he'd been taught at the beginning of the lesson. First he lifted one ski an inch from the ground and turned it slightly, putting it down so that the back of the ski almost touched the one that hadn't yet moved. He then moved the other one and repeated the process until he'd completely faced about. The section of disturbed snow seemed impossibly distant, and his mouth hung open for a moment before he replied.

"Wow! You can really get somewhere on these things!"

"That's the idea, Desert Man." She ran her hands through the thongs of her two standing poles and brought them to her sides. "Had enough?"

"Heck no!" Jack pushed off again, but slowly, balancing on his lead leg until the ski almost came to a complete stop. He'd traveled almost two yards, and when he slid the other ski forward he covered the same distance. "I may just be getting the hang of this!"

Kelly glided past him easily, the goggles still on her forehead. "That's not what I meant. I think we might be finished for right now —the Mayor's headed our way."

Jack looked across the common in the direction of the Visitor's Center, sighting Tillman's red and black coat as the dentist came across the walkway they'd used to cross the square on his first day in town. Jack and Kelly pushed off together, taking their time as they skied over to the mayor. Still unused to the speed with which they covered the ground, Jack found himself comparing the sensation to riding in a boat that was approaching the dock too fast.

"Well look at you! Been here three days and you're getting around like a local! Wait 'til we strap a set of snowshoes on you!" Tillman called out merrily. He wore only a baseball hat despite the cold, tan with the patch of a local tractor dealership.

"He's a natural, Marv. Can't tell his left from his right, but I guess that doesn't really matter in cross-country."

"I've got a good teacher." Jack gave Kelly a smile which she returned. "So where are these scenic trails I've heard so much about?"

"Hold on there, cowboy. I think it'll be better if you spend a few more hours cruising around where we can all keep an eye on you."

"What is this? Some kind of communal playpen for the new guy?"

"Well now that you mention it, I did get some calls from the local shopkeepers telling me they were having a lot of fun watching you . . . which brings up why I'm out here. Patrice Lawton called just a few minutes ago. A few members of our theater group are getting together to start work on the scenes for Mr. Barron's Mystery Weekend class, and they'd just love for you to drop by."

Jack's elation at gaining a new skill evaporated quickly. The local players were a wild card in every engagement, and Death Troupe writers had to walk a tightrope between alienating them and getting too close to them. Jack remembered that they were preparing two scenes from *Macbeth* for Barron's symposium in March, and recognized the danger of getting in the middle of that.

"I'd be happy to do swing by, but they have to know that I'm not a director. I'm just a writer, and frankly there's a lot about this business that I don't understand at all." The excuse flowed out smoothly, like a ski skimming over hard-packed snow, and Jack recognized it from previous engagements.

"Oh I'm sure they just want to show you what they can do, is all. They're getting together at six. I'll email you the address as soon as I get back to the office."

Jack frowned as Tillman departed, unsure of how many times he would have to repeat his honest denial of any understanding of Barron's mind. It was a full five seconds before he registered what the mayor had said at the end.

"Address?"

It was one of the things Jack had forgotten during his hiatus from Death Troupe: Much of the early preparation for a community theater performance takes place in someone's home. That was how he came to be standing on the stone front stoop of the Riley house a little after six that evening. The Rileys both taught at the Schuyler Mills Elementary School, and their modest place was only a block away from that.

Glenda Riley answered the door wearing a frilly apron over a dark dress. Jack remembered her from his welcoming party at the theater, and was surprised to see that the trim redhead was even better-looking up close.

"Come in, come in, Jack! Welcome to our home." She motioned him inside, and he found himself in a small living room cluttered with a playpen and many toys. A young man with curly brown hair and round glasses gave him a small wave from a reclining chair across the room, where he was holding a baby that looked as if it had just dropped off to sleep. Though childless, Jack had the sense to simply wave back.

Another child, the boy he'd seen run into Glenda at the party, was seated in front of a television set near the room's front windows. He was absorbed in a cartoon movie where a horde of jungle animals was singing and dancing, and Jack now saw that the older child had his mother's red hair and his father's curls. Sliding out of his heavy jacket, he carefully walked forward to get a better look at the baby.

"Come on back when you're ready, Jack." Glenda said evenly, heading down a short hallway toward what was probably the kitchen. He could hear Dennis Lawton's voice from back there, answered by a male voice he didn't recognize.

"She's just dropped off." Whispered the brown-haired man, who was wearing a sweater vest and an open-necked shirt protected by a throw-up rag. "I'm Curt Riley. I teach over at the elementary school."

Curt's voice was soft and measured, and Jack believed it wouldn't be much louder even if he weren't holding a sleeping infant. Although he was seated, he looked tall and thin like his wife. Everything about him suggested an abiding calm, and Jack decided to spend a little time in this oasis of peace before facing the questions in the next room.

"How old is she?" he asked as he settled into a wing-backed chair that had seen better days.

"Eight weeks." Riley looked down at the tiny face. "A Thanksgiving baby."

"That's wonderful." Jack didn't know what else to say, but that seemed to work with the young father. Riley looked up and smiled.

"You have any? Kids, I mean?"

Allison's face flashed before his eyes for an instant, making a connection which he had seldom considered. With their separate careers, it had always been an unspoken fact that they weren't likely to have a family in the near future. Now, only recently reunited and for God-only-knew how long, the chances seemed even more remote.

"No . . . not yet, anyway. Guess I'd have to get married first."

"Says who?" Riley gave him a wink, and they both shared another smile. Knowing small towns and the high standard of conduct expected of their teachers, Jack felt a small flush of pride that his newest acquaintance would utter such heresy in his presence.

"I'll tell my girlfriend that one."

"Oh no . . . that won't work at all. Take it from me—" he cast a conspiratorial look toward the kitchen "—you've got to trick them." He delivered this last with a look of such straight-faced sincerity that Jack had to struggle hard not to laugh. Riley broke the expression a moment later, allowing his voice to approach a conversational tone. "Honestly, now, I can't tell you how happy Glenda is to be included in your show. She was in tears when they announced that Schuyler Mills had won the engagement."

"Everyone I've met has spoken very highly of her acting skills, so maybe we should be thanking you. I understand she studied drama in New York City."

"That's right. We were classmates at NYU. I was after a teaching degree and she was heading for the stage, but when I popped the question she packed up and came back home with me instead. To be honest, I've always felt a little guilty about that."

"Well have no fear." Jack leaned forward and then stood. "By the time Barron's done terrorizing your players, every one of them will be thanking their lucky stars they didn't make theater a career."

It was Riley's turn to subdue a laugh, but he did it in such a relaxed, natural way that it was as if he'd simply let go of an unpleasant thought. Jack gave him a small wave as he turned toward the kitchen, but he froze halfway down the short, darkened hall. In a flash of inspiration, he'd seen the investigator character he'd been trying to create for Ryan Betancourt's Depression-based mystery. Unconsciously looking for guidance from his dead partner, Jack had been trying to build a character obsessed with solving the decades-old family scandal. Now he saw a different way to go that he much preferred.

Phrases filled his head as he went down the short hallway toward the light of the kitchen, and he longed to take out his notebook and capture them. *Calm confidence. Glacial machinations. Deadly patience.* Jack hated the way moments of inspiration like these so often found him when he couldn't retreat to a quiet spot and truly develop them. He heard several voices ahead, however, and tried to refocus his thoughts on the job at hand.

The kitchen was small, which shouldn't have been surprising given the size of the house, but it was well organized and very clean. An oven, microwave, coffeemaker, and sink area faced a full-size refrigerator decorated with magnets of the alphabet and the older child's drawings. Just after that a small dinner table sat next to a curtained back door, and he recognized three of the five faces seated there.

"There you are, Jack! Pull up a chair." Dennis Lawton said this from the far corner, where he was hopelessly hemmed in by his wife and an older man and woman. Glenda Riley, *sans* apron, rose from the chair closest to Jack.

"I'm so sorry for the cramped space here, Jack, but why don't you go ahead and take my seat—"

"I wouldn't think of it." Jack put a hand on Glenda's shoulder, pressing her back into the chair. With a quick look around, he decided that a seat on the countertop would put him in a good spot for providing what little input he could, and also an excellent egress point when the chance presented itself. "I'm not going to break anything if I hop up here, am I?"

"See? I told you he'd fit right in." Patrice Lawton said this to the unidentified man and woman, and then proceeded to make introductions. "Jack, these are two of our mainstays, Albert and Sarah Griffin."

"Albert? My mother calls me Albert. Call me Al." The male mainstay waved at Jack, smiling from behind a graying moustache and goatee. Despite the man's bonhomie, Jack immediately identified him as Macbeth and then wondered if Sarah would be playing the role of Lady Macbeth.

"Al it is, then."

"Al and Sarah are two of our group's founders, and we'd be nowhere without them." Patrice continued as if none of the intervening byplay had occurred.

"That may be true, but we're very concerned about the small number of roles in the scenes that Mr. Barron has selected for his Mystery Week class." Sarah Griffin spoke in a slow, measured tone that Jack normally associated with the southern part of the country. Sarah was probably fifty, with blonde hair going gray that hung down to her shoulders. Two slight lines crossed her forehead and some minor crow's feet were evident at the corners of her eyes, but she didn't look like the type that got easily excited. "We've got some wonderful people in the troupe and we don't want to see anyone left out."

As if on cue, every face at the table swung toward Jack. He'd just swung up onto the counter, but wasn't caught unawares. "Oh, I wouldn't worry about that too much. How many scenes did he ask you to prepare?"

"Two. Well, three maybe. He wasn't specific with numbers. He asked us to prepare the scene where Macbeth and Lady Macbeth discuss murdering the king, and as you know that's in two scenes, one where they first consider the idea and then another when Lady Macbeth convinces her husband to go ahead and do it."

"It's been a little while since I've read it, actually—" Jack now recognized some of the papers on the table as copies of the pertinent segments of the play, and held up a restraining hand when Dennis reached for them. "—but I get your meaning. Sounds like two players max. What's the other one?"

"The scene where Lady MacDuff and her son are murdered." Glenda answered this time, and Jack began to piece the problem together. Clearly the Griffins would handle the first sequence, and if the group was to make full use of Glenda's talents she would have to play Lady MacDuff.

"Got it. That scene's got what, three people in it?"

"More, if you count the murderers, but we don't think that's a good use of our other players." Al said this in a conciliatory tone, tipping his head to the side to take the sting out of the words.

"Oh, neither do I. Here's why I ask: I've been working with Barron for a long time, and he's never been known to spare the horses. So I expect you're going to get additional requests from him as the weeks go by, for more scenes from this play and maybe even others, with little rhyme or reason to any of it."

"I'd say these scenes fit the theme of a Mystery Weekend, don't you think?" Patrice Lawton offered, and Jack had to remind himself that the Lawtons were very literal people.

"Yes they do, yes they do. And you can bet all the others will as well, in their own way. But what I'm saying is, don't expect to be able to connect the different scenes in the hope of figuring out Barron's point in selecting them for his seminar. He's done a fair amount of teaching, and I'll see if Berni—his assistant—can scare up some tapes of any of that, but it's not easy to predict where he's going most of the time. I know I've never been able to do it."

The response to that last statement was a mix, and Jack saw that he'd have to dial down the hyperbole around the Lawtons. The Griffins seemed to take it in stride, nodding politely, and Glenda appeared genuinely excited by the idea of such an unpredictable rehearsal environment, but the Lawtons looked uneasy. As the original writer for Death Troupe, and having left many interim meetings with Barron feeling the same way, Jack knew he had to reassure them.

"But then again, no one's ever had to *wonder* what Barron wanted. He's very clear in his direction, and if you just prepare the scenes he's requested the way you know how . . . he'll be able to shape them any way he wants." He tried to adopt a look of gentle reassurance. "Remember, it's a seminar and not a performance. He may ask some of your players to go over the top just for the sake of demonstration."

This didn't seem to satisfy the Lawtons, so he took out the big gun itself, the ugly truth about Jerome Barron that always tided him over. "You wanna know the secret of dealing with Jerry Barron?"

The mention of the forbidden truth, as well as the offering of an ironclad approach, seemed to do the trick. Both Lawtons looked up in keen anticipation.

"Just remember that Barron is the star of the show. I know that he's not supposed to be, but he doesn't agree with that. That's why he takes a curtain call with the players. That's why he's the only one who knows who the killer is until the very last minute. Personally, I think that's why he developed Death Troupe in the first place: He doesn't like taking his hands off the wheel. So don't worry about the seminar. That's one place where he'll have the spotlight on him the whole way. And he'll tell you exactly what he wants."

There was a palpable relaxation in the room, and Jack noted the changed body language with pleasure. As a writer he wasn't supposed to like extemporaneous speeches, but if he couldn't string the words together when he needed them, he'd be a poor playwright indeed.

A small red warning light began to flash in the back of his mind, and he remembered, even after two years' absence, to provide the final admonition. "Now do me a big favor, and don't ever repeat what I just said around a member of the Barron Players or, for God's sake, Barron himself."

Jack was just reaching the hotel's back door when his cell phone went off. He'd spent a couple of hours at the Riley house, and shouldn't have been surprised to find that he'd enjoyed it. After calming their fears about Barron's seminar, he'd been asked his impressions of the main characters in the requested *Macbeth* scenes and had offered what little he could. He hadn't read the play in years, but in a dedicated group like that it wasn't necessary.

It was a familiar pattern, and it truly didn't bother him. He didn't consider himself an expert on any play other than the ones he'd written, and even with those he found the impressions of others to be a fascinating thing. Some of those outside observations were mere flights of fancy, but most of them came from careful study of the words which, even when applied to other writers' plays, he found flattering.

In the end he'd been required to offer very few ideas regarding such items as Macbeth's motivation and had, instead, listened to the group batting around their sometimes conflicting impressions. They'd all been taking notes regardless of their minor disagreements, and when he'd finally made his escape it was with the certainty that this was one community theater group which Barron would not find wanting.

The new idea concerning the Depression theme was still rattling around in his head, and he'd jotted down a few notes before starting up the truck and heading back down the road toward the town center. He'd had every intention of locking himself in his room with these latest notions, but the voice on the other end of the cell phone had been Kelly Sykes. She was over at Maddy's, ready to buy him a drink, and he idly wondered if this might not be some tricky way for the mayor to find out how the new guy in town had fared with the local theater group.

91

That didn't appear to be the case, however. He'd been greeted with loud good fellowship by some of the bar's regulars when he'd come stamping through the door, but once he'd settled into a booth with Kelly he'd discovered that she wasn't terribly interested in events at the Riley home. After some small talk about his cross-country skills, she'd asked him how the Schuyler Mills engagement compared to the ones before it. In no time at all he'd been regaling her with tales from Death Troupes past.

"—you need to know that Ryan had a bad habit of not hanging around in the host town. He was always jetting off someplace—" frequently to wherever Allison had been performing, but Jack hadn't found that out until it was far too late "—and, being a rich kid, he could afford it. Now, I did enjoy spending time with him and thought he was a heck of a writer, but to be honest I didn't mind it when he played hooky. It gave me a chance to get my own ideas straight without him constantly arguing that my scenes were flat or that certain characters weren't being written up to their full potential.

"The problem with that particular engagement was that Barron was really playing around with the introduction of the clues, and with very little warning."

"That's bad, right?" Kelly was wearing a white cable-knit sweater and had her hands folded under her chin, enjoying the story. They'd both had a couple of drinks by then, and her cheeks bore a rosy color that he'd only seen when they'd been skiing on the town common. She'd let her hair down, and Jack was having no trouble looking at her.

"Oh you bet it is. There really needs to be tight coordination there, or you can end up with a player handing out clues that don't follow what the writer is putting together." *Or that the Director has decided he likes better, disseminated in a way that neatly forces the writer's hand.* "Which was exactly what happened there. Ryan had missed the last meeting with Barron, but that didn't really matter because Jerry had decided to do his own thing with the next set of clues anyway.

"Ryan and I were walking through the park, headed for dinner, when out of nowhere Puff Addersley hops up on a wooden crate and begins this rousing political speech from a hundred years ago. That locale had been a hotbed of union organizing in the early days, and Puff is dressed up in this great 1880s workingman's outfit. It's early evening and the weather's gorgeous, so there's all sorts of people out and about. Ryan and I slip into the crowd to hear what we *know* is a nice, straightforward back story, but all of a sudden I see that Puff isn't saying anything I recognize!"

"Let me guess: Ryan didn't recognize it either—and he thought you'd changed it!"

"Bingo." Jack touched his nose with his left index finger, while pointing the right one across the booth. "Puff finishes up, and he's nailed this speech so completely that the crowd goes wild. You'da thought they were going to march on the local sweatshop, he'd gotten them that worked up. Although I was confused, I'd gotten caught up in the story myself and hadn't noticed that Ryan, standing right next to me, has been getting madder and madder with every word of Puff's speech.

"So when I turn to ask him what he thinks, he shouts, 'What the fuck was *that*, Jack?' so loud that every head turned."

"You must have been mortified."

"Baffled is more like it. I didn't put two and two together until it was too late, and by then he's shouting at me about how this wasn't what we'd agreed on, how did I dare do something like that on my own, all sorts of sh— . . . nonsense . . . like that. Anyway, Ryan was taller than I am, and so he got a little carried away and actually poked me in the chest."

"What did the crowd think of that?"

Jack stopped in midsentence, one hand frozen in the act of mimicking Betancourt's jabbing finger. He looked confused for a split second, and then asked in a low voice, "You've heard this story before, haven't you?"

"No, no! I already said I didn't! It's just that it's logical to assume the crowd must have thought you were part of the act."

"Well it is . . . and they did, too." Jack paused again, peering at Kelly as if trying to probe inside her mind. "You're one intuitive lady, Miss Chamber of Commerce Liaison."

"That's true. So go on. What happened next?"

"I was already fed up with Ryan's coming-and-going by then, and the finger jabbing was the last straw. So I hit back in kind of a reflex action."

"You hit him?"

"Well, it was more like a slap . . . at first I only pushed his hand out of the way, but he put it right back in my face and so I really smacked it. It made a sound like I'd just popped him a good one, and people in the crowd thought I'd punched him. We knew a lot of the folks in town by then, and so three or four of the local guys grabbed hold of us and pulled us apart."

"Did you say anything?"

"Oh you bet I did. I was yelling at him that this wasn't my idea at all, and that if he'd just hold up his end of the workload maybe he'd know what was going on. Things like that. And of course he was yelling right back at me, saying I had no imagination and couldn't write . . . well all of a sudden he realizes that he's lost it in public. Now that's something that Ryan Betancourt simply *did not do*, and so in the space of a few seconds you could almost see him change.

"First he looked shocked, then he looked scared, and then . . . they'd let go of us by then, and he just took my hand like this—" Jack reached across with his left hand, taking Kelly's right before shifting so that he was sideways in the booth "—and turned so that we were both facing the same direction, and raised my hand like I'd just won some prize fight.

"Out of the side of his mouth he said, 'curtain call' and we both took a bow as if we'd just performed a bit we'd been rehearsing for days. We straightened up, and you should have seen the faces. They just weren't buying it, and I was already thinking, 'Oops' when Ryan takes this little hop backwards like some kind of circus tumbler finishing up a run, brings his hands to his mouth, and blows them all a kiss like they'd been applauding for five minutes."

"No! And how'd they take that?"

"It was amazing. It was like some kind of programmed response. They saw him smiling and blowing that kiss, and they all started to clap their hands. We both had the sense to get out of there right away, but they were still clapping when we turned the corner."

"Wow. Talk about fast on your feet."

"He was like that."

"No, I mean both of you. That was really sharp, the way you picked up on what he was doing. A bad straight man would have blown that whole act right there." She held up her hand, as if to stop him from breaking her concentration. "But just a second. What was Puff doing all this time?"

"Like I said, he's a real pro. One of our biggest concerns for players dropping clues in public is their escape route. We've had actors who were followed and others who got mobbed, so it's important for them to have an exit strategy. Puff had a little closing segment that he was supposed to deliver, something that was going to get the crowd looking around for something that wasn't there, but when he saw how our little shoving match had distracted everybody, he just hopped down and took to his heels."

"How did Barron take it? The news that his two writers got into a fistfight?"

"The D's a funny guy, and it's hard to know how he'll react to anything. Several people reported the incident on the Rumor Control page of our website, and so of course he heard about it . . . I think

Puff told him as well. Anyway, it put him in a tough spot because he was basically at fault for making the change without telling us. So he did what he usually does, which is to claim it as his own. He said it was a great new method of helping the players get out of town once their clue-dropping performance was finished and that he was surprised we carried it off so well."

"He sounds difficult to work with."

"He is. I swear he spends most of his time in a different world, one where everything is exactly what he says it is, and he wants to have it that way in the real world as well." He stopped himself, taking a drink while polishing his ending. "We put up with it because wherever he gets his ideas, the real world or his fantasy world, they're usually very good."

"You said you learned a lot from him."

"How could I not? The guy's been in theater for decades, he's celebrated across the globe, and you tell me what Broadway director could go into murder theater without getting laughed off the planet? Sure there was some criticism when we started out, and our first performances were a little rocky, but Barron's a very bright guy who doesn't make the same mistake twice. He learned, we learned, and the end result isn't half bad."

He stopped talking intentionally, aware that he was starting to go on and on. The drink did that to him sometimes, but they hadn't been at Maddy's long enough for that to be the reason. Two different hockey games were on the big screens at either end of the bar, and there was a lot of background noise around them, but to Jack it felt as if things had suddenly gotten very quiet.

Kelly ended the moment. "It must be very difficult to write a creative piece on a deadline the way you do. I've never heard of a group like yours, where they write a new piece for every place they go."

"That's why we only do one show a year." They both laughed lightly at that. "But you're right—it can get a little nerve-wracking. Time may fly when you're having fun, but it *vanishes* when you've got a deadline."

"Do you really feel that you're writing in collaboration with Jerome? You said you did, in an interview a few years back." That was artfully done. She knew she was getting close to the line where he'd have to shut up, and so she'd neatly placed her question within bounds by quoting him. Even so, he felt compelled to explain something to her that he'd never put into words before.

"You know, when he and I started this thing—" it was a phrase he'd stopped using when Ryan came on board, but it was true; in the

95

beginning Death Troupe had been just him and Barron "—some of the critics were really down on us. They were heavy into that 'discovery through rehearsal' stuff and felt that there was no way for the players to fully develop their characters when they were preparing multiple endings on a play they'd never seen before."

The writing of different outcomes for the plays had never been a secret, but Jack cautioned himself again. He was treading dangerously close to the truth with an outsider.

"So Allison did this beautiful interview where she just gushed about how refreshing it was to break out of the mold and work without a net, not knowing until the last minute just how things were going to work out. Rehearsing conflicting scenes over and over again until they could play them in their sleep, all within a three-week period. Talk about a deadline.

"It was an excellent performance, and she really shut up the critics with that one. But what she didn't mention was that the work that Barron and I do in the very creation of the play is partly rehearsal itself. I remember one time, late at night, when I was arguing with him over some nitpicky change in a throwaway line.

"He said—" Jack dropped his voice into the gruff imitation of the Director— "'Think of the rehearsal process in other plays; it's meant to *explore* a story, not just memorize one way of telling it. So when I ask you to re-write different acts and consider alternate paths to take, think of it as part of the rehearsal. We're taking the benefits of rehearsal back a step—into the writing itself.'"

That seemed to have a real effect on her. She'd placed her palms on the table, and when he stopped speaking her mouth was open just a hair. He settled back and took another drink, letting her turn the whole thing over in her mind.

"Wow . . . I never thought of it that way."

"Neither had I, until then. Barron's a lot of things: A prima donna, a pain in the ass, a manipulator, even a slave driver . . . but he's also original. Once you fight your way through all that other stuff . . . it's well worth it."

Kelly came out of her reverie as if she'd just caught her reflection in a mirror, with an embarrassed gasp that shut her mouth. She quickly looked around, as if checking to see if anyone else had seen her, and then took a long drink of her own. By the time she put it down, her earlier expression of happy entertainment had returned. She put her chin on her hands again.

"So tell me about those early performances. The ones that didn't go off so well."

Back in his room, Jack sat down at the desk and thought for a long time. The reminiscing about Barron and Ryan had awakened some unexpected feelings, but he found that he didn't mind exploring them —after all, it was part of his job. His resentment of Barron's domineering ways hadn't stopped him from praising the Director to Kelly, and he believed that he'd given her an honest appraisal of the man's talent. Likewise, he'd always respected Ryan professionally and his reading of the dead man's journal had only served to reinforce that. He'd mentioned Ryan to Allison exactly once, in Maine, and she'd flatly stated that she didn't want to talk about him.

Jack scarcely noticed now that a single conversation with a stranger had granted him more clarity on that subject than an evening with the woman he still believed he loved. Instead, he moved on to the obvious conclusion that reviewing Ryan's notes and regaling Kelly with tales of their work together had confirmed his genuine affection for the man who had stolen the love of his life. Despite that betrayal and his related periods of truancy, Ryan had been great company during the two engagements they'd worked together. His gift was undeniable, his wit was sharp, and his recklessness was fascinating.

This last thought echoed in Jack's head, and so he turned it over a time or two. For a rich man, Ryan had seemed to hold his life and safety in slight regard. He'd sailed the oceans by himself, engaged complete strangers in heated arguments, and bedded any woman who caught his eye. That wildness had also appeared in his writing, particularly when he took a perfectly acceptable scene and turned it into something that practically jumped from the stage to seize the audience by the throat.

Jack knew when his stream of consciousness was taking him somewhere, and so he went with it now. Ryan had fashioned himself the wiser member of their team, but the truth had been different. Jack had always been the one to cancel the last round of drinks, to put the acceptable scene back the way it was so that it wouldn't overshadow the bigger ones to follow, and to counsel against traipsing on local sensibilities. That caution had carried a price, as it had allowed Ryan to play the role of mustang to Jack's plow horse. It had also blunted his writing, and could even have helped Ryan to steal his girl.

But there was clearly something bigger to be found here, and Jack closed his eyes to let his mind show him what it was. It came through slowly, having been blocked until then by the years of resentment and loss. Jack now saw that his pleasure at Ryan's passing had not been genuine, and that it had masked an even more painful feeling. What had Wade said, about Ryan's reaction to the suicide in Red Bend? *We should have listened to Jack.*

He'd felt a dull, predictable satisfaction when he'd heard that, but hadn't known until that very moment why a stab of guilt had followed it. It was clear now, here in this snow-covered village, why he'd experienced that contrary emotion. It wasn't enough to have been the voice of moderation when dealing with Ryan; he should have seen the man's attraction to Allison just as he'd seen the danger of using local scandals as part of the play. If he'd only kept his eyes and ears open, as Wade had so often suggested, he might have prevented the betrayal that had set the stage for the many wicked events that had followed. He might even have saved Ryan's life.

Standing slowly, as if recently recovered from a long illness, Jack walked into the bedroom and opened the laptop bag where he'd thrown it on the bed. He selected a large writing tablet, the kind he used when he wanted to really let his mind roam. A big canvas was required for that, because he would fill it with every idea that came to mind. He'd end up scratching out most of them, but it was the best way to discover the ones worth keeping.

Sitting back down at the desk and uncapping a pen, he began scribbling out small phrases describing the Depression-themed play and the ways in which it might recreate the awful tragedy that had occurred in northern California. Glancing over at the dying arrangement of black roses to his left, he smiled for a moment and then began drawing tiny skull-and-bones symbols next to the ideas which he considered most likely to cause trouble.

"Now," he said aloud, breathing easily and sticking the end of the pen between his teeth. "How do we adjust this so nobody else gets hurt?"

Chapter Eight

"You know, Jack, just for once I'd like to see you develop the things I asked you to."

Jerome Barron leaned back in a cheap office chair on the other side of a cheap conference table. He had summoned Jack to a small hotel on the outskirts of Ticonderoga, a town made famous by the colonial-era fort that bore its name. Meetings like these were standard during the writing phase of an engagement, as Barron preferred to learn that a play had wandered off track sooner rather than later.

Jack nodded evenly at the Director from across the table, a Styrofoam cup of coffee in one hand. Despite the verbal fireworks and exacting changes that always accompanied these meetings, they were a nice break from the host town and always well catered. Berni was the only other individual in the small conference room, and she was patiently feeding papers of various sizes into a digital scanner at the far end of the table. Jack had brought along some pictures to help sell his new idea, and had followed an old Death Troupe practice of sketching his more developed concepts by hand. Although no hacker could steal something that had never been on Jack's laptop in the first place, the sketches still had to be digitized for the meeting. A laptop and projector sat next to the scanner, and each image appeared on the wall to Barron's right as the machine assimilated it.

"Hear me out. I liked Ryan's idea, but nobody in Schuyler Mills has mentioned the Depression even once. They talk about mining, the silent film era, and—" he swept a hand toward the blank wall, where the latest image suddenly took its place as if on cue "—Prohibition."

The vertical blinds on the room's windows were all drawn shut, and the picture stood out in black and white against the gloom. It was a police lineup that could have been straight out of a Roaring Twenties movie, with a group of disheveled hoodlums slouched in front of a series of horizontal lines meant to establish their height. The American melting pot hadn't melted these men much, and the age before cosmetic surgery had left them the noses and chins they'd been born with. The staff at the Schuyler Mills Library had helped him select this photo, and he felt it provided a good backdrop for his pitch. Jack stood up and approached the projection.

"The Adirondack region was a major transshipment point for bootleg liquor coming in from Canada, and there was a whole sub-industry that sprang up in support of it. Garages that suped-up the cars and repaired the trucks, boaters who moved the stuff on the rivers, and of course clubs where the gangsters partied down with their customers.

"So instead of using a Depression-era story about someone losing the town's nest egg, I'd like to shift it to something a little more interesting. Most people are intrigued by organized crime, so let's use a theme that says most of the town was in bootlegging. It's still similar to Ryan's idea, but instead of losing their nest egg in the Crash of 1929 they lose their livelihoods when Prohibition is repealed in 1933. It's just as big a catastrophe: No more fat fees for fixing trucks or hiding hooch. No more gangsters with big wallets spreading their money around at the clubs. And there's conflict, too: A big scramble to see who's going to control the legitimate flow of booze that replaces the criminal sources."

"Go on." Barron wore a dark green turtleneck that morning, and had draped a gray tartan scarf over his shoulders even though the room was quite warm. It should have been, as both doors were locked from inside and the heat had nowhere else to go. Security was a concern even this early in the brainstorming process, and Barron had kept the location secret until the previous night, when he'd summoned Jack over the secure cell phone provided by Wade. As for the advance man, Jack wasn't sure if the Director knew he was investigating the events in Red Bend and had decided not to mention it. Barron had grumbled something about Wade not being available to sweep the room for bugs, but Berni had already performed that task before Jack arrived.

"So I was thinking . . . the Adirondack area wasn't just a gangster playground. This was a time before air conditioning, and a lot of wealthy people had summer homes up here where they could escape the heat. We'd have to pretend Schuyler Mills was bigger back then than it actually was, but that's okay. My thought is to create a setting where there are a few rich families in the area and some of them were in the bootlegging business.

"With the repeal of Prohibition there would be a rush to get licensed and secure a legitimate source of liquor, and in that scuffle some families would win and some would lose. So how about if one of those families made darn sure that they won?"

"I'm not following this, Jack."

"Remember that in real life the gangs tried to make the leap from bootlegging to legal alcohol distribution and that the authorities tried to keep them out. So what if one of the rich families in the town hooked up with one of the bootlegger gangs? The gang muscle discourages the other families from competing for the legal contracts, and the rich family acts as their front."

Barron laid one large hand flat on the table next to a writing tablet and an assortment of pens and pencils. Jack had identified this as one of his tells, an indication that he was considering what was being proposed. Jack paused as if gathering his arguments, letting the Director digest what he'd heard so far.

"Okay. I'm seeing it. Everybody likes gangster stories. But where's the murder?"

"That's where we come back to the original idea, the Depression theme." It was important not to completely jettison the original assignment, which Barron would probably take as a personal rejection no matter whose idea it had been. "Ryan's modern-day investigator character, coming into town to ask questions about a disgraced ancestor, is a great role and we can do a lot with it. As a Prohibition story we can have an earlier murder, say an Elliot Ness supercop who was killed in the area and framed for being dirty in the bargain. The current-day investigator could be his descendant, trying to set the record straight."

"Ryan's original idea had a missing confession angle—"

"I love those."

"I know you do. So we could throw that in here. One of the killers admits on his deathbed that the murdered supercop wasn't dirty, but someone else conceals the confession. Or maybe the supercop had a casebook that could show who killed him and the investigator is looking for that." A new idea popped into Jack's head, and he offered it even though he knew the hazard of mixing unprepared proposals with Jerome Barron. "Heck, maybe the supercop's casebook got buried with him in an unmarked grave and so the guy's descendant has to find out where that was and dig him up."

"No digging." Barron raised an index finger as if pointing at something on the room's tiled ceiling. "Don't forget that one nitwit years ago, the one who spread the rumor that we were burying clues around town. Place looked like a mole colony before we could quash it. And we had to pay to have them filled in."

"Got it. No digging. Although I don't think they'd get very far —the whole area's frozen rock solid." As usual there was a fair amount of embellishment in Barron's memory. The aforementioned holes had been concentrated in a just a few spots, and Jack certainly hadn't been paid extra after he and Wade had repaired the damage. "But here's where we get to the fun part: We can go with just the one murder of the supercop, or we can add another one on top of that in the current day, maybe a local who was trying to tip off the modern-day investigator. Either way, it all comes back to a gang that I like to call—" Jack nodded at Berni, who hit a button on the laptop to bring up another picture, one showing liquor barrels being offloaded in a dark cove by the dead of night. A hand-written caption named them, and Jack read it aloud: "The Seven Seas Gang."

Barron squinted at the new picture in the darkness, and Jack didn't wait. "I did a little reading on the various bootlegger outfits, and they had all sorts of exotic names like that. The Sugarhouse Gang, the Broadway Mob, Egan's Rats . . . lots of others. Now a fair amount of the liquor moving into and out of the Adirondacks went by boat on the rivers and lakes, and so it's not a stretch that a group of inland waterway thugs would give themselves an inflated name like The Seven Seas."

"This was a real gang?"

"No, I made it up, but that's where it gets good: Their name is a play on words. Everyone thinks they're called The Seven *Seas*, as in the seven main oceans of the world, when actually it's Seven C's, the third letter in the alphabet. It's a clue because the gang was founded by seven guys whose last names all started with the letter C. Over the years that fact gets lost, and so when the investigator discovers it—I haven't decided how he does that yet—it helps him figure out which family took over the bootlegging. And their descendants, whether they want to or not, might be able to help him figure out what happened to his supercop ancestor."

"That's it, that's it . . ." Barron seemed to be muttering, but Jack knew it was a sign that the Director's imagination had just kicked in. Taking a sip from his coffee, he sat down and prayed that Barron wouldn't completely run away with his concept.

Berni slid out of her chair and over to the side wall, where she raised the lights a bit. She'd given up her preferred business attire for jeans and a tight sweater, and Jack was again reminded how much she physically resembled Kelly Sykes. The projected image was still visible on the wall where Barron was now standing, and Berni returned to the laptop to take down the Director's thoughts. The picture of the bootleggers disappeared, to be replaced by a blank page where Berni rapidly typed, 'Schuyler Mills In-Progress Review Brainstorming Notes'.

Barron had been waiting for this to finish, and now he started speaking with his arms crossed over his chest. Berni typed in pace with his comments, and the words began appearing on the wall as if the laptop were transcribing the Director's speech.

"Bootleggers theme. Seven Seas Gang, spelled out. Seven C's Gang, with a C. Seven local families involved in bootlegging, surnames all begin with C. Prohibition ends and the gang chooses one family to act as their front in the legitimate sale of alcohol. Treachery. Betrayal. Other families shut out of the business. Resentment. Rivalry." He looked back at Berni and said in a soft voice, "New page."

The screen went blank again, and he continued. "One murder at least. Prohibition agent, local boy who was trying to clean up his hometown—"

Oh, boy. Here we go.

"—agent is murdered and made to look corrupt. Body buried in a concealed spot, possibly with the agent's notebook. Notebook could establish his innocence, and perhaps identify his killers . . . or the family that took over the liquor business in the area. Question mark: Agent killed after Prohibition is over? Perhaps killed by the family that fronts for the Seven Seas Gang, and they make it look like the gangsters did it? FBI gets involved and puts the gangsters behind bars, leaving the front family with the business?

"Agent's family leaves the area, and we move to the modern day. Descendant of the agent comes to town doing research on his ancestor. Locals unhappy with the questions. The family that took over the bootlegging is still there, very wealthy and respectable. Afraid of scandal."

Barron turned away from the screen to face Jack, his left arm still across his chest and his right hand raised with the fingers spread as if he were physically trying to grasp something. "This Seven Seas thing intrigues me. Whenever one of the actors says it out loud the audience will think of the oceans, so we'll need some way of giving them the letter C as a clue."

"How about having someone explain it during the introduction, back when it was common knowledge? The current day investigator wouldn't know, but the audience would."

"Maybe. Maybe. But you know I don't like spelling things out like that . . . literally, in this case."

Berni spoke up, having supplied the answer many times before. "What about presenting it in the form of newspaper copy? It could be part of the prologue film, or splashed across the screens behind the players. Use a combination of them, from spelling out Seven Seas, then spelling the word Seven but using the letter C after that, and then representing it as the number 7 and the letter C."

"I like that." Jack turned in his seat, pointing at Berni with his index finger. "In newspaper copy it might just look like a space-saver. Not so obvious."

"Newspaper copy. Newspaper copy." Barron slowly walked toward the windows and stood there as if they weren't shuttered. After a moment he turned around and spoke to Berni. "Type it up there just the way you said it."

He then took a step toward Jack, his mouth open as if an idea had somehow become stuck trying to exit. "And how about this? A little more misdirection. We actually show them the letter C version a few times, but the calling card for the gang isn't focused on that at all. It's on the number seven. Say they leave a seven of hearts playing card on their victims' bodies—"

"—or mark their territory with seven bullets from a tommy gun."

"Maybe in the shape of a seven? Or is that too similar to Zorro?"

Barron glanced over at Berni, who gave him a pleasant, pursed-lips smile. "Don't ask me. Zorro's *way* before my time."

The Director cocked his head to one side, donning a hurt expression. "Mine too, sweetheart!"

Berni shook her head impishly and began typing the latest comments under her own.

"I like this idea, Jack. Lots we can do with it." Barron sat down with a sigh, as if the brainstorming session had been physically draining. "But I want you to keep going with the Depression theme as well."

"What?" Jack tried to keep the exasperation out of his voice, but he'd been taken by surprise and failed miserably.

"Oh, it's not that much more work. It's the same historical timeframe, and I'm sure you could fit this Seven Seas Gang into both versions. In fact, I think you'd be surprised at how similar the two ideas are, and how much they could satellite off of each other."

"Until we drop one of them, right? You're the one who said we're operating under a deadline here. How long are you going to play with these before you pick one?"

"Oh, don't worry about that. There's always plenty of time."

"Thank God you're back, Jack." Berni raised both arms over her head and stretched, a yawn elongating her features even more. Coming back down, she looked at the door through which Barron had exited after announcing that they were on break. "I don't want to speak ill of the dead, but these sessions were absolute hell when we did them with Ryan."

Jack slowly broke apart one of the croissants he'd snagged from the snack table. This kind of commentary was a departure for Berni, as she normally tried to stay away from the troupe's personality disputes. Though she got along well with most of the company, and particularly the costume designers who treated Barron as a savant, her first loyalty was always to the Director. Jack couldn't remember her confiding something like this before, and had to believe that the previous two years had been quite a trial.

"It's good to be back." He buttered a flaking piece of roll, studying it while deciding whether to push. He'd intended to ask Barron about Ryan's unpopularity, but perhaps Berni would be a better source. "I couldn't help noticing, up in Maine, that the rest of the troupe was . . . not unhappy."

"It was hard to miss, wasn't it?" She gave a helpless little laugh, a pained expression rising up on her face. "The engagement after you left was the difference of night and day. I thought Jerome was going to pull his hair out. Ryan kept leaving the location . . ." she seemed to be searching for the right words, and Jack knew she was trying not to say that Ryan had been jetting off to see Allison. "And of course he wasn't prepared for any of our meetings."

No good. Jack hadn't spent much time around other directors, but he knew that Be Prepared stood first among their ten commandments, just like the Boy Scouts. He popped the piece of the croissant into his mouth, and Berni continued.

"And what he was writing was just all over the place. Please don't repeat this, but Ryan couldn't put one of these things together without you. He could write great dialogue and big scenes, but he couldn't build a working mystery to save his soul. Jerome said that was what made you two such a good team. You wrote a great mystery, and Ryan polished it up."

There was a sound in the hallway outside, and Berni cocked her head to one side in a fashion that was almost identical to Barron's. Munching on the food, Jack had a moment to wonder if she'd been told to flatter him this way, but he truly couldn't see any reason for that. He was already committed, and used to Barron's idiosyncrasies, so there seemed little point to such blandishments.

"Jerome had to basically re-write the first play we did without you, the one outside of Muncie. These in-progress reviews turned into full-on writing sessions, and even with that we weren't ready when the troupe came to town." Her face darkened, confirming that he wasn't being sweet-talked. "The actors *really* didn't like that. I suppose I can't blame them; they have so little time to get the script in hand and develop their characters . . . and then to arrive and find there were still gaps in the story . . . even Puff spoke up."

"Wow." They looked at each other like the parents of a well-behaved child who has suddenly acted out in school. "That is bad. I've seen Puff step up and take over rehearsals before, when things were getting a little hot and Barron got called away . . . but he always sided with the Director, even while straightening out whatever was wrong."

"I'll tell you a little secret about that." Berni grinned at him, breaking the tension. "Puff and I have a little signal, whenever Jerome and one of the actors—usually Kirk—are starting to go round and round. Puff gives me the sign and I come up with an excuse to get Jerome out of there. Then Puff smoothes things over while he's gone."

"And I thought I knew how this outfit operated." They smiled at each other again. "Well at least Barron's as much in the dark about that as I am."

"Oh, Jerome's not fooled. He knows what's happening, but it's a face saver for everybody and it gives him a break as well." She dropped her eyes to the table at that point, and the smile fell off. "But the Indiana show was a real chore. Did you see the tape?"

"Of course." Jack had detected tension on the faces of the actors, but he'd chalked that up to his own all-too-human hope that Death Troupe would experience just a little trouble without their original playwright. He now remembered that he'd correctly guessed the play's culprit and that he'd felt the underlying mystery hadn't been very artful. Looking back, he understood just how hard the actors had been forced to work in order to dress up a script that had been weak from the start.

"It was especially hard on Allison. Ryan had written some wonderful scenes for her character, but they didn't mesh with the rest of the play at all. He wouldn't rewrite them, either, and so Jerome switched Sally Newsome into the role." Another piece of the puzzle fell into place for Jack. He'd noticed that Sally had been in over her head. "I thought Ryan was going to quit right then."

"That show was a big hit, from what I read."

"I think that was the only thing that kept Ryan on board. Jerome wanted to let him go, that very night, but Allison came to see him right after the show and he changed his mind. I don't know what she said, but his whole demeanor around Ryan changed after that. The California engagement was no picnic, but we knew what to expect from Ryan by then. Jerome was much more relaxed around him during those sessions, and they were almost as tough as Indiana."

"But that Red Bend show was really good, you have to admit."

"Red Bend had a very spooky vibe to it, Jack. Bad juju. I think that helped a lot."

"You want me to shoot a *silent* film short to start my play?" It was midafternoon and Barron was clearly getting tired, but his reaction still wasn't as bad as Jack had feared. It smacked of interest, and Jack went in for the kill.

"Sure. You've opened the last five plays with great little movies, using the local theater group. It got them all involved while still keeping them away from the main performance so they couldn't find out anything they weren't supposed to know."

"You know it wasn't the last five. We didn't do it in Florida; crazy theater-in-the-round doesn't lend itself to that kind of intro."

"I know. I was there. But here's my point: You've got a great film crew, you know how to direct one of these, and if you do it as a silent movie it'll be a great homage to the silent picture industry that existed in the Adirondacks before talkies moved everything to Hollywood."

"That really true?" The Director glanced at Berni, who nodded from her station at the laptop. She'd worked through the lunch break, checking much of Jack's research. "Hmm. Wonders will never cease. But that local troupe's not gonna like the idea of having no lines."

"Didn't you once say that the best actors can do their scenes without the lines? Communicating only through expressions and action?"

"I say a lot of things. But in this case I do stand by my words. As in these people aren't top-tier actors. They're a community outfit that probably couldn't bring it off."

"You should see them. They're chomping at the bit with those two scenes from the Scottish play. You'll have the entire Mystery

Weekend to coach them, and I think a director of your caliber could get them where they need to go."

"I hate you, Jack Glynn." Barron tipped his chair back, reached both arms over his head, and stretched. "But I'll admit this has potential. I was getting tired of the standard introductory shorts anyway. And who knows? Maybe they're such dreadful actors that we're better off not hearing them talk."

Jack knew when to move off a subject with Barron, and flipped a page on the pad in front of him. Somewhere deep inside he was laughing out loud, though, having finally stolen a march on the overeager film crew that had made his life so difficult in the past. *Let 'em dance to* my *tune for once, see how they like it.*

"I've got some clue ideas, things we can use right away while I develop both of the two themes." He was careful not to overemphasize the word 'both', knowing he'd lost that argument and fearing that a sign of pugnacity might overturn his victory with the silent movie idea. "There's an unused billboard by the side of the main road between the town center and the Playhouse. I checked it out; there's a ladder attached to it and the platform looks stable enough for a crew to climb up and paste something on it in the dark of night."

Berni's fingers danced across the laptop's keys, recording the suggestion, and Barron picked up the thread. "Any idea of what to put up there?"

"I was thinking maybe a lineup photo, something that could get more specific as time went by. Kind of like that rogue's gallery we posted on the town hall bulletin board in our first engagement."

"That mess."

"Yes, that mess. But I think we've learned a few things since then. I hadn't thought of it earlier, but since the Seven Seas Gang is going to be part of whichever theme we ultimately choose, we could use that lineup photo, the one of the gangsters, to start. Enlarge it and hang it up there, just to get things going. Later we could hang one using our actors and their characters' names, as a way of introducing the suspects."

One of the rules of the game specified that the troupe had to identify a maximum of seven characters in the play who could be the murderer. It was meant to give the audience a sporting chance, but designating those roles early on usually had the opposite effect. With plenty of time for debate and little information, many of the locals chose a favorite suspect from the list and stayed with it no matter how the play or the clues unfolded.

"All right. Let me think about that one. What else?"

"Not much so far. There's a spot on the far side of Long Lake—
that's the one next to the town center—where the ground slopes up to
form a big empty hillside that's currently buried in snow. There's a
bunch of canoes and rowboats stacked near that, and if someone took
those and arranged them to spell something it would be seen from the
entire town."

Barron snapped his fingers, sitting up straight. "The Seven Seas.
A big number seven and nothing else. It's generic enough so it
doesn't box us in, but it introduces the gang at the same time. And at
first they won't know what the heck it means."

"I hadn't thought of that . . . but it's good."

Barron cocked his head to the side. "Of course it is."

It was late afternoon, and Jack had a long ride ahead of him when
Barron walked him to his truck. The parking lot was well plowed, but
Jack still crossed the icy blacktop gingerly in his new boots. Berni
had bundled up the Director in a heavy coat and a brimmed hat, and
Jack wondered what Barron wanted to say to him. He decided to beat
him to the punch.

"Jerry, can you tell me why you're insisting on two themes? We
don't really have a lot of time, you know."

"Are we back to this again? When you wrote *Wind in the Palms*
you started out with three radically different concepts—and look
what happened there."

"Yeah. It was the best play I've ever written, and it earned me a
partner who stole my girl."

Barron stopped when they reached the truck. His lips parted
inside his beard, and he shook his head as if at a loss for words.
"Look how long it took you to get that out. The night I told you I'd
hired Ryan I thought you were going to explode . . . and yet here we
are, how many years later, with the man dead, and you're raising the
objection *now*?

"You're the one who mentioned *Wind in the Palms*."

"All right." Barron sounded like Jack's mother when her
patience had finally been exhausted. "You want it, so here it is. When
I recruited Ryan, I didn't know you were capable of something as
good as that play. You'd been our writer for three engagements, and
even though you developed by leaps and bounds at first, you really
plateaued after that.

"Don't misunderstand me. When it comes to the nuts and bolts
of writing mystery theater, you're the best there is. But you didn't
show any ear for the high notes. You could write a nice central
melody with a consistent backbeat, but when it was time for the

crescendo, you simply didn't deliver. A play's like a song, Jack; sure it has to hang together, and one note has to lead to another, but there's got to be a point where everybody listening is sitting on the edge of their seats, just *knowing* the big moment is only a few notes away.

"I was willing to supply those at first, but I got tired of waiting for you to learn to do it and that's why I hired Ryan. Talk about a polar opposite: The guy had no sense of melody and his timing was atrocious, but man could he hit the high notes. And the two of you together . . . well, before he turned out to be a rat, the pair of you wrote some beautiful music."

"And *Wind in the Palms*? The one I did all by myself? What was that?"

"That's a question you should have asked at the time, Jack. *Wind in the Palms* was simply amazing. You outdid yourself. But you didn't recognize what you'd accomplished, which means you damn sure didn't know how you did it. And when it became a hit, you should have dug into that play until you figured out what you'd done." He raised a gloved hand and pointed at him. "That's why you had so much trouble adapting it to the screen. You never understood how you wrote something that good in the first place, so how could you translate it into a different medium?"

The words hung in the frosty air, but Jack didn't respond. Barron gave him several seconds, but when he didn't make a sound the Director continued. "Do me a favor, Jack. Get yourself a nice set of headphones and listen to a few classical tunes. Pick something that really hits you, that gets your blood going or the tears flowing, anything you like as long as it's got a lot of different instruments.

"Here's why I say that: While you're listening, shut your eyes and try to pick out some of the moments when the song's building, like where an oboe hops in or a fife flutters a few notes and then disappears. Be honest with yourself, and ask if you ever noticed those things before. Then go back and listen for the big moments, those soaring, sweeping passages where you feel like your heart's going to explode in expectation.

"And after that, start writing. Write this play like a composer. I've always said that the best members of this troupe came from musicals, and I stand by that. To do what we do, you gotta be able to hear the music—even when it isn't there."

It was well past dark when Jack pulled into Schuyler Mills. Of course that didn't mean it was very late, as the sun had gone down before five o'clock. The ride had been uneventful, and had given him a chance to ponder the day's developments.

Why had the Director insisted on keeping the Depression era theme when the Prohibition idea was so much better? It had sparked his interest as soon as Jack had proposed it, and Barron had even admitted that the two concepts were similar enough to have interchangeable parts.

And what was that business about listening to music? Barron often compared plays to symphonies ("after all, they're both run by Directors") and musical terms were common in theater, but his suggestions this time had been much too pointed. It was almost a warning that he planned to exercise much closer supervision of the writing process than in the past.

That brought the discussion with Berni back into his mind, and he considered that the Director's bad experience with a lone Ryan Betancourt was why he was now treating his original writer like a complete rookie. Although that might be part of the reason, Jack still feared that the Director harbored real doubts about his abilities. If that wasn't the case, why had Barron voiced that hurtful assessment of his early days with the troupe? As if any of that mattered now; he'd written *Wind in the Palms* all by himself after those earlier efforts, and he was now an established screenplay writer in Hollywood. Leave it to Barron to suggest that *Wind in the Palms* had been a fluke, neatly taking the wind out of his writer's sails and resurrecting Jack's own concerns about having lost his touch.

Lost it? According to Jerry, you never had it in the first place. At least now you know what he was getting at back in Maine. He really was just asking if you can still do the job.

More of the Berni conversation drifted into his consciousness, enough for him to wonder again if Barron had put her up to it. Berni might not miss much, but that didn't mean she shared what she found. It was very unusual for her to have dished this much dirt, but he now understood the company's lack of grief over Ryan's passing. They'd resented the extra work forced on them by their undisciplined writer, and they'd openly revolted over his bias toward Allison.

Apparently Allison had interceded for Ryan at the end of his first solo engagement, and this made Jack curious. What had she said to get her boyfriend off the hook? Wade had been correct in his assessment that Allison's first love would always be the stage, so it didn't make sense for her to shield the playwright at the expense of the troupe. That is, unless she'd detected something in Ryan that showed he was in particular need of protection. Had she sensed the thing that Jack had missed, the hairline crack in Ryan's psyche that had caused him to kill himself?

Jack came into Schuyler Mills from the east, the part of town that lay on the other side of Round Pond. He'd driven through there on the way out that morning, and had been struck by how different it looked. Whereas the town center was composed of older buildings, the eastern half of Schuyler Mills consisted of newer construction that explained its pet name among its inhabitants, Newville. Even the shops in Newville seemed more modern, as if telling the tourists and the campers to go west if they wanted a more traditional Adirondack experience.

He noticed a large number of cars and trucks parked off to his right, near a club called Sal's, and decided to pull over. At first he had no intention of going inside, really just wanting to take a moment to call Allison, but when he turned off the engine he could feel the pulse of the music coming from inside the long, low building. A pair of twenty-somethings went by on their way inside, and he remembered hearing that Sal's was considered a younger, hipper hangout than Maddy's.

At first he didn't recognize the male voice that answered Allison's cell phone, but Mickey quickly set him straight. It was still early in Vancouver, but Allison wasn't available and her assistant promised to tell her he'd called. The cab of the truck was cooling off quickly, and Jack's mood wasn't improved by his failure to get through. He didn't call often when they were apart—neither of them did—and he would have hoped that Allison's helpers would have considered such an unexpected occurrence important enough to put him through.

The door to Sal's opened to admit more patrons, and the blast of light was inviting. A strange thought came to him just then, and he hit another number that he had on speed dial. After three rings, Kelly answered.

"Hi Jack! This is an unexpected surprise."

"Yeah, well, I was out cruising around and ended up over at Sal's and wondered if you might want to step out for a drink."

"Oh, I'd like to, Jack, but I'm not in town. I'm in Binghamton, visiting the folks."

Idiot. Now you really *look like a loser. Can't raise your girl on the phone, and no one to drink with.*

"I'm sorry, I didn't know that. Is everything all right?"

"It's just a visit. Too bad I'm not there; I'd definitely have joined you."

"Well, again I'm sorry I bothered you. I hope I didn't interrupt."

"It's fine, Jack. Really, I should have told you I'd be out of town, but you've done so well making new friends that I didn't think of it." The words sounded like a mild rebuke, but her voice was light enough so he couldn't tell. "Hey, I've got to run, but I'm sure you'll meet plenty of people there at Sal's. Take a rain check on that drink?"

"You got it."

He closed the phone and looked at the now-menacing door of the unknown bar. He had more than enough work to do, and wanted to go over Ryan's Red Bend notebook again to see if it contained anything else that might help him develop the still-living Depression concept. He looked down at the phone in his hand, annoyed by his prior two calls. Barron's suggestion to put on some headphones came back just then, as if riding the steady thump of music on the other side of Sal's door.

"What the heck," he said aloud, tossing the phone onto the passenger seat. He covered it with his coat, not wanting to haul the heavy garment around inside the club. "He did say I was supposed to listen to some tunes."

"Naw, they started imagining they were surrounded by witches because it was the middle of a long, cold winter just like we got here."

Jack listened with a look of contentment, having found a safe haven shortly after entering Sal's and finding it was much more than an eastern version of Maddy's Place. Whereas Maddy's was a cozy sports bar and a good spot to get a bite to eat, Sal's was clearly meant for dancing and drinking. The heat inside was overwhelming, but it all seemed to be human-generated. He'd had his behind pinched twice while working his way through the crowded dance floor, where a host of people clad largely in denim were whooping it up to the strains of a live band.

He'd been waved over to a booth shortly after that, recognizing Lynnie the Wicked Wanda's counter girl by her blonde locks and good looks. She was sitting with two other men her age, one large with a well-trimmed beard and the other thin with spiked hair. They were having a good time, and had launched into several spirited arguments after he'd bought a round.

"I dunno . . ." the spike-haired one offered doubtfully. His name was Tadd Wilkinson, and he worked at a computer store two towns away whenever he wasn't designing online games of his own. "I guess there's something to that. I mean, strange things do seem to happen around here during the winter. There are girls that I wouldn't even look at in the summer who start lookin' mighty tasty come the middle of February . . ."

Tadd's voice trailed off, and he glanced at Lynnie to his left. She gave him a playful slap, further confusing Jack as to the relationships in the booth. As far as he was concerned, she was well ahead of Tadd's wintertime schedule. That night she wore a tight dress of a sheer dark fabric that showed off her figure nicely, and her bare arms proved to Jack that he'd been wrong about the tattoos. On her arms, anyway.

"That reminds me." The big man to Jack's left turned as much as the narrow booth allowed. He'd identified himself as Gary Price the Cable Guy, and still wore a shirt sporting the logo of the local television service. Apparently he was of an electronic bent the same as his roommate Tadd, as he'd boasted that he could hook up everything from a sound system to a personal computer. From the grin he'd shown under his dark brown beard, it had been clear he meant to indicate that he hooked up much more than equipment. "I've got an idea for you, Writer Man.

"There's been a lot of disappearances right here in River City over the years, and I think you could work this into your story." Jack nodded pleasantly, already on his guard. Gary leaned closer, as if to be heard over the noise from the dance floor. "There's a segment of the population that's particularly susceptible. They seem normal for a long time, eighteen or twenty years maybe, but then all of a sudden they get transported to this . . . other place . . . called . . . College."

"Or to its evil sister kingdom, Marriage." Lynnie interjected sweetly, giving Jack a quick raise of her eyebrows when he glanced at her.

"Or marriage. Anyway, they disappear into these strange places, and after that they're never . . . heard from . . . again."

They all laughed heartily at that, even though it wasn't particularly funny. Jack had tactfully switched to drinking the same Canadian beers the others had ordered, but even so he was feeling the one bottle he'd consumed. He was surprised to be relaxing this much in such a noisy setting, but perhaps that was it: He wasn't the center of attention here and could stop performing.

It was impossible to ignore the bodies hopping or swaying on the dance floor, and his eye strayed to the abundant female skin on display. Looking back across the booth's scarred table, he noted that a dress, a ribbon around the throat, and just a little makeup had transformed Lynnie from a cute coffee server into something quite interesting. He still wasn't sure of the relationship between her and the two boys, but they appeared to have been lifelong friends and little more.

Not that he had any intentions of cheating on Allison. Allison, who hadn't trained her staff to immediately bring her any phone calls from Jack Glynn. Allison, who had refused to discuss the dead man who had been her lover for over two years. She'd refused to even speak Ryan's name, and a dark thought suggested itself when Jack considered that fact.

She left me for Ryan, and then came back on the very day she buried him. Talk about cheating.

He shook the notion out of his head with disgust, and consciously took up the conversational glove that had been dropped on the table much earlier. "So Tadd, tell me about these games you design."

He wasn't toying with the young people; he'd envisioned an electronic game based on Death Troupe's plays a few years earlier and still thought it was a good idea. After all, the troupe sold copies of the script, videos of the performances, and a host of Barron Players regalia, so why not go the rest of the way? Besides, his new friends honestly intrigued him. They had the easy confidence of youth and an offhand disdain for conformity, but they blended it nicely with an active intelligence that suggested they might not be in the same spot ten years later.

"Aw, it's nothing really, at least not yet." The thin man seemed a shade embarrassed, and Jack was just starting to fear he'd said something wrong when Tadd continued. "I'm a programmer, so I can write code that makes a game do just about anything. Lynnie draws the figures that I use, and I code 'em in. She's really good; you should see some of the stuff she paints."

"Forget the painting," Gary interjected, "You wanna see something? Get her to do you an ice sculpture. Girl's murder with a chainsaw."

"Yeah, that's me—the original ice queen." Lynnie gave Jack a quick wink, but she was blushing happily at the compliments. She nudged Tadd lightly, as if to get out of the spotlight. "Go on, tell him your idea."

"You see, your whole approach to a mystery play really lends itself to gaming. From what I hear, you've got a bunch of different endings that you could throw out there, and that's what the best interactive stuff does. It's much more realistic that way. Say a player decides to ignore the door in front of him and goes out through the window. He might miss a pot of gold, but he might also have avoided a fucking dragon." He seemed to get flustered, and reached for his beer. Without looking up, he half-mumbled, "You should swing by our place and check 'em out."

115

"We live right next to the bridge between here and Old Town." Gary explained, using a term that Jack already knew was the Newville residents' name for the town center. "You can't miss it. It looks like an old firehouse because that's what it is."

"It was a jail before that. You can still see where they had one of the cells in the downstairs." Tadd offered this as if it were a major selling point. "The upstairs is our apartment. It's not much, but it beats living in my parents' basement."

"That's where Tadd does most of his designing." Gary added. "Games made right here in the good ol' US of A."

"And stolen by the good ol' PR of C." Tadd replied, raising a finger to his lips. He noted Jack's consternation, and explained with an impish look on his face. "People's Republic of China. They don't just hack the Pentagon, you know."

"How many times I gotta tell you that your stuff hasn't been hacked?" This came from Gary, who shied a hand at his roommate. He turned to Jack, but seemed to be looking past him at the dance floor. "I do it all in my job, from phones to televisions to computers. I've got every computer security machine known to man, but my roommate here still insists the boys in Pyongyang are stealing his ideas."

"Beijing. Pyongyang's in North Korea." Lynnie corrected him with a small giggle.

"Don't get me started on the Koreans . . ." Tadd seemed ready to do just that when he suddenly looked up at a spot just behind Jack's shoulder. Seeing the look of surprise, Jack remembered the scare which Ryan had experienced on a crowded dance floor in California. Trying not to show his concern, he turned in his seat to find his vision obscured by a large set of breasts that were trying to escape a red top worn by a middle-aged blonde woman leaning into the booth.

"Hey Gary, how's about a dance?" she asked sweetly, with just a slight slur in her words. Despite his limited field of vision Jack could tell she was quite attractive, and so he pressed backward as far as he could to let Gary respond. The big man answered in a plaintive wail.

"Oh come on, Mrs. Trainor, I've already been written up once this month for fondling the customers."

"I haven't been Mrs. Trainor since Mr. Trainor ran off to Ottawa with that stripper." The blonde woman took a step back as if to make room for the motionless Gary to join her. "And I think I'd like to know who else you've been fondling."

116

She stood there with her hands on the hips of her jeans, her hair flowing over her shoulders, and just when Jack thought Gary was going to decline the offer the big man indicated he wanted to get out. Jack got to his feet with difficulty, trying not to bump into the obstinately motionless blonde. Turning back to the table, Gary repeated as if in a trance, "I will not sleep with the customers. I will not sleep with the customers."

The former Mrs. Trainor slipped a hand between the back of his shirt and his jeans, grabbing his belt. Without a word she turned and half-dragged him into the crowd while Tadd and Lynnie waved farewell. Jack slipped back into the booth just in time to hear the other two simultaneously pass judgment on the scene.

"What a whore!" The two began laughing heartily, clutching each other's arms.

Jack thought that was a bit harsh, and tried to be diplomatic. "Well, if her husband really ran off on her . . ."

"We're talking about *him*." Lynnie managed to blurt this out, but it sent both of them back into hysterics, and Jack decided this was probably a good, high note on which to exit.

"Well as they say, three's a crowd." He stuck his hand across at Tadd, holding one of his business cards. "Give me a call when you want to show me some of your stuff. I can't make any promises, but the troupe has a pretty good website and it wouldn't hurt us to branch out a little."

Lynnie leaned across the table and gave him a quick hug. "Thanks, Jack. He's really good; you won't regret it."

"I'm sure I won't." She was still holding him, so he slid his arms around her and gently squeezed back. She gave an approving murmur just before whispering, "Next time we need to see how well you dance."

He gave her a wink as he pulled away, and suffered a couple more pinches, these much more aggressive than earlier, as he maneuvered through the dancers. The memories of Ryan's Red Bend dance club experience came back to him again, and he had to force himself not to swing around to make sure it wasn't a tall man in a dark suit and a mask.

And once he got back out to the truck, so chilled by the short walk across the lot that he practically dived into his overcoat, there was no message waiting from Allison.

Chapter Nine

Two days after his meeting with Barron, Jack came skiing into the town center under an ineffective midafternoon sun. The television weathermen had explained the deep cold that had swept into the region as having come from Canada, but Jack believed it was probably Siberia. He was relatively warm now, having pushed his cross-country skis halfway to the Playhouse before his burning calves had forced him to turn back. Though disappointed at the way his runner's muscles failed to translate into the different demands of skiing, he was proud of the effort he'd put in.

Allison had finally returned his phone call the day before, but by then he'd decided against quizzing her about Ryan's difficulties with the troupe. She'd sounded busy, and he'd felt like a fool now that his reason for calling her had been discarded. They'd chatted a little about the film she was working on, and then a bit about the play, but after that the conversation had dragged enough for him to let her go.

He was just about to cut across the common toward the welcome of the shower in his room and the beer in his refrigerator when he saw the black-and-red form of Marv Tillman waving at him from the Visitor's Center. The mayor was walking down the snowy street toward him, but without the telltale hunting jacket he would have looked the same as any other tall man (or woman) in the area. A red knit cap was pulled down low over his ears, a black scarf was up over his nose, and a set of dark glasses completed the disguise. Jack took pity on the way Tillman's boots kept slipping on the hard pack, and started sliding the long skis down the road to meet him.

"You're looking more like a pro on those things every time I see you, Jack!" Tillman greeted him with a muffled voice. "Before long you'll be all over the trails around here."

Jack felt a slight rush of anticipation despite his fatigue. During his many lessons on the common with Kelly he'd frequently looked up at the surrounding hills and imagined what it would be like to finally get up in the woods. "They tell me there's a trail right in back of the Great View that I could try."

Jack's stay at the Schuyler Mills Hotel was coming to an end, and his next place of lodging was the Great View Motel, so named because of an ancient sign above the motel offices that promised a GREAT VIEW. It stood by itself as a string of single-story cabins looking down on the town square, and in that direction it lived up to its name. Densely forested hills rose up right behind the cabins, and the whole place fit the bill for seclusion.

"Yeah, beautiful area back there, too. You can see a long way from a couple of spots. I've always found it inspirational—not that you need anything like that."

A drop of sweat rolled down the canal formed by Jack's spine, and didn't stop until it slid into the light ski pants he wore. His gray sweat top was damp under the down vest he'd bought for skiing, and he now became aware of the wetness of his socks inside the narrow ski boots. Even so, he wasn't fooled; Tillman's supportive comment had chilled him with the reminder that he'd made no headway on either of the themes approved by Barron.

"Yeah, well, just let me know the moving day and I'll have my stuff together." He looked up at the hotel's corner window where he'd spent much of the last two nights, taking in the idyllic setting and searching the darkness for an idea.

"Oh, that's not why I came out. I wanted to show you this." Tillman removed one glove and rummaged around in his pocket until he produced a cell phone. He flipped it open, hit a succession of buttons, and held out the tiny display screen for Jack's perusal. "Let the games begin."

Jack squinted behind his sunglasses. The dull sun still managed to reflect off the whiteness that surrounded them, and he had difficulty seeing the picture. He transferred one of the ski poles into his other hand, took the phone from Tillman, and turned it until he finally made out the image before his eyes.

"Bring me the head of John the Baptist, huh?" He breathed, unsure of what he was looking at.

"Excuse me?" Tillman asked brightly, clearly enamored of the photo.

"It's a head on a plate, right? You know: 'Bring me the head of John the Baptist on a platter' . . . you didn't pay much attention in Sunday School, I'm guessing."

"Hey, I *teach* Sunday School." Tillman took the phone back and regarded the photo for a moment. "Now *that's* good. I didn't see it that way—good on ya, Jack! You have an artist's eye."

"Thanks, but can you tell me what it really is?"

"Sure. I apologize for the lousy picture. Melanie's emailing it to you even as we speak, so it should be easier to see on your laptop." Tillman stamped his feet absently, like a horse swishing its tail in fly season. "You don't recognize it?"

"Should I?"

"I figured you would . . . it's our first clue, isn't it?" He extended the phone again, and Jack took it back. "It's a fake head, sitting on a plastic disk that looks like an ice-fishing hole. It was out on Tannhauser Lake, right where Matt Gearey likes to fish. Matt always sticks an overturned bucket in his hole to mark his spot, and you can imagine his surprise when he lifted it up and saw that."

The tiny photo seemed to expand right before Jack's eyes, as if rising up to engulf him. He'd identified the facsimile head and the beard, but he'd mistaken the fake hole for some kind of platter. All at once he found himself alone on a frozen pond, pulling an overturned bucket out of the place where it had spent the dark night, only to be confronted by what seemed to be a dead man floating underneath.

"My God."

"Really? That's not yours?"

"I'm sorry, Marv . . . Mr. Mayor . . . it, it might be." His mind seemed to stutter right along with his tongue. Death Troupe clues could be a bit grisly, but they weren't meant to actually scare people. He searched his memory and realized that he'd mentioned ice fishing to Barron at their meeting two days earlier. "Sometimes the team runs with a new idea that they don't share with me. I've had to look these things up on the website a few times myself in the past, to see which ones were genuine."

"Oh, yeah . . . your Rumor Control page. We didn't check that, but I suppose we should have."

"It probably won't be up there for awhile. Sometimes it takes a day or two for the team to admit that a clue is real."

"If that's the case, it may be up there already."

"What? How old is this photo?"

"Uh . . . that's where things get a little foggy. Matt took that picture, and a couple more, right when he found the thing. He thought it was cute. But then he remembered that he owed Noah Sanderson a prank, something Noah did to him at the Fourth of July picnic . . . anyway, he planted the thing out where Noah does his fishing and . . . so now it's making the rounds."

"Making the rounds?" This was an entirely new reaction to what might be a piece of Death Troupe evidence, and Jack thought he'd seen them all. He'd been shaken out of bed in other locales, and even dragged half-running down the street by people who were convinced they'd found a clue, but he'd never seen one re-used as a practical joke.

"Yeah, the fishing crowd has a sense of humor all their own." Tillman shook his head behind the scarf and glasses. "Hey, I'm gonna go check the website. You better get inside. You're gonna catch your death, standing around out here after a workout."

Jack handed the phone back. "Yeah, good idea."

He almost promised to find out if the fake head was bona fide or not, but stopped himself at the last second. It was important not to upset the Director's plans, and sometimes Barron left a legitimate clue in limbo for long periods. Taking the pigstickers back in his hands, he turned and began slowly pumping his legs back up the empty road. A second reason for not making that promise occurred to him then, one that he didn't like.

If it isn't ours, whose is it? And what kind of sick message was it meant to convey?

"That is simply brilliant. Why didn't *you* think of it?" Barron's rough voice came over the phone even as Jack studied the picture on his laptop. He'd sent the photo to Berni as soon as he'd had a chance to slip out of his wet clothes and into a bathrobe, and his phone had rung shortly after that.

"So it's not ours?"

"More's the pity. It fits the locale to a T. Everybody there can relate to the ice fishing angle, and the image is priceless. We need to think of a way to work this into the play."

"You're not serious."

"Of course I am. I've always wanted to have a creative interaction with the locals, just to see what they'd come up with. Well this is one potent image, and I'm not above stealing it." This was yet another aspect of Death Troupe over which he and the Director disagreed. Barron had always been enchanted by the amateurs and pranksters who'd tried to horn in on the act.

"So you're not going to disavow this on Rumor Control."

"Oh, sure I will. But not for a while. You're not exactly burning up the track with clue ideas, so there's nothing wrong with letting the punters carry the load for us until you get in gear." Someone, probably Berni, spoke in the background and Barron muted the phone for a few seconds. When he came back he was clearly trying to sign off. "So when am I going to see some fleshed-out concepts from you? Time's going by."

Jack restrained himself, dying to point out that time wouldn't be going by half as fast if he didn't have to work on two different themes. "Workin' on it."

"Well work a little faster, all right? How many times I gotta tell you that nobody writes a great first draft? Just get some basic plots down, and we'll go from there."

"That how it worked with Ryan?" Jack had wanted to ask this ever since their last meeting, when he'd learned the truth from Berni. He wasn't disappointed in the answer.

"Of course not. That was one writer that never needed a kick in the ass."

The line went dead, and Jack dropped the cell phone into the plastic bucket which had held the now-departed black roses. He'd cleaned the container after dumping the wilted flowers, keeping the skulls and the chaff and now using the bucket as a cradle for his keys, wallet, and phone. Instead of making him mad, Barron's parting words had given him an idea. Reaching into the laptop's carry bag, he removed Ryan's notebook and opened it to the very first pages.

Ryan had always maintained that writing a good play started with the envisioning of the big moments, from dramatic confrontations to passionate revelations. Jack hadn't agreed with that, preferring to build an interconnected framework of relationships based on the locale and then seeing how those could lead to murder. He now confirmed that the first half of Ryan's notebook consisted of phrases and sketches representing the initial glimmering of the high points around which he'd planned to construct his play. Perhaps it was time to take advantage of them.

The heating vent near the sitting room's ceiling began to hum as warm air gently drifted down on him. Snow had begun to fall outside, and the streetlights were already coming on. He'd intended to take a shower before getting back to work, but the robe was cozy and his muscles were giving off an ache that was not unpleasant.

Taking the notebook and a large sketch pad, he walked into the bedroom and flopped on the bed, stomach down. The binding of the Red Bend journal was well broken in, and he let it decide which set of doodles it would display. Flipping open the cover of the large pad, he began writing in a large, rapid hand. Any and every thought relating to the Great Depression flowed out onto the page, mere phrases such as 'bread lines' appearing alongside sketches of stockbrokers leaping from Wall Street windows.

"Well whaddya know?" he exhaled quietly, unwilling to stop his hand as it filled yet another page with emotive words and pictures. "That rich prick might have been on to something after all."

"Hi stranger." Kelly Sykes whispered to Jack as she carefully eased herself into the seat next to him. The lights were up in the Schuyler Mills Playhouse, and Jack was silently watching the first rehearsal of the *Macbeth* scenes requested by Barron. He'd spent the late afternoon drawing up a tentative outline for the Depression play, and had been so exhausted by the effort that he'd gladly accepted Patrice Lawton's invitation to attend the practice.

He smiled at Kelly in return, though torn by her arrival. Long exposure to stage professionals had made him view an outsider's attendance at even the earliest rehearsals as a privilege, and he was alarmed by the idea that Kelly might want to hold a conversation. Though they were several rows back from the stage, Jack considered it the height of rudeness to demonstrate inattention when actors were working hard right in front of him. Besides, he knew it royally ticked most of them off.

At the same time, though, he was pleased to see her. She hadn't been around much since his abortive drink invitation, and Jack had feared he might have somehow crossed a line. Her happy demeanor and casual dress of jeans and black sweater suggested otherwise, and his doubts were replaced with the vain idea that she might have tracked him there. He couldn't help noticing that she'd taken the seat right next to his instead of leaving a space, and thought he detected a slight scent of perfume.

Up on stage, Dennis and Patrice Lawton were working with Al and Sarah Griffin as they felt their way through the first stand-up read-through of the scene where Lady Macbeth convinces her husband to murder King Duncan. Earlier, Dennis had asked Jack if it might not be wiser to prepare all of the scenes from the beginning of the play, to provide context for the assigned portion and use more of the available actors. Ruefully thinking of his last meeting with Barron, Jack had reminded the four Schuyler Mills thespians that the Director was very likely to add other requirements as time went by. They'd seemed satisfied with that, and had gotten down to the work of reading the words aloud on the stage where they would be performed.

Jack liked the way the Lawtons operated. They made good use of the experience which Al and Sarah clearly brought with them, and stood on stage with their two actors instead of sitting out in the audience. This wasn't unusual, given the small number of players and the basic nature of the night's work, but it showed they were without pretension. They also had a light way of directing, and performed the minor roles in the scene without referring to notes. Although the four of them were dressed in street clothes, when Jack closed his eyes he had no trouble envisioning them in period costume.

Settled in his chair, warm in a fleece pullover with two roomy pockets, he recognized that this was his first live rehearsal in over two years.

Kelly listened to the back and forth for several minutes before sliding down in her chair and propping her jean-clad knees against the seat in front of her. She steepled her fingers in front of her mouth as if in prayer, and when she spoke it was almost inaudible. "I love watching them rehearse. I've read this play over and over and still get something new every time I look at it. And even then, when they start dissecting the lines, it's as if I never read it at all."

Jack was pleased by her display of etiquette, and slowly raised the papers he was holding so that they blocked the players' view of his mouth. He replied without looking at her, in a tiny whisper. "They've been debating one of the biggest questions about this play. Macbeth gets the idea that he'll be king from the three witches, and thinks of killing Duncan all by himself, but somehow Lady MacB gets the blame for pushing him into it."

"But she does push him into it."

"I know that. But Dennis makes a good point—does Macbeth communicate the idea to his wife, or does she think it up on her own the same way he did?"

"You got me there. I'd have to reread it."

He handed the script pages across, and they fell silent again while the work continued on stage. It was fun to see a real-life husband and wife playing a pair of murderous spouses, made even more so by Lady Macbeth's manipulation of her husband's self-image. Jack knew a few actors who embraced their roles so completely that they sought out emotions from their personal experiences to evoke the feelings they would display on stage. He doubted Al and Sarah had ever conspired to murder anyone, but even so their first rehearsal came across as genuine.

"See what I mean?" Patrice Lawton asked no one in particular up on the stage. "Lady M gets blamed for the whole murder just because she has to buck up her husband at the moment of truth, but the play shows that Macbeth thought of killing Duncan when he was still miles from home."

"It's not the first time a woman took the fall for her husband." Sarah Griffin answered sweetly, smiling across at Al-Macbeth.

Dennis Lawton tried to keep the discussion on track. "I still say it's a moot question, because of the degree to which she blames herself later on. That's the whole point of the 'bloody hands' dementia. She feels overwhelming guilt and loses her mind."

Al Griffin was still a beat behind, clearly responding to his wife's comment. "'This woman you put here with me'—she did it."

"That's Genesis, not *Macbeth*." Sarah.

"Hi Madam, I'm Adam." Al.

Out in the seats, Jack stifled a laugh at the Griffins' repartee. He enjoyed the freewheeling nature of early rehearsal, but Kelly misread his mirth.

"Al and Sarah are quite a pair, aren't they?" She whispered from behind the script. Casting him a sly grin, she continued. "They've got a resounding sex life, by the way."

Caught off guard, Jack was forced to disguise a startled cough as a normal one. The onstage discussion continued as if he hadn't been heard, and he had to remind himself that there are no secrets in small towns.

"It's interesting you mention the story of the Garden of Eden." Dennis went on patiently. "Both tales are quite similar, with a supernatural motivator for the evil deed. The serpent prompts Eve to convince Adam to eat the fruit, and in the Scottish play the witches prompt Macbeth to consider killing the king."

Patrice Lawton seemed intrigued by this line of thinking. "Are you saying, 'The devil made me do it'?"

Seeing that she'd hit Jack's funny bone, Kelly pressed on. Hidden by the pages that no longer camouflaged Jack's reactions, she let her face go from an elfin smirk to a full-on leer. "And I do mean resounding. Their neighbors have actually complained about them."

Knowing he was in full view of the stage, Jack bowed his head and brought a hand up to rub the bridge of his nose while trying not to laugh. "Cut it out. I'm begging you."

Taking pity on him, Kelly split the script pages and handed two of them over. Jack quickly raised the papers in front of his face, turning an expression of amused disapproval toward her. All he got in return was the briefest display of the very tip of her tongue before she settled back in to look at the stage.

Jack shut the door to his pickup quietly, having grown aware that noise travels much further in cold air than hot. He took a moment to stand next to the truck in the hotel parking lot, looking up at a sky that was now free of clouds. The frigid air felt good in his throat as he inhaled, and it seemed that he could make out every star in the firmament.

He'd enjoyed listening to the rehearsal, feeling energized by the enthusiasm on stage. He'd watched Barron and the Death Troupe actors doing similar work many times, breaking a scene down until they were minutely examining single words and, more often, the spaces between them. Dissecting the words was a good way of reaching their intended meaning, and also a start point for coordinating the actions of the speaker and the other players on stage. This could be quite a balancing act, moving people around without distracting the audience from the spoken words, and it never failed to spark his imagination.

The Griffins had suggested the entire group go to a coffee shop in Newville, and Jack had been secretly pleased when Kelly had first looked at him before answering in the affirmative. It had been a rollicking good time, and although nothing overt was said, Jack could not escape the feeling that the two older couples were trying to play matchmaker.

The cold slowly began penetrating his new boots, and Jack crunched across the parking lot toward the back door with a sense of accomplishment. He'd covered a lot of ground that day, from his first excursion on skis to the rough outline of the Depression-era play to his acceptance by the town's community theater group. He unconsciously avoided acknowledging his growing interest in Kelly Sykes, but not the many small indications that she reciprocated the feeling.

He was careful to be quiet in the rear hallway, unsure if the hotel had rented out any of the back rooms in his absence. No sound came from the television when he emerged into the dark lobby, and as usual no one stood vigil behind the front desk. He was halfway to the stairs when he sensed a presence in the room, and turned to look back at the stuffed chairs arrayed near the fireplace. A lone figure sat in one of them, wearing a trench coat, a necktie, and heavy boots.

Wade Parker spoke from the shadows, and Jack's good mood evaporated with the words.

"Hi Jack. We need to talk."

Wade put a hand on Jack's arm just as he unlocked the door to his room, and when the writer looked back the investigator had a finger to his lips. Wade slid past him, holding a device that Jack had recently seen in the hands of Berni Fitzgibbons. It was a small box with a needle that jumped under the right circumstances, and it was used to detect listening devices.

Wade nodded at Jack's empty desk in passing, as if relieved not to see the laptop sitting there when it was supposed to be in the safe. He slowly moved around the sitting room, sweeping the box back and forth like a divining rod, before passing through the connecting door into the bedroom. Jack hung his overcoat on the back of the door after closing it, and sat at the desk to wait.

When Wade returned, he'd lost both the box and his trench coat. He was still in his normal attire of a jacket, tie, and dress trousers, and Jack observed his black winter boots were not new. Wade settled into the reading chair to face him, wearing a blank expression.

"You want a beer or something?" Jack offered, trying to break the tension.

Wade reacted as if he hadn't spoken. He leaned forward with his hands clasped, resting his forearms on his knees. "Jack, we've been friends a long time and I want you to know you can tell me anything —as long as it's the truth."

Though knowing what was on the way, Jack tried to keep his voice calm. "All right. What's going on?"

"Jack, have you ever been to Red Bend, California?"

As ready as he was to hear the words, Jack still felt the unmanning jolt of guilt. The shame at being discovered rose up in his throat, so he just answered.

"Yes."

"When did you last go there?"

"In November, because I wanted to see the show." *And because I was lonely and I really missed my ex-girlfriend and Red Bend was just too damned close to Arizona.* "I've only been there that one time."

"That's what your credit cards say. Long drive from Arizona?"

"You can do it in a day. But I broke it up, stayed overnight in Monterey."

"I know."

"Let's cut to the chase here, Wade. What did you find out in Red Bend?"

"One thing I learned was that the original writer for the Barron Players drove into town without making any effort to see his old friends and then left the very night of the performance."

"Let's not forget those old friends included my ex-girlfriend and her new boyfriend."

"Who used to be one of your buddies." The unspoken words hung in the air anyway. *The guy who stole your girl. The guy who killed himself after an ugly stay in Red Bend. The guy whose job you now hold.*

Jack's eyes widened, as embarrassment was quickly replaced by fear.

"Now just one second. You *know* I wouldn't do anything to harm Ryan, Allison, or the troupe! *You know that.*"

Wade lifted his arms from his legs, and leaned back into the reading chair like a man who'd just come home from a long day. He raised a restraining hand. "Of course I do. Even a guy who kills people in fantasy murder plays doesn't use his own credit card. But I needed to hear you say it."

He gave Jack a brief smile, kicking his anger up a notch. What kind of game was this? The fear turned to annoyance, and that was turning to anger when it was stopped cold by a question he'd already asked.

"What *did* you find out in Red Bend?"

"I now know why the people running the retirement home didn't want to pursue this thing." Wade rested comfortably in the chair, his tie loosened and a Canadian beer in his hand. "Turns out there was a door leading up onto the roof that was left unlocked because a number of the residents liked to go up there to have a smoke."

"I thought the guy jumped off the fire escape."

"So did I. The night attendant heard a noise on the escape and thought it was the sound of the old man going off, but the local cops are sure he went off the roof. Officially the staff doesn't know anything about that unlocked door, but I bought a few drinks for one of them one night and he told me they routinely left it open. They got tired of walking up there to unlock it every time one of the rich retirees wanted to go smoke a coffin nail."

"But you said the dead man was senile."

"Very much so. Apparently he'd follow the others from time to time, and he'd even been found up there alone once. The whole thing starts shaping up into an unhappy accident until you remember the newspaper in the guy's room."

"The one with the article about the play's connection to his family."

"Yeah. The poor guy was so out of it that they doubt he could have read the thing, or even understood if someone read it for him. So I'd dearly love to know how that newspaper got in his room."

"Think somebody planted it?"

"I think that's possible. It's such a direct connection between the play and the old man's family . . . and if somebody pushed him, they'd want to give the authorities a reason to say it was suicide."

"Did anybody benefit from his passing? An inheritance, maybe?"

"That's where it gets goofy. His money had already been divvied up among his heirs, and they were footing the bill for his care. It's a top-notch facility—if you ignore the octogenarians sneaking smokes on the roof—but it wasn't a financial strain for his people to keep him there."

"How about a different reason? Some other way to benefit?"

"Now why didn't I think of that? You oughtta write mysteries for a living, Jack. You're really good at this." Wade shook his head. "There's a lot of potential suspects here if the goal is to get the troupe in trouble: Somebody in the town who thought the performance was a waste of money, maybe somebody from Barron's past who's fed up with his continuing success, or maybe somebody who didn't like Ryan Betancourt."

Stung by Wade's rebuke, Jack didn't respond. He picked up his own beer from the desk behind him and took a long pull while waiting for the advance man to continue.

"That list is too long for a lone investigator to tackle, but I found out something that made it shrink quite a bit." He paused, as if considering his words. "I'm sorry to tell you this, but Pauline Scott is a missing person. She disappeared shortly before the show in Red Bend and hasn't been seen since. There's been no activity on her bank account, her credit cards, or her phones. Her parents are worried sick."

A memory: A young woman, dark hair and dark eyes, dressed like an Ivy League co-ed in a pleated skirt, tweed jacket, and matching scarf. Walking up to his table outside a sandwich shop where he'd been eating lunch. *Hi, my name's Pauline, Pauline Scott, and I've been dying to meet you! This is my second Death Troupe show and I just love what you do!"*

"My God. First Ryan, and now this. What's going on, Wade?"

"Hey." Wade's voice took on the slightest hint of sternness. "Right now she's just missing. I'll grant that it doesn't look good after all this time, but until they find a body there's always hope. And even if they do find something, there might not be any connection between what's happened to her and what happened to Ryan."

Another memory: Pauline's first time meeting Ryan. Yet another lunch table in yet another small town. A pleasant meal with plenty of laughs, until Ryan excused himself for a few minutes. *I don't like him, Jack. You be careful around him.* She'd been right not to like Ryan, but was it because she saw him for what he was, or because he was Jack's new friend?

"That's possible, I guess. I mean, you said she hadn't shown up at any of the engagements since I left."

"Right. I spent some time with her myself, and I never thought she was much of a danger."

"Really? You never mentioned that to me."

"No reason to. You had enough on your mind writing the plays. It's just that she started appearing at every engagement and I wanted to know what we were dealing with."

"And what was that?" Jack kicked himself mentally, seeing for the first time that he didn't know half as much about Pauline as she had known about him and the Barron Players. Even the troupe's security man had paid more attention to the girl than the man who'd obviously entranced her.

"She just really liked you, is all. That's what I thought then, and it's still my opinion." Wade let out a long exhale. "I interviewed her parents, and it turns out we were a little off the mark when we thought she was some kind of groupie. Eleven months out of the year she had a nice, responsible job as a financial consultant. High-paying, too. When we saw her she was on vacation—apparently she scheduled it around the performances. She wasn't so much a groupie as a buff. Her parents knew all about the troupe, but here's something funny: They'd only heard your name in passing. Seems she kept that to herself."

Jack frowned, recalling the four engagements Pauline had attended. Although she'd visited once or twice when he'd been alone in the host town, she hadn't exactly hung around on those occasions. She was most in evidence during the two or three weeks prior to the show itself—which fit the story that she'd been on vacation. He'd once asked her what she did for a living, and when she'd replied that she worked in a bank he'd assumed it was a low-paying job with little responsibility.

What an ass I am.

"So they have no idea what might have happened to her?"

"None. She had a pretty steady routine, put a lot of herself into her work. No boyfriend at the time she vanished, and doesn't seem to have done high-risk stuff like picking up strange guys at bars."

Jack forced the third memory away, the picture of Pauline in a black leotard so sheer that it was practically see-through. She hadn't picked him up in a bar on their one night together, but she hadn't behaved like a novice either. *Those great tricks of hers were probably something else she didn't mention to her parents—along with where she learned them.* Suddenly uncomfortable, Jack decided to change the subject.

"So have you come to a conclusion about Ryan?"

"What, whether he's dead or not?" Wade deadpanned that one, but it made him sound as if he was reconsidering his doubts about Ryan Betancourt's mortality. "He hasn't shown up alive anywhere, but I'll still be damned if I can prove he's actually gone. I only learned one thing more about him, but it's pretty odd: His name was in the visitor's book at the retirement home, a few weeks before the troupe got to Red Bend. I showed his photo to an attendant and he swore it was him."

"But didn't he believe that whole family had died out?"

"That's what he said." Wade briefly raised both hands, palm-up. "Look, people keep things from me all the time, and often for very little reason. The attendant I talked to recognized his picture right away."

"I've been reading Ryan's journal from Red Bend . . . didn't he say that the stranger who grabbed him at the Halloween party looked just like him?"

"Yeah, well . . . you had to have seen Ryan when the cast finally came to town. He was a wreck. He got really drunk that night, and I gotta confess I didn't believe much of that story about a doppelganger. No offense, Jack, but you creative types are subject to flights of fancy. You let your imaginations run away with you."

"That's our job."

"And you're all very good at it. The thing is, none of the witnesses who saw the tall man screaming in the street weeks earlier said that he resembled Ryan. And no one at the party remembered seeing this strange masked man at all."

They both lapsed into silence at this point, as if the amount of information was too vast to assimilate. A wind had sprung up outside while they were talking, and a gust threw ice crystals against the sitting room window. Wade looked up at the sound, and then sat regarding the darkness for a long moment.

"Tomorrow's the last day of January." He stated flatly. "Some month, huh?"

Chapter Ten

On the morning of Groundhog Day, Jack Glynn emerged from his wintry den and saw his shadow. He didn't spot it right away, as a light fog obscured much of the view from the front porch of his new dwelling. He'd moved into the Great View Motel the previous night, and had found the ramshackle arrangement of single-story cabins to his liking. They didn't look like much, but his unit was well insulated and so far everything worked. He now had a front porch that looked out over the town except where the view was obstructed by the two-story building that served as motel office and home to the Great View's owners, Wally and Delilah Emerson.

Rates at the Great View were low, so Jack found that several of the other cabins were occupied by skiers whose cars and trucks were parked haphazardly around the motel's gravel parking lot. In the dead center of the lot, on a circle of snow that probably had grass underneath, sat a structure that looked like an enormous wooden keg laid on its side. A large heating unit was connected to the keg, and a man-sized door was set into the circular wall facing away from Jack's unit. Wally had proudly told him that the keg was the motel's sauna.

"Don't let 'er looks fool ya." The fat, balding fifty-something had told him in the office, making Jack wonder for a moment if he was referring to his portly wife Delilah, who was walking past the sauna at the time. "There's plenty of room, it's hotter'n Hell once the generator's been goin' long enough, and there is *nothing* better than runnin' outta the sauna on a cold winter's night and dropping face-down in the snow."

He'd leaned across the motel's scratched-up front desk at that point, even though Jack was the only other human present. "Don't be surprised if you see me and the missus do that of an evening. We're not much to look at in our birthday suits, but we do provide fair warning before we come out. If you hear a couple of mad fools hollering outside your place one night, it's probably best to stay away from the windows for the next minute or two."

The desk in his cabin looked out the aforementioned windows, and while the unit wasn't as spacious as his rooms at the hotel there was still plenty of room for one man working alone. He had a functioning Internet connection, the shower water was blazing hot, a hand-stitched comforter had kept him warm the previous night, and a back door opened out onto a long, steep hill that was covered with snow and dormant trees.

On Groundhog Day he'd brewed himself some coffee on waking, and then decided to brave the elements for a moment. Wearing a full set of long underwear recently purchased at Bib's, his fleece pullover, and a pair of heavy socks, he took his steaming mug of coffee out onto the porch and was pleasantly surprised to find that it wasn't all that cold. The cabin's sloping roof extended over the front deck, and he walked out to the two-by-four that served as a railing. His cross-country skis stood up proudly against the railing off to the side, and he felt they helped him fit in with the other guests. The air was heavy with moisture, and the mist gave the site a ghostly appearance. He could barely make out the silhouette of the units on the far side of the parking area, and if he let his mind loosen up he found it easy to imagine the mist as steam instead of condensation.

Sipping from the mug, he turned and looked south toward the town. He could identify the roof of the movie theater, and the front of the library just beyond that, but something further out caught his eye. The Great View backed against the top of one of the larger hills north of town, so he could see over the Visitor's Center and to the other side of Long Lake. The mist around him was shifting just a bit, and the trees on the ridgeline south of the lake slowly came into focus. It was then that Jack Glynn got to see his shadow.

The distant ridge sloped gently down to the lake, and every other day it had been an unspoiled blanket of white. Now something sat in the dead center of the expanse, something large and angular which Jack didn't recognize even though it had been his idea.

The rising sun burned off a little more of the ground fog while he waited, and Jack was finally able to see that the slope beyond Long Lake was now the site of a very large, blood-red number seven. It was hard to know what the numeral was made of from that distance, but he saw nothing that resembled a hull or a mast and had to think that Barron's agents had rejected his suggestion to use the nearby boats, parked for the winter, to construct the clue.

He held a thumb up as if to gauge the size of the symbol, but lowered it when he realized just how silly that was. A thrill passed through him all the same, as it did every time Barron's minions struck without his knowledge. It was as if an army of phantoms was operating all around him, with calling cards like the large seven giving the only indication of their presence.

The front door of the Great View's office opened with a bang, startling him, and then Delilah Emerson emerged in a heavy bathrobe and boots. A large fur-lined hat with flaps that hung down over her ears completed the ensemble, and she was holding a set of binoculars.

Seeing him, she gave a friendly wave and called out. "Well hello, Jack! Looks like you were busy last night!" She didn't wait for a response, training the field glasses on the newest monument in Schuyler Mills.

"Actually I'm not usually in on things like this," he called back, not quite as loud. "But this one was my idea."

"Looks good! A big upside down letter L!" The binoculars came down just long enough for Delilah to throw him a mischievous glance, and then she went back to viewing.

"Can you tell me what it's made of?"

"Yeah—two long sheets of some kinda fabric. Nylon, probably. Looks like somebody staked 'em in place so they wouldn't blow away." The field glasses came down again, and she turned to look in his direction. "It's a good effect. Can you tell me what it means?"

"We never know what any of this stuff means until the night of the show." Delilah's doubtful expression told him that wouldn't be enough, so he tried again. "The first clue always has the same meaning: Game on."

"This is just fantastic." Mayor Tillman was on the phone for the third time that day, and with each call he had grown more excited. "The whole town's talking about the clue. Half of them are trying to figure out what it means, and the other half just love the way it appeared so suddenly. *Very* mysterious."

"We do aim to please." Jack replied airily, looking at some of the pictures posted on the Rumor Control page of the troupe website. Berni was obviously being bombarded with photos, but she had an eye for this sort of thing and had chosen some good ones. She'd also taken the opportunity to lightly disavow the almost-forgotten severed head while sweetly complimenting its unidentified author. The explanations on the Rumor Control page were always written very tongue-in-cheek, almost like a gossip column, and it was sometimes hard to tell if a clue had been completely disowned. "And we try to get everybody involved right away."

"Well you certainly did that. Miriam from the library's getting tons of requests about the significance of the number seven in the town's history."

"Tell 'em to pace themselves. There'll be plenty more of these by the time this is over." Jack was feeling a pleasant glow from the reception his idea was getting. He'd spent the day in his cabin, fleshing out the pair of storylines that, though not brilliant, were good enough for his next meeting with Barron. He didn't like to adopt that kind of passive attitude in his work, but it was hard not to when dealing with the Director—particularly when he changed the good ideas as much as he changed the bad.

"I'll pass it on, but I doubt it'll make any difference." Tillman cleared his throat. "I'm gonna sign off here, Jack, but please tell Mr. Barron that we do appreciate the effort. You're really livening up the winter."

Jack turned off the cell phone and put it back in the bucket. He'd received other complimentary phone calls from people like Bib, the Lawtons, the Griffins, the Maddens, Lynnie and both her buddies, and also Kelly Sykes. Kelly had wrangled a dinner invitation out of him, but it was still too early to start getting ready for that. The sun was dipping near the trees, turning the sky behind the cabin a dull orange, but that only meant it was late afternoon. Glancing at the clock, he saw that it was even earlier than that and guessed that the clouds bearing some promised snow flurries had already moved in.

Rising, he walked to the back door and pushed it open. A hard kiss of cold air brushed both his cheeks, but he stood there anyway, looking up the tree-covered slope to a stretch of level ground that he now knew was the beginning of a cross-country ski path. He'd picked up a trail map from the Visitor's Center before moving to the Great View, and had already selected a nice, easy two-mile loop that would take him up into the hills a short way before turning in a circle that would deposit him at his back door.

It had been a good day, and the delivery of the first clue had recharged the battery so recently depleted by Barron. Looking at the sky, he decided he had plenty of time to gear up, ski the two-mile loop, and then get ready for dinner with Kelly. Pulling the door shut, he reached for the sweat top and ski pants that had become his cross-country rig.

"Plenty of time. Plenty of time." He muttered to himself as he began to change.

The climb out of the motel's shadow was a bit more challenging than he'd expected. So far he'd practiced on generally flat terrain, and just getting out of the hollow which was the Great View's home required him to walk sideways up a deceptively long dirt road. Apparently the sun didn't reach the back side of the complex much, as the road itself was practically sheet ice. Just for fun, Jack had tried to push himself straight up the incline using the poles. He'd gone about five yards when gravity and the nearly frictionless surface had combined to send him sliding backward to the bottom.

He covered only a few inches with each sidestep, but the edges of the skis kept him from sliding and after a time he reached the top. The cross-country trail was marked as such by a red wooden disc, affixed to a nearby tree, that bore the white silhouette of a skier. A red wooden arrow just above the sign pointed skyward, as if to suggest the route went straight up in the air. The path was level at this point, and he could see the tracks of other skiers fossilized in the ice. The hill sloped upward on the other side of the trail, and he briefly admired a tall, dead tree which stood among the white-coated evergreens. Its derelict trunk was cracked and denuded of bark, but it still held a single branch suspended high over the path. He imagined it as a cartoon, a laughing toll taker raising the branch to allow him to pass.

The motel quickly disappeared on his right as he picked up the rhythm, and he took in the scenery as he moved. The trees on either side of him stood straight up no matter how sharp the incline, and he wondered if the ground beneath the behemoths ever gave way to the strain. He knew that the trees were supported by massive, interconnected root systems, but he let himself imagine one of the mighty trunks crashing across the road in front of him, just missing him by inches.

The ski trail entered the forest a few hundred yards out, and he left all signs of civilization behind. The ground took on a gentle decline, so he tucked the poles under his arms like a downhill racer and laughed as the skis slid along beneath him. His momentum ran out quickly once he hit a level patch, and he took up the sliding cadence yet again.

The trail turned and took him through a notch between two small hills, and he hadn't gone far when he saw that the snow-burdened trees were almost completely blotting out the fading sun. Knowing that the heat generated by his exertions was the only thing keeping him warm, he congratulated himself on choosing a short route that would have him back at the motel in less than an hour. His ski pants were of a breathable fabric with a light cloth lining, and he wore a down vest over his sweat top. A wool hat and ski gloves completed the ensemble, but he'd already learned that these would become wet with perspiration after a short time. That wasn't bad as long as he kept moving, but he'd been warned that this was not the attire for standing around outdoors in an Adirondack winter.

The evergreens gave way to larger trees surrounded by a wide variety of skeletal bushes that scratched against his ski pants with surprising resiliency. The bushes sported just a few leaves apiece, most of them a sickly yellow, and he wondered why they hadn't joined their fellows under the snow during the fall. Here and there he spotted taller bushes that seemed composed of nothing but vines and a scattering of blue berries. Beginning to labor now, he imagined the berry bushes as some kind of vegetative spider's web, with the frozen fruit representing the cocooned insects unfortunate enough to have become ensnared.

His breath puffed out in front of him in small clouds, and Jack chided himself for thinking the real experience of trail skiing would be as easy as coasting along the flat, sun-covered roads of Schuyler Mills. *This was what you wanted to see*, he had to remind himself, and he forced his eyes off of the hypnotically reciprocating skis and onto the white landscape that surrounded him.

And it was beautiful. Snow partially wrapped the trunks of the trees, camouflaging them against the wintry backdrop. Even the stringy bushes held clumps of the white stuff aloft, and he now spotted some of the deadfall he'd imagined at the beginning of the trip, their jagged splinters standing out from the blankness like the spars of ships crashing through the waves. The ground about him opened up further on, and he could easily imagine some settler having built a tidy cabin in this comfortable dell. As if to confirm his fantasizing, a low wall made of ancient rocks materialized out of the snow as he slid on by.

The sun was disappearing behind him, and he might have been concerned by this if it hadn't been accompanied by a gently falling snow which drifted down like pollen. He decided this was the flurry activity forecast earlier in the day, and that it was painting an erroneous picture of a setting sun. Besides, he was certain that the map—left behind because it was paper and he didn't want to ruin it—had indicated that he would soon encounter a fork in the trail that would start him on his way back.

Right after that he spotted the red disc in the distance, nailed to a tree and partly hidden by snow which had frozen across the brave skier emblazoned upon it. Hustling forward, unaware that his fatigue had already reduced his energy-saving strides to a shuffle, he saw with satisfaction that this was indeed a fork in the trail.

Pleased as he was to find the marker, Jack might simply have obeyed the arrow nailed to the tree above it, directing him to the fork on the right. The lowering sun was turning the snow from white to a bluish gray, but he could still make out a fresh set of ski tracks leading down the right-hand trail. That seemed wrong, however, as he was almost certain that the map back in his cozy cabin had split off to the left at this point. He now regretted the decision to leave it behind.

The new snow was beginning to collect on his shoulders, and the dampness of his clothes began to chill him as his body heat dissipated. He raised first one ski and then the other, shaking off the snow and trying to decide if he should obey his memory or the wooden arrow. Jack recognized how stupid that sounded even as he thought it, but then he questioned whether he'd yet reached the map's promised fork.

What if he was still shy of that mark, and took the wrong branch in ignorance? His estimate of how far he'd traveled was based on his experience on level ground, and he'd already learned that skiing in the real woods was much harder. That being the case, it was possible that he still had a distance to go before the left turn he wanted. The map was small and covered many miles of trails, so didn't it make sense that some branches weren't significant enough to appear on it?

"Well . . . the signs are here for a reason." He said out loud, sticking the poles into the snow to get himself moving down the right-hand trail. It felt good to be in motion again, and he quickly worked off the cold that had been seeping into his clothes. In no time at all the blue-gray blankness, aided by the thickening snowfall, had enfolded him

The trail he now followed lay between two long hills, granting him an extended stretch of flat travel. The path zigzagged every hundred yards or so, and Jack imagined that a stream probably ran along this channel at other times during the year. The snowfall became a bit more determined, starting to fly in at an angle and hitting him directly in the face. He observed with pride that the flakes were not accumulating on his arms, where the heat of his effort melted them before they could coalesce. This was not true of the ground in front of him, however, and he began to see that the tracks of the previous skier were beginning to disappear beneath the new carpet of gray.

And gray it now was, here in the low ground between two ridges cloaked by snow-burdened trees. The sun was probably close to setting by then, but he wouldn't have known it because his vision was so obscured. He momentarily considered turning back, but that awakened a strange memory from his early childhood that quickly displaced the sensible notion of retracing his steps.

He'd been young enough to still be riding a tricycle, and his mother had sternly warned him against leaving the driveway in their suburban yard. The family car had been parked there, and so it had left a disappointingly small area for him to use. He'd given himself a bigger circuit by going around the car a couple of times, cutting around the high fender where it almost touched the garage, but that had quickly lost its appeal and his eyes had wandered to the sidewalk.

It was a safe, quiet neighborhood where almost nothing ever happened, but the prospect of crossing onto the no man's land of the public walkways was still daunting. He knew that the cracked and bumpy sidewalk went all the way around the small block of houses, and he was reasonably sure that he couldn't get lost if he simply followed it. He imagined the thrill of pedaling that entire distance, ducking his head as he passed exotic mailboxes and braving the threat of the neighbors' dogs.

Even so, he almost didn't try it. He'd received strict instructions, and he knew that his mother frequently checked on him from the front windows. He rolled the three-wheeled bike to the border, where the driveway meshed with the older concrete, and stood up in his sneakers to look down this beckoning superhighway. He supposed, later on, that if one scary-looking dog had been nosing around out there he probably would not have gone, but the tricycle rolled forward a few inches on its own, and by the time his feet had found the pedals to stop it he was already on his way.

It had been a magical trip, and Jack considered the exaggerated tale of this journey, springing full-blown from his mind even as he pedaled, to be his first work of fiction. He'd manfully ducked all of the mailboxes although in no danger of touching them, and believed he'd reached an incredible speed when Mrs. Dobson's aged poodle had raised its somnolent head to look at him. He'd felt like Columbus standing in the surf of the new world when he'd reached the far corner, and for many years after that had considered the street sign there to be his pennant of ownership of the land he'd claimed as his discovery.

That spot also marked the furthest extent of his nerve that day, however, as the planned circumnavigation of the block had encountered a snag when he'd realized that turning the corner meant he would actually lose sight of his own yard. With the easy flexibility of youth, he'd told himself that he'd only meant to go this far anyway and that he'd better get back before his mother became concerned. Turning the tricycle around, he'd raced past the now-sleeping Dobson poodle, and even managed to reach up and swat the last of the mailboxes with an open palm before returning to the safe port of his own yard.

He'd received a mild scolding for this transgression, but his mother had seen this as the first of many such trial excursions toward manhood and had secured his promise that the next time he wanted to go outside the yard he would not go alone. Laboring down the darkening ski trail, the memory of that discussion reminded him of Mayor Tillman's advice not to venture into the hills alone until he had sufficient knowledge of the area. Strangely, he didn't make the connection between the wise decision to turn back that he'd made as a child and his current circumstances until much later.

Even without being able to see it, Jack knew the sun had set and decided to give Kelly a call to let her know he might be delayed. His pride hurt just a little at the notion that word would get around that he'd become disoriented on his very first foray, but he still felt it was the right thing to do. He pulled Wade's cell phone out of his vest pocket, and was comforted to see the bright glow as its display screen lit up.

He wasn't as comforted to see that the phone was having difficulty finding a cell connection, and he watched in dismay as it cycled for many seconds and then gave up. Not believing the message that no signal was available, he scrolled through his contact list and clicked on Kelly's phone number. The phone sat mute in his hand as it tried in vain to connect the call, and after a few seconds it again told him that there was no signal to be had.

The grayness around him was now taking on a shade of black, but he decided to quest onward in the hope of finding another trail sign or even, miraculously, arriving at his destination. Although he'd lost his bearings early on and knew in his gut that he was nowhere near the motel, Jack still allowed himself the hope that this would soon be over. He began planning what he would order for dinner, and imagined himself in one of the area's better restaurants, seated near a roaring fire with Kelly and surrounded by people.

A line from *Macbeth* came to him as he put the phone away, and he tried to remember the exact words. It was the moment when Macbeth commits himself to whatever bloody course will keep him on the throne, stating that he's already done such terrible things that there is no going back. Taking the pigstickers in his clammy hands,

Jack gave up on remembering the exact phraseology. Instead, he began repeating his best estimate of the verses under his breath, keeping in time with the surging skis. "Waded in so far . . . that returning . . . would be as hard . . . as going forward."

Roughly forty-five minutes later the binding on his left ski let go. One moment he was stubbornly sliding along through the growing darkness, and the next he was on his face. The left ski slipped out from underneath his backward-pushing foot, and he wasn't able to get his weight onto the other one in time. Neither pole kept him upright, and as Jack hit the ice he heard a cracking noise that he momentarily feared was one of his bones.

He tried to roll over into a seated position, but the still-attached right ski had tangled with the poles hanging from his wrists. The snow on the trail was ice-cold, and his painful fall sent his emotions brimming over. He ended up flailing around madly, finally yanking the pole tethers off one at a time and casting them away in spite. Not satisfied with that, he reached down and popped the clip on his right boot-toe, releasing himself from the equipment and kicking it away as if rejecting the entire sport.

Sitting up, he now saw that the left ski was several feet back down the darkening trail. For a brief moment he felt relieved at no longer being encumbered by the devices, but then the cold biting into his thinly protected backside reminded him that he was far from civilization in the middle of winter. Rising painfully, he determined that he was still able to walk even though he'd banged his left knee hard against the ground. Gingerly stepping to the left ski, he lifted it from the trail and tapped it butt-first on the ice to shake off the new snow. He found the other one and set the two skis side by side in preparation for putting them back on.

He slipped the metal bar protruding from his right boot into the binding on that ski and clipped it into place with a loud snap. He tried to do the same thing with the other ski, but there was no sound when he pressed down on the black plastic clip. Instead, it went into position and immediately popped back out. This had happened once before, usually when his toe hadn't been properly seated, so he put his weight on his left foot and pressed down hard on the binding clip.

It popped right back out again, and Jack felt the first feathery brush of fear in his throat. The snow around him was providing some kind of reflected light from a moon that he could not see, so he wasn't in complete darkness, but if the ski were actually broken there was no way he would be able to fix it there. Taking his boot out of the binding, he raised the ski so that he could peer at the clip itself. He hoped to see a mass of jammed dirt or ice, but nothing like that obstructed the fastener's operation. Turning the ski sideways, he held it up close to his eyes again and felt the tickle return to his throat: The hook portion of the clip was completely gone, obviously broken off when he'd fallen. He could press the thing into place until doomsday, but it would never fasten.

And without a way to keep his boot in contact with the ski, he was going to have to walk the rest of the way in footwear that wasn't in the least bit designed for that. All thoughts of embarrassment now fled, and he pulled out the cell phone yet again. This time he tried several different numbers, from the mayor's personal cell to the bar phone at Maddy's Place, but all he got in return was the same message that the device wasn't receiving a signal.

With the cold eating into his pathetically thin and dangerously dampened clothing, Jack stood there on a frozen trail in a steadily darkening world and spoke aloud in a voice that cried out for water. "Some great phone you gave me, Wade. A real lifesaver."

He abandoned the skis an hour further down the track, after trying to carry them slung over his shoulder. They were quite light, and he'd been able to fashion a bundle of sorts by feeding the skis through the wrist thongs of the poles, but the four pieces kept shifting around and he finally couldn't bear to continue.

He hadn't seen a trail marker in miles, but he still hoped he was traveling a known pathway that might be used by the rescue party that he had to think was coming for him by now. Selecting a large tree close to the frozen avenue, he propped the equipment against it so that it would be visible to anyone coming down the trail. Lurid stories of wilderness survival situations had been coming to mind as he walked, and he remembered how pieces of the lost individual's belongings, recovered by desperate searchers, had helped them determine which direction to follow.

Jack had finally admitted that it was indeed a desperate situation somewhere after breaking the ski binding. The cross country boots weren't meant for regular walking, and even though the soles were flexible they had almost no tread to them. Apart from a notch running from the toes to the heels which mated with a raised ridge on the ski itself, the boot bottoms were almost smooth. After slipping several times, he'd been forced to adopt a tentative lurch where each foot was raised and lowered without pushing back on the ice beneath it.

"This is gonna take all night." He muttered to himself, and the idea that he might actually be out there until daylight increased his now-constant sensation of dread. His feet were beginning to develop

142

hot spots that he knew would become blisters, and there was nothing he could do to prevent it. Every now and then he rapped the heels of the tiny boots against the hard pack, temporarily relieving the pressure on his swelling toes. It maddened him to think that somewhere, not many miles away, people were safely indoors or even asleep in snug beds. Looking at the dormant trees, it was hard not to believe that they were all dead.

He'd noticed the absolute stillness that surrounded him, and had started talking to himself as if to fill the void. "Why don't they sell some kind of fanny pack with these things? At least I could be carrying a change of socks . . . and a flashlight."

He began imagining the items that might have ridden in this imaginary pack, and it quickly changed from a hip bag to a large rucksack. Now walking with his gloved hands jammed in his armpits, Jack conjured up an image of a cozy emergency campsite, complete with a ground mat, a poncho shelter, and a small stove on which he could heat up water or even a meal. The thought of food set his stomach to growling, and he checked his watch to see just how much time had passed since he was supposed to have met Kelly for dinner.

The missed date was a mainstay of Jack's hope, as he didn't believe Kelly would just assume he was busy and forget all about him. No doubt she had tried to call and, being charged with his safety by the now-clairvoyant Mayor Tillman, had then swung by his new digs to see what was up. She would have found his truck there, and might even have noticed that the cross-country skis were missing from his new front porch.

"No she wouldn't." he told himself glumly, trying not to stray into self-delusion. "You just moved there, and she hasn't even seen the place yet."

This spooked him even more, knowing that he was such a recent arrival at the Great View that no one had gotten used to the sight of his skis propped against the cabin—or even of his presence. Jack had tried to remember if anyone had seen him leaving, but the cold had penetrated his mind to the extent that he couldn't be sure. Even if they had, why would they notice he wasn't back yet? And even if they noticed, why would they be alarmed?

The snow let up for a bit, and a glowing disc behind the clouds told him that the moon had risen above the snow-frosted hills. Jack took comfort from the illumination this provided, and finally allowed himself to ask the obvious question about Kelly and possible rescue. It took him a long time to utter it, but only because he'd tried so hard to keep it out of his mind.

"What if she just plain forgot about dinner?" he queried the gray world around him, but the only reply was near-total stillness.

The survival stories came back then, but now they were the bad ones, where the victim was found after it was much too late. Trudging along, with his shivering back hunched against the vest and his frost-covered wool hat pulled down as far as it would go, Jack Glynn began wondering just when the people in the survival tales, the ones who hadn't made it, had recognized that they were going to die.

Jack had spent a lot of his life outdoors, and although he was more familiar with the desert he did know what to watch for in the cold. Mucus had frozen inside his nostrils, but apart from that he was mildly pleased to note that he still had feeling everywhere else. He worked his jaws frequently, knowing this would pump blood into his exposed cheeks, and stopped every now and then to wiggle his toes and fingers. His feet were complaining mightily by then, but he took the sharp stabbing of the blisters as a sign that he wasn't yet a candidate for frostbite. His fingers could still tell him that the insides of his gloves were a clammy refrigerator, and his weary legs were yet able to warn him that they were slowly becoming exhausted.

His mind had begun jumping around, returning him to the tricycle voyage of his childhood and the legend he'd concocted of the exploit. He now began questioning whether that had indeed been the first story he'd ever invented, and pondered the idea that he might have dreamed up many more wondrous tales before he was old enough to remember them. This raised the idea that perhaps he—and every baby from time immemorial—might have comforted themselves in the middle of long, scary nights with imagery and characters so fantastic that they dwarfed any of the paltry efforts of later life.

He liked that notion, and kept with it even as he saw that the trail was narrowing. He'd encountered a large piece of deadfall a while back, broken in pieces straight across his path, and had taken that as a bad indication that almost no one used this route. Pushing that thought away, he grabbed instead at the happier concept of the newborns spinning yarns inside their bald heads, laughing at the amazing stories while the oblivious adults nearby wondered what they found so funny.

"Maybe they come up with these tremendous storylines, because . . . because . . . because there's no one there to tell them that it doesn't make sense . . . or that their work is *pedestrian*."

That had been one of Barron's favorite criticisms in the early days, a disdainful dismissal that had finally annoyed Jack so much that the Director, in a rare display of tact, had stopped using it. The thought of Barron and his never-ending changes angered Jack as he walked, and he switched back to the child-writer idea.

"—no brainless critics, no prima donna directors, just a one-man show. One writer, one performer, one member of the audience . . . and they're all the same guy."

The new concept seemed a thing of genius to him, and he wished for the thousandth time that night that he wore some kind of pack. This time, instead of lusting after energy bars and coffee, he imagined the bag containing a notebook and a pen—anything that would allow him to record this breathtaking discovery before he forgot it entirely. The ground tried to slip out from under him just then, and he came back to reality enough to see that the trail had been shifting to a steep decline for many yards.

There was an explanation for this, and he saw it with a resigned sort of dismay. Though shadowed by the hills and trees which pressed in on three sides, the end of the trail was plain to see. It was a mass of large rocks, pushed there by whatever earth mover had cut the road many decades before, and it rested against a hill that looked like it rose up to the heavens.

Jack slowly bit into his lower lip, as much to see if he could feel the pain as to express disappointment. He was astounded by the totality of the silence that surrounded him once he stopped moving, and it frightened him because it was confirmation that he was completely alone. He stamped his feet gently, and when he spoke again it was in the voice of a child.

"So tell me a story, Jack."

"—and even though the snow was deep . . . and his feet hurt like Hell . . ." Jack's bone-dry voice rasped as he climbed, but he kept on with the narrative anyway. Having reached the end of the trail, and knowing he didn't have the strength to go all the way back to the start, he'd made a decision. He knew it was the same bad choice that so many of the victims in the survival tales had made, the one where they left the wreck or the highway or the trail and so made it impossible for the searchers to find them, but he felt he had little choice.

He had no idea where he was, and it infuriated him that the hills so completely blocked his vision. For all he knew, an isolated house or maybe even an entire town might be on the other side of one of the looming ridgelines, and he was determined to find out. Aware of the great distances between habitations in the Adirondacks, he rationalized that he would at least be able to get his bearings once he reached the top of the hill.

"... Jack kept on moving ... upward ... using the trees to help him along."

The climb had turned out to be even harder than he'd feared, as the narrow cross-country boots drove deep into the snow with each step. His legs ached from all the walking, and now the uphill plodding was almost more than they could bear. To make matters worse, this particular slope was covered with rocks that varied in size from boulders to baseballs, and he couldn't see them because of the snow and the darkness. His legs, sinking through the wet, embracing cold, scraped painfully against these unseen tormentors. Each time he encountered one of the boulder-sized rocks he had to slide himself up and over the thing, reaching out for tree branches because the soles of the boots could gain no purchase.

"The snow sat heavy on the trees, and so it was hard for Jack to know if he was getting close to the top ..."

Some of that snow came down on his head in a great, wet clump as he grabbed hold of one of the thinner trees to keep from falling over backward. His chest was heaving with the effort now, and he propped his back against the quivering sapling to catch his breath. There was no wind, and for the briefest moment he thought he heard something that sounded like a motor. He stopped breathing and froze there, hoping to hear it again, but after a minute of silence he knew he had to keep moving toward the top.

"Sounded like a snowmobile." Jack told himself, even though he knew it was a lie. It could have been a trick of the wind, or maybe an airplane miles away, and even if it was a snowmobiler out cavorting late at night, what good would that do him? It was ludicrous to imagine himself running down the other side of the hill, barking his shins on the unseen rocks and tumbling over the boulders, trying to get the attention of someone who couldn't possibly see or hear him.

"No, what you need is something . . . that doesn't move. A house . . . or a gas station . . . or an all-night restaurant." He whispered, pushing off of the tree and grabbing the branches of the next one. Red and blue flashes flickered before his eyes, and he felt faint as he clutched this new purchase. As if mocking him, the bough twisted under his weight, almost spilling him over before he caught his balance again. Releasing the uncooperative limb, he lurched forward again in a spray of snow that finally took him around the tree and onto a patch of ground that, in the darkness, seemed almost level.

His lungs and legs burning, he tottered forward far enough to see that the whiteness ahead was finally below him instead of above.

He was at the top, in the middle of a stand of evergreens so dense that the snow was barely two inches deep for a dozen yards in every direction. His voice had been reduced to a croak, but he continued the story as he stumbled across the small clearing, straining to see.

"And when he finally made the top, Jack looked out . . . and down below, not far away at all . . . was a road that led to a small town where there were lights . . . and people . . . even though it was late."

Pushing the branches aside, he found himself standing on the edge of a sheer drop-off that allowed him an excellent view. At any other time he might have appreciated its beauty and its stillness, but what he saw didn't match the story he'd been telling and so he didn't like it.

Collapsing against the bole of the nearest evergreen, hugging it so close that its stone-cold bark rasped against his cheek, Jack looked out on an endless vista of snow, trees, and frozen lakes so devoid of civilization that it could have been the time of the glaciers.

If the clouds hadn't parted again, just for a few moments, he never would have seen the towers. Collapsed against the tree, trying to summon the will to accept that he would have to retrace his steps all the way back to the motel, he barely noticed that two of the stars just over the nearest hill were blinking in unison.

"Gotta be a rescue party out by now . . . if I go back up the trail I'm bound to run into them . . ." he mumbled, swaying slightly in the modest shelter of the tree line. The evergreens were cutting the wind, and even the bitter cold wasn't quite as sharp as it had been. "Maybe sit down here for just a moment . . . rest up and then get going."

The deadly notion had just taken root in his brain when he detected the simultaneous wink of two dots of light that stood close together against the night sky. More confused than anything else, he pushed away from the tree trunk and squinted into the distance. After a few seconds the two stars flickered again, both at the same time, and he tilted his head as if dumbfounded. Gazing at the spot just above the nearest hill, which might have been a mile away or ten, he slowly detected the shape that supported the two stars.

It was some kind of tower, and cables drooped away from it on both sides. To his exhausted mind, it looked like the supports of a suspension bridge. "But there aren't any bridges like that out here . . . I don't think."

Understanding came to him when he tried to remember the scale model in the Visitor's Center, the one that showed the region as a summer paradise. To the northeast of Schuyler Mills, how far away

147

he didn't know, ran a power line that he'd once compared to a column of giants trooping across the land. On the model the giants had appeared to have trampled all the trees in their wake, and Jack pictured the wonderfully, mercifully cleared ground that went the length of every set of power lines he'd ever seen. He remembered seeing the corridor on his last trip east, where it crossed the highway headed toward Ticonderoga, and he almost wept for joy.

"I'm gonna make it. I'm gonna make it." He rasped, and then had to stop himself from blindly running away from the cliff in a mindless effort to get off the hill. He memorized the ground before him, noting the notch he would have to follow to hit the power lines, and even then recognizing that he would have to cross yet another long stretch of Adirondack ground buried in snow.

"Doesn't matter. Doesn't matter." Jack turned and began stumbling along the cliff face, looking for a way down. Though almost consumed with the effort, he allowed himself the small hope that someone, a joy rider perhaps, would be snowmobiling along the corridor when he finally emerged. For some reason he decided that it would be a lumberjack, returning to some lonely mountain camp from a night of drinking in town. He imagined the logger driving up on a snowmobile as he started his descent, and in his mind his rescuer had the face of a Saint Bernard dog.

The terrain punished him cruelly on the final leg, as the pass between the hills turned out to be a frozen stream choked with rocks of all sizes. He used up the last vestiges of his strength getting through the notch, and his battered mind conjured up a strange pairing that wouldn't depart no matter how hard he pushed them away. Ryan Betancourt and Pauline Scott drifted around him with the newly returned snow, and after awhile he stopped trying to dismiss them.

Both faces elicited the same feeling, a deep-rooted guilt that he hadn't known he carried. Now, drained of energy and stripped of pretense, he saw what he'd done to each of them. No matter how badly Ryan had wronged him, his former partner had been all alone at sea when his demons had come calling. Jack's thoughts of Pauline were even sharper. Outside of work, the one thing she'd had in her life had been Death Troupe—and he'd taken that from her when he'd quit.

'Quit' my ass. When you ran away.

"I'm sorry." He moaned in time with the throb of the blisters, no longer aware that the stabbing pain was a sign that he had not yet developed frostbite. "I'm sorry."

Frozen bushes reached out for his weakened legs as he left the trees and finally stood in the giants' corridor, looking up at the massive towers that rose above him like angelic sentinels. The lights at the top of the nearest one blinked through the falling flakes, and he bent over to rest his hands on his knees, too tired even to sit. Blowing hard, he turned to his right just in time to see the headlight of his lumberjack rescuer's snowmobile approaching.

The light bounced up and down violently, and even in his debilitated state Jack could tell that the vehicle was moving at breakneck speed. He managed an understanding smile, and whispered, "Yep. Ol' Paul Bunyan really tied one on tonight."

The machine materialized out of the swirling whiteness, and he saw that its pilot was no lumberjack. He seemed to be an enormous creature, completely white and absurdly bug-eyed. It took a moment to see that his rescuer was a polar bear, which gave Jack a hollow pang of fear that it was all a mirage. He pushed that thought away with a giddy laugh.

Maybe this is how it ends after all. No blaring trumpets, no flaming chariot. You get picked up by a myopic polar bear driving a snowmobile.

Swaying gently, he returned to the words which had brought him the last mile. "I'm sorry. I'm sorry."

The roaring machine skidded to a halt a few yards in front of him, and the polar bear leapt off with considerable dexterity. It reached up two snow-covered paws and seemed to scalp itself, pushing the top of its head back to reveal a bright orange skull. The bug-eyes went next, swept up on top of the orange, and only then did Jack recognize the face of Bib Hatton over his snow-frozen moustache.

The giant ran toward him, holding out an enormous blue parka. In an instant Jack was inside the covering, sinking against Bib's chest while the other man held him in a crushing embrace.

"Oh thank God, Jack! Thank God!" Holding him up with one tree-sized arm, Bib shouted the words while wrestling something out of his pocket. It must have been a cell phone or walkie-talkie, as he began bellowing into it while Jack's exhausted mind slipped toward blackness. "I've got him! I've got him! I'm on the power lines near Little Beaver Creek!"

Bib dragged him to the snowmobile and tried to get him to sit across it, but the legs that had carried him through the night had finally given out. Almost falling off the machine, Jack vaguely detected the approach of more lights as they bucked through the drifting snow. His eyes refused to remain open, and Bib's words came at him from an impossible distance.

"Stay with me, Jack! You're gonna be all right! We gotcha, buddy! We gotcha! Everything's gonna be fine!"

Part Two

The Script

Chapter Eleven

"I have to take him."

The words floated nearby, as if he was underwater and they were just above. Jack's brain tried to tune in the sound, but he felt himself sinking into the depths and the words passed out of reach for the time being. He unconsciously knew that he'd been hearing the same phrase over and over for some time, but in the darkness he couldn't understand why.

After a while he seemed to rise toward the surface again, and he heard the maddeningly familiar voice once more. He knew he should have been able to identify the speaker, but the blackness of the water and the heaviness of his body made it difficult. This time he detected a note of urgency in the words, and remembered them as part of a brief argument that he'd barely heard.

"I have to take him."

His mind changed gears on him, as if swimming away from the sounds, and now he began to feel wet fabric against his cheek. He understood this sensation even less than the unidentifiable voice, but at the same time he found it strangely comforting. The darkness around him shifted, and he saw a bright orange glow as if someone were holding a match directly in front of his eye. His focus narrowed, and he made out several rows of tiny holes in the orange, black against the glow.

"Stay with me, Jack. I can't do this alone."

The sentence was new, but he was sure he'd heard this one before as well. The voice was the same but much louder, fighting to be heard above a mechanical roaring in his ears. He felt his head turn and look down, but instead of more blackness he saw light. A field of gray spread out beneath him, and he feared for just a moment that he was upside down in the water, trying to swim toward a surface that was actually behind him. Even this was only troubling in a dull, distant way, and he found the same comforting feeling when the phrase came back again.

"Stay with me, Jack! I can't do this alone!"

The whole thing came into focus at once, the memory bursting into clarity as if he'd just been slapped. He was on the back of a snowmobile, crashing along a tree-lined avenue of gray under a black sky. Something was pressing against his back, and he couldn't move his arms or his legs. In the moment's consciousness caused by the bumpy ride, he saw through the fake fur of a zipped-up parka hood that he was riding double with someone, someone wearing an orange reflective vest over a dark blue coat.

The earlier fragment came back, and he recalled the terse argument between Bib and someone else, one of the other rescuers who had ridden up out of the storm. Something about Bib being too big for Jack to ride double with him, and then many hands lifting him onto a different machine, constricting straps wrapping around him and fixing his appendages to the driver.

"I have to take him."

He finally recognized the voice just as he broke the surface, waking up in the small, deliciously warm hospital room. He spoke the name before seeing its owner a few feet away, slumped in an armchair as if dead.

"Kelly."

Her brown hair was loose and tangled, and she wore a heavy sweater that quickly disappeared into the bottom half of a blue snowsuit whose suspenders passed up and over her shoulders. His voice had rasped in a way that took him back to the endless trek through the whiteness, but it woke her anyway. Her eyes darted around crazily for just a moment, and then she sprang across the room at him.

The tangled hair was in his eyes and over his nose, and the arms of the sweater were wrapped around his neck. He couldn't see her face, but she sounded close to crying. "Oh don't you ever do that again, Jack. Don't you even think about it."

With his head pinned so that he could only look behind her, Jack's eyes widened in amazement as he saw the dark blue fabric of a heavy winter coat in the chair she had just vacated, still covered by a bright orange reflector vest that glowed in the room's dull light.

Wade Parker got to the hospital two hours later, in the early evening. During that time Jack had eaten two complete meals, had his intravenous tube removed, and hosted what turned into a small party. Mayor Tillman had been in the hospital cafeteria when he awoke, but the others had to come all the way from Schuyler Mills. Tillman had done his best to list the host of volunteers who had turned out to comb the woods the previous night, but the room had filled with Jack's rescuers before he could finish. A hip flask or two had made an appearance, and in no time at all the room was filled with mildly tipsy well-wishers.

Bib Hatton had turned up still dressed for snowmobiling. Leaning in, he'd confided to Jack that he'd spent the day trying to find his missing ski equipment. Tears had glistened at the corners of his eyes, and his cheeks were red from the additional time he'd spent in the elements.

It was only then that Jack made the connection between the skis and the man who had sold them to him, and saw the mountain of misplaced guilt on Bib's shoulders. Gripping the big man's arm, he'd whispered, "Hey, you found the only important thing out there—me."

That had seemed to ease Bib's mood, and none too soon because the Lawtons and the Griffins had arrived about then. The room wasn't big enough for this gathering, and an annoyed nurse had quickly sorted the mob into a rotation. Even Lynnie Eckart had showed up, with Tadd Wilkinson in tow. The cable company still had Gary Price on the clock, but the two youngsters had proudly informed Jack that all three of them had driven snowmobiles in the search.

Jack hadn't had time to feel true embarrassment at the fuss he'd caused, and the general merriment of his visitors quickly made that a moot point. His one attempt to apologize, made when the room was still full, had met with such a storm of rejection that he'd dropped it from then on. His rescuers seemed unaware of his many mistakes, from not turning back at dark to stupidly leaving the trail, and instead found the distance he'd covered simply amazing.

"Honestly now, Jack, I put some riders up on the power line as an outside bet at best." Tillman had explained above the din. "My money would have had us finding you on one of the trails, but Bib and Kelly were both sure that's where you'd end up. 'He camps in the desert all the time', they said, 'and if he was in trouble in the desert he'd head for a main road. Well the power line's the closest thing to a main road out here, and it's got big honking markers you can't miss' and so I sent 'em up there with a few others."

Tillman had then fixed him with the same appraising look he'd used when they'd first met. "Pretty smart move, goin' up on the high ground so you could find those towers."

Yeah. Except I didn't go up there for that. And I almost missed them. And if I'd turned around on the trail I'd probably have been picked up hours earlier.

All that was true. From the description of the search, Kelly had become worried when he hadn't called for dinner and had gone to his cabin at the Great View. Wally Emerson had let her in, and a quick check of the building and Jack's truck had revealed the absence of his cross country skis. A full-scale hue and cry had gone up immediately, and snowmobiles had roared into life for miles around. Tillman had directed the search from the town's ambulance, using a mix of radios and cell phones, and then roared off toward the power lines when Bib called in.

Although many of the rescuers had driven over the wrong path Jack had taken, there had been no sign of his ski gear. This proved to be a topic of great interest to Wade Parker when he diplomatically shooed off the last visitors.

Shutting the door, Wade pulled the room's one chair close to Jack's bed and spoke in a very low voice. "They tell me you tried to use your cell phone out there, but couldn't get a signal."

"That's right."

"Tillman gave me your phone—he secured your laptop safe as well—and so far I can't tell what went wrong with it. This afternoon I had one of the locals drive me out where you were, and it worked just fine. I called all over the place, and from the middle of some pretty big hills, too."

"Well it sure didn't work fine last night. Did you monkey with it at all?"

"I did have to change the battery, but only because it was almost dead when the mayor gave it to me. Assuming you'd kept it charged, it should've been fresh when you first tried to call out, and for long after that. Can you remember if you'd charged it recently?"

Jack's eyebrows came together as he remembered the day spent typing at his desk with the cell phone ringing every few minutes. He'd fallen into the habit of leaving the phone with his keys and wallet in the plastic bucket that had housed the black roses, and honestly wasn't sure of the last time he'd plugged it in.

His mind, just getting back to normal, had trouble processing this. Was it possible that he'd put himself through hell just from plain laziness? "I'd been using the thing most of the day, and I hadn't been putting it back in the charger . . . but I know I had a strong battery signal. I checked it more than once out there."

"I'm sure you did. And even after using the thing all day we still should have been able to pinpoint your location. Heck, we should have been able to find you even when it wasn't on. That's one of the reasons I got that model in the first place, out in Red Bend when Ryan got his case of the jitters. It's hooked into a service that I can call from anywhere in the world to find out where that phone is . . . but they couldn't get you."

"What'd they say?"

"They said it must have been blocked somehow. That's why I took the thing out there today." Wade looked discouraged for an instant, and Jack noted the stubble on his cheeks. "If they're right, whatever was stopping that signal last night isn't doing it now."

"So what do you think happened?"

Wade raised a hand with the fingers spread, as if showing his palm to someone behind him. "Not sure. But it's disturbing as all get out. And speaking of disturbing, they said you thought you were following a trail sign when you took that wrong turn."

Burning embarrassment rose up in Jack's throat, now that no one was there to say it wasn't his fault. He was just about to confess his shame at having dragged half the town into the woods late at night when he took notice of Wade's phraseology. "Think? There's no 'think' about it—I followed the arrow pointing to the right."

"Are you sure?"

"It's about the only thing I *am* sure about. I thought it was wrong when I did it, but I figured the arrows are there for a reason and off I went." His face flushed for a moment when he considered just how stupid that sounded. "But you were out there. You must have seen it."

"I did. It was pointing to the left. And a couple of the searchers from last night told me it was pointed to the left when they went by too."

Jack sat upright, reflexively grabbing handfuls of the covers. "I didn't imagine this, Wade. That arrow pointed to the right. I stared at it because I knew I'd have to take a left to circle back. I'd studied the trail map before I went out. I'm not a complete idiot."

Wade raised his hand again, this time palm out as if telling him to slow down. "I believe you, Jack. The arrow's just nailed to the tree, so it wouldn't be hard to turn it the wrong way and then turn it back again. I poked it with a long stick and it moved freely."

Jack eased back against the raised portion of the bed, feeling the tension drain a little. What happened was bad enough without being accused—

His voice was weak when he asked the question. "Wade, what are you saying?"

"Some of the locals think somebody might have switched the sign for fun and then turned it back the right way later on. According to the mayor, you saw recent tracks on the right-hand trail—" He raised his eyebrows, and Jack nodded. "—which means somebody went that way just before you. So the easiest explanation is that you got caught in somebody else's practical joke."

"What do you think of that explanation?"

"It would work for me if your phone hadn't gone on the blink at the same time—or if we'd recovered your skis. But with all those things happening at once, it's hard to write this off as an accident."

The room's heater had been set at a high temperature, and Jack was tucked in under several layers of bedclothes, but he still felt a chill. "So what do you think it all means?"

"At the very least, I think it means you weren't out there alone."

When Jack awoke, the clock on his hospital nightstand said it was almost one in the morning. He wasn't surprised to be awake at that hour, as he'd slept most of the day and his circadian rhythm was probably out of whack. It didn't bother him that the room was even darker than he remembered, as he saw that someone had thoughtfully closed the door. The hallway outside had been poorly lit to begin with, but he'd found the dull glow comforting and had left the door open.

Despite all that, Jack slowly peered around while he waited for his eyes to adjust to the dim light from the room's narrow window. Wade's words of concern came back to him now, and he was just about to chide himself for being a scaredy-cat when he made out the figure of someone sitting in the chair facing him. He didn't start at first, thinking for an instant that it might be Kelly standing (or sleeping) guard over him, but then he noticed that the figure was sitting bolt upright and that it was too tall for the Schuyler Mills publicity officer.

He made plenty of noise fumbling for the switch to the single tube-light over his bed, but the figure didn't move and so he flipped it on. It was a weak bulb, and barely reached the seated individual, but it was still enough for him to make out the bemused smile of Ryan Betancourt.

158

The rich man was much thinner than Jack remembered, and he was bundled up in an odd combination of what looked like surgical scrubs and a long winter coat. Ryan stared back at him just long enough for Jack to consider that he might be seeing his first ghost, but then his visitor proved he was flesh and blood.

"Hello, Jack. Long time."

"Not as long as I thought it would be."

"Because I'm supposed to be dead?"

"Because I swore I'd never speak to you again."

Ryan gave his head a dismissive tilt to the side while briefly pursing his lips. Jack grinned at this, having watched it become one of Ryan's mannerisms during the time they'd written together. As for his recent feelings of remorse over Ryan's passing, he found them robbed of their power now that the other writer wasn't dead.

"What's the smile for?"

"Oh, just that tilt-the-head-and-flatten-the-lips thing you just did. You picked that up from the Barron and never even knew it."

"It's nice to think I got *something* from that old bastard."

"From what I've heard, you were *about* to get something from him: A pink slip."

Ryan flashed the wide smirk that had always heralded the delivery of an argument-winning line. After a slow look at the door, he rose and carried his chair right up to the bed. Sitting down again, he leaned forward in a way that reminded Jack of his earlier visit with Wade.

"Jack, people always say nasty things about the last guy to leave the group. You should have heard what they said about you." Another look at the door. "Now ask yourself something: Do you think I'd fake my own suicide when all I had to do was wait to get fired?"

"Maybe you should ask yourself something instead: Do you think that your old writing partner might have finally realized that everything you say is a crock?"

Ryan straightened slowly. Now that he was so close, Jack was able to see just how much weight the other writer had lost. Ryan had always been lean, but back then it had been a robust kind of thinness while now he appeared to be actually sick. His pale cheekbones stood out like the hills which Jack had traversed the previous night, and the single worry line which had dared to crease his forehead was stretched so tight as to be almost invisible.

Ryan noted the perusal and mistook its subject. He raised his arms as if to show off the green parka, a thrift store relic with a ripped inner lining. A dark, unbuttoned cardigan was beneath that, flanking an illegible identification tag hung around his neck on a black

159

lanyard. "You like the disguise? If I bumped into anyone in the hall they'd just assume I work here."

Jack now saw that the other man wasn't wearing surgical garb at all. His trousers were a set of gray pants that had been washed so many times that they could have been made from a bed sheet. The shirt under the cardigan looked the same way, and Jack had to agree it was good camouflage. In that rig, Ryan could be mistaken for anything from a doctor to a janitor, and yet if he were questioned closely he could not be accused of impersonating either one.

"Not that I saw anybody on my way in." Ryan dropped his arms and settled back into the chair. "It's amazing how dead these places are after hours."

"Now that we're back on the topic of death . . . what kind of game are you playing, Ryan?"

"Oh it's a game all right, but I'm not the one playing it." He seemed to reconsider his words for a moment. "At least I wasn't playing it at first. I don't know what else you might have heard about our last performance, mixed in with all that character assassination about my impending dismissal, but somebody was having a lot of fun with me in Red Bend."

He raised a bone-like finger and pointed.

"And now they're having it with you."

"I'm sure Wade filled you in on this." Ryan continued. "Somebody was hounding me out there in California. It all started innocently enough, with little pranks that were so clumsy that the local school kids wouldn't have claimed them. But then it got a little more serious. Somebody doped my drink one night when I was trying to mingle with the locals . . . probably hoping I'd flip out or something."

"You didn't?"

"Well . . ." Ryan smiled whimsically. "I experimented with a few things when I was in college. I recognized the symptoms right away, and got back to my room before things got out of hand.

"It never really got control of me, so it must have been a low dosage . . . or maybe they didn't know I'd already played in that league."

"So how did that convince you to drop dead?"

"It didn't." The heater next to Ryan gave off a sharp metallic click just before hot air began blowing from its vents, and Jack was surprised to see his old writing partner start in fright. Ryan's normally composed expression turned to one of genuine fear, and he did a quick two-step movement, his head jerking toward the heater and then back at the door.

160

He composed himself quickly, and continued as if nothing had happened. "I'm sure Wade told you about the guy who killed himself in Red Bend after the troupe left town."

"Yes."

"Barron had fed me a rumor about a local scandal—you know, the sexy stuff you always hated—and I looked into it. It was old news, legend mostly, and nobody I talked to knew anyone who'd be offended. So I used it, and then that old fart did his nosedive while a newspaper article about the show was sitting on his bed.

"That was all I needed to tell me this was going to get very ugly very fast. But even before then, I'd figured I was going to have to split for a time."

"And why was that?"

"The same reason you're the target now that I was then. It has nothing to do with you or me personally." He paused for effect. "It's about Allison."

To Jack, seated in the bed, the tiny room seemed to get just a little bit smaller. "Allison? How could anything that's happened be connected to her?"

"Easily. Whoever was doing all this wanted to scare me, and the most obvious response for a man in my place would have been to quit."

"Okay. And what would that have to do with Allison?"

"I'm her boyfriend. If I quit the troupe she's probably going to quit too." The tense Ryan had selected stung, as if the night Allison had spent with Jack in Maine had already been nullified by the return of her dead paramour. She'd called the hospital shortly after Wade had departed, but he'd been too embarrassed to let her make much of his misadventure. They'd made pleasant small talk until she was called away, and it was only after hanging up that Jack realized he'd blown a chance to get her to visit for a day or two.

Receiving no response from the man in the hospital bed, Ryan went on. "At first I figured it was those two ridiculous lickspittles she picked up as assistants after her first film. They latched onto her because they thought she was going to drop the stage and head for Hollywood."

"I've met them."

"Well you should have had to deal with them as Allison's boyfriend. It was hard enough getting time with her when we were both on the road, but it was practically impossible once those two got control of her phone. I swear they saw splitting us up as a way to pry her loose from the troupe."

"Wade thinks they want her to do that. Drop the troupe, that is."

"Yeah, well, I'll get to Wade in a moment." Ryan's washed-out face had darkened noticeably at the mention of the advance man's opinion. "I was almost convinced that Allison's lackeys were behind all this when the stranger popped up in Red Bend. You hear about him?"

Jack nodded, unwilling to tell Ryan just how much of his journal he'd read.

"Guy scared the heck outta me. First he shows up screaming his head off in the street one night, which was spooky enough. But then people began telling me what he'd said, and it really got scary. He *knew* what I was doing with the script. He guessed the culprit before I'd even written the first version of the third act, and long before we gave out any clues that would have pointed at that character." His face darkened again. "I almost rewrote the whole play . . . what a shame. I had some beautiful little nuances in that version.

"But that's what told me it wasn't Allison's assistants. They were always with her, so they'd need some major league help to be pestering me like that. And let's face it; they're just not smart enough to figure out a Death Troupe play in progress."

Jack nodded again, feeling a bit of the heady camaraderie of the old days, when he and Ryan had misled entire towns together. Although he'd rejected most of Ryan's big-city snobbery, Jack knew he'd adopted his intellectual snootiness when it came to Death Troupe.

"So you figure it was somebody in the troupe."

"Yes I do." Ryan's expression turned somber. "There are a lot of people in the organization who could be behind this, but only two have enough motive. Wade . . . or Barron."

"You really did do a lot of drugs in college, didn't you?"

"I didn't say it was *easy* to believe."

"Just why would either of them go to these lengths to run you off? Barron could simply have fired you, and Wade knew enough about you playing hooky to get you tossed any time he wanted." He thought for a moment, struggling to follow Ryan's logic. "Besides, what's the connection between Wade and Allison?"

Ryan's eyes came alive, and he leaned forward again in a movement that was almost convulsive. "Bingo, Jack. Bingo. You want a connection between him and Allison? It's all a question of motive: You see, he's fallen for her.

"Hear me out: Whoever's doing this has to be able to sneak around in the shadows, and nobody ever knows for sure just where Wade is. That guy in Red Bend guessed which direction the play was going, and the best way to do that would be to hack our computers.

And who handles security on those? Wade." He stopped for a moment, pretending to gather his thoughts, but Jack could tell Ryan was gauging the effect of his words. "But as I said, it all comes down to motivation. Which brings us to his attitude toward Allison: He was always telling you to get away from her, even before I came on board. Probably doing it now."

Jack fixed him with his best poker face, and Ryan continued.

"Wade's always known more about Allison than he should. I used to think he learned about her travels while tracking my little side trips, but that's what finally made me suspicious."

"I'm not following you."

"Sure you are. You must have thought of this at some point. If Wade was tracking me when I was supposed to be working with you, he must have known I was sneaking off to see Allison. So if he knew, and he was your great buddy . . . why didn't he warn you?"

Jack's stomach tightened at the mention of his final days with the troupe, and those memories gave Ryan's crazy story a flimsy sort of credibility. At the time, he'd been so utterly confounded by Allison's revelation that he wouldn't have been a bit surprised if the ground beneath his feet had opened up and swallowed him. He'd stumbled though the first few weeks in Arizona in a daze, and when that had lifted he'd found the time to wonder if others in the troupe—especially Wade—had known what Ryan was up to all along.

"The answer's simple. Like just about every red-blooded man in America—" Ryan's whisper took on a hint of contrition "—including me, Wade fell for her. He wanted her for himself, which is why he kept trying to get you to dump her. When that failed, being Wade he just bided his time and, sure enough, I came along.

"I bet he thought I'd be some short-lived thing and that he'd step in once Allison came to her senses." He gave off a short snort. "As if that would ever happen. But a year went by and he saw what we had was real, and he couldn't take it anymore. So he cooked up this plan to scare me off, and when it didn't work he convinced a senile old man to jump off a roof. Or pushed him himself."

"You do know Wade's investigating that, right?"

"So he says. Listen, I've got a nice discreet team of investigators, PIs to the rich if you will, who are working with me on this. Wade's spent a little time back in Red Bend, but they tell me he's not really digging into the old man's death.

"What they do tell me is that he's gone on to Idaho and started the advance work on the next town. That's all well and good, but they tell me something else along with it: He's spent a fair amount of time right around here." Ryan paused to let this sink in. "Bet you didn't know that. And if you haven't thought of it yet, isn't it a coincidence that Wade was here a couple days before your little accident . . . and that he got back here just a few hours later."

"Now hold on. You can fly across the entire country in a few hours. The mayor called Barron as soon as he found out I was missing, and Barron called Wade."

"And what did Wade do then?"

"He tried to locate me using the cell phone . . ." Jack's voice trailed off weakly, and he saw Ryan fighting to hide a smile.

"Yeah. That special cell phone he gave you, right? He gave me one, too, out in California. So how'd that work out?"

"It didn't . . . but how'd you know that?"

"As I said, I've got people in the area. Not a lot of them, but then again there wasn't a need for a lot of them when the alarm went up last night." Ryan offered him an affectionate look. "The locals always liked you better than me. Half of Schuyler Mills took to the woods looking for you, and the whole place has been retelling the story ever since. Just think how many of them would have spent a quiet night in bed if Wade's locator hadn't picked that moment to go on the blink.

"And speaking of that, where's this great cell phone now?"

"Wade's got it."

"What a surprise. Want another? When he got here, he hired a guy to take him out on the trail you'd been on. He told everybody he wanted to see this crazy sign, the one that pointed you in the wrong direction, but then he had the guy take him out looking for your skis. I wonder why he'd do that."

"Because he thinks someone monkeyed with the sign, and the tracking service says something was blocking my phone. One of my bindings broke on me out there, which is pretty strange because the things were new. Add that all together, and you can't blame Wade for suspecting someone was out there with me."

"He have any suspects? Beside the boogeyman, I mean."

He's gonna put you *on the list as soon as I tell him you're alive.*

"Remember Pauline Scott? He says she disappeared just before the Red Bend performance and hasn't been seen since."

This news appeared to have a real impact on his visitor. Ryan's gaunt face went slack for an instant, and his mouth stayed open a while after that. His eyes took on a distant cast, and he seemed to shrink down into the big coat and second-hand clothes. Jack didn't say anything more, merely observing the reaction and trying to understand it.

"Pauline?" Ryan spoke the word as if Jack had suggested that Bigfoot was behind everything that had happened. "And she's been missing all this time?"

"That's what Wade says."

Ryan looked down at the floor for close to a minute. His earlier nervousness had been erased by this latest information, as he didn't look up when someone pushing a cart passed on the main hallway. When he spoke again, his face was resolute.

"Jack, I'm going to have to ask my people to look into that. This may be even more serious than I thought." He leaned forward again, with an earnest look in his eyes and his hands clasped as if in imprecation. "If something happened to Pauline, it's probably connected to whatever's going on here. But if she's actively involved, it makes it all the more important for you to pack up your stuff, quit the troupe, and go home to Arizona."

"Quit? Who said I was quitting? You're jumping all over the place."

"Maybe I am, but it's not my fault. You see, I actually had a plan when I disappeared. I wanted to take myself out of the equation and watch what happened after that. I believed I could figure out who was behind all this based on what certain people did once I was gone. Once *Allison's boyfriend* was gone.

"But somebody ruined my plan by bringing you back. They replaced Allison's dead boyfriend with her ex-boyfriend, neatly recreating the situation that put me in the grave.

"And if your old groupie Pauline is mixed up in this, she's not gonna be happy that you're back writing for your old sweetheart. That's one of the many reasons why you've got to quit, Jack. Your being here puts Allison in danger. You've got to quit for her."

Chapter Twelve

It was impossible to reconcile all the competing thoughts. As a mystery playwright Jack felt he was able to juggle many different concepts and potential outcomes, but this was simply too much. He considered himself well grounded in reality, and believed strongly in simple coincidence. Prior to Ryan's appearance, he'd almost been willing to accept the notion that he'd bought a defective set of skis, that he'd failed to keep his emergency cell phone properly charged, and that the trail sign had been switched—and then switched back—by someone playing a joke on a fellow skier.

But now all that was in doubt, and he was left in a darkened hospital room feeling as if he were still wandering in the wilderness. He was only mildly intrigued by his easy acceptance that Ryan was still alive, and ascribed that to the many years he'd spent twisting reality with Death Troupe. When they'd been a writing duo, Jack and Ryan had spent innumerable evenings brainstorming in each others' rooms, and it had not been unusual for Ryan to wake him in the middle of the night with a new idea.

Many of those ideas had involved the ensnaring of their audience in a web of deception, and for several minutes after Ryan left—promising to be in touch—Jack wondered if he might be the unknowing servant of Barron's latest outlandish scheme. The Director was always looking for ways to top the previous performances, so a fake suicide by his famous Broadway writer and the return of his original scribbler, even as a dupe, wasn't beyond the man's nefarious imagination.

He doubted that idea, however, feeling it would require the cooperation of so many people (including Ryan's Death Troupe-hating sister) that it was almost impossible. That left him with Ryan's

166

belief that his continuing presence represented a threat to Allison' safety, but he found that notion to be simply unacceptable. If Ryan was correct, it meant he had to quit the troupe, and Jack wasn't going to do that. Not again.

Ironically, his resignation two years earlier had placed him outside the boundary of Ryan's far-flung suspicion. After telling the dead man that he had no intention of leaving, he'd asked the obvious question of just why Ryan trusted him enough to reveal his presence.

"That's easy; you quit this rotten outfit. Of all the people I could suspect, you're the only one who washed his hands of the whole thing. It couldn't be you."

That made about as much sense as any of Ryan's other conclusions, but Jack felt duty bound to consider them. He was greatly troubled by Ryan's insistence on Wade as the likely perpetrator, and so he tried to imagine who else would meet the dead writer's criteria. If the phantom in Red Bend had guessed Ryan's intentions for the play, it had to be someone familiar with how the company operated. Although that reasoning strongly hinted at an insider, they'd been in operation long enough to have attracted the malicious attention of a studious stalker.

That thought, of course, dredged up memories of Pauline. Ryan had been intrigued by the news of her disappearance, but Jack felt he was in a better position to judge. Like Wade, he had never sensed a dangerous thing about her. She'd been terribly interested in the whole concept of Death Troupe, but in an admiring, analytical fashion. She'd spent many hours with him, asking questions about the methods they'd used to trip up every audience they'd met so far.

All of which, of course, qualified her as the knowledgeable outsider who might be dogging their every step.

A new, even more disturbing notion followed on the heels of that one. Could Pauline's disappearance be every bit the fraud that Ryan's had been, and for similar reasons? Although that question meant she was still alive, it also made her exactly the kind of lunatic that Jack had always feared.

He pushed these unsettling feelings away and forced himself to accept that if Pauline wasn't behind the plot that Ryan was investigating, it was likely that she'd become its victim. In either case, it made a convincing argument for Jack Glynn, past and present boyfriend of the now-threatened Allison Green, to pack up his things and head for home. He was a playwright, not a PI, and even the egotistical Ryan Betancourt had hired professionals to aid him in his quest.

But maybe that was all a little too pat. Jack's reborn relationship with Allison was a tenuous thing, so he had to wonder if Ryan might not be trying to trick him as he had before—and for the same reason. Perhaps the rich playwright had only been telling a half-truth, like so many of the villains he'd created: Genuinely spooked by the suicide in Red Bend, he could have decided to take himself off the playing field for awhile. Then, distressed that Allison's former boyfriend was back with the group as his replacement, he could have decided to resurface and send Jack packing yet again with a made-up story about the threat to her safety.

But how would that mesh with his mistrust of Wade? He'd said he believed the advance man secretly wanted Allison for himself. He'd sounded annoyed that Barron had returned Jack to the troupe's —and Allison's—embrace, but only in as much as it interfered with his original plot: By pretending to die, he'd left Allison available. With Wade as his prime suspect, Ryan could have been waiting to see if the advance man would take the bait and make his feelings for Allison known.

Barron had unwittingly foiled that plan when he brought Jack in as Ryan's replacement. That had forced the inconveniently deceased writer to remain in the shadows, wondering if the phantom from Red Bend would try to work his black magic in Schuyler Mills. He'd interpreted the skiing mishap as the work of that phantom—or, more specifically, Wade—and emerged to warn Jack away once the threat had become real.

In spite of his distrust, Jack had to ask one question about his old writing partner: What if Ryan was right about that?

He now remembered how Wade had set him on edge in Utica, telling him to keep his eyes open and to report anything unusual. The pokerfaced advance man had been uncharacteristically ominous that night, and had made a special trip to Schuyler Mills to relay the news of Pauline Scott's disappearance. Then, just after Jack's rescue from the cruel wilderness, Wade had suggested someone might have tried to kill him out there. Wade, who seemed to know so much about Allison and had so frequently counseled Jack to break up with her. Wade, who had given him the emergency phone that hadn't worked.

He let those disturbing theories drift off after only a little more consideration, and replaced them with the suspicion that no one would ignore. He now reviewed the many reasons to believe that his midnight visitor, the man who'd once betrayed him, who claimed he'd risen from the dead only to protect the woman they both loved, was behind the whole thing.

Ryan's resurrection proved many of the things that Wade had already found questionable about his suicide. Wade had made it his business to know where Ryan went when he wasn't at work, and the advance man openly doubted Ryan's description of events in Red Bend. He'd also said that the playwright had visited the demented old man who would later jump off the retirement home roof—and had lied about it.

He'd really *have something to chew on if I told him Ryan's alive.*

Jack had been sure, from the moment he'd first seen the apparition, that he would tell Wade about Ryan's visit—but now he began to doubt that. Deceitful or simply delusional, Ryan had shown himself to Jack in a way that made it hard to prove he was still among the living. No one else had seen him, and Ryan had enough money to ensure that finding him would not be easy.

An easier thing would be to doubt a man recently rescued from the frozen wilderness when he began insisting that he'd seen and spoken with a ghost. Giving himself a small smile in the gloom, Jack had to admire Ryan's foresight. Playing out that scenario, he considered that Ryan might have hoped he would make that mistake all along. Raving about a dead man in his room late at night, especially after waking from a deep sleep, could accomplish Ryan's stated objective of packing him off to Arizona.

The room's heater began pinging again, but even with two heavy blankets Jack Glynn was still cold. Events were taking control of him, and he found he didn't like it. How many plays had he written for Death Troupe where some sap was made the fall guy in the devious plots of others? Or worse, where a character who thought he was the one setting the trap was the one who ended up ensnared?

"May I speak with Jack alone, Mr. Mayor?" Wade Parker asked this from the door of Jack's room, where he stood wearing a long trench coat, a jacket and tie, and boots.

Jack had been cleared for release that morning, but finding a doctor to sign the papers had turned out to be a major administrative matter and it was now past noon. Tillman, casually attired and waiting to drive him back to Schuyler Mills, sat in the room's only chair while Jack sat on the bed, fully clothed and anxious to leave. The Mayor had brought Jack's boots and other attire from his room at the Great View, and his shame-covered cross country skiing clothes were stuffed in a plastic bag next to the bed.

"Sure thing." Tillman stood up with a slight groan, stretching his legs. "From the look on that face I'd say you've got some company business to discuss. I'll see if I can scare up somebody who can finally sign Jack out of here."

He passed Wade at the door, which the advance man closed behind him. Although Wade's usual deadpan expression was in place, Tillman must have caught the same emanations which Jack had already detected: Wade had something on his mind.

He knows about Ryan's visit.

The idea brought a mixture of guilt and anticipation with it, and those feelings were heightened when he saw that Wade was carrying a green canvas bag. It was neither big nor small, and collapsed on its contents when Wade dropped it on the chair that Ryan had occupied a few hours earlier. Tossing his trench coat on the far side of the bed, Wade retrieved the bag and then sat.

"Bring me a present?"

"Sort of." Wade made a move as if to open the bag's fasteners, but then stopped. Resting his hands on the carrier, he gave Jack a look that was part pity and part accusation.

He knows.

"Jack, I think I already said you can tell me anything, as long as it's the truth. Right?"

"Yes, you said that."

"Okay then. Early this morning I went back out on the trail you followed, and I found something we overlooked yesterday." He popped open the buttons that held the bag closed, and removed a contraption that looked like some kind of animal trap. It was fixed to a narrow board that was splintered at both ends, and a broken piece of plastic with a spring attached to it jutted up from the surface. It took a moment for Jack to recognize it as the binding portion of a cross-country ski.

"Is that mine?" he asked bloodlessly, the very sight of the binding throwing him back onto a dark, frozen trail in the middle of a nightmare.

"You tell me." Wade spoke softly, extending his hand so Jack could take the unwieldy fragment. He recognized the color as matching his own set, and lifted the badly damaged clip from the spot where it would have fastened his boot to the ski. The tooth which would have held it in place was missing.

"It could be mine. The left binding broke so that it wouldn't seat anymore . . . but what happened to this thing? Did you run over it?"

"That would have been impossible. It was off in the woods."

Bib had gone looking for his gear and hadn't spotted it, and Jack's antennae came up. "So how'd you find it?"

"I went over every inch of the trail you were on, starting where it dead-ended. I'd drive the snowmobile up a hundred yards, dismount, and then search both sides of the road. I kept repeating that until I came across what was left of your skis. I was hoping they'd just fallen over and been covered with snow, but they weren't."

Jack held up the fragment, which looked like it had been smashed with a sledgehammer. "My skis were like this?"

"Yes. I only found bits and pieces of that particular ski, but I did find the other one and both poles. Somebody really whacked those things against a tree out there."

Jack stopped inspecting the fragment in his hands, slowly coming to understand what Wade was saying—and why he'd asked the mayor to leave.

"I didn't do this, Wade."

"It's all right, Jack. I was alone out there this time, so nobody knows what I found. It's perfectly understandable. You were exhausted, you were lost, and you had trouble getting the binding to sit down." He gave an apologetic shrug. "Heck, we've all thrown things when we're mad, and you were in a dire situation. Kelly and Bib both say you were babbling away, making no sense at all, when they found you."

"I did not do this. And the binding wasn't . . . malfunctioning. It was *broken*." He held up the splintered ski. "See here? There's supposed to be a piece that locks in here, and it's gone. It was missing when I tried to put the ski back on. And I didn't lose my mind and start smashing things up out there. I wrapped the skis and the poles up together and tried to carry them out with me, and when I got tired of doing that I braced them against a tree, so that they were on the trail. I was hoping somebody would see it."

Wade gave no reply, instead fixing him with a noncommittal stare that he'd probably used in many a witness interrogation. Jack knew his face was reddening, but he couldn't help it. He'd meant to tell Wade about Ryan, but now he knew he couldn't. The advance man believed he'd lost his composure and destroyed his one means of conveyance in a survival situation, and that he was either lying about it or had repressed the memory. There was no way he was going to tell him he'd seen a ghost under those conditions.

He was still turning the binding over in his hands when Wade reached across and gently took it, returning it to the confines of the bag. When the investigator spoke again, his voice was solicitous, like a parent suggesting that a weary child head off to bed.

"Jack, have you thought about maybe dropping out of this one? Maybe going home?"

Tillman drove him back to Schuyler Mills under a dull gray sky. Jack sat in silence through much of the trip, grateful that the normally loquacious town mayor was leaving him alone. Melanie Archer's observation from his first minutes in the town, where she'd said that Tillman should have been a psychiatrist, now proved its accuracy. The mayor could see that he was sorting things out in his mind, and Jack didn't have to guess at what he thought was bugging him. The desolate hills and snow-coated trees quickly took them back into their embrace, and more than once he caught the dentist studying him out of the corner of his eye.

He thinks I'm afraid of the woods. Good.

If Ryan's visit had been a bombshell, Wade's had to qualify as a nuke. He'd intended to tell the advance man that Ryan was alive, but all that had changed when the investigator had produced the broken ski. Although Ryan's resurrection had raised too many questions to count, the sight of the mangled binding in Wade's hands had brought Jack's very concept of reality into doubt.

As exhausted as he'd been out in the woods, he knew for a certainty that he hadn't smashed his equipment. He vividly remembered wrapping the skis and poles together and then propping the bundle up against the largest tree available so that it was clearly visible on the narrowing trail. Was it possible that one of the searchers, frantically trying to locate him, had run over the bundle and not even noticed? It seemed unlikely, even if his carefully prepared marker had fallen onto the path and been covered with snow. And even if that had happened, would a snowmobile have kicked all of the pieces off the trail and into the woods?

Bib had gone out looking for his gear just after daylight, while Jack was comatose in the hospital, and hadn't found a thing. Just a few hours later Wade had hired a driver to show him the route Jack was believed to have followed, and he hadn't seen anything either. Having traversed the snowy wilderness himself, Jack could accept that people driving on the trail might overlook something off to the side, and that only a determined hunt like the one carried out by Wade would find them. But how had the gear ended up out in the trees? And who had smashed them in the first place?

As a writer he was careful to notice when the boundary line between his imaginary world and the real one began to blur. His craft not only required him to imagine settings and events which he'd never actually encountered, but it also asked him to step into the shoes and minds of people who had never existed. In many cases these were personality types which were utterly foreign to his own

172

experience, and sometimes they were psyches which he found completely repugnant. It took a powerful imagination to do something like that, and he knew that such free-form creativity could assume a life of its own.

Jack didn't reject the idea that his imaginary world could overlap the real one, largely because he knew how far he traveled on the other side. He didn't just dabble in subterfuge and deception; he analyzed them down to their tiniest parts and took them into his own heart. When the writing was going well, it practically immersed him in a world of shady deeds and dark malice, and it was sometimes difficult to remember that it was all make-believe. During one engagement he'd become so geared to trickery and betrayal that he'd caught himself questioning the motives of real-world people who'd done nothing more sinister than hand him incorrect change.

Remembering that incident, he forced himself to entertain Wade's suggestion. In the extreme circumstances of his trek through the woods, where he'd comforted himself with a fable about his impending rescue, was it possible that he might have repressed the ugly moments when he'd lost his composure, ruined his skis, and tossed them into the darkness? He tried to visualize himself doing just that, but the musing never took on the color of authenticity. The stark moment when he'd identified what was wrong with his broken ski was so firmly emblazoned on his mind that he actually felt the same sensation of soaring fear all over again.

Jack caught himself shaking his head, his blind eyes seemingly fixed on the snowy landscape rushing by. He was now sure that he hadn't destroyed the equipment, but the answering of that question had given him another: Could this mean Ryan was right about Wade?

That would explain the ruined skis, as an Allison-obsessed advance man might have smashed the equipment to make her current boyfriend appear unstable and untrustworthy. Jack didn't believe that a snowmobile could ruin a set of skis in that way just by running over them, and he shook his head again when he saw how well this solved the mystery of how the equipment had come to be destroyed. And in Wade's hands after Bib had failed to find them.

He found himself back in the same circle of confusion that had swamped him after Ryan's departure that morning, except to a much greater degree. He didn't want to believe that any of these ugly possibilities might be true, and that stubbornness suggested a possible resolution: What if Wade and Ryan were the ones who had let their imaginations run away with them?

If the old man in Red Bend had simply fallen, and Pauline had tragically met with foul play unrelated to the troupe, the maneuverings of both men began to look almost silly. Adding a cell phone with an uncharged battery, a trail marker that might have been blown around by the wind, and a set of broken skis that might have been scattered by the snowmobiles of his frantic rescuers, Jack was left wondering if he might be the only rational member of the trio.

What had Ryan said, about why he trusted him?

"That's easy; you quit this rotten outfit. Of all the people I could suspect, you're the only one who washed his hands of the whole thing. It couldn't be you."

Was it possible that, despite the events of his long hiatus, he was now the sanest one of the bunch?

Jack hadn't noticed how long they'd been driving when he was shaken back into reality by the sight of a long break in the woods and a line of giants marching off into the distance. Tillman had slowed the car, and now he pulled off to the side of the empty road. The grayness was nearly total, and Jack slowly ticked off its different shades in the naked trees, the rolling snow, the dead grass, the leaden sky, and the frosted power lines.

"Sorry to disturb your thoughts, but I didn't want to just ride by this." Tillman pointed past him, to where the right-of-way disappeared over a horizon that was hard to distinguish from the whitened sky. "Just a few miles north of here there's a stone bridge that crosses Big Jumper Creek. That's where I was with the ambulance and the Maddens. Poor Tammy was beside herself; she practically ripped you off the back of Kelly's snowmobile when you got to us."

Jack let his eyes wander over the undulating terrain, noting how deep the snow was and remembering the way the scrub brush had pulled at his ski pants when he'd stumbled out into the open. He was intrigued that the sight of the location held so little fear for him now.

"As you know, we're still a long way from town. Everybody's amazed by how much ground you covered. They're saying you're one tough guy, Jack Glynn. And they're impressed that you had the sense to climb that hill to find a way out."

"Leaving the trail was a major screw-up and you know it. So do they. By climbing that hill I could easily have gotten so lost out there you never would've found me."

Tillman put the car back into gear and slowly pulled away. "Oh . . . we were gonna find you . . . it was just a matter of time. But here's something you might not have considered yet: You had a rough experience out there, sure, but as a writer you're probably much more in touch with this place than you were just a few days ago. At the very least, you now know something I know.

"I like to compare our winter to the ocean. It's majestic, and beautiful, and it can be a lot of fun. But if you underestimate it . . . if you turn your back on it . . . it may just jump up and kill you. I think you have a genuine feel for that now . . . and if you don't mind my saying so, it might help you write your play."

Jack waved at Tillman from his front porch while the mayor drove out of the Great View's parking lot. They'd transferred the safe containing Jack's laptop back inside, and Tillman had invited him to dinner at his place that night.

"I'm sorry, Marv, but I still owe Kelly a dinner." Tillman's words of advice had reminded Jack of how many new acquaintances had rushed to his aid, and he felt the need to reach out to them now. Compared to his closest associates from Death Troupe, the colorful denizens of Schuyler Mills seemed almost normal.

Tillman had seemed pleased by his answer, and had only offered his opinion that Jack owed Kelly a lot more than dinner before driving away.

The sun was just sinking below the tops of the trees, reminding him that he'd headed out on his fateful trek at about that time two days before. It seemed as if he'd been gone much longer. Stepping inside, he took out the cell phone which Wade had returned to him and noted with chagrin that it had already acquired a signal. He dialed the first number on his list, and a gruff male voice answered after two rings.

"Bib's Outfitters. Bib speaking."

"Hey there, Mr. Outfitter! I lost my cross country skiing stuff and was hoping you'd sell me a new set."

"Jack! You back in town?" Bib laughed as he spoke, but the relief in his voice was audible. "I figured you'd be taking a few days off . . . like in Miami. I know I would."

"Don't tempt me. You gonna be there tomorrow? I'd like to swing by and get a new set of skis, poles, and maybe even a small pack for emergencies . . . not that I need one."

"I think we can do that, and seeing as the first set almost dusted you, this one's on the house."

"What? You give free merchandise to every tenderfoot knucklehead who gets lost in the woods? Charge me full price or I'll never learn my lesson."

Bib laughed heartily at that, and Jack could almost feel the last traces of guilt flowing out of the man who had sold him the faulty skis. "You got it, tenderfoot. See you tomorrow."

"You bet."

The next call was to Kelly, who gave him some coquettish static about a crushing load of work she had to finish before ultimately agreeing to meet for dinner. While talking with Kelly, Jack had absently looked out the window in the direction of the motel office and realized that there might be another needlessly heavy conscience over there. Putting his jacket back on, he limped across the parking lot and grunted his way up the short flight of stairs leading onto the building's front porch.

Wally Emerson was standing behind the front desk when he walked in, and the chubby older man almost flinched at seeing him. It was touching and troubling all at once, to know how many people who had done nothing to put him in peril counted themselves among the culpable. Jack put a big smile on his face as he approached, and shook Wally's hand fraternally.

"I took the long way home the other night, and I'm still a little sore from the workout," he began. "So how about turning on that sauna I've heard so much about? I'd like to give it a whirl."

Wally's smile looked the way Bib's voice had sounded, and he gave Jack a grateful nod. "You got it, Jack. Damn it's good to see you."

"It's good to see you too, Wally. Just go ahead and give me a wave when it's ready." Jack looked out the side window, to a spot on the other side of town where a large number seven was barely visible in the gathering gloom. "And you and the missus are welcome to join me . . . as long as you keep your clothes on."

Chapter Thirteen

"That's a lot of good work, Jack. Maybe you should get lost in the woods more often." Barron spoke from yet another chair in yet another hotel conference room, this one near Schenectady. He was wearing a bright red turtleneck that day, which Jack knew to be a sign that he was in a good mood.

Jack turned away from the last wall projection of his presentation and sat down wearily. He'd been standing and talking for close to an hour, but for once he had to agree with the Director. His near-death experience, and the jolts that had followed it, had greatly stimulated his imagination. Tillman's advice had also proven a tonic, as his new work now portrayed the bootleggers of the Seven Seas Gang as a hidden, understated menace just like the one he'd encountered on the trails near Schuyler Mills.

He'd spent the better part of a week scratching away at notepads, filling the pages with characters and motivations for his Prohibition idea. Berni had fed these into the scanner that morning while gushing over his sojourn in the woods, and he'd reviewed them with her before Barron came down from his room. He'd also brought along some halfhearted notes on the Depression theme, but hoped that the Director would see that the gangster play was the way to go.

"I like what you've done here," Barron said, rising and walking toward the glowing rectangle on the wall. Jack had finished with the vintage police lineup photo, and the disheveled group of gangsters looked at Barron as if awaiting some dire punishment. "And we're going to hang onto it for a later performance. It shouldn't be too hard to transpose to a different location."

Before Jack could respond, the Director waved an index finger at Berni. The gangsters all vanished, and a typed introduction to the Depression theme took its place. From the look of it, Barron had been doing some in-depth brainstorming of his own and was well on the way to developing a full-on outline. Flummoxed, Jack cast a questioning glance at Berni only to discover that he could barely make out her silhouette in the gloom. He then noticed that Barron's Gal Friday had turned the room's lights down as far as possible, and understood it was for a reason.

Bernice Fitzgibbons, there are times when you're the most devious member of this whole shifty outfit.

Barron hadn't waited to regain his attention. "You'll of course notice that I've kept some of the features from the Prohibition concept. I was noodling around with some of the concepts we discussed, and things just began falling into place for me. And judging from the amount of time we lost while you were at wilderness survival school, it's a lucky thing I did."

"I was in the hospital for just over a day."

"I would have thought you'd be happy that I'd gone ahead with this. It's a fully formed concept, and with just a little work I think you can take it straight to a rough draft."

So that was it. Barron wasn't taking any chances with Jack's rusty skills. Or maybe he'd gotten used to taking the lead when Ryan had proved unreliable. Either way was an insult, even for Death Troupe, so Jack folded his arms across his fleece top and leaned back. The chair's worn-out springs creaked in eloquent protest, but Barron pretended not to have noticed.

"This one has two murders in it. The first takes place during the Stock Market Crash of 1929. The high-powered, never-miss stock broker investing the town's money is found dead in his office, looking as if he'd shot himself. His assistant tells everyone that the broker was despondent over losing their money in the Crash, but a short while later evidence surfaces that suggests the broker had taken most of their funds out of the market.

"This raises the question of what happened to the fortune that he'd converted into cash and gold. The assistant finally breaks down and admits that the broker was laundering money for the notorious Seven Seas Gang, and he suspects they took the money and committed the murder. That scares everybody into silence, and in the meantime the money's gone, the country's on its economic backside, and they've got bigger things to worry about than chasing something that they'll never get back."

The Director signaled to Berni with another flick of his finger, and the slide changed.

"Present day. An investigator comes into town, having heard of the legend and wanting to try and figure it out. He's a bright young guy, and he's learned that the broker had indeed moved most of the town's money out of the market. Over the years the story got a little smudged, with the townsfolk insisting the broker had lost all their money, either in the Crash or through nefarious activities.

"But our investigator doesn't believe any of that. He thinks that one of the town's currently-wealthy families got hold of the money and kept quiet about it. The dead broker's assistant is the scion of one of those families, and there are other remnants as well. One of the meaner clans still in town is descended from the Seven C's Gang. They've changed their name from one that starts with a 'c' to roughly the same name starting with a 'k', but we of course don't reveal that until much later."

Despite his annoyance, Jack couldn't help but be pulled along. Barron had made a deft expansion of Ryan's original notes, and was quickly establishing a storyline where any number of people could be guilty of stealing the money and killing to cover it up.

"Is the investigator somehow related to the dead broker?"

"I'm leaving that open, but it does strike a nice poignant chord: A great-grandchild, come to set the record straight and clear the family name."

"You said there were two murders. Where's the second one?"

"Modern day. The investigator comes to town and starts nosing around, but he's running into a lot of people who don't want to discuss ancient history. Everybody involved in the original events is dead, and the people in the area who inherited their fortunes from bootlegging don't want that dredged up. Our man starts feeling as if the entire town knows what actually happened, and that they're keeping quiet because they all benefited in some way in the end."

"Even though it was their money that got stolen to begin with."

"Very good. That can go a lot of places, from a deal-with-the-devil to a downtrodden, that's-the-way-of-the-world attitude. As the play develops, some of the locals could start to find their moral compasses—or just see a chance to besmirch the reputations of some rich folks."

Barron nodded at Berni, and the slide changed to a cartoon of an informant whispering in a trench coat-attired gumshoe's ear. "Enter the one guy in the town who knows what happened and is willing to talk about it."

"Victim number two."

"Exactly. I want this guy to end up floating in a frozen lake, with his head sticking up out of an ice fisherman's hole. Just like that plastic head they found before you decided to ski to Canada. We can get the film crew to do a great visual display of the body from underneath the ice, unidentifiable, surrounded by blue water, spread-eagled. Later we can show what it looks like from the surface." Barron paused. "That plastic head was a great visual. Wish I knew who came up with it."

"You sure it wasn't you?" Jack asked in a sly voice. "You liked that one right from the start, and the only things you've ever liked right from the start were your own ideas."

"No reason we can't use it." Barron paused, his bearded face taking on a contemplative look. Abruptly turning to Berni, he spoke in an excited voice. "Blank page. Make a note: Use the undersea view of the floating dead man as part of the ad campaign . . . posters, the website, and maybe even the cover of the program."

Jack let his mind run over the illustration as described by Barron. It really was a great visual, eerie and intriguing at the same time. Seen from below, the victim was just a dead body who could be anyone from the cast. It was automatic for people seeing the picture to wonder who it was, and what had happened to put the body there. Using the undersea viewpoint was an added effect, as the viewer was placed in the frozen water with the corpse whether they recognized it or not.

"Design could play around with the surface of the ice as seen from below." Berni offered quietly. "It could be white, or it could be almost transparent . . . it could be night time . . . maybe even have a lightning storm passing over the lake."

"I like that. Type it in." Barron strolled past Jack to the room's windows. Pushing back one of the closed blinds, he seemed to be taking inspiration from the snowscape outside. Jack gave him time to think, and then added his own idea.

"If the ice is transparent—or close to it—you could show a pair of boots, someone looking at the hole from above. Several, of you wanted to give the impression that there were numerous culprits."

Barron released the blind, cutting off the light from the snowy world beyond the conference room's walls. "Put that down too. It might clutter up the image a bit, but we could always have different versions . . . or an animated clip that runs in a web advertisement. Rig it up so people don't notice the boots until they walk away . . . could be very effective."

The Director returned to his seat while Berni typed. There were no doubt more slides to be shown regarding his new vision, but he didn't call for the next one, or say anything, when Berni's fingers stopped moving.

Jack had placed the bland expression on his face once more, and planted vacant eyes on the edge of the table closest to the projection. He knew that he was being observed, and wasn't willing to give Barron a hint at what he was thinking. He knew he didn't have to.

"I'm getting a feeling here," Barron announced, spinning a hand on his wrist as if to dispel whatever unseen forces were assaulting his senses. "I think you'd like to say something, but instead you're just sitting there looking like a guy who froze to death."

Jack had to laugh at that. The Director didn't let anyone sit and stew, and so now it could come out. He kept his voice conversational. "I think this is a fine idea, and it'll work. What bothers me is that you've never gotten this involved this early. Usually you let me write most of the play before you start making arbitrary changes."

"Arbitrary!" Barron raised his voice in mock outrage. "Arbitrary! I'm a director. I'm *expected* to be arbitrary!"

He enjoyed a laugh with Berni, and Jack joined in out of politeness. He knew there was no way of convincing Barron to reconsider the Prohibition theme, but he needed to keep the atmosphere social. He waited for more.

"You raise a good point, so let me explain." Barron stood up, and Jack settled in for what was bound to be a great—and well rehearsed—performance. "This goes back at least one engagement. I've been shaping and correcting these mystery plays for a bunch of years now, and I finally realized that I was basically rewriting other peoples' work. I don't mind doing that, but since I'm being reduced to the level of a mere playwright I began to wonder if maybe I should try and cobble one of these things together myself."

Barron had never expressed any desire to write, and even now his suggestion that he'd caught the bug was steeped in disregard. The mystery writer in him knew that it didn't logically follow, and Jack found himself straightening up just a little.

"Look at it from the perspective of the rough draft. You've told me, I don't know how many times, that the first thing you write is absolute garbage . . . and that that's okay. It's only once you look at your first attempt, kick it around, determine what *makes* it garbage, that you start to see how to make into something *more* than garbage. It's like a gold sample, when they just get it out of the ground. Ugly as sin. But work on it, separate the good parts from the bad, shape them, polish them, and then . . . then you've got something."

"Shouldn't Berni be writing this down?" Jack asked innocently, and was rewarded with a stifled laugh from the shadows. "Sounds like gold to me."

"No. It's a rough draft, and it won't be gold until I polish it." Barron resumed his speech without losing step. "You and Ryan used to come up with competing versions of the same scenes, and did you ever completely choose one over the other? Of course not. You took the best parts of both and ended up with a scene that was an amalgamation of your separate talents. An alloy, if you will."

"I'm sensing a theme here. Gold . . . alloys . . . dirt." Berni managed to make her giggles sound like a coughing fit, and Jack reiterated his observation about her acting skills.

"You could say that. In that when I talk, I usually do dispense some gold. So that's a theme whenever I open my mouth." The Director was getting annoyed, so Jack interlaced his fingers over a knee and quieted down. "My point is this: So far we haven't got a single word written of what will ultimately be our script. I've become enamored of this area and its history, and I think the Depression-era theme is well advanced already. Advanced enough where a *competent* writer could start putting words on the page.

"That's what I'd like you to do with the next few weeks. We have a rare opportunity here in that I'll be in Schuyler Mills for the entire Mystery Weekend—my God—in March, conducting my symposium and getting to know the local community theater group." Unlike Jack's barbs, this last comment seemed to derail Barron's train of thought. "You did say they have some modest level of talent, didn't you?"

"From what I've seen so far, yes."

"Good. Although I'm not saying you'd know what to look for. At any rate, I plan to arrive in town a few days before Mystery Weekend. At that time I'd like to huddle with you, comparing what you've written to what I've written. We'll pick the parts we like the most, meld them together, and *voila!* We'll have our play."

Jack didn't respond at first, and Barron returned to his chair to signify that he was done talking. He didn't wait long to prod his writer for a response.

"Well? What do you think?"

"I think that's a way to end up with two radically different plays that have so little in common that one of them is going to get chosen in its entirety. So if that's the case, why don't I let you write the one that's going to be chosen and save myself a lot of time and effort?"

"They won't be that different. I've got a lot more guidance to give—" a wave at the wall projection "—and I think you'll be surprised at how closely our two efforts will resemble each other if you stay within the boundaries. And even if they don't, we need more than one Act Three, don't we?"

"Jerry, you and I both know that you're going to pick your scenes over mine."

"Well of course—if you're going to approach this with an attitude like that. Assume you're going to lose, and that's exactly what you'll do."

"What's goin' on here, Berni? You can tell me." Jack asked this as he slid into a booth in the hotel's restaurant. Barron had stayed in the conference room to make a few phone calls, and Berni had suggested they walk to a nearby strip mall where they'd have their choice of places to eat. Unfortunately, the shuttered conference room had kept them from noticing that heavy snow had started to fall during the morning and so Jack had suggested they stay in the hotel. Berni hadn't been terribly pleased with that idea, but had gone along anyway.

"What's there to say? Jerome's an artist and he wants to try something new. I told you he wrote a very big part of the two plays we did with Ryan. Maybe he finally saw what you writers find so appealing."

"He's never had anything good to say about a living playwright —and the dead ones don't get much respect, either." Jack nodded at a young man who handed each of them a menu while saying that their server would be right with them. He waited until the man had moved out of earshot, cursing Wade for having passed this irritating trait onto him. "Besides, anybody could tell how much he enjoys making the writers jump through hoops. Why would he want to pitch in on the first script when he knows how much it changes?"

The genesis of the script was one of the facets of Death Troupe that was both good and bad. It was good in that the Director was involved in the play's creation right from the start and would have his vision established well before the players arrived in town. It was bad in that most playwrights didn't have to deal with outside advice until they'd completely finished the work. During an argument over this very topic, Barron had once listed some noted writers who had rewritten plays at the request of their directors, but it was hardly standard practice.

"Come on, Jack. You've heard the explanation a million times before. One of the things Jerome wanted to create here was a non-stop brainstorming session, from the writing of the play to the final rehearsal. That was why he picked the mystery venue in the first place: Trying to trick an entire audience means shifting things around almost to the night of the performance, so why wouldn't that all start with the play itself?"

"We don't actually have to trick the entire audience."

Berni gave him a friendly smirk just as a middle-aged waitress approached. The dark secret of Death Troupe had less to do with changing the play's ending (which was almost never done) than with manipulation of the voting process. To qualify as having correctly identified the play's culprit, more than fifty percent of the voters had to have selected the true murderer. With a maximum of seven suspects and an entire theater troupe trying to confuse the issue, it was statistically remote that any audience would even reach the required majority.

"My my! Fancy meeting you here!" Exclaimed the waitress, pulling Jack's attention away from his inquiry about Barron's motives. She was slightly overweight, with blonde hair tied back in a ponytail and dancing blue eyes. A plastic nametag hanging from her uniform's shoulder strap said her name was Imogene, and Jack didn't recognize her at all.

"Yeah . . ." Berni sounded uncertain for the first time since Jack had known her. "I told my friend here how good the food was, and he insisted on stopping by."

"Now isn't that nice?" Imogene's voice rose an octave on the last syllable, and she focused the blue eyes on Jack. "Well she should know. She's eaten breakfast and lunch here three days running!"

Jack raised his eyebrows at Berni while silently mouthing the question, "Three?"

"Yes, three." Berni let an edge creep into her words while meaningfully reaching across her chest to squeeze her own elbow. It was the version of the 'outsider' warning used when the signaler couldn't physically touch the recipient. "Our last day in New York suddenly freed up on us, and so we decided to get up here a little early."

Jack let the topic go with reluctance, and they ordered their meals. Once Imogene was far enough away, he took it up again. "So you found yourselves with a free day, and your response was to get out of dull old New York City as fast as possible."

"Jack, I know you've never written for Broadway—" It was one of Barron's favorite jibes, and for an instant Berni sounded just like him "—but if you had, you'd have gotten as sick of the Big Apple as I am."

They both laughed at the parody, and Jack knew Berni well enough to truly let it go. If Barron had honestly decided to try his hand at penning an entire Death Troupe play, why was it unbelievable that he wanted to get out of the city to write it? As if to show that he was content to let the matter drop, he turned in his seat and slowly surveyed the restaurant. It was only separated from the hotel lobby by a low wall, so he was able to get a good look at everyone around him.

It was a habit he'd developed after getting out of the hospital. Ryan had been nowhere in evidence in town, and so Jack had tried to see if he could identify the rich man's operatives. Ryan could certainly afford the hefty price tag such assistance would require, but after a time Jack had decided that he wasn't being followed.

"Looking for somebody?" Berni asked with a touch of ridicule, as if questioning his sanity.

"Nah. It's just that this engagement's felt weird right from the get-go . . . and it keeps getting stranger."

She misunderstood this, and reached for one of his hands. "Anyone could have taken that wrong turn in the woods, Jack. And most people would have gotten hopelessly lost out there. I know I would have."

"No, that's not it . . . well, not all of it, anyway. It's just that this one's been off-kilter right from the start." He wasn't sure he could say Ryan's name while keeping a straight face, so he decided not to try. "Throw in this Mystery Weekend concept, and the compressed timeline . . . I guess I'm just not used to it."

"The timeline's certainly a challenge, everybody recognizes that. We didn't know they start summer theater classes in early June, which means we've got to be done and gone by the middle of May . . . or wait until the fall."

"Fall would have been a full year since the last one. Why not wait and do it then?"

Berni looked down at the table and then back up again. "We didn't think May was going to be a problem . . . until we lost our writer."

The food arrived just then, providing an excuse for both of them to fall silent. Shaking out his napkin, Jack took another quick look around. Berni's pointed mentioning of Ryan, coupled with his unconscious search for the man's operatives, came together in an almost mystical way. It gave him an idea, and he turned it over in his head.

Berni hadn't wanted to eat in the restaurant, ostensibly because she feared the wait staff would reveal just how long she and the Director had been staying there. That had been two days already, and her embarrassed explanation had meshed with Barron's surprising decision to pen a version of the play himself. Her excuse for that strange development had been Barron's efforts to help Ryan in the prior two engagements, and now she'd gone out of her way to mention that Ryan was dead. Had that been a slip?

Barron's been pushing two versions of the play right from the start, and now he says he wants to write one of them himself.

That makes sense only as a cover for someone else writing it for him.

Maybe a guy who's supposed to be dead.

It was late when he drove into Newville that night. He'd spent the afternoon hunkered down with Barron, hashing out the Director's nascent concept of the Depression-era play, and the longer they were at it, the more Jack suspected that Barron wasn't working alone. It didn't surprise him that a man of Barron's talent and experience could create a basic concept, but his notes were much more detailed than they needed to be at that point. Barron had always embraced the notion that a play evolved in the hands of its actors, designers, and director, so it was quite unusual for him to be giving such thorough guidance at this stage of the game.

Though piqued that his Prohibition theme had been rejected, for once Jack wasn't feeling put out by an in-progress review with Barron. He found it humorous that the Director was pretending to write a play, and could only explain the subterfuge as a clumsy attempt to hide Ryan's presence. The reappearance of the dead writer had been a bad shock at first, but the intervening week had lessened that feeling greatly—particularly because Ryan hadn't resurfaced. That interlude had given Jack time to think, and to recognize that much of the cloak and dagger stuff he'd experienced on this engagement could be explained if the Director were behind it. Barron loved unusual publicity, and a scheme requiring one of his writers to vanish into a pine box was entirely fitting to the theme of Death Troupe.

If that was the case, it stood to reason that other members of the company were involved, and Jack found that notion disquieting. Wade took great pride in being a professional investigator, and he'd never demonstrated anything more than a grudging respect for the troupe and its leader, so his participation in such a plot would be far out of character. And if Wade were in on the charade, was it possible that Allison was too?

As usual, the crazy switchman in his mind directed his train of thought straight from Allison to Kelly. They'd spent a cozy dinner together when he'd gotten out of the hospital, but since then she'd been busy every night. The ad campaign for the approaching Mystery

Weekend had picked up steam, and she was still working on the publicity for the show itself. He hadn't seen her around town much, but then again he'd been holed up in his cabin working on a concept that would never see the footlights.

The road curved slightly as it approached the bridge that unofficially separated Newville from Old Town, and Jack noted a large number of cars and trucks parked in the vacant lot next to the ancient firehouse that Tadd Wilkinson and Gary Price called home. He hadn't made it out to see them yet, and was feeling slightly guilty about that when he detected the first vibrations of powerful music coming through the chilly night air. His windows were up and his radio was on, but clearly they were throwing a party.

Pulling to a stop across the street from the old stone building, he saw that the roll-down front door which had once allowed access to the town's fire truck was open a good two feet. Bright light spilled out underneath, as did the music, and he was now able to make out the footwear of several people who were obviously dancing.

"Well, you did promise to stop by." He told himself as he shut off the engine and reached for his jacket.

The street was deserted in both directions, so he stopped for a moment to look at the bridge leading into Schuyler Mills proper. Slightly humped in the middle and flanked by steel guardrails, it spanned a stretch of black water that was considered treacherous even when frozen over as it was now. He was startled out of his reverie by the sound of a loudly slamming door, and turned to see two women, both without jackets, emerging from a large pickup truck parked well back in the dirt lot next to the firehouse. One was short with long red hair, and the other was just a little taller with blonde hair done in corn rows. They both wore tight jeans and high boots, and the black tops they wore competed for how much cleavage they could show.

They didn't seem to notice the cold even though they stepped out smartly across the frozen ruts next to the building. The redhead was saying something disparaging about a man named Randy, and the blonde was laughing under her breath as they moved. Looking at them, Jack noticed a covered staircase that went up to the firehouse's second floor and presumably to Tadd and Gary's apartment. The two girls went right by that and wrenched open a side door leading into the dance area, letting still more light and sound blast out into the darkness. He wasn't sure they'd seen him, and was going to wait for them to get inside before deciding whether to just walk in or try the stairs when the blonde turned and asked in a slightly slurred voice, "Ya comin' in or not?"

He obediently hustled across to where they were holding the door for him, and even though he was immediately assaulted with the smell of beer and human sweat, he couldn't miss the scent of marijuana that clung to the two girls. He thought he detected it inside as well, but at least he now knew what they'd been doing in the pickup truck.

You're getting good at this investigations stuff.

The room he'd entered ranged roughly fifteen yards across from where he stood and twenty yards back, and he now understood why the rolling door was raised. At least twenty people, most of them young, were crammed together in the space, dancing and colliding with each other while swigging from bottles of various kinds. Beer was the libation of choice, but he did see a pint of bourbon and a fancy bottle of a very nice liqueur bouncing about in the crowd. Denim and cleavage seemed to be the dress code, and the dancers were generating so much heat that he quickly removed his coat.

The fire truck garage had two windows on the river side that were boarded over, and in the rear he spotted a homemade bar that looked like it had once been a large packing crate. Gary Price was standing behind the box, clad in a long-sleeved t-shirt that showed off his physique, talking with what looked like the Schuyler Mills chapter of the Hell's Angels. The three biker men were all older, and one of them had gray hair that went halfway to his belt, but they all sported some variation of a motorcycle vest with the Harley Davidson logo on the back. Heavy biker boots and chain wallets completed the rig, and for a brief moment Jack wondered if he should have called ahead.

"Jack!" Gary had spotted him, and the big man waved a friendly hand from across the room. Seeing a mountain of winter jackets stacked on some kind of work bench, Jack added his coat to the pile and walked around the border of the dance floor.

"Guys, this is Jack Glynn, the writer I told you about!"

While shaking hands with the bikers and discovering with astonishment that they were following the play's evolution with great interest, Jack noted that the back wall of the garage was not the rear end of the building as he'd supposed. It may have been so originally, but it was now made up of exposed brick of unknown age fronted with a latticework of two-by-fours and an uneven opening that served as a door. Through the doorway Jack could see an unfinished stairway that went both up and down in a small passage also made up of old brick. A nice draft came up from below to combat the heat generated by the dancers and a potbelly stove that sat in the corner across from the bar.

He made loud small talk with the bikers and Gary for a while, drinking a beer and then being cajoled into doing shots of a brown liquid that the quartet would only identify as "shit". Whatever it was, it had a kick like a mule and had him searching for a polite way to avoid having any more when Gary asked if he wanted to see the rest of the place. He gratefully accepted, although the bikers sent the two of them up the stairwell with a chorus of jibes questioning their manhood and demands that they eventually return to drink some more shit.

The rough stairs ended at a scuffed-up white door, but that opened onto what turned out to be a cozy and well-maintained apartment. The entire place was covered in brown carpet that looked new, and it was spacious enough for a kitchen, two modest bedrooms, and a living room with large windows looking out on the river. Although two bachelors lived there the place was reasonably neat, and several other partygoers were gathered on the sofa and chairs in the living room. This was a slightly more sedate group, but the age range and attire was similar to the crowd downstairs.

Tadd was seated on the couch, and he jumped up when he saw Jack. He wore a black set of jeans and a dark sweater that made his already thin frame look like a rail, and he gave Gary a pleased look. "See? I told you he'd be by."

Gary left them talking, reaching to open a narrow door onto a small wooden porch that appeared to be tacked onto the building's rear wall. Several cases of beer were stacked out there, and he took two off the top. The one he handed to Jack was so cold it was hard to handle, but surprisingly the contents wasn't frozen. The three men touched cans fraternally before drinking, and Jack decided not to stand on ceremony.

"So Tadd, you feel like showing me some of these computer games you been workin' on?"

"His stuff's really good, better than a lot of the things I've seen on the market." Jack commented later, sitting on the railing that ran along three sides of the suspended porch. He'd spent close to an hour with Tadd, and had come away impressed. "He's got a great blend of animation and storytelling, which of course is what we'd be looking for if I can convince Barron to consider it."

Gary nodded pleasantly, having come back up from the party to rescue Jack from Tadd's clutches. His roommate, flushed with Jack's compliments, had disappeared downstairs when he'd seen that the other partygoers had abandoned the upper floor. "He really does know his stuff, and of course the artwork is Lynnie's. I know there are no promises in this business, but it sure would be nice if you could get their feet in the door."

The porch was actually the top end of a fire escape formed by a wooden ladder built onto the side of the firehouse. It was covered with a small shingled roof, and Jack imagined it was quite a comfortable spot to sit and watch the sun go down in the warmer weather. It didn't seem all that cold even then, late at night in the middle of winter, but he attributed that to the amount of alcohol he'd consumed.

"I suggested a Death Troupe game to Barron many years ago, but we'd just started out and he was a little concerned how it might affect his reputation."

"I thought you said he got credit for being some sort of visionary, with the things you guys have done."

"Oh, he sure did, but it could have gone either way. Theater's a funny world. Anyway, he's got so much online merchandise connected to Death Troupe, not to mention the DVDs of the performances and his own instructional videos, that this might be the right time to approach him again. I'll see what I can do."

Gary nodded pensively, and Jack waited to hear what was on his mind. He'd originally believed that the telephone man was embarrassed to be throwing a business proposal at the town's visiting celebrity, but now he could tell that wasn't it. Gary finally took one last sip of his beer and began to spill his secret.

"You know, I really wanted to get out to the hospital that first day, but I had to head off to work right after they found you." Jack nodded, giving him time. "I only just heard that they never found your skis. And that Bib Hatton went out lookin' for 'em at first light and didn't have any luck."

Jack nodded again, unwilling to tell any of the locals about Wade's alleged discovery. "I gotta think that somebody came across them and just took the things."

"That's what I wanted to tell you—I'm pretty sure that's exactly what happened. I was riding around out in the open, about a mile north of the trail you were on. The mayor had posted some of us in kind of a worst-case safety line in case you covered more ground than they expected—which apparently you did, but in a different direction. Anyway, I saw another guy on a snowmobile way in the distance, and he had a pair of cross-country skis on his back. I yelled at him, but he didn't seem to hear me.

"So I got on the cell phone and asked the mayor if anyone else was near me, and he said no. That made me think it was just some stranger who was out driving around, but then I got to thinking it was awfully late—or early, I guess—and why would he have the skis? I mean, you can carry 'em that way for awhile, but if you go near anything with branches you're gonna get hung up. And it's not really comfortable, either."

"You know, I hadn't thought of that. How *do* people carry skis on a snowmobile?"

"There are different ways, but most folks strap 'em onto the machine itself. I pretty much forgot about the guy after they located you, but then I heard they never found your stuff."

Jack kept his face blank while looking down at the top of his beer. The ski that Wade had shown him had been badly mangled, and he'd come up with several ways that might have happened. In addition to the explanation that he found most plausible—that a snowmobiler had run them over—he'd pondered the frightening possibility that someone had smashed them to make him look like he'd gone nuts in the woods.

Doing that kind of damage to the skis would take time, however, and breaking them against the trees would make a fair amount of noise. With a search party combing the woods, anyone coming across his gear would have been hard pressed to do this without running the risk of being detected. It made more sense, and explained Bib's inability to find them at daylight, that the skis had been removed to a place where they could be destroyed—and then returned.

But who would do that? And why?

Gary took his silence for skepticism, and looked down at his beer. "Anyway, I thought you'd want to know. And it might not have been your stuff, either."

"Forget about it. We'll never find 'em now." Jack was just about to launch into a round of thanks for Gary's participation in the rescue when a buoyant voice chirped up right next to him. "There you are!"

He turned to see a widely smiling Lynnie standing in the doorway, dressed in jeans and a flower-patterned top. The neck of the blouse sported a drawstring of black ribbon that had come undone, and she looked like she'd been dancing up a storm. Tiny drops of sweat stood out on her cheeks, and her face was flushed under her blonde hair. She turned to Gary. "They can't find that bottle of Daniels you mentioned."

The big man took his cue, sliding off the railing onto the porch's weathered planks. Instead of stepping back inside, Lynnie slid out onto the tiny structure so that the seat of her pants pressed up between Jack's open legs where he sat on the railing. Gary passed by her with difficulty, and she took the opportunity to devilishly grind her hips back and forth. The girl's maneuver had taken Jack completely by surprise, but when she delicately laid the fingers of either hand on his spread thighs he responded in kind. Squeezing her upper arms, he inhaled the mix of perfume and sweat that she'd brought from the dance floor.

He'd expected her buttocks to be doughy, but found to his delight that they were not. Her legs felt rock hard against him as well, and he decided that she must have been dancing a long time before coming upstairs. He pressed his nose into the blonde hair, and without a word she let her head loll back onto his shoulder. It suddenly got extremely quiet up there, and Jack was sure he heard the branches creaking on the nearby trees. After a bit she turned in place and kissed him on the tip of his nose. "I heard you looked at Tadd's ideas. You're the best."

Though tipsy himself, Jack could detect the odor of hard liquor on the girl's breath and wondered just how drunk she might be. He was just about to tell her that it was nothing when she slid her hands around his waist and covered his mouth with her own. A wave of excitement coursed through him at the contact, and he followed suit when she slid her tongue into his mouth. Two warm hands began massaging his lower back, and she leaned into him with her pelvis. His hands slid up her arms and into her hair as if moving on their own, and he used one of them to cup the back of her head.

They kissed for some time, and when she drew away he felt true disappointment. The dancing light had left her eyes, and he felt a stab of doubt that said she'd found the experience unsatisfying. He needn't have worried, however, as she took one of his hands in hers and silently led him back into the house.

The living room was empty, and even the music from below felt somehow muted. After the cold of the outside the heat of the interior felt deliciously warm, and Jack followed the girl like a schoolboy. She pushed open a thin door into what he had to guess was Gary's room, and twisted the lock on the door knob when they were both through. A weak gray light came in through the room's one window, and he was just able to make out the dimensions of the bed before she pulled him down onto it.

She was amazingly strong, and not at all passive. Despite being pinned by his weight, she slipped her blouse up and over her head easily, revealing a bra that even in the dim light looked very black and very lacey. Maddened by the sight, he planted his mouth between the two mounds while she cradled his head and softly moaned.

His hands slid under her back, searching for the bra's fasteners, but something about the fabric triggered a memory. Even as he'd been fondling and kissing her outside he'd been telling himself that

Allison would not approve, but that objection had held little weight. Kelly's face had entered his thoughts just after that, but his tongue had been revolving with Lynnie's and that image had been brushed aside as well. And yet now, with the hard metal hooks in his hands, something made him stop and lift his face an inch from her flesh.

"Want me to get it for you?" she whispered, but by then he knew what it was. The light from the window showed that the bra was a nearly transparent black, and it took him back to the drunken night with Pauline Scott. Pauline's body hadn't been similar to Lynnie's at all, but the fabric of their undergarments was almost identical. Other similarities to that other evening, like the level of his intoxication and their tenuous connection, replaced the smiling blonde's face with the vulnerable, yearning image of a brunette. Waves of shame swept over him, and he exhaled loudly before pushing himself up.

"Hey, hey, what's wrong?" She asked with real concern, taking hold of his shirt and trying to pull him back down. A second passed that way before she arrived at what she thought might be the problem. "Um . . . if you want protection—" she caught herself at the last second "—I'm sure Gary has some here. Shouldn't take us long to find them."

Jack rolled off of her, but just to the side. This wasn't going to be easy, but he had to come up with an excuse for not continuing, something that would fend off the girl's wrath and salvage her pride. "Hey, listen, you're really wonderful, but this is all a little sudden . . . and I'm thinking I might be too old for you—"

She gave a short laugh, reaching out a hand to stroke his arm. "That's nice, Jack, but I'm asking you to screw me, not marry me."

If at first you don't succeed, lie lie again.

"And believe me I want to . . . in the very worst way." His mind raced madly, but then he remembered an excuse that Ryan claimed to have used when brushing off girls he found unappetizing. That was not the case here, but it was worth a try. "You see . . . I'm here in town on a job, and my boss takes a dim view of this kind of thing."

The hand left his shoulder and she reached across him, burying his face in that wondrous décolletage for an instant more. He heard a click, and the room was suddenly bathed in the rays of a floor lamp next to the bed. The girl was regarding him with an expression that was half disbelief and half pity, and he braced himself for a slap or for shouting. The moment passed when her face dissolved into a helpless smile, and she pulled him into her arms as her body was wracked with laughter.

"Oh, you poor baby! Your boss takes a dim view of *sex*?"

Chapter Fourteen

"—but you have to give them a fair hearing. I've seen some of the games this guy Tadd's put together, and I think they could do a good job for us." Jack spoke with a voice roughened by the previous night's drinking. Safely back inside his place at the Great View, he'd awakened with a bad hangover that had so far surmounted his every attempt, from water to coffee, to defeat it. He'd waited until mid-morning to call Barron, wanting to make sure he got his friends from Newville an interview.

"I already said I'd see them, didn't I?" Barron sounded very bright and chipper, and Jack found it annoying. "A computer game could satisfy a real need. Some people don't like it that we only perform the play once, so maybe this'll make them happy. Hey, here's an idea: Ask your buddies to work up a way for the players to see their favorite suspect become the actual killer. That should calm down all the sore losers out there."

"They're way ahead of you on that. I'd like to have them show you a demo at some point during the Mystery Weekend."

"Sure. We'll be coming to town a little early, so there should be time. Arrange it with Berni."

"I will . . . where are you now?"

"Still in Schenectady. I've got a thing in the city in a couple of days, so I thought I'd stay put and get some words on paper. You know, like you should be doing."

"How do you know I'm not?"

"Your voice sounds like you're choking on steel wool, and I can practically feel your headache all the way over here. You know I want my writers to get in good with the locals, but you need to remember we're operating under a deadline."

I almost got in very good with one of the locals last night. Jack allowed himself to smirk at that, having parted with Lynnie on amazingly good terms. Remembering his paltry excuse of the prior evening, he decided to tweak his Director just a bit.

"Speaking of the citizenry, I want to warn you that you may take some heat for your 'No Fraternization' policy."

"No fraternization? That's half the fun of being a road show! When have I ever pushed something crazy like that?"

"I remember a couple of times when you mentioned it to Ryan."

Barron didn't miss a beat. "Ryan could always handle the girl situation. It was about the only thing he was actually good at. If I did say something like that to him, it was probably meant for you to overhear."

"Then there it is: You told me I couldn't fraternize with the locals."

Barron laughed lightly, making Jack wonder just what had put him in such a good mood. "All right, use me as your excuse . . . you wanna tell me what happened? No, on second thought don't. Just be careful out there. Word travels fast in a small town."

The Director hung up, and Jack set the cell phone back in its cradle. Rubbing his temples, he spoke aloud. "That's exactly what worries me."

Armed with the good news that Barron would consider Tadd's proposal, Jack got in the pickup and headed to Wicked Wanda's. Lynnie had actually been laughing when they'd parted the night before, but he was no stranger to the vagaries of women and wanted to ensure that good will still abounded.

Lynnie was behind the counter when he entered the shop, wearing a sleeveless shirt that made her look like she was clad in only her Wicked Wanda's apron. Though tending to a diminutive woman in a parka, she threw him a bright smile when he slid through the door with his laptop bag.

"Hi Jack! Good to see you!" she called out in a voice that was not too loud and not too soft, a greeting that could have been applied to any of the coffee shop's regulars.

Immensely relieved, he was just about to reply when the patron ahead of him turned around. Jack knew she was the leader of the town's sewing club, the ones who had made the banners for the theater, but fumbled for her name. He needn't have worried, as she had something to say.

"There you are!" She happily brandished what appeared to be an old newspaper at him. "This is wonderful, simply wonderful. And using the old *Spillway* to put out the clues is just perfect!"

Having just been saved from a potentially uncomfortable scene with Lynnie, Jack found himself utterly unprepared for this new, albeit happy, onslaught. His eyebrows moved closer together as he tried to identify the item the woman was holding and to remember her name. He was coming up short in both endeavors when Lynnie came to his rescue.

"Theresa, Jack might not know what the *Spillway* is." She gave him a mischievous wink. "According to him, sometimes he doesn't even know some of the clues."

Theresa Gardner. That was it. He'd promised to attend one of the sewing club's biweekly get-togethers, but so far hadn't managed to keep his word. The elderly lady's face squinched up in consternation for just a moment, and then she was opening up the item in her hand. It did turn out to be a newspaper of sorts, a single sheet folded double and printed on paper so yellowed that it could have been a museum piece. Looking at the front page, Jack finally recognized the item as an imitation of the old *Spillway* newspaper which had kept the denizens of Schuyler Mills informed back when it had still been a mill town. The aged paper was also a facsimile, and he recognized that Barron had dropped yet another unannounced clue in the vicinity.

No wonder he was in such a good mood.

"May I look at this?" he asked, gently taking the broadsheet out of Theresa's hands.

"Is that true? You didn't know this was going to be arriving today?" Her words only dimly registered as he first digested the date, printed in an old script. February 10th in that cold, uncertain winter which had followed the Stock Market Crash of 1929. The phony parchment crinkled a little in his hands when he realized that this particular clue release must have been planned for quite some time— and that his Prohibition angle had been vetoed long before he was informed of that fact.

"From the look on his face, I'd say no." Lynnie offered, allowing an impish smile to slide across her lips. "I can only remember one other time when he looked that confused."

Even that barb didn't penetrate Jack's concentration, as he quickly found the article that pertained to Barron's Depression-era theme. Headlined with, "Dreaded Bootlegger Gang Suspected in Missing Funds Case" it went on to describe how the vicious Seven Seas Gang (alternately spelled out and represented as '7 Cs') was believed to be somehow connected in the suicide of the town's money manager the previous November. It said the broker was believed to have killed himself after losing the entire town's nest egg in the Crash, but now there was reason to believe he may have been murdered.

Looking up from the prop with an expression of utter helplessness, Jack still managed to stammer, "Pretty good, huh?"

"It's better than good—I remember watching my father reading the *Spillway* when I was a little girl, before the mills went under. Everybody knew what these were the moment they appeared. A big truck pulled up outside the Visitor's Center not even an hour ago and dropped off five bundles of these." She reached up and gently pried the paper from his reluctant hands. "So if you don't mind, you're going to have to get your own."

When Jack drove back to the Great View, it was with the air of a retreat. The newspaper clue had jolted him in more ways than one: First, it showed that Barron had already set the Depression theme in motion before their meeting the day before. Second, he feared he knew the source of the newspaper itself. He'd stayed at Wicked Wanda's long enough to tell Lynnie the good news about Tadd's game idea (which had earned him a long hug and a kiss on the cheek that had lasted one heated second longer than it should have) and then headed to the library down the street.

He'd found the big building's small staff in a state of near-ecstasy at the way their archives had been included in the play. They'd been comparing the facsimile broadsheet to the original, commenting with great pleasure at how seamlessly Jack had fit the clue article among the genuine news of that long-ago day. He hadn't bothered to set them straight on that, and a brief discussion had revealed that Kelly Sykes had checked out the original copy roughly two weeks earlier.

Feeling confused and outnumbered, he'd had the sense to pick up a pizza on his way back up the hill in the gathering darkness. That precaution had proved wise, as one of the phone messages waiting for him had been from a jubilant Kelly. He'd returned the others, mostly congratulatory calls from the mayor and other fans, before steeling himself to call her.

"Jack!" she sounded like a schoolgirl who'd just been invited to a very important party. "Tremendous job on the copy! I didn't know why Mr. Barron wanted that old newspaper, but you fit your story in perfectly—and now we know what that big number seven meant!"

That was simply too much. Too much information from someone who'd just picked up the phone, and too much of a connection to his conniving boss. Jack's stomach churned slightly as he fought the waves of suspicion which crashed against the shore of affection and gratitude which he honestly felt for the woman on the other end of the line.

Stay cool. Figure it out. Don't overreact.

"Yeah, it really does get the ball rolling, doesn't it? Although I've got to admit that I had very little to do with this one . . ."

"You're just being modest." Was there a trace of mockery there? Barron had never involved anyone from the host town in the troupe's machinations this directly before, and Jack's brain twisted in the effort to understand it. Clearly the Director was playing some sort of game, between his crazy offer to pen a script and his failure to warn his writer-in-residence that he'd requested help from a local. "The copies are all over town by now; everybody's talking about it . . . so you wanna catch a bite, maybe soak up some of the adulation?"

A bewildering series of images trouped across the stage of his mind. Kelly seated next to him at the Playhouse, carrying on a complete conversation while appearing to be sitting stock still. Laughing at him during his first cross-country ski lesson as he floundered about while trying to regain his feet. Asleep in the chair in his hospital room, and then draped over him like a blanket.

He had to clear his throat before he answered. "Uh, I'd love to, but I'm really a little behind here and if I go out tonight I know I won't get back until late."

The silence from the other end lasted a very long time, but she recovered quickly enough. "Oh, yeah, I understand. Deadlines . . ."

"Well you know what they say: Time may fly when you're having fun, but it vanishes when you're under a deadline."

"Sure . . ." Disappointment flowed out of the phone like sound. "Hey, you want me to pick you up something? I could bring it by."

A quick, guilty look at the slowly cooling box sitting on the cabin's small table. "No, I picked up a pizza on the way back here. Let's shoot for tomorrow night, okay?"

As if I'll have this all sorted out by then.

"Okay." The voice had become softer, like she'd taken a step away from him. "If you want a break and feel like catching some air, let me know."

"Sure. Talk later."

"Bye bye."

Putting the phone back in its cradle, he looked at the pizza-alibi again. For a guy who'd been away from Death Troupe for two years, he'd certainly fallen back into their deceitful ways with little difficulty.

Damn you, Barron. What the hell are you up to?

It hadn't been a total lie. He did eat some of the pizza, microwaving individual pieces over the hours that followed, while working on the Depression era theme.

He'd fired up the laptop to find that Berni had emailed him an encrypted set of Barron's Depression notes. No matter how confused Jack might be about Barron's motives, he did have a play to write, so he opened up the file and got to work. He'd picked up three copies of the *Spillway* clue sheet earlier, and now thumb-tacked the appropriate article to the wall over his desk.

Despite his irritation at being led around by the nose, Jack could easily see a good mystery play in the framework provided by Barron's notes and the latest clue. Taking the deceased broker as his start point, he'd quickly built a cast of likely characters surrounding the dead man's disappearance. He enjoyed this kind of exercise, where he seemed to pluck fully-formed human beings out of thin air, and in no time had created a leader for the Seven Seas Gang, two wealthy Schuyler Mills families whose last names began with the letter C, and a young, treacherous assistant for the doomed financier. That would all be part of the play's introductory film, and he could see Glenda Riley in the role of the dead man's widow, broken in heart but nowhere else, as she took her young family out of Schuyler Mills with the promise that someone, someday, would clear her husband's name . . .

He actually jumped in fright when he heard the knock at the cabin's back door. It wasn't loud, but it was definitely human. For the first time since he'd moved in, he noticed how easy it would be for someone to enter the small building unnoticed from the forest side. It was one in the morning, a little late for visitors, and his nagging doubts about his closest associates preyed on his imagination.

There was no reason for anyone to come around to the back, and he quickly looked about the small room for something heavy. Nothing more lethal than the narrow desk lamp came to mind, and his hand was reaching out to pull the power cord out of the wall when he stopped himself. Someone seeking to do him harm wasn't likely to knock, and the door was so fragile that a good tug would probably have opened it even when locked. He took a step toward the curtain that covered the door's single-pane window, and detected the shape of a human face just behind the gauze-like barrier. No assailant he'd ever created would have approached the victim in that way, and he quickly surmised who it was likely to be. Kelly would have come to the front door, but someone with more amorous intentions might not.

Fully expecting to see the prurient smile of Lynnie Eckart, and not sure how he'd respond to that, he was more than a little let down to see the knowing smirk of Ryan Betancourt when he pulled the door inward. For a split second he regretted not bringing the desk lamp along, but the other writer came up the two steps and slipped past him with only the admonition that he close the door.

Ryan wore a long military-style greatcoat over a set of old dungarees and a pair of snow boots that had seen better days. He went to the rocking chair in the nearest corner and sat down, slowly pulling a black neck gaiter up and over his head. A matching black watch cap stuck out of one of the greatcoat's pockets, and he stuffed the gaiter in the other. Throwing Jack an impish grin, he spoke in a voice that was just above a whisper. "Miss me?"

Jack waved a hand at the brown coat while moving across the floor to the desk chair, which he reversed to face his visitor. "You still in disguise?"

"Have to be. I'm not supposed to be here, remember?"

"What is that? Salvation Army?"

Ryan had unbuttoned the long jacket by then, and held up one side by its wide lapel. "Belgian army, I think. I got it in a secondhand store. Pull the gaiter up over your nose and the watch cap down over your ears and you're the Invisible Man."

Even underweight and wearing thrift store clothes, he still looks good. Bastard.

"So did you walk here?" Jack let a note of derision slip into his voice.

"Some of the way. I'm parked up the road, and this place is lit up well enough that I could find it through the woods." He folded his hands in his lap and leaned forward. "So how did Wade take it when you told him about me?"

"Pretty well, considering I didn't tell him." He almost added that he hadn't told anyone, but decided that might be inadvisable. Ryan was just as gaunt as he'd been in the hospital, and his breezy demeanor didn't change the fact that once again he'd gotten into the same room with him unobserved.

Ryan's expression shifted abruptly, taking on the look of a man who'd just received good test results from the doctor. His lips parted, and he seemed to breathe out a silent sigh of relief. The moment didn't last long, and he replaced the expression with one of businesslike concentration. He leaned back into the rocking chair and crossed one leg over the other. "So you're staying."

"Jury's still out on that."

"Come on, Jack. We've known each other too long for that. You're staying."

"All right. I'm staying."

"And why is that—exactly?"

Jack moved his head from side to side, as if deciding whether or not to make on offer on some part of Ryan's wardrobe. He was good and tired of being one step behind just about everybody, but the rich man's question suggested that he might be catching up. Having failed to run him off, why would Ryan care about his reasons for staying?

He's not sure if I'm back with Allison.

"Oh, there's this very nice twenty-something local gal who's got a yen for me. You know how it is."

The angular face relaxed again, as if the good news from the doctor's office had been followed by the announcement that he'd won the lottery. It was gone an instant later, and Jack was pleased that he'd been watching. The feeling didn't last, however, as a crafty, almost lupine expression found its way onto Ryan's features.

"Aw c'mon, Jack, that's not you—that's me."

"Let's just say I've spent a long time in the desert."

Ryan nodded at this, his lips parting yet again and his eyes taking on a distant look.

"Me too. Me too. Lonely out there." The eyes came back to the room, sweeping over the modest furnishings and then back to the desk. Rising, Ryan slowly removed his coat to reveal a bulky fleece pullover while staring at a spot on the wall behind Jack's head.

"This the new play?" His eyes took on a hopeful interest, like a frustrated jobseeker hearing about a possible opening. He started across the short distance, but stopped abruptly when he saw the thinness of the curtain on the front door. He took a step backward, like a vampire retreating from unexpected sunlight. Standing almost against the far wall, Ryan raised a finger. "Can we do something about that? I really can't be seen."

Concern over the other man's behavior melded with an unexpected feeling of sympathy when Jack took in the look in Ryan's eyes. What was going on here? If Ryan was working some kind of elaborate publicity prank, probably at Barron's behest and with Wade's consent, he wouldn't have been actually scared by the notion of being seen. Cautious, yes, but not frightened. The writer he'd known had been a man born to privilege and authority, and seeing him reduced to this fearful scarecrow tugged at his conscience.

"Sure, sure. Sit back down." Surprised at the consoling nature of his words, Jack rose and went into the cabin's small bathroom. Reemerging with a heavy towel, he tucked it over the flimsy support rod holding up the curtain on the front door. While he was doing this, Ryan took the big army jacket and hung it on a peg stuck in the back door, blocking the small aperture there. A heavy set of blinds covered the main window, and Jack had already pulled them tightly shut that afternoon.

Appearing relieved, Ryan picked up the rocking chair and moved it close to the desk. He'd done something similar so many times in their writing years that Jack felt a twinge of déjà vu. Giving his old partner one last look of appraisal, Jack picked up one of the extra broadsheets and handed it to him. "That's the latest clue."

Ryan's eyes devoured the copy, and Jack was forced to accept the idea that he wasn't faking. Ryan was a natural actor, but his behavior that evening had been so disjointed that it had to be real. He'd switched from grinning puppet master to frightened marionette and then to mere spectator, and all in the space of a few minutes. Watching him, Jack felt another wave of pity welling up.

But that was crazy. If Ryan wasn't working with Barron, that meant he honestly believed he was on the trail of whoever had been shadowing him in Red Bend. Him and his helpers.

That thought raised a question, and Jack didn't wait for his guest to finish reading. "Ryan, didn't you say you've got a bunch of PIs helping you?"

"Yeah. A whole team." He answered without hesitation, still reading.

"Wouldn't they be able to make sure you were safe here?"

He looked up at that, but with the face of a disappointed school teacher. "What are they supposed to do, Jack? Stand out in the parking lot and stop people from looking over here?"

Jack's professional pride stung at that, so he let Ryan finish digesting the document. Like the moving of the chair, the quick rebuke had also been a replay of events in the past. Ryan had always couched his editorial comments in condescension, and once again Jack wondered at the man's mood swings.

"This is really very good." Ryan stated, looking up from the newspaper. "I like what you've done with my idea—thanks for keeping it."

"I didn't. Barron wanted to stay with it. He says he's going to try and write a script on his own, as a way of broadening his horizons."

Ryan gave off a brief snort, his face pinching up with smothered laughter. "Jerry? Writing a play? *That*'ll be awful."

"You never know. He's been in the business a long time."

"Yeah, cracking the whip at other people while they do the work. And criticizing the results no matter what they are." He stopped, as if considering a new idea. "But why would he want to write one of these things? He lose confidence in you?"

"Are we back on this? You're the one he lost confidence in."

"Says you." The words came out lightly, the way playground buddies would disagree with each other. He tossed the newspaper onto the nearby bed and pointed at the laptop screen. "You working out a concept of your own?"

"I kind of have to. Jerry says he wants to compare his script to mine and then pick the best parts of both."

Ryan's mouth opened in a silent laugh, and Jack found himself joining in. "He's going to pick the best parts of both, huh? You shouldn't bother writing a word."

"I know."

"So why do it?" The unspoken suggestion hung in the air: *Why not go home to Arizona?*

"Because he's no writer, and in the end he'll need something to salvage. And because I said I would."

Ryan sat back in the chair, resting his hands on its arms and beginning to gently rock. "What do you think he's up to?"

"You know Jerry; he may really want to try something new." *I sound like Berni.* "He's done it in the past."

"No he hasn't. He's tried a new way of directing a new kind of play, but it's still directing. And he's never done anything outside of that, so I wouldn't expect him to do it now." Ryan paused again, his lower lip momentarily disappearing between his teeth. "Whatever he's up to, it's not what he's telling you."

Jack briefly fought the impulse that made him want to hear more. If Ryan and his helpers were questioning Barron's unusual behavior, it might not hurt to hear him out. It was yet another replay of a past relationship, with Ryan once again playing the omniscient mentor. No matter how much that bothered him, Jack still wanted to know what the rich man and his cohorts had discovered.

"Why don't you just come out and tell me what you're thinking?"

"It's not what I'm thinking. It's what I know." Ryan reached into one of the fleece top's pockets and pulled out a folded piece of paper. He handed it across, and when Jack opened it he saw that it was a printout of a photograph. It was taken outside the hotel in

203

Schenectady where he'd recently met with Barron, and it showed the Director warmly shaking hands with Kelly Sykes.

"I remember her from Red Bend. Publicity chick for this little burg right here, but she spent a *lot* of time with Barron out there. My guys took this photo a few days ago, before you went to meet Jerry." He pursed his lips in regret, his eyes blinking rapidly. "You're being outmaneuvered, Jack."

"—no, no, that's the wrong way to depict the gangsters. These guys were devious and tough, and they made their livings from crime. They'd have seen right through a scheme like that. And they would have handled it the old-fashioned way, with a Tommy gun."

Ryan was perched on the edge of the motionless rocking chair, his face less than a foot from Jack's. They were both hunched over the laptop, and Ryan was reacting to Jack's first attempt at fleshing out Barron's ideas. As usual, he strongly disagreed with everything the Director suggested—and most of what Jack had conceived.

"You don't get it, do you? The Seven Seas Gang is made up of seven families whose last names begin with the letter C. So it's not a gang of bootleggers getting outfoxed by the civilians. It's one family of thieves turning the tables on six others."

"So what are you telling me? One crime family saw its chance to steal the entire town's savings, and the other six just said, 'Oh well, looks like our money's gone, better luck next time'? That's not the way these guys operate. Maybe it would take them awhile, but they'd keep on the lookout and eventually they'd figure out who took the loot. Being criminals, they wouldn't accept the idea that the broker killed himself—because a phony suicide right after the Crash is exactly the kind of thing they would have thought up themselves."

Jack folded his arms and looked away, considering Ryan's point. His eyes drifted over the empty pizza box and the three crushed beer cans sitting on his bed, a scene that could have been plucked from any night when he and Ryan had worked together. Concerned over his thinness, Jack had convinced the other writer to eat most of the pizza and, while Ryan had been dining, they'd started discussing the new play.

Considering Ryan's unsettling news and quasi-fugitive status, Jack was amazed to find himself enjoying the time. The more they talked, the more convinced he became that Ryan had never seen Barron's notes before. His fellow writer's disrespect for the Director had lightened Jack's mood considerably, and reminded him of Ryan's skill at denigrating the opinions of authority figures.

"Okay . . . okay. I see that. I don't think it's a guaranteed reaction, but it does open up a couple different ways for the story to go. So what are you thinking? That one or all of the remaining Seven Cs families figured out what happened?"

"Absolutely. They get the tables turned on them in 1929, losing the booze proceeds they were investing with that broker, but then they realize that one of their own actually took the money. You could go in a lot of directions here: The guilty family already thought of this, so they try to pin it on one of the others. Maybe they succeed, and maybe that family holds a grudge to the present day. Or maybe the other families aren't able to exact revenge, but they teach succeeding generations that Family X needs a beat-down if the chance ever comes up."

"So they could be the ones helping the investigator, the one who comes to town researching what happened to the broker?"

"Absolutely. Conversely, they might be the ones behind the killing of his informant. Let's say they patched things up over the years, that Family X let them in on a few deals later on. That would give them a reason to keep the secret, and if the legend says they were victims of the theft, it wouldn't be apparent to the audience that their descendants were in cahoots with Family X."

"I like that." Jack swiveled toward the laptop and began typing. Ryan's idea would even let him use part of his Prohibition story, relating the end of the bootleggers' livelihood to their reconciliation with the offending family. He was just getting the last notions down when Ryan stood up and carried the rocking chair back to its place by the back door. Looking up in surprise, Jack saw that it was almost five in the morning.

"I gotta get out of town before the sun comes up—not that that's going to happen soon." Ryan was already climbing back into the thrift store greatcoat, peering out the back door window into the pitch darkness beyond. He turned to Jack with a happy smile. "This was fun, ya know?"

"You know, it really was."

The neck gaiter slid down over Ryan's blonde hair, and he took the watch cap in both hands. "We need to stay in touch, Jack. If you're going to stick around, you'll need to know anything else my guys dig up."

The intrusion of coarse reality, not to mention Ryan's role as Keeper of the Secrets, robbed the moment of its warmth. Even if the rich man wasn't working with Barron, why trust him?

"I know what you're thinking. I did you in once before, so why believe anything I say now?" The tall man crossed the room to the desk and reclaimed the picture of Kelly and Barron. He held it open for a second, displaying the image, before folding the paper and tucking it in a pocket. "You at least have to agree that I'd be much better off if I hadn't let you know I was alive. I took a big chance that you'd tell Wade or Jerry. Even if you couldn't show them any proof, it still would have thrown a big monkey wrench into what I'm trying to do."

"And what is that, Ryan?"

The hat covered the blonde hair, and he took another quick look out the window. "I already told you. I need to know who was ghosting me in Red Bend. And after what happened to you in the woods, you do too."

"That was just a bad combination of a guy who didn't know what he was doing and a faulty ski binding."

"Really?" Ryan pumped a gloved thumb at the new skis and poles standing near the bathroom door. "You need to understand something: The bindings on those things don't break on their own."

"That's what the guy who sold them to me said. But that's why he thinks they were defective from the get-go."

"The guy who sold you the skis told you that? Come on, mystery playwright, what did you expect him to say? Of *course* he's gonna blame the factory!" He shook his head a couple of times before pointing a finger toward the back door. "You know that stone barbecue out back? The one that's closed for the winter?"

"Yeah."

"Next time you go out skiing, rest your stuff against the back of that thing while you put the skis on. When you bend over to fasten those fragile bindings, look at the base of the barbecue for anything that could keep a message watertight. An aspirin bottle, something that won't stand out against the snow. If I've got a message for you, it'll be in something like that."

"Since when did you turn into a spy?"

"Since I learned that someone was trying to frame me for an old man's death." The gaiter went up over his nose, and he opened the door. With a silent wave of a gloved hand, he disappeared.

Jack sat regarding the door for some time, imagining Ryan skulking through the shadows behind the other units, his emaciated frame bundled up in castoff clothing, as he hurried toward his car. His eyes came to focus on the small window in the flimsy back door, and he slowly rose. Walking to the cabin's small closet, he took out a warm-up jacket and hung it on the peg over the tiny aperture, blocking it.

206

He turned and looked around the small space, aware that it felt a little better now that he'd shut out the prying eyes again. His gaze fell on the new skis and poles in the slim corner next to the bathroom door. Though narrow, the equipment consumed a fair amount of the cabin's limited space and should have been outside. The gear stood there in mute testimony to the thought which had built in his mind over time, the one Ryan had put into words.

The bindings on those things don't break on their own.

Two days later, Jack was sitting in the back of a coin-op laundry in Newville when Mayor Tillman finally found him. A freezing rain had been dropping all morning, and it was turning the main road outside the laundry's windows into a gray mess of half-frozen slush.

Despite the weather, or perhaps because of it, Jack found the place calming. The humming machines kept the place warm, many people were coming and going, and there was a table in the rear where he'd set himself up with a large cup of steaming coffee and a writing pad. He was actually doing his laundry, and had decided that the laptop was simply too pretentious for the venue. The floor was a hard, dingy concrete with drains strategically located in case of overflows, and three ranks of washing machines stood on raised pads. Whirring dryers lined one wall, facing a plywood service desk where the lady who ran the place accepted wash deliveries or handed out the cleaned product in mesh bags.

Just above the fray, a variety of antique laundry tools had been hung on the walls. He couldn't identify most of them, but he did recognize an old hand washboard that looked like a torture device. He found the effort to dress the place up quite laudable, and was trying to think of a way to put it in the show when Tillman came through the door.

The mayor wore a long slicker over his hunting coat, and a wide-brimmed rain hat that looked like a fedora from a distance. He shook the water off the hat while vigorously wiping his feet on the rubber mats by the door, and walked toward Jack after greeting the lady behind the desk by her first name.

Tillman hung his dripping coat on a hook with the other jackets and sat down heavily in a folding chair opposite Jack. Although customers ranging from senior citizens to young mothers roamed among the machines, they were alone at the small table. Looking up with an amiable expression, Jack suddenly became aware of the dull electric buzz from incandescent lights directly over his head.

"Hello, Mr. Mayor. Nasty day out, huh?"

Tillman gave him a weak smile as he removed his glasses and began wiping them with a handkerchief. "It certainly is. Lots of black ice today that wasn't out there yesterday."

He finished cleaning the lenses and put the glasses back on. "I haven't seen you around lately. Everything all right?"

You gotta love small towns. The word's out that Kelly and Jack are having a spat. I wonder how long it'll be before it's chalked on the wall of the elementary school.

"Actually, yes. I've reached a breakthrough in the writing and it's moving along really well."

"Good, good . . . but the laundry's no respecter of a man's time, is it?" Tillman's tone was conversational, even approving, but he clearly wasn't buying the explanation. He set about straightening his burgundy sweater, the one that hadn't bunched up anywhere.

"In every Death Troupe show I've done, there have been a few places where you can really get a feel for a town. The local watering holes and diners are always good for meeting people, but if you want to see them going about their business, go to the laundry." He threw Tillman a disarming grin. "Besides, I needed a break."

"That's kind of why I'm here. People miss seeing you around on the other side of town. Maybe you should take your break at Maddy's or Wanda's or . . . heck, just take a walk around the common."

"I'll do that. I didn't know I was causing a stir."

"No stir. Everybody knows you're busy." Tillman seemed uncertain for the tiniest instant, but he decided to plow ahead. He dropped his voice to a near-whisper. "Jack, if this is none of my business just say so and I'll be on my way. It's just that you and Kelly seemed to be getting along so well and all of a sudden it's like somebody really took the wind out of her sails." He caught himself, realizing that he was telling tales on one of his employees—as well as a citizen of the town. "Not that she's moping around or anything, the kid's not like that, but I just wanted to know if there's anything I could help you smooth over."

The last bit came out in a rush, and instead of sounding like an older man offering relationship advice, it reminded Jack of a much older man, the one who'd warned him about the mayor before he'd ever met him: *Watch this guy, Jack.*

The memory lasted only a moment, and was quickly replaced with gratitude for Tillman's role in his rescue from the wilderness and his kind words when Jack had returned to the town.

"I'm sorry if I missed something, but I can't think of anything that would need smoothing over." He mixed mild surprise with gentle concern, and thought it came out well enough. "We spent a lot of time together, sure, but that's because we've got a lot in common . . . there's really been nothing more than that."

Tillman blinked a few times, as if waiting for him to continue, but when that didn't happen he gave a small nod. "I figured as much. I was just concerned that maybe our helping your boss with that example newspaper might have annoyed you. When he asked for it, I thought he was going to use it for advertising, maybe as part of the show's poster, so I didn't give it a second thought when I told Kelly to handle it . . ."

He's a good boss. He's taking a hit for someone on his team. But he's also lying just a little bit.

" . . . I guess I'm saying that it's my fault if that bothered you."

"Oh that?" *Who's lying now?* "I was a little surprised, but I think I've mentioned before that the final presentation of a clue is the Director's decision. I'm sorry if that came across wrong."

Tillman nodded again, getting ready to leave without accomplishing what he'd come to do. He stood slowly, and reached for the still-dripping raincoat. "Do me a favor, and come into town for dinner tonight. Or give me a call and I'll meet you with the missus."

"Sure. You want to meet at the diner? Say six?"

"That'd be great." Tillman smiled, appearing slightly relieved. He picked up the hat and was just taking the first step toward the door when he stopped. "So this is the place for taking the town's pulse, huh?" He put the hat on. "You'd think I'd know something like that, wouldn't you?"

The afternoon passed quickly back at the Great View. The rain hadn't stopped, but it hadn't risen in intensity either and simply kept up a gentle drumming on the cottage roof. Jack typed steadily for at least two hours, fully aware that the bizarre occurrences around him had helped the writing immeasurably. Perhaps it was the unsettling feeling of not knowing who was telling him the truth, or even who he could trust, but he now found it easier to imagine the deception and uncertainty which surrounded the characters in his play.

Although he considered his own experience with the theater to be fairly narrow, Jack had spent a lot of time with actors over the years and had paid attention to the things they said and did. He knew that some of the Method actors would relate to his current circumstances, as they often tried to find something in their personal experiences to fit the roles they were playing. He'd heard them advising each other to "use" events from their real lives that related to their characters, and even though that wasn't a popular phrase with Death Troupe he liked it anyway.

Whatever was happening, his work was clearly benefiting from it. He'd built a rough outline and, instead of his normal turn toward fleshing that out, simply began writing bits and pieces of dialogue around the high points of that loose framework. It was a trick that Ryan had tried to teach him years before, but he hadn't found it useful until now.

As for Ryan, there had been no further indication of his presence. Jack had donned a rain jacket after lunch and taken a short stroll behind the cottages, aimlessly kicking at the snow around the stone grill until satisfied that it was not home to one of the other writer's message drops. He'd looked uphill at the cross country ski trail once or twice, but the idea of giving that another try wasn't appealing. In fact, the skis in the corner of his room were still brand new.

He was just about to take a break when the cell phone went off. It identified Kelly as the caller, and he picked it up with some trepidation. If Tillman and the others had considered her demeanor alarming enough to speak to him about it, she was probably aware of it. He didn't have to wait long to find out.

"Hey Biff, I heard my old man gave you the third degree about why you haven't been around the malt shop lately." Her voice was light, and more mocking of Tillman than solicitous of Jack's feelings. He took the joke as a good sign and went with it.

"Sorry Mary Sue, my mom must have put him up to it. Grown-ups."

She chuckled back at him, lightly. "They make a federal case out of everything, don't they? What a drag."

He dropped the Fifties banter and resumed his normal voice. "It wasn't that bad."

"Of course it's not bad for you, Superman; you can just run off to your fortress of solitude. Me, I've got to be right here in the middle of it." A brief laugh. "Wanna know something weird? I'm a town employee, but when I told them I haven't been around at night because I was busy with town business . . . they didn't like it. Everyplace else the civil servants are asleep, but me . . . I live in the only town where you get in trouble for being busy."

They both laughed at that, and Jack felt the tension easing. Clearly Kelly had moved past his reaction to the newspaper clue, and for reasons he couldn't explain he found himself hoping that he hadn't been written off completely. The words came out of his mouth before he had a chance to reconsider.

"I'm having dinner tonight with the Tillman's at the S&M. You're certainly welcome to join us—"

"Hang out with the squares? Not me, daddy-o. I was serious when I said I've got a ton of work to do."

He didn't know why the words stung the way they did, so he chalked them up to payback for his rudeness a few nights before.

"Whatcha workin' on?"

"There's this play, see . . ."

"I know, I know. I'm working on the same thing."

"Oh, I doubt that. I doubt that strongly." The voice trailed off at the end, almost disinterested. "Listen, Jack, I gotta go. I *am* going to see you around the schoolyard, right?"

"Count on it."

"I will."

It was only then, and for reasons he didn't understand, that he glanced at the calendar and noticed that the previous day had been Valentine's Day.

Chapter Fifteen

Jack's phone rang at five the next morning, startling him out of a deep sleep. He'd dined with the Tillman's the night before, but hadn't stayed out late. He'd written until midnight and, eyes drooping, crawled under the covers of the cabin's big wooden bed.

"Hello?" he asked weakly, seeing through the blinds that it was pitch dark outside.

"Hi Jack, it's Marv Tillman. Sorry to wake you." The man on the other end of the line was one Jack had never met before, all business. He came to a sitting position as if on command. "I'm up at the Campion Hill fire tower, and there's something here that we think might be one of your clues."

Oh God. What did Barron do now?

"Really? What is it?"

"It's a mannequin, hung from the tower. From a distance it looks like somebody hanged himself. You sure you don't know anything about this?"

Lord I wish I did.

Wide awake now and aware of how cold the room was, Jack decided that he needed to match the mayor's tone. "I do not, and unless I'm very mistaken that is not one of our clues. We don't do things like that."

Tillman made a sound like a sigh, but then again it could have been the wind up on the big hill. Jack tied to imagine what it must look like up there at that hour, surrounded by darkness and cold air.

"Listen, Jack, this thing is a little spooky and I'm definitely going to have the boys take it down." That was probably a reference to one of the two men who made up the small town's Department of

Public Works. "But before we do that, would you mind coming up here and having a look? The boom's open and you can drive right up. This thing's coming down either way, but I'd like to make sure it isn't connected to the show."

Me too.

"I'll be right there."

Kelly had taken him up the tower during his first week in town, but that had been in broad daylight. The road leading to the fire tower was very different in the dark, and Jack drove the truck slowly. The headlights reflected off of the snow and ice that covered the road, making him think of films he'd seen of the ocean floor, shot from within deep-diving submersibles. The trees on either side hemmed in the thoroughfare, reaching for him as they had during the night he'd spent wandering through the wilderness. He turned on the radio and had to hit the seek button a few times before finding a station. He was more than a little relieved when he reached the top.

Tillman's SUV was parked at the base of the tall tower alongside a dump truck that bore the town's symbol and a pickup that had seen better days. Parking nearby, Jack zipped up his jacket and pulled his hat down over his ears before hopping out into the snow. As he walked by, he noticed that the battered pickup had once been painted brown and that an empty rifle rack was visible in the rear window of the cab.

It struck him as funny that the room at the top of a fire tower was also known as a cab, and he looked up as he came to the bottom of the metal stairs. A dull light glowed from the windows high above, but he was unable to see if anything was hanging somewhere over his head. He'd observed the tower from the Great View parking lot just before setting out and hadn't even seen the light, much less a body. He started up the stairs, the soles of his boots ringing against the steel lattice of the steps. The tower's four support legs and reinforcing cables were open to the elements, and it was cold as he climbed. Once above the level of the surrounding trees, he was surprised by how much of the town was still lit up and how much of it he could now identify. This growing familiarity with the area pleased him, but his struggle for breath was an annoying reminder that he hadn't gotten any exercise since his sojourn in the woods.

Winded, he stopped on the stairs as soon as his head rose above the level of the cab's floor. A metal table was bolted to the center of the floor, but there was still plenty of room to move around. The strip bulb at the ceiling's apex didn't throw much light, but he was able to see an obviously cold Tillman, a young town worker whose name escaped him, and an elderly man who regarded him with an unfriendly stare. Tillman and the town worker were both bundled up for the cold in long coats, but the older man was wearing a full-body camouflage suit of the type worn by hunters. A camouflaged hat with ear flaps was perched on the man's head and, from floor level, Jack could see that his hunting boots were covered with frozen muck.

"Thanks for coming up here, Jack." Tillman was rubbing both gloved hands together, and tilted his head toward first one and then the other of his two companions. "You might have met Ned Waters already. He's one of our public works guys." Waters looked to be very young, probably just over twenty, when he raised a mitten in mute greeting. "And this is Charlie Fannon. Charlie saw some lights up here a few hours ago and decided to come up and have a look. Right, Charlie?"

"Absolutely, Mr. Mayor." The voice was rough with age, but he replied with the obedience of a schoolboy being given a second chance by the principal. Jack didn't need any more than that to guess that Charlie had been doing something wrong when he noticed the lights—if that was, in fact, what had brought him up there. Given his own inability to detect any illumination as he approached the tower, Jack had to believe that Charlie had been very close to have detected a flashlight up there. Given his attire, it seemed likely that he'd been skulking through the woods nearby, holding one of the items from his truck's now-empty rifle rack.

"Okay." Jack responded in a tone of intentional disinterest, indicating that whatever town rule had been broken was no business of his. "So where is this thing?"

"Over here." Tillman led him across the creaking floorboards to the side of the cab furthest from the stairwell hatch. The entire window segment covering that wall had been propped open, and it took Jack a moment to see that it was hinged at the top. Getting his bearings, he decided that during daylight hours anything hung from that side of the tower would be in view from the center of town.

"Back when this was a functioning watch tower, this was how they got supplies up here." Tillman pointed overhead, to a thick pipe affixed to the ceiling. The pipe's telescoping segments had been extended into the darkness, and presumably had supported a pulley system for hauling things up to the cab many years earlier.

Tillman took a small flashlight from his pocket and pointed it into the darkness. Though forewarned, Jack almost jumped in fright at what was suspended outside.

The effigy hung from the end of the pipe as if wearing a noose, clad in light blue pajamas, dark slippers, and a rich red bathrobe that gently flapped in the breeze. Jack got the message immediately.

It's supposed to be the old man from the rest home.

"This isn't some teenager's scarecrow." Tillman kept his voice calm once they'd hauled the thing in, but he was clearly alarmed. "And I can't help noticing that it's missing a head."

The mannequin lay sprawled on the scuffed boards of the cab's floor, illuminated by two flashlights and the overhead bulb. It was constructed of a lifelike plastic, its limbs were able to move on their own, and it was indeed headless. Squatting down, Jack flipped aside the glossy red robe so he could inspect the cheap pajamas beneath. He half expected to see the name of an expensive old-age home in California emblazoned on the pocket. It wasn't there, but it didn't have to be. The robe was cashmere and of a kind that only a wealthy man could afford.

But the guy from Red Bend didn't hang himself. And why is he headless?

Jack gathered his thoughts before standing. The Red Bend connection was obviously meant for him, but there was no reason to communicate it to the whole town.

"You know Death Troupe has seen some pretty elaborate pranks over the years, right? Well I think this is one of them."

"A prank? Look at that robe, Jack; it's gotta be worth five hundred dollars at least. And it's brand new. Helluva lotta money for a prank."

It is indeed. And whoever put this here meant for someone like Tillman to notice that.

"I'd say that points even more to a third party. We try to keep the clues inexpensive." That was true. The people paying for the show didn't like being billed for pricey hints when a cheap one would do the job just as well. "And I wouldn't be surprised if this body matches the head from that ice fishing hole."

He didn't have to point out that the townspeople had originally supposed the ice fishing head to be a clue—or that it had turned out to be a joke.

Tillman was rubbing his gloved hands together again, and the other two seemed anxious to wrap this up. The mayor pursed his lips hard one more time while studying the effigy, but when he spoke he sounded slightly mollified. "Yeah. I thought the same thing. That head's been making the rounds and getting a lot of laughs. You think maybe somebody was doing an encore?"

"Probably." *The Hell I do.*

"Okay, let's get out of here. Put the thing in my truck for now." He raised an index finger to all three of them. "And not a word to anybody. This show's supposed to be fun, and I'm not going to have the town turned into some kind of Halloween fright night for the next three months."

The town worker picked up the limp form like it was a diseased corpse and headed for the stairs. Charlie Fannon went next, but when Jack started after him Tillman's hand landed on his arm. He turned to see that the look of concern was back.

"Is there something you're not telling me, Jack?"

Watch this guy, Jack. The Director's words came back to him, a reminder that Tillman, mayor or not, was just one more local who might be trying to trick him. A stark denial would raise suspicion, though, and Jack felt he did a credible acting job when he told the corners of his lips to rise just a bit.

"Of course there is, Mr. Mayor. I'm the writer for Death Troupe."

"That's not what he was wearing." Wade had answered the phone on the second ring even though it was still the dead of night in Idaho. "Were there any markings on the clothes, anything specific to the location?"

Jack had described the scene at the fire tower as best he could without coming out and actually saying the words. It was an old Death Troupe practice, talking around the topic in case the conversation was overheard.

"The place out west? No. But it was a cheap pair of pajamas, like hospital issue. And the robe was expensive . . . a man's robe. What else am I supposed to think?"

"I dunno . . . maybe that we recently dropped a clue about a money manager who killed himself when he lost a bundle in the Crash—and that any joker with an imagination might think of hanging?"

"The thing was missing its very top part."

"So it's the same funny man who did the trick in the lake. Even more reason to think it's a local with a sense of humor. The D would have liked this . . . maybe you shouldn't have let them take it down."

"I didn't have any say in that. Speaking of the D, should I call him?"

"At this hour, even on eastern time? Forget it. Besides, he's not keen to hear anything more about the place out west. Let me handle that."

216

"Fine by me."

"Look, it's still pretty early here so I'm gonna try and get some more shuteye. Anything else going on out there?"

Jack's stomach muscles clenched involuntarily. He'd dialed the number while cautioning himself not to accidentally reveal Ryan's presence, but the question still caught him unawares. More confused than ever concerning who might know about Ryan, Jack still didn't like the flippant way the private investigator had asked that last question. Having rejected the connection to Red Bend that Jack saw in the effigy, Wade was now fishing to see if anything else was going on. Strange behavior for a man trying to get back to sleep.

"Nah, nothing else . . . sorry to wake you."

"No problem. Listen, just for giggles, get a picture of this thing and send it to me. I'll tell the D next time I talk with him." There was a pause, and Jack imagined Wade rubbing the sleep out of his eyes. "Listen, I hope you aren't still sore about our last conversation. It's my job to evaluate things, and I have to call 'em like I see 'em."

"I didn't listen to you, so how sore could I be?"

Wade gave a little laugh. "That's the spirit. Write something good today."

He hung up, and Jack put the cell phone back in its cradle. It was almost full daylight outside, and he heard the short cough of a car door being shut. He drank the last of a cup of instant coffee he'd made before placing the call, and swiveled the chair to look around his tiny abode. His eyes fell on the brand-new skis in the corner, and he was ruefully reminded of how winded he'd become when climbing the fire tower stairs.

Standing, he went to the closet and found the ski pants and sweat top from his last foray on skis. He laid them on the bed and began taking off the jeans he'd worn during his predawn trip. "What the heck. How lost can I get in the daylight?"

Once dressed, he picked up the skis and the poles and carried them out to the stone barbecue. Leaving them there, he went back inside for the map (now encased in a plastic bag) and the cell phone before locking the back door and heading back to the skis. It felt strange to be wearing the same boots which had pained him so much during his last excursion, but he was only going a short distance and felt his feet were healed enough to handle that.

Besides, he needed to clear his mind before deciding if there was indeed a link between that morning's experience at the fire tower and the dead man in California. It was maddening that he had no one to talk to, but Wade had scoffed at the connection and Barron didn't want to hear anything about Red Bend. He felt an unusual pang, regret that he couldn't discuss it with Kelly or Tillman, and marveled that he would feel an impulse to discuss troupe business with a local. He reminded himself that the isolation was symptomatic of the standard progression, where the writer became so familiar to the townspeople that they forgot him. In the past it had allowed him room to write, and he'd been doing just that when this latest distraction had popped up.

Leaning down to snap the binding down over the first ski boot, he took a moment to look for any sign that Ryan might have left a message. There was none, but before he set out he admitted to himself that for the first time in two years, he wished he could talk to Ryan Betancourt.

Jack was gone for less than an hour, but he found the exercise invigorating on many levels. He was pleased to learn that his leg muscles, badly strained during the ordeal, had healed in the interim. Even the blisters on his feet seemed to have recovered, and it made him think of an old hiker's admonition to break in a new set of boots by suffering a long distance in them. He'd never agreed with the explanation that the resulting blisters would create even stronger tissue when they healed, but now he had to wonder.

He found himself gliding along smoothly in the bright whiteness of the woods, enjoying the rich blueness of the new day's sky. Fresh snow had come in overnight, and it coated the tree branches and bushes like white frosting. The sun warmed up the air nicely once it was above the trees, in sharp contrast with the cold he'd encountered at the top of Campion Hill earlier that morning.

The memory of the hanged man should have bothered him, but instead he found it almost as stimulating as the physical exertion. Tillman had been quite concerned by the mannequin, even without knowing what Jack suspected about the pajamas and the robe. Wade, though slightly more friendly than he'd been at the hospital, had been out rightly dismissive of a connection, and that made Jack consider the possibility that the mannequin was indeed nothing more than a prank.

Even that was unacceptable, however, as it added yet another player to the game that was unfolding around him. The Director was basically challenging him on his home field of writing, the advance man believed he was unstable, and the previous writer had turned up alive when he was supposed to be dead. Although Jack found little credence in their excuses for what they were doing or thinking, at least he knew what that was—and who they were. If the jokester who had planted the severed head had also provided the decapitated hanged man, he or she represented a range of unknowns too broad to contemplate.

Sliding through the virgin snow, Jack only knew that he didn't like any of it, and mostly because it was impinging on his own position as the supposed author of that year's mystery show. He stopped in mid-stride, having reached the point on the trail where he'd taken the wrong fork on Groundhog Day, but it wasn't to look at the arrow pointing (this time) to the left. Standing very still, he listened to the near-silence that surrounded him. He sniffed the early morning breeze, detecting nothing, and slowly ranged his eyes over the whitened landscape.

This is what I was supposed *to be doing. Getting the scent of the place. Taking its pulse. Observing, and then letting the inspiration come to me. Instead of getting tangled up in everybody else's weird conspiracies.*

He slowly lifted one ski, turned it away from the other, and set it down. Then he lifted the second one, following the first, and repeated the process until he was pointed back down the trail the way he'd come. His tracks were the only thing before him, and he fitted the skis into the shallow glistening grooves like a scout in enemy territory, retracing his steps to disguise his direction of travel.

That's what I am. The real *advance man, all alone out here, figuring the place out. That's why I write the script, the plan everybody else follows. That's why, no matter how Barron changes it or the actors interpret it, it's my show. It's always my show.*

So forget what everybody else is doing, saying, or plotting. It's my show.

Picking up the glide, he began sliding one foot forward at a time. The new skis hissed against the snow like a backbeat, and he picked it up, repeating the new thought out loud, over and over, gaining strength as he headed back.

"Forget the rest. It's my show. Forget the rest. It's my show."

His cell phone rang while he was in the shower, and when Jack emerged he was in no hurry to answer it. The short trip in the woods had flooded his mind with new ideas, mostly unrelated to the writing of the play itself, and he was anxious to explore some of them. Toweling off his hair, he played the message on the phone and discovered it was just Mel Archer, saying how much she liked the art work on the Barron Players' webpage.

"At least it's not a picture of a guy swinging from the fire tower." He muttered as he opened up the safe and set up the laptop. He'd changed into jeans and a sweater and fixed a cup of coffee by the time the machine was ready, and so he typed in the address for Death Troupe.

Instead of the pitch dark background and the sequential appearance of the double-masked Janus faces, a swirling background of dark blues, blacks, and grays manifested itself across the screen. At first it gave the impression of rolling surf as seen from underwater, but then the cascading effect slowed down and the richer colors leached out of the panoply. The display resolved itself into an off-kilter whitened patch that took up the top third of the screen and, below that, a dull gray area that still appeared to be in a mild form of motion. The shifting colors under the stationary white area lightened just a bit, and a cross-like shadow began to rise from the bottom of the display.

Even though Barron had described this at their last meeting, Jack was still baffled until the murky cross took on the indistinct shape of a dead man, floating under the ice with arms and legs spread wide. The blurry image ascended close to the barrier above it, and rays of dull gray light shone through the whiteness of the ice after all the motion had ceased. The ice had resolved itself into different-shaded swirls of gray, and he thought he could make out a shadowy number seven above the corpse, as if written there by whoever had put the body under the ice. A tiny menu of options then appeared at the bottom of the screen, rocking back and forth slightly until they came into focus, like sediment at the floor of a frozen lake.

"Wow." The word came out on its own, and Jack hit the refresh button to watch the introduction all over again. The people who handled the graphics for Death Troupe's website were true artists, but even this was a step up for them. Thoughts of the designers, mixed with the image of the ice, gave him a sudden inspiration that was so perfect that he experienced an actual thrill.

He reached across for the phone, and hit the speed dial for Lynnie Eckart.

"Now here's the secret to selling this to Barron: Show him something that he'll want to play with."

Jack lifted a can of soda to his lips after imparting his wisdom. He'd spent much of the afternoon at Tadd and Gary's firehouse apartment, looking at the prototype game that Tadd was preparing for Barron. Lynnie was due to drop by later, and he'd taken the opportunity to critique Tadd's presentation.

"But it's a game! Of *course* he'll want to play with it." Tadd's eyes were red from lack of sleep, and he was having trouble following some of Jack's comments.

"That's not what I mean. Barron's never just accepted a single thing I've shown him, no matter how good it was. So use that to your advantage, by giving him something that interests him enough to want to change it."

"I had a boss like that once. You'd write him a program that did everything the client asked for, and still he'd screw with it. I swear the guy was just trying to justify his existence."

"I know the type—but that's not Barron. He's a legitimate genius, and there's only been a few times when I thought his ideas were actually wrong." He looked at the computer screen, where a spectacular sunset was turning the sky orange on a beach lined with palm trees. Tadd (or Lynnie) had chosen *Wind in the Palms* for the demonstration, and had been working on it night and day.

It's nice to see that somebody *can bring that play to the screen.*

The animation was very lifelike, and the characters that Lynnie had drawn up were a true revelation. Although he could usually guess which Death Troupe actor would play a certain role, Jack seldom wrote a play with a living person in mind. He usually had a fully-formed image in his head, frequently bearing no resemblance to the player ultimately assigned to the role, and Lynnie's rendering of those characters had come surprisingly close to his own.

"So here's what we want to do: Barron loved *Wind in the Palms*, but he had a couple of different ways he could have gone with it—"

"I know; they were both in the video." Tapes of the performances had sold well once the troupe became famous, but the true money-maker had been Barron's instructional videos concerning the evolutions of individual plays. They were loaded with directorial gold, but badly divorced from the reality of how the shows being discussed had actually developed. It was yet another of Death Troupe's dirty little secrets, and so Jack had to be careful.

"Right. And you've done a great job incorporating those into the game." Tadd and Lynnie's working demonstration included Jack's own alternate endings, as well as two more scenarios which Barron had touted in the video. On nights out in the desert when he'd been feeling particularly low, Jack had taken to lighting a roaring fire and then playing that tape. He'd laughed mightily at the endings that he'd never heard of before, even as Barron had said they'd come within a hair of being used in the actual show.

"But he had a couple of other ideas early in the process, ones that aren't on that video. I remember when those other endings first popped up, and I think I know what triggered those thoughts in Barron's head. What we're going to do now is write those triggers into this demo, and hope they set him tinkering like they did before."

"You remember stuff that made him think of something else? That's like four, five years ago."

"That kind of thing—having your hard work altered for no apparent reason—happens a lot when you work with a guy like Barron. Remembering what set him off on a tangent was a good way to keep it from happening too much."

"Wow. He really does sound like my old boss." Tadd's face was somber, his voice doubtful. "So I'm supposed to get him to remember those other ideas?"

"Not necessarily. It's almost impossible to predict Barron's reactions. All we want to do is show him something that gets his gears turning. It does have a tradeoff, in that he'll want to change a lot at first, but it'll get you the gig. And the changes will drop off after a while. With how busy he is, he's not going to spend a lot of time managing a videogame."

"What if he catches on to what I'm doing?"

Jack smiled at this. "That's easy. If he asks you something like, 'Did that no-talent bastard Jack Glynn tell you to put that in here?' don't answer it. Just open your eyes as wide as you can, keep your face blank, and ask, 'Ya like it?' just like that."

"Just like what?"

"Like I just did. Don't overdo it; you've got that wide-eyed innocent thing going on anyway, so just be yourself and you'll be fine."

"I dunno . . . this guy sounds a little scary."

"He's a lot scary, but remember the worst thing he can say is no." That was meant to reassure the young computer genius, but clearly the late nights had taken their toll. His face fell at the prospect of coming up empty after so much effort, and Jack saw that he was going to have to do some coaching. "But hey, that's not gonna happen. Chances are he's gonna see one of these triggers, take the hook in his mouth, and you'll have made the sale. But if he smells a rat, just hit him with that 'Ya like it?' line, he'll laugh, and everything'll be fine."

Tadd blinked several times while swiveling his head in a clockwise fashion, obviously trying to get into character. His reddened eyes rounded just a little more, and he asked in a dry, ordinary tone, "Ya like it?"

"That was . . . good. But really, don't try so hard. Just do it naturally."

"Ya like it?"

"Better. Put the accent on the second word: Ya *like* it?"

"Ya like it?"

222

"Ya like it?"

"Ya like it?"

A blonde head appeared at the small room's door, and Lynnie adopted an exaggerated expression of relief. She put one hand on the front of her coat and rested the other on the door frame before speaking. "Whew! You have *no* idea what I thought I was walking in on!"

"I can get a truck to move these things for you." Gary Price, still attired as a representative of the cable company, looked down on a sketch that was spread out on the living room's coffee table. "Depending on how big they are, it can even be covered."

"That would be best," Jack answered from an armchair opposite the trio on the couch. He'd asked Lynnie to work up a diagram of a special piece of art—two, in fact—that he'd commissioned her to create. "You'll be putting these out in the dark of night, and believe me you don't want to get seen doing this."

"Don't worry about that; whole town's asleep by one in the morning." Tadd observed happily, energized by the escapade which Jack had requested. He was sipping from a mug of strong coffee, and the caffeine seemed to be affecting his judgment.

"I don't know about that." Jack murmured, remembering the morning's trip to Campion Hill. "I understand there are some hunters who get a little too close to habitation some nights."

"You must have met Charlie Fannon." Lynnie's bubbly demeanor had been transformed by Jack's commission, and she now spoke in a low, almost analytical tone. The gears in her head were already in motion, and Jack marveled at the change. By profession he spent most of his time with artists, and he drew energy from them whenever they were creating. "He likes to bow hunt a little too close to the town, in-season or not. Drives Marv Tillman crazy."

"How'd you bump into Charlie, Jack?" Gary asked, reaching for his own mug of coffee. "Get lost in the woods again?"

This provoked a few good-natured titters among the youngsters on the couch, but Jack couldn't tell them the truth about how he'd met the hunter.

"Yeah, I was lucky he was nearby." That didn't seem to satisfy Gary, so he waved a hand at the diagram on the table. "I was scouting locations for our little presentation here and was trying not to be seen. It's amazing, who's up late at night around here."

"Don't want to take any chances anyway." Lynnie spoke as if in a trance, her eyes trained on the paper but seeing something else entirely. Jack imagined her envisioning a fully-formed image, rising up from the two dimensions of the sketch as the art took shape in her mind. She appeared to snap out of it with a slight nod, but he figured she'd simply decided how she was going to proceed. Giving a gentle elbow to Gary, she resumed her normal voice. "You never know who might come running down the road half-naked because somebody's husband came home early."

Gary blushed at the remark, elbowing her back. "I was fully clothed. You have to have your escape planned out in advance." He put questioning eyes on Jack again. "I don't know what you're cooking up here, but it sounds to me like you're putting out a couple of clues all your own."

Jack had considered lying to them, saying that Barron had asked him to handle the creation of the two new items, but he'd realized that a careless comment from Tadd during the presentation of the game prototype would boomerang badly.

"Yeah, you could say that. That's why you can't mention this to anybody—especially from Death Troupe."

Lynnie's eyes found his next, and they'd resumed their devilish, seductive challenge. "You bein' bad, Jackie?"

"Very."

It was late in the afternoon of the next day before Jack Glynn came to understand that he'd created a minor schism in the town of Schuyler Mills. He'd written steadily through the day, armed with the ramifications of the two clues that his youthful co-conspirators were creating. If he hoped to force Barron's hand (or, more realistically, give it a nudge) he would have to build those clues into his version of the play in a fashion that Barron would find irresistible. Even while coaching Tadd in the fine art of manipulating the Director, Jack had wondered if he was the right man to be giving that guidance.

He'd been preparing a late lunch when he'd suddenly remembered that the community theater group would be meeting that night. Initially reluctant to get too involved with them, he'd become intrigued by the assignment Barron had asked them to prepare for his Mystery Weekend classes and wanted to see where they were with the scenes from *Macbeth*.

Setting his lunch aside, he picked up the phone and dialed the Lawtons at home. No one answered, so he found Patrice Lawton's cell phone number in his own device's memory. She answered after the first ring.

"Hi Patrice, it's Jack Glynn."

"Jack! How is the play coming along?"

"It's finding its way. But you know Barron; nothing ever stays the same."

"Oh, do we now!" A slight shade of chagrin came over the airwaves, but Patrice didn't sound overly worried. "He's asked us to prepare two new scenes, both from *Hamlet*, and as you can guess it's a lot more work."

Typical Barron, changing things at the last minute. And why Hamlet?

"I didn't know about that. What scenes?"

"Oh, I'd have to look up the exact numbers, but they both involve Ophelia. We're not complaining, mind you. We were concerned about getting Glenda some stage time and this fits her perfectly. Of course she was up to playing Lady Macbeth, but she's closer in age to Ophelia."

Maybe that's the reason. But since when has anything Barron's done been logical?

"I'm sure that's what he's got in mind. Are you working on it tonight?"

There was an uncomfortable pause at the other end, and Jack felt an unreasoning sensation of concern. He didn't have long to wait before finding out it wasn't that unreasonable.

"Why yes, we are, but honestly we've been feeling a little guilty about taking up your time when you've got so much work to do."

A torrent of doubts and questions exploded in his mind. It was absurd that they felt they were taking up his time; he hadn't dropped in on them since getting lost in the woods weeks before. They'd practically twisted his arm in the early days, and he'd never suggested that he had better things to be doing.

What was going on here? Jack had told Barron that he'd been lassoed into helping out, and the Director had been scornfully amused that a writer would be of any value in such an undertaking. There had been no leak about the hanged man from the fire tower, including Rumor Control on the troupe's website, so it couldn't be that. He was still pondering the question when Patrice supplied the answer.

"Kelly's been giving us some wonderful feedback, so we thought it would be better to let you alone to work on the play."

His mouth hung open as he sought the appropriate response to that piece of information. His phone call might have caught Patrice off guard, but not unprepared. She was telling him that his presence at rehearsal might be awkward for Kelly, while also reprimanding him for failing to pursue the young lady.

"Oh . . . oh . . . well it sounds like you've got everything under control there, then."

"I think so. But we'll be sure to call you if we run into anything."

"Please don't hesitate to do that. I'd be happy to help." He answered like some kind of etiquette robot, his mind already racing with the other implications of this new wrinkle.

"Oh we won't." *What does* that *mean? That they won't hesitate to call, or that they won't be calling no matter what?* "I have to go, Jack. I'm sure I'll see you around town."

"Sure. Bye now."

Hanging up, he marveled at the speed with which his situation had changed. Despite his long history with small towns and his genuine affection for them, he now saw that he'd committed the cardinal sin of a Death Troupe writer. He'd alienated part of the community, and in a way which forced some of them to feel they had to choose a side.

He sat back heavily in the chair.

Oh my God. I'm becoming Ryan Betancourt.

The show must go on.

The concept that the show waits for no man was one of the earliest facts about live theater impressed upon Jack as a writer. Even in dinner mystery theater, where he'd originally expected a little flexibility with the timing of events, the performers had stuck to that age-old maxim. When he'd become involved with Death Troupe, he'd detected its presence even in the way Barron ran rehearsals: They began on time and—for the most part—ended on time. Even dress rehearsal had been treated like a real performance, with one of the managers backstage announcing the time warnings of half-hour, fifteen minutes, and then the one-word command of "Places".

Those time checks were like a dinner bell for most of his actor friends, whetting their theatrical appetites, but Jack considered them a thing of dread, the final elapse of the time that had been available to him as a writer. Just thinking of that ominous countdown, and the knowledge that the curtain would rise at the prescribed time, usually jolted him into greater efforts during the writing phase.

That evening was no different, despite the cavalcade of distractions that had slowly piled up over the previous weeks. Though some were of his own making—like the unauthorized clue provision scheduled for late that night and the prickly situation with Kelly—most of them were not and he now found he resented them. He couldn't figure them out, and in one part of his mind he suspected they were the product of overwrought imaginations and competing egos. Didn't they see he had a play to write? Didn't they understand that nothing could commence until a completed script was finally approved by the Director? The show might go on, but it wouldn't be very good without the words he was tasked to create.

Jack had always taken a workmanlike approach to writing, and relied on several techniques which had served him well when he'd been at a loss for inspiration. Reviewing the work he'd already done usually provided something else to do, be it the next logical step in the mystery or the development of a character that needed fleshing out. Barron's process of building a play—providing general guidance and refining rough ideas—had worked in concert with that approach and Jack had never failed to meet a deadline.

Even so, he'd come to consider Barron's method a crutch on which a lazy writer could lean once too often. The Director's penchant for unpredictable changes had initially caused Jack to put forth less than his greatest effort, as he'd come to expect his work to be modified whether he agreed or not. That attitude had allowed him to drift along in Barron's slipstream for their first two shows, but somewhere in the middle of the third engagement Jack had decided to give his imagination free reign.

Wind in the Palms had been the result, and even though the Director and the players had added their own modifications the resulting performance had been substantively what Jack had written. It had received great praise from the audience and the critics, and he would have felt he was actually getting somewhere if Barron hadn't then brought in a second writer, someone to help with creating the big moments that had eluded Jack until the extraordinary script he'd just penned.

As much as he'd fought it, the addition of Ryan had slowly put him back in the original mode of not caring if his bigger ideas were accepted or not. He'd retreated into building sensible frameworks for the mysteries they wrote, abandoning the high drama to the new writer from Broadway. He still didn't know it, but that decision had begun a slow process of disengagement which had ended when he'd quit the troupe over what Ryan and Allison had done to him.

Tapping away at his desk in the Great View, Jack was equally unaware that the events of the past few weeks were threatening to do the same thing to him in Schuyler Mills.

It was nine o'clock when Jack walked into Maddy's Place. It was packed, but the prevalence of broad-shouldered hockey shirts told him that an important contest was taking place on the ice somewhere. Both television sets were broadcasting the same game, and Jack was pleased to see the large number of female residents who were also giving the contest their full and rowdy attention.

The game also gave him the chance to get well inside before being detected. He'd wanted to gauge the reception he'd receive, now that people were allegedly choosing sides in his nonexistent love affair with Kelly. Maddy greeted him in the middle of the floor, and seemed happy to see him in Old Town once again. Tamara made a similar comment after giving him a big hug, and he briefly pondered the notion that his growing connection to Newville might be the root of the problem after all.

If that was the case, the items that Lynnie, Gary, and Tadd were preparing weren't going to improve things—if they were identified as having provided them.

He was casting about for a place to sit when he felt a rough finger poke him in the back.

"Hey Jack, I'd like you to meet my better half." Bib's voice came from behind him, and Jack turned to discover he was seeing double. The infamous severed mannequin head from the ice fisherman's hole was perched on Bib's shoulder, and Bib was leering at him with a drunken smile.

Jack could see the rubber disc which had served to imitate the hole cut in the ice, folded on one side nearest Bib's neck so that the monstrosity could be attached to his shoulder. One strap of the big man's overalls was fitted over the disc, but a wide strip of silver duct tape ran from the other side and disappeared inside Bib's shirt.

"Um, Bib, that thing's not taped to your chest hair, is it?" Jack asked, stepping closer as if to inspect the area where the tape vanished inside his shirt. Bib swept a hand up to block the view and stepped away.

"Hey, I'm not that kinda gal, mister . . . at least not until I've had a drink or two!" The crowd gave up a loud yell at that point, and Bib swung around to look up at the television. The opposing side had scored a goal on the town favorites, and Bib grimaced as if in true pain.

"Oh, don't look!" He advised in disgust, raising a large hand to cover the mannequin head's eyes before moving off through the crowd.

Jack found a spot in a booth with a few locals who weren't completely consumed by the game, and discovered that his failure as a match for Kelly Sykes hadn't made it all the way around town yet. He chatted with them for awhile and then offered to buy a round. The Maddens' wait staff was badly outnumbered, and so he squeezed out of the booth to make good on his offer.

As Jack approached the end of the bar furthest from the televisions, he saw the wide expanse of Bib's back, now minus the plastic head. It sat on the bar next to him, facing in Jack's direction as he approached, and he could easily imagine how it would appear to be a human head floating in an ice fisherman's hole. He hopped up on the bar stool in front of it.

"You two have a falling out?"

"I don't know what we're even doing together anymore. We just don't see eye to eye on anything." Bib glanced at the trophy. "But you know, a little time apart can be good for a relationship."

Jack picked up the head, surprised at how heavy it was. He flipped back one of the two long strips of duct tape in expectation of seeing thousands of Bib's chest (and perhaps back) hairs. Instead he was presented with another strip of duct tape, mated to the first one to sandwich a bungee cord which had obviously kept the thing fastened to Bib's overalls.

"You son of a bitch."

"Hey, you mystery guys aren't the only ones who can play a joke." Bib downed a shot of some brown liquid and signaled to the bartender. "Don't you go tryin' to take that, Jack Glynn. I've grown very attached to it."

Jack flipped the head over and saw that its insides were solid. He couldn't see any manufacturer's marks, and his roving fingers found nothing stamped or embossed to indicate its origin. He finally put it back down, and when he turned to Bib he saw that the big man had bought him a shot of whatever he was drinking.

"What's this?" he asked, indicating the short glass.

"Some nice Kentucky bourbon. Puts hair on yer chest." Bib reached across and flipped one of the phony duct tape fasteners in the air. "Or back on it, if need be."

"Oh, I dunno about this . . . I grew fangs and claws last time I drank that stuff."

Bib studied him for a moment, as if considering whether or not to tell him to hit the road. "Ya know, we got a few gals in this town who've got fangs and claws . . . maybe you should drink that and go find one of 'em."

Jack returned the stare as long as he deemed wise, and then downed the drink in a gulp. It left a pleasant sting, but he knew it would quickly jump on top of any other alcohol he might consume. "What makes you say something like that?"

"You disappoint me, Jack. I thought you writers were supposed to be fun. You're a pantywaist drinker, you can't ski for shit, and you're a wallflower to boot." He reached across him, turning the mannequin's head so that it faced away. "We can't stand to look at you."

The bartender approached and asked Jack if he wanted something more, and he remembered his thirsty friends from the booth. Bib had gone back to watching the game, so Jack paid for the drinks when they arrived and gathered them up in his hands. Slipping off the stool, he mumbled something to Bib about talking later and had almost made his escape when the big man spoke again.

"Hey Jack."

He turned to see that Bib was holding the mannequin head in front of his own, as if he'd been replaced by the trophy. "Write a good play, buddy. It's your only hope."

Chapter Sixteen

He barely slept that night, but the phone didn't ring until after dawn and so he had to believe that his trio of conspirators had accomplished their mission without being detected. When it did ring, it was Kelly Sykes inviting him down to the volunteer fire department to see the latest clue. He was so pleased to hear her voice that at first he didn't ponder her assumption that he was unaware of the troupe's new hint.

He did consider that, however, after dressing for the cold morning and driving the short distance downhill to the fire department. The building housed the town's one fire engine, assorted firefighting gear, and a large exercise room in the back which the town offered to its residents as a sort of civic gymnasium. Jack had run on one of the treadmills there when he'd first arrived, and had decided that the fire station would be a perfect place for one of the new clues.

The item stood in the snow-covered grass bordering Main Street where it forked for the Playhouse or out to Newville. The woods closed in on this spot, and so Lynnie and the guys had placed the clue as close to the road as possible. The large firehouse building was visible through the trees, and Jack had little difficulty imagining the scene at three o'clock that morning: Gary parking the truck where it couldn't be seen from the road, and then using a two-wheeler to wrestle the thing into place with Tadd's help and Lynnie's direction.

Kelly was wrapped up in the olive drab comforter coat again, and wearing a kind of peaked knit cap that Jack always associated with pictures of Nepalese mountain climbers. The cap covered her ears and then ended in two tails that could be tied under her chin. She was sipping from a large Styrofoam cup of coffee while a gaggle of the town's citizens, also dressed for the elements, snapped pictures of the newest monument in Schuyler Mills.

"My my my!" Jack announced appreciatively as he approached. "This is a first for the Jerome Barron Players: An ice sculpture clue!"

"Hello, Jack." Kelly gave him a suspicious smile. "It *is* nice, isn't it?"

The sculpture stood five feet tall, but fully half of that was its base. The foundation was almost three feet across and three deep, and the object carved out of the top half of the ice was a large violin. Jack had expected it to be simple, envisioning the instrument standing vertically on its frozen base. Lynnie had outdone herself, however: The ice-blue violin was canted from left to right and also slightly back, and the detail was exquisite.

The strings, though not carved individually, stretched across the raised bridge in the narrowest part of the instrument's body and gracefully reached up to the scroll at the top. A reed-thin bow had been carved out right next to the violin, as if laid on top of the foundation, and Jack pretended to be looking at it when he moved a little closer.

He really wanted to see the only part of the clue that he'd actually specified, and again he wasn't disappointed. The S-shaped holes cut into the violin's body on either side of the bridge had been modified, and he found he didn't have to explain them.

"It's a clue all right." Kelly decided, stepping up next to him and pointing at the notches in the ice. "These here are called F holes on a normal violin, because they resemble the letter F when it's written in script. The one on the left's been changed to look like a dollar sign, and the one on the right's a seven. The symbol for money, and the symbol for the Seven Gang. Clever."

Jack nodded, trying to hide his satisfaction. Kelly continued.

"There's another one of these, not an exact replica, standing in front of the bowling alley in Newville. So we have two violins."

Close. Very close. But not exactly right.

Kelly turned interested eyes toward him. "Like to give me a hint what they mean?"

"Aw, that would be cheating. Besides, I only make suggestions about these things. Barron makes the final decision."

She was still staring into his eyes, and her lips curled in disbelief. "So it *is* a clue."

"I learned a long time ago not to make that assumption until the thing was confirmed on Rumor Control." *And I doubt this one's gonna get confirmed anytime soon.*

Her half-smile teetered on the brink of a full-on smirk, and she turned away after studying him a few seconds more. "Well whatever it is, it'll last a while in this climate."

She stepped back, produced a cell phone camera, and began snapping pictures.

That's exactly what I was thinking.

Jack would have liked to observe the commentary on Rumor Control from a table at Wicked Wanda's, but he didn't want to do anything that might draw attention to Lynnie and the guys. He'd received a tame email from Tadd after returning to the Great View, a friendly note with photos of the two violins that said the latest clues looked great. Jack hoped Lynnie wasn't behind the counter at Wicked Wanda's with bags under her eyes, but he'd have to wait to find out.

He knew of a small bookstore in Newville that offered Internet access and coffee, so he packed up his laptop and headed over there in the midmorning. Although Rumor Control was largely a static presentation of photos and Berni's commentary, there was a live chat bar on one side that sometimes got quiet lively. Berni hadn't made a ruling on the authenticity of the new clues, and Jack felt cautious optimism that Barron was even then trying to determine their meaning. If he could figure that out, or if he simply liked them, there was a chance that the Director might incorporate them into the play. In that case Jack would have managed, for the first time that engagement, to influence his headstrong boss.

The chat room discussion of the sculptures had been moving right along when Jack accessed the site, and numerous pictures of the two violins had been posted. The debate had startled him at first, as the size of the ice violins had confused some people into thinking they were cellos. Fearful that Tadd or Lynnie might intervene to set the others straight, he'd been relieved to see how many people knew that a violin has a chin rest and a cello does not. Lynnie had been exact in her reproduction, and the chin rest was clearly visible in the photos.

The discussion updated frequently, and Jack was complimented by the seemingly endless supply of interpretations, some of which he found quite intriguing. The dollar sign and the number seven on both violins had been taken as intended, meaning a reference to the Seven Seas Gang, but a rather obvious conclusion that he'd overlooked was soon being offered. Several people thought the violins were a reference to the old gangster movies, where the criminals had used violin cases to carry their Thompson machineguns.

Jack was enjoying that particular line of speculation when a new player entered the fray. The identifying names in the chat were all pseudonyms, and the new participant went by the moniker of Scarlet. That didn't catch Jack's eye at first, but the newcomer's question did. Popping up on top of a long list of comments about the violins, it asked bluntly:

Has anyone heard anything about a clue that was supposedly displayed on the Campion Hill Fire Tower? It was a dummy of some kind, hung from the tower, but someone took it down before anyone saw it.

The discussion of the violins continued for a few more entries before the fresh topic received a response, and several of the participants expressed both ignorance and interest in the allegedly missing clue.

Scarlet only made one more contribution, but it was a big one. After being asked how he or she had heard about this missing clue, Scarlet answered simply:

Maybe you should ask Jack about that one.

Somehow the steaming mug of coffee in his hands stopped transmitting heat, and Jack felt the hair on the back of his neck rising as if someone were staring at him from behind. That was impossible, as his back was to one of the sitting area's walls, but Jack looked around nonetheless. The bookstore had few patrons at that hour, and none of them paid him any mind, so he looked back at the chat bar in time to see that Scarlet had gone offline.

Scarlet. Red.

Red Bend.

It took two days before the full ramifications of Jack's violin clues were evident. Though sorely tempted to call Wade or Barron about the appearance of the Scarlet entity, Jack knew that he'd well and truly cornered himself with his unauthorized hints. Barron and Berni were no doubt trying to decide on a proper response to the intriguing ice sculptures, but a sudden phone call from their headstrong writer might connect the dots for them. He'd contacted Wade regarding the Campion Hill effigy on the morning it had appeared, and it stood to reason that questions regarding its alleged disappearance would be directed at Tillman.

But that wasn't what Scarlet had suggested. Jack had returned to Rumor Control several times to see where the discussion was going, and had been relieved to see that the violins were still its primary focus. Finding no more comments from Scarlet, he'd re-examined the mysterious communication and been impressed by its phrasing.

Its first part had been conversational, and had even suggested it was a Schuyler Mills resident asking if anyone else had heard the rumor. Death Troupe had fans all over the globe by then, so it wasn't unusual to get people chatting who weren't associated with the host town. People identifying themselves as outsiders had taken up the issue of the missing dummy, but it was the second part of Scarlet's missive that now occupied Death Troupe's playwright.

Maybe you should ask Jack about that one.

Scarlet hadn't sounded like a resident with that comment. Whoever it was, the entity was telling the people in Schuyler Mills to ask the troupe's writer. Not 'maybe *we* should ask Jack' but 'maybe *you* should ask Jack'. It smacked of manipulation, and Jack began to consider the possibility that Scarlet had put the effigy on the tower in the first place.

Berni, in her role of anonymous arbiter of the Rumor Control page, had finally addressed the mounting questions about Campion Hill. Continuing the off-hand tone of previous denials, she'd politely dismissed the issue of the allegedly missing clue. Her gossip columnist alter ego laughingly suggested that someone had been watching too many horror movies, and Jack wondered just how Scarlet, or whoever had put the thing up there, was taking that insult.

He didn't get to wonder long, as the marvelously unexpected consequences of his ice sculpture clues began unfolding shortly after that.

He'd written steadily for most of two days, and even though he found the results dissatisfying he now had a concept that went all the way from start to finish. It was mid-afternoon, and he wouldn't have answered the phone except he was exhausted and didn't want to write anymore. He'd been bombarded with questions about the sculptures and the hanged man on the first day, but shutting the phone off had passed the message that he wouldn't be providing any answers.

The voice on the other end was Lynnie's, and she sounded like she was in seventh heaven even though her artwork had been on display for days. She'd phoned from Wicked Wanda's, but had been interrupted before being able to say why she'd called. Ending the conversation abruptly, she'd simply told him she had a customer and that he should take a drive down to the town common.

She hadn't seemed frightened or even mildly disturbed by whatever was happening, so Jack approached the town center without trepidation. Even so, he selected a side street that took him through much of the housing on the slope of Campion Hill, in order to get a look at the common from above. Startled by the amount of activity on the white expanse below him, he climbed out of the truck and studied the scene.

The sun made the snow glisten, but it reflected much more strongly off of the items that were being deposited at intervals on the common's outer edge. Figures in parkas and winter hats were circulating among a variety of trucks and cars, and he even made out the image of a stepladder next to one of the new objects. A roaring sound came to him then, and he realized what he was seeing.

The Schuyler Mills town common had been transformed into a workshop and display station for over a dozen ice sculptures. Some were arriving as the finished project, others were being created before his eyes, and still more stood out as large, unsullied blocks of frozen water. Squinting in the glare, he recognized Tillman's jacket and, next to him, the smaller figure of Melanie Archer. They didn't seem exercised by the events taking place before them, and just before he started up the truck again Jack was sure he saw Tillman applauding something one of the artists was doing.

He pulled up outside Wicked Wanda's and waved inside at Lynnie, who was standing by one of the display windows. She actually hopped up and down when she saw him, and then disappeared. He decided she was grabbing her coat, and turned to marvel at the group working twenty yards in front of him.

Their block of ice was ten feet tall at least, and one of the artists was carving off the top-most corners with a light chainsaw while someone else held his stepladder steady. A few yards further down another crew was putting the finishing touches on a bird that Jack finally recognized as a phoenix, its wings spread in the flames and a tongue of fire leaping from its upturned mouth.

The door opened behind him, and Lynnie emerged in a long red parka with the hood up. Her mouth was open, and she looked right past him at the sight of the sculptures in progress. Looking down, he saw an enchantment on her face that he normally associated with small children at Christmastime, but then he corrected himself. For an artist like her, this experience was probably very similar to Christmas.

"Great job the other night." He muttered, after making sure no one else was near them on the sidewalk. More cars and trucks were arriving around them, onlookers now, and he knew he had to be careful. "You do beautiful work."

"They did come out well, didn't they?" she gave him a glance and then looked back across the common. "We almost got spotted at the bowling alley, but Tadd and Gary just froze in place and whoever it was drove right by them."

"All three of you did a great job. The website's burning up with questions about the sculptures."

"I know!" she exclaimed, giving him her full attention. "I've *never* gotten this much publicity. Too bad I can't claim it."

"You will. Right after the show, if not sooner." He pumped a thumb at the carnival erupting in front of them. "So what exactly's going on here? Did we start a feud or something?"

She laughed as she answered. "In a way, yeah! There's a lot of people who cut ice around here, and they don't sit still when they think they've been called out. These here—" she tossed her head "—they're only the latest. They started popping up last night, some at the bowling alley, a few by the supermarket, but now it's wide open."

The consequences for his own ice sculpture clues, and in fact many of the other hints that the troupe had yet to provide, now began to take shape in Jack's mind. Over the years, Barron had developed only one concern about third parties providing clues, and this was it: He could deny a small number of them, but if they became legion the whole distribution was in danger.

"Maybe you should have warned me about that." He said in a musing voice.

"In case you forgot, I'm a *woman*, Jack." She stated proudly while bumping him once with her hip. "I'm not gonna warn you about anything."

Events took on a life of their own for several days after that, and Jack watched it all unfold with rising satisfaction. He drew a perverse pleasure from the knowledge that he'd unwittingly unleashed a tide of creativity on the town. He was also reasonably sure that he'd greatly complicated the schemes of whoever was toying with him, and found that pleasurable too. Having spent so many of the previous weeks as an unwitting pawn, he now found that pulling other people's strings made for a pleasant change.

The ice sculpting community had led the charge, but they were closely followed by the wood carvers. Jack had seen many of their wares on display all over the Adirondack region, and had been mightily impressed by their creations. At first he'd thought they restricted themselves to larger-than-life depictions of the many animals that lived in the area, but he now saw that they were just as versatile as the people who worked with ice. Tillman had encouraged the first wave of artists to show their handiwork on the town common, and soon the many glistening statues left by the ice sculptors were joined by similar-sized works in wood.

Jack had taken to skiing down to the common to view the array, and he was even more impressed to see that the newer arrivals were very much attuned to the play he was writing. Tommy guns and violins abounded, sacks of money spilled from open safes, and the emblem of the Seven Seas Gang (sometimes represented as the 7 Cs) was stamped on most of it.

It didn't end with the chainsaw brigade, however. The ladies of the sewing club had been laboring on an enormous banner for the approaching Mystery Weekend, to be strung across Main Street near the common, and had no intention of being left out. Jack was told that they'd rushed their masterpiece to completion with an all-night session and then enlisted their male friends and relatives to hang it. Their handiwork was now stretched across the road near the sign announcing that this was indeed Schuyler Mills, and Jack found the banner a thing of beauty.

Kelly Sykes had designed an ingenious logo for Mystery Week, and the sewing ladies had emblazoned the banner with Kelly's symbol at either end. Admiring the work one day, Jack saw that the design was meticulously needle-pointed onto the streamer with nylon thread. The logo itself was a rough-edged oval of gold meant to represent the illumination thrown by a single candle standing upright on a rough wooden table. The candle was flanked on the right by an old parchment book laid on its side and on the left by three short (and partially collapsed) stacks of gold coins. In front of the candle—and partially obscuring it—was a crystal skull that appeared to be bleeding onto the table. It took a second viewing to see that the skull was actually made of ice and that the pool of blood was the water melted by the candle.

Even the less artistically inclined residents of Schuyler Millers got into the act, as one group of enthusiasts adopted the large number seven overlooking the town from the opposite side of Long Lake. Originally created with two broad stretches of red fabric staked to the ground, the brand of the Seven Seas Gang had started to shift around over time. In an operation that would have done justice to the cleaning of a Renaissance fresco, the recreationists had delicately removed each of the retaining stakes and then fastened the freed fabric to a red-painted hay bale. Proceeding down the length of one arm and then the other, they'd realigned the entire seven and then staked the hay bales in place for good measure. The gangster emblem now stood out in three dimensions on the hill, a mutely powerful statement of ownership.

Tillman had greeted the town's artistic reawakening like an early spring, and had done everything in his power to encourage further civic participation in the days leading up to Mystery Weekend. The town movie theater, already prepped to show mysteries non-stop for the entire event, began running classic murder films for free every other night. Lunch specials from Old Town to Newville were renamed to honor great detectives and villains of the genre. Finally, in an act that was not detected for a full day, Tillman had the town workers erect a chain link barrier topped with barbed wire around the base of the Campion Hill Fire Tower. When questioned about this, he'd motioned to the explosion of artistry on the town common and asked if anyone felt a hanged man had a place amid such beauty.

And best of all, the exuberance of the town's citizenry had so covered Schuyler Mills with arcane symbols that any further clue distribution Barron might have been contemplating was out of the question. He'd finally broken down and called Jack once the situation in town had been fully explained to him.

"What the heck are you doing to those poor people, Jack?" He'd asked in a tone that was only half-kidding. "They've all gone murder-happy."

"Oh that's not necessarily true. Some of the sculptures are of angels, or bears . . . hey, I just remembered, they've even got one in wood that's a small car!"

"Good Lord. And just how are we supposed to seed the area with clues if the place is already littered with angels and bears and small cars?"

"Ooh." Jack knew he couldn't fool the Director with his acting, so he'd decided to pretend ignorant amusement. "I hadn't thought of that . . . what if we just pick a few of them, build the story around the clues they might represent, take their pictures, and put them up on Rumor Control as our own? Save us a heck of a lot of effort."

There was a long silence, and he envisioned Barron rubbing his forehead with his eyes clamped shut in pain. "And what would we do when the people who made those items came forward and said they weren't clues at all?"

Jack let a couple of beats go by before answering. "Hey, how about the two violins then? The ones that started the whole thing? Nobody's claimed them yet, so how about we say they're ours?"

"Are you just playing with me, or have you actually lost your mind?"

"No, seriously, here's what I'm thinking for the clue: There were two of them, and even though everybody thinks they're violins, what's another name for a violin?"

"A Stradivarius?" It was Barron's turn to be sarcastic.

"No, that's a brand of violin."

"A fiddle?"

"Yes! And there's *two* of them . . ."

"Two fiddles. Fiddling around. First and second fiddle. Playing second fiddle. A character who's sick of being unappreciated. Is that what you're thinking?"

"Exactly. I've got a character in my version of the play who's an assistant to . . ." Jack caught himself, remembering that someone might be listening in. ". . . well, you know who. Anyway, we could claim the two violins as legitimate clues and then massage the story so the assistant is one of the suspects. Whaddya think?"

"Great, except we have the same problem. What do we do when the clown who put them out there in the first place claims them as his own?"

"Oh, I don't think we have to worry about that." Jack let the rich insinuation of the words drip from his mouth, and it didn't take Barron long to catch on.

"You son of a bitch." He exhaled in a low growl. "She *said* you were behind this!"

"She? Who's 'she'?"

"Berni, of course. Who else would it be? And don't try to change the subject! You did this?"

"Maybe we shouldn't discuss this over an open line . . ."

"Screw the open line! You planted a clue without consulting me?"

"Why yes, Jerry, I did. I just thought it up and did it, and to hell with the consequences. I guess I wanted to be just like you."

The Director began coughing loudly, and Jack recognized this as his patented means of hiding that he was laughing. "*That*'ll be the day . . . so I bet you've already got a nice little story rigged up behind this rotten-assistant character, eh?"

"I've got some ideas." Although Barron sounded mildly intrigued by the 'second fiddle' clue, Jack decided to force the issue. "So what about it? You gonna have Berni put the company stamp on those two marvelous ice sculptures?"

"I'll think about it. Just tell me one thing: Where'd you get them?"

The explosion of self-expression which gripped Schuyler Mills spared almost no one, including Jack Glynn. He'd noticed this effect in the past, as a fledgling writer huddled with like-minded scribblers, during his time with the murder dinner troupe that had introduced him to Barron, any time he came into contact with Barron himself, and through most of his collaboration with Ryan.

Long a student of inspiration, Jack believed there was more to this phenomenon than shared learning and peer rivalry. Privately he believed that the world contained a creative energy that had no physical form (and therefore no boundaries) and that this power sometimes reached out and tapped into real human beings walking the planet. He suspected that the gathering of creative minds can attract that energy the same way a cluster of positively charged particles near the ground can summon their negative counterparts from a cloud overhead—and frequently with similar results.

Right or wrong in that belief, he now found himself in one of those exhilarating periods when he'd rather be writing than doing anything else. Times like those didn't necessarily guarantee a product that was great or even good, but the desire to create was so strong that it hardly mattered. In fact, he found a thrill in the recognition that the passages he knew to be mediocre did not strike fear into his heart the way they normally would have. The words of his various writing instructors and professional mentors over the years came back to him at times like these, and he found a new understanding in their advice: Writing is rewriting. The rough draft is just that. You can't polish what you haven't written.

Things that made for a normal life—like a daily routine that followed the sun—took a back seat to times like these, and he exulted in that change because it served as proof that his writing was indeed the most important thing in his life. It wasn't a conscious choice on his part, like deciding to repaint the bathroom or go buy the groceries, but an overarching reallocation of his existence that was as undeniable as breathing. Day turned into night, breakfast turned into dinner, and the laptop or the writing tablet beckoned even when he was asleep. He would often awake with a new idea—as if he'd merely been on a break and not unconscious—and he would see the empty seat before the desk not as his station in some pointless assembly line, but as the pilot's seat in a ship that could go anywhere.

Despite the mind-blowing implications of all that, his body did require exercise and he obeyed it without question. He'd taken to skiing down to the common late at night, to enjoy the latest additions to the exhibit, and to take a few laps in an area that was safely lighted.

It was one in the morning when he got there, and the square was deserted by then. Maddy's was dark and quiet, but that wasn't surprising because Barron was due to arrive the next evening and even though it would only be Wednesday it would kick off the non-stop flurry of activity that promised to be Mystery Weekend. He glided around the entire perimeter of the square, stopping frequently to view the artwork more closely. Many of the wood carvings towered over him, from intricately etched totem poles to life-size bears and a marvelously constructed Eiffel Tower. In between these longer-lasting works stood the ice sculptures, glistening swans and translucent angels, a man-sized penguin and an ingenious waterfall that would actually come into motion as the artwork melted.

He was more warmly dressed on these short forays to the town center than in his regular trail skiing, because it was bitterly cold at that hour and because he wouldn't be exerting himself as much. Although he enjoyed seeing the latest sculptures and carvings deposited on the fringe of the large field, Jack found greater pleasure in simply coasting around, marveling at how much he felt at home in a place he'd never visited until a few weeks before.

He looked at the hotel, up at the corner room that he'd first occupied, and remembered the long nights looking out that window, sorting out his feelings toward Ryan and his concern over the play he was tasked to write. Gliding along effortlessly in the direction of the Civil War monument, he thought of the many pleasant hours he'd spent on that same ground with Kelly. He hadn't seen or heard from her since the violins had appeared, and could only conclude that she was busy with preparations for the big weekend.

He was lost in thought about the pretty publicity specialist when another cross-country skier appeared out of the darkness beyond the edge of the common. The street lights ringing the expanse illuminated the long row of artwork, causing the ice sculptures to twinkle when Jack moved about, and he'd only detected the other man's approach after he'd actually crossed onto the square.

Jack had seen this lone skier before, from the hotel's corner window, and recognized the man's easy grace as he drew closer. He didn't glide as much as roll, his shoulders swaying from side to side, and Jack felt a moment's fear when he saw that the man was headed straight for him. He was standing between a carving of a stag rearing on its hind legs and an ice sculpture of The Phantom of the Opera, both life-sized, and suddenly experienced the desire to be more fully visible. His eyes moved to his left and right several times as he slid out into the open, and he saw with alarm that there wasn't a set of headlights anywhere around.

The approaching skier's dark clothing stood out against the snow, making Jack notice that a single action would remove the reflective vest from his torso and allow him to easily escape into the nearby shadows. Both of the skier's hands were wrapped around the handles of the pigstickers, but he wore a loose top with big pockets that could hold anything.

Standing there feeling like a fool, Jack now realized what he'd sensed the only other time he'd seen this skier, weeks before: The man's athleticism reminded him of Ryan Betancourt. Only his belief that Ryan was dead, and his ignorance about the writer's claim of a doppelganger in Red Bend, had prevented him from seeing this similarity at the time. The figure's face was almost invisible behind dark ski goggles, but his chin and sallow cheeks resembled Ryan's.

Jack looked about him once more, this time for a weapon, but none was at hand. Trying to stay calm, he quickly slipped the thong of one pigsticker off his left wrist and leaned the pole against the now-disquieting image of The Phantom of the Opera. He flexed his left hand as if working out a cramp while changing his grip on the remaining pigsticker so that he could use it to defend himself if necessary.

The other skier, as tall and thin as Ryan, slid on by and then stopped between the two large sculptures behind him. Jack turned in place, and the new arrival fixed him with a blank stare that seemed to last an hour. The dark ski hat was pulled down so far on the man's head that it was impossible to see the color of his hair, and to Jack he appeared to be almost a skeleton. He finally reached up with the poles still hanging from his wrists and raised the goggles, convincing Jack that he was in the presence of the man that Ryan Betancourt had described as his double.

"What's the matter, Jack?" The thin man asked, his breath turning to fog as it emerged from his mouth. "Don't you recognize me?"

"Hello, Ryan." He managed to get that out after listening to his heart thunder for a second or two. When he spoke again it was with quiet indignation. "For a moment there I thought you were that twin of yours, the one you saw in California."

The corners of Ryan's thin lips flashed up and down, once, in what Jack perceived as an involuntary admission that he'd intended that very effect. "Sorry about that. I've been traveling around all wrapped up like this for so long that I forgot how it looks." The words were distant and bleached out, and so unlike the man he'd known that Jack took a moment to inspect him more closely. Though preoccupied with his own survey of the area, Ryan caught the scrutiny and slowly replaced the goggles.

"Ryan, I saw a man skiing down this very road the evening I arrived in town. About this time of night, too, and dressed just like you are."

"It *was* me. I've been all over this town, and nobody's been the wiser."

"That's not what I meant. Why were you outside my hotel in the middle of a freezing cold night?"

Ryan cocked his head to the side, his lips taught with disapproval. "What have I been trying to tell you, Jack? As long as you're the troupe's writer, you're in danger. Me and my guys have been watching over you most of the time you've been here."

"Except that one unlucky night out in the woods."

"You'd been on your own for more than one night when that happened. Wade had been in town, so we had to lay low." He looked around him again, appearing impatient to go. "Which is why I'm here now. With Barron due to arrive, I'm gonna have to stay away for awhile. At least until this 'Mystery Weekend' is over."

"That mean your guys are going to be gone too?" Jack asked this in a low voice, having drawn a feeling of security from the idea of Ryan's helpers even if he'd never been able to see them.

The question obviously caught Ryan off guard, as his head jerked back in Jack's direction before he corrected himself and resumed his scan of the area. Jack's eyes narrowed as he registered the idiosyncrasy that he'd most disliked in Ryan: The man couldn't bear to look flustered, or un-cool in anyway, and could never admit that it had actually happened. The years he'd spent with Ryan raised a second question before the first one was answered.

Is he alone *here?*

"Yes, Jack, my guys will be out of town too. People in Wade's profession have a knack for picking their own out of a crowd, and there's too big a chance he'd spot one of them." He leaned far out on the skis, looking up the road from behind the Phantom. "So watch your back for the next few days. And keep checking the message drop."

He planted the ski poles in the snow and was just about to push off when Jack spoke in a low, solicitous voice. "Ryan."

"I'm a little exposed here, Jack, so make it quick."

"Been a little tough on you out there, hasn't it?"

Ryan's head swung toward him, but it was impossible to see what was going on behind the goggles. His jaw tilted toward the ground for an instant, and Jack could almost feel the weariness seeping out of the man. When Ryan replied, it was with a tone of exhausted concern that he'd never heard from him before.

"Like you'll never know." The light reflecting off of the goggles made his face look even more like a skull. He recovered quickly, and spoke with a fierce conviction.

"That's why we have to *get* this guy, Jack. You and me. For what he's done to both of us . . . and what he might do to Allison and the troupe." He pushed off with an effort, and said over his shoulder as he slid up the road, "You and me, Jack. You and me."

Chapter Seventeen

As was usually the case with Barron, time seemed to speed up around him. He wasn't due to arrive until Wednesday evening, but Jack had watched the remaining hours slip through his fingers anyway. He'd spent the morning preparing his Mystery Weekend presentation, a two-hour workshop that he hoped would be sparsely attended, and then headed over to Newville to help Tadd and Gary get their place together for the Director's visit.

The two bachelors had proved themselves adept with a vacuum cleaner, but it took Lynnie's direction to get the kitchen cleaned properly. Jack had helped the men transport what seemed like a thousand empty beer cans to the reclamation center, and had then manned a mop as they cleaned the stone floor of the garage.

Tadd had wanted to move his computer out into the living room, but Jack had counseled against it. "Barron's going to want to see the demo the same way a gamer would see it, so it'll just be you and him in your room, sitting in front of your machine. He might not know much about technology, but he knows everything there is to know about dress rehearsals—and those have to be as close to the real thing as possible."

He did have an ulterior motive for that decision, though, and pulled Gary aside when Tadd and Lynnie went to pick up the pizzas they would have for a late lunch. "Listen, I know you think you haven't got a speaking part in this thing, but you're wrong. I've got a very important role for you. You're going to be our gigolo."

"I can do that."

"I know you can. Barron's got a ferocious assistant named Bernice, a very pretty young lady, but with a mind like a steel trap. I don't want her throwing questions at Tadd—"

"*That's* why you want him to do the demo in his room!"

"Mostly. The part about Barron and dress rehearsals is true, but I really don't want Berni in a position to interrupt. So I want you to dress up nice without overdoing it, and separate her from the group as soon after they get here as you can manage. Give her a tour of the firehouse, take her for a walk down by the river, anything that keeps her from squeezing into that room."

"You did say she was pretty, right?"

"Very. But she's a friend, too, so don't get carried away with your performance."

"You'd make a good director, Jack. Ever think about that?"

"Yes, but it's usually in the middle of a nightmare."

He'd left the firehouse gang late in the afternoon, changed into a pair of gray dress slacks and his maroon sweater, and then driven to the Visitor's Center to be on hand when Barron got to town. Mel Archer had been the only one on duty when he'd arrived, and he'd made small talk with her while looking down on the scale model of the woods northeast of town, imagining his pitiful figure stumbling over the harsh terrain. Tillman and Kelly had arrived a few minutes later, and had convinced him to sit with them by the fire while they waited.

Tillman had decided to keep the reception committee small, having guessed that Barron would be seeing plenty of the Lawtons over the next few days and wanting to get him and his party settled in before the welcoming dinner at the Playhouse. In addition to Berni, Barron would be accompanied by the troupe's film crew. They'd been through the area in the fall, when the changing of the leaves had transformed the region into a red, orange, and gold paradise, but now they needed some shots in the dead of winter. Barron was going to personally direct them to a few locations, and had also commissioned them to record his symposium.

Mel had joined them by the crackling fire, and they'd spent a pleasant half hour reminiscing about the two months Jack had been in residence. Though keyed up about the Director's arrival, Jack felt a comfortable lethargy coming on and didn't try to fight it. The degree to which he was accepted in a host town might vary, but there was one thing that always stayed the same: When the troupe finally arrived, he was surprised by how much his reaction resembled that of a local.

It was always an eerie transformation: Initially feeling like an intrusive outsider, he would move through the stages of familiarization with the locality and acceptance by the residents until he'd almost forgotten he belonged to Death Troupe. Although

247

Mystery Weekend was interrupting that process, he still experienced a quaintly disturbing feeling from other engagements, when he'd seen the arrival of the troupe and thought, "Who are these strangers? And when are they leaving?"

A sudden question jolted him out of his drowsy daze, and he found himself reflexively looking at Kelly without knowing why. The question made no sense, and there was no reason to fear the answer even if it was yes, but still his first reaction had been to look in her direction.

What if Allison's with them?

They'd communicated sporadically by email over the past weeks, and Allison had been neither surprised nor angry that he'd forgotten to send anything for Valentine's Day. He'd never made that mistake in the past, and now pondered why it didn't bother him more.

He didn't get a chance to consider this for long, as Mel announced that she'd heard something and went to the now-darkened window to look out at the parking lot. She called out that the group had arrived, and they all reached for their jackets in response. Following the others out the door, Jack discovered that his concern over Barron's presence in the town had been erased by his consternation at the question of Allison's unlikely presence. Clomping down the wooden ramp at the back of the group, he couldn't take his eyes off the back of Kelly's head, and even more disconcerting, he couldn't understand why.

As was his habit, Barron quickly took control of the evening. After all the hands had been shaken inside the Visitor's Center, he'd made a brief speech about how happy he was to be there and how much he was looking forward to the Mystery Weekend. Intrigued by the artwork on the common, he'd dispatched Berni to get him moved into the hotel and then led the rest of the group across the street as if he'd grown up there. Jack and Kelly had peeled off to help Berni, and they'd managed to register both her and Barron before the art aficionados caught up with them. Barron would have the corner suite Jack had occupied when he'd first arrived, and Berni would have the room directly across the hall from that. The film crew's vehicle had been left in the Visitor's Center parking lot, saving Jack the effort of refusing to move their belongings.

Tillman and Mel Archer had excused themselves after bringing Barron over and making sure that Jack or Kelly would guide the newcomers to the Playhouse for dinner that night. Kelly had split off to help the film crew find their rooms, giving Jack a chance to update Barron on the status of the play and remind him of the videogame presentation the next day in Newville. Barron had confidently informed him that his own version of the play was nearing completion, and Jack had experienced a sinking feeling regarding his draft's chances of survival.

The party at the Playhouse was a mirror image of Jack's own welcoming, except the crowd was bigger and Barron was the center of attention. The building's electronic marquee played a continuous loop of the Barron Players' Janus masks followed by a dynamic version of Kelly's Mystery Weekend logo, with the light of the candle flickering and the pool of ice-blood slowly expanding across the table top. Two streamers adorned the flagpole atop the cupola, the Death Troupe flag Jack had seen weeks before now joined by another pennant with Kelly's crystal skull.

Inside, Jack discovered that he wasn't the least bit hurt by the crowd's reaction to Barron. The Director was a magnetic presence and a lifelong showman, and on top of all that he was The New Kid in Town. In previous engagements Jack had salved his wounded pride with that observation, but this time he found he didn't need it. He quietly moved through the buffet line and the crowd, more on the lookout for Ryan's operatives than for attention. The wraith's promise to pull them out of town for the next few days hadn't rung true for Jack, but once again he failed to see anyone who was both a stranger and a candidate for an undercover investigator. He supposed, once again, that they wouldn't be very good at their jobs if they could be identified by an amateur like him, but he wondered, once again, if his sudden suspicion from the night before might not be true: What if Ryan was all alone up there?

The man's gaunt appearance and his near-obsession with Allison and Wade had worried Jack right from the start, but now he was moved more to pity than true concern. After watching Ryan ski away the previous night, he'd imagined him returning to a lonely motor home, parked in a deserted campground somewhere near the town. Such a recreational vehicle would provide both anonymity and mobility, and Ryan could certainly afford a good one, but if he was indeed alone, what could all that isolation be doing to his mind?

A member of the community theater group touched Jack's arm at that point, offering hopes for a good experience with Barron, but it didn't distract him from his line of thinking. On the contrary, it made him even more aware that, despite his self-imposed exile of the past few weeks and the minor schism over Kelly, he was surrounded by people who more or less enjoyed his company. He had only to pick up the phone to have a dinner date or a drinking buddy, and he feared that Ryan was in no such position. With Barron in town, the reclusive rich man couldn't even wander around in disguise for fear of being spotted.

At this point Barron stepped up on a platform erected for the occasion and made a few comments using a microphone. He wore a bright red turtleneck and black dress trousers, and held every eye in the room. The phrases of compliment and gratitude flowed from his lips with ease, and Jack knew most of them to be genuine. Though at least a hundred feet away from the Director, he could still feel the energy the man generated. The Mystery Weekend wouldn't officially begin until Friday, and Barron wouldn't hold his symposium until Saturday, but there was an air of anticipation that Jack recognized as part and parcel of the cyclone that was Jerome Barron.

The crowd was eating it all up, and the Lawtons looked ready to petition the court to adopt the Director at any moment. Jack could see Glenda Riley's red hair and hope-filled face next to the Griffins, and was relieved that the older couple appeared to be taking it all in stride. Barron would be working with the community theater group starting Thursday night and through most of the day on Friday, prepping them for his symposium and adjudicating their skills for the show. Thinking of his own minor duties for the weekend, Jack felt a low sense of dread as he turned toward the exit that would take him up to the balcony.

He was perched on the railing again, watching the dance of the roving lights on the closed curtain in a replay of his own welcoming party, when Kelly continued the theme and joined him. The crowd in the lobby was getting louder, and the noise coming through the open balcony door sounded both happy and expectant. Kelly had chosen a gaily colored dress for the occasion, and she smiled broadly as she hopped up on the rail to face him.

"That Jerome." She exclaimed, pointing a thumb behind her. "What a ham he is! I've never seen him operate in front of a crowd before—is it always like that?"

"Worse, sometimes. He's one of the few directors who take curtain calls, and he's always center stage when he does it. I swear he developed the whole Death Troupe concept just because it lets him stay in charge all the way through the show."

She slid a little closer with an almost perceptible light in her eyes. "Isn't a director always in charge?"

"They've got near-total control right up until that curtain rises, and then almost none at all. The actors take over then, and the director might as well be part of the audience for all the influence he or she can exert."

She seemed to like that, and he thought she was going to pursue it when she next opened her mouth to speak. He couldn't have been more wrong.

"So what's this I hear about you spending a lot of time at a certain old fire station in Newville?" The light was still in her eyes, but they'd changed from enchantment to challenge. Her lips were slightly parted, and she turned her head just a bit as if to say that she expected an answer right away. The question couldn't have been more direct if she'd actually asked if he was sleeping with Lynnie Eckart.

Instead of surprise, Jack felt a slow rush of male vanity topped off with the unusual sensation of knowing more than Kelly Sykes. As much as he tried to keep a straight face, her probing eyes and the flash memory of what Lynnie had looked like stretched out on Gary's bed were too much for him. A silly smirk began curling the corners of his mouth and he decided that for once he was going to have to simply tell the truth.

"Can you keep a secret?"

"You have no idea how good I am at that."

"All right." He beckoned with a finger, and she leaned over willingly. He placed a hand on her shoulder as if to steady himself on the rail, and moved his lips close enough to almost touch her ear. "Tadd Wilkinson had an idea for a videogame version of Death Troupe that he pitched to me, and I thought it sounded pretty good. I told Barron about it and he asked to see a demo. So I've been helping Tadd get a presentation together, and we're showing it to the Director tomorrow."

He released her and straightened up as if finished telling the tale, but she barely moved. Her eyes were still locked on his, and a questioning look danced across them. "So that's what you find so interesting at the firehouse."

"It's actually an apartment now, but you're right—the building itself is very intriguing."

The smirk she'd been fighting blossomed into a full-blown, derisive leer. "You really are a terrible actor, Jack Glynn."

He remembered Barron saying something similar up in Maine, just after he'd seen Kelly for the first time. *That's what I love about writers—they're such lousy actors.* The memory fled just as a mechanical whirring came at them across the empty air of the auditorium. He recognized the sound of the curtain opening even before he turned his head to see the red barrier separate and then disappear on either side of the brightly lit stage.

251

The sight of the polished wood never failed to excite him, and Jack felt a catch in his throat as people began trooping down one aisle. There weren't more than a dozen of them, Tillman and the Lawtons and a fair number of the community players, but they were led by Barron. His red turtleneck fairly bounced at the head of the column, and he mounted the stage with a few quick steps that seemed to tell the others to hold up.

Turning to face the group, he smile broadly and then did a modest dance, the old soft shoe, his shoulders and arms shaking back and forth as if he were loosening up. The small audience brimmed with excitement, and someone began to clap even before the Director stopped moving. The others joined in briefly, but stopped when he raised a peremptory palm toward them. Still smiling, he said in a voice that reached all the way to the balcony, "I love the sound of wood."

Tilting his head back, he opened his mouth in a circle and sang out in a honed, echoing baritone. "Do-re-mi-fa-sol-la-ti . . . dooooooooooooo!"

This started up the applause again, and more people began drifting down the aisles to see what was happening. Looking down on the group, Jack realized he was probably the only one there who knew this was Barron's ritual for taking control of a new theater. Most people mistook it for a test of the acoustics, forgetting that Barron really couldn't gauge the effects of the sounds while standing center stage.

The Director closed his mouth and brought his head back to level, but then something in the back of the auditorium caught his attention and he raised his chin again. Sitting on the balcony rail with Kelly, Jack knew that he and the publicity officer had become the object of the Director's gaze. He was surprised to feel a child-like warmth at being recognized, but that left a moment later.

Down on the stage, Barron raised both arms before him as if he were claiming the entire room as his domain. More people gathered at the front of the auditorium, and to Jack it resembled a scene of near-idolatry even though he knew most of the partygoers were simply curious. Barron seemed not to notice them anyway, instead standing there with his arms spread, his eyes fixed on the balcony, and his lips curled back in an expression that was at once pride and possession.

The next morning started early, with Jack guiding Barron and the film crew to various points around town. Although passersby approached without hesitation whenever they were in the town proper, it was considered cheating to follow them and watch what they were choosing to shoot for the show. As a result, Jack was able to drive Barron and Berni to the old firehouse shortly before noon with no one the wiser. Even if they'd been spotted, most people were likely to assume Barron was intrigued by the aged structure and its location near the bridge over the frozen river. Having decided not to take that chance, Jack drove straight into the newly cleaned garage and watched with approval as Gary and Tadd pulled the door down behind them.

After initial introductions, Tadd beckoned them toward the stairs leading up to the apartment. Jack stepped behind Barron at just the right moment, giving a well turned-out Gary the opportunity to fall in beside Berni. He'd followed Jack's advice and was wearing a set of blue dress pants, black shoes, and an olive sweater that showed off his physique without being pushy. Jack heard them chatting pleasantly enough as the group clomped up the unfinished stairs, but he still wondered if he was going to succeed in keeping Barron's inquisitive assistant out of the demonstration.

He needn't have bothered, as Lynnie had outthought him once again. A platter of cheese and crackers was arranged on the coffee table in the living room, but no one noticed it at first because they were all looking at the blonde hostess standing next to it. Jack actually felt his breath had been taken away, and his face colored slightly when he saw that the ice sculptress had already solved the problem of Berni.

She wore a dress that was a businesslike gray wraparound with a red leather belt that accentuated the swell of her hips, and the wraparound portion of the outfit left just a hint of cleavage before hugging her chest quite nicely. Barron had been reserved in his greetings until then, but he now stepped from behind Tadd and extended a hand toward the blonde.

"I'm guessing you're the designer I've been hearing so much about." He said brightly, taking her hand in both of his own. Lynnie replied that she'd only provided Tadd with the basic character figures and the scenery for the presentation, but the Director had already taken the bait.

Still holding her hand, he turned to Tadd and said, "Of course she's going to help you with the presentation, right?"

The programmer gulped for a second, but Lynnie was more than up to the task. "I'll be glad to sit in, although I'm afraid there might not be much room. We thought it would be best to show you the demo the way a gamer would see it, so we're set up in Tadd's bedroom."

She helped Barron remove his long coat, exposing a navy blue turtleneck and khaki trousers. Absently handing the coat to Jack, she took Barron's arm and steered him down the hallway while Tadd followed. Jack had advised him to dress casually, completing the image of a videogame player enjoying the new software in the comfort of his home, and Tadd's choice of outfit was nearly as inspired as Lynnie's. He wore a pair of white cargo pants so new that a store tag should still have been pinned on them, and a long-sleeved black t-shirt with the Mystery Weekend logo on the chest. He'd kept his hair spiked, but looked far from confident.

Tossing the coat aside, Jack stopped him just short of the bedroom door. Leaning in close, he whispered, "Ya *like* it?"

The sound of Barron's gruff baritone inside the room was followed by a titter of laughter from Lynnie. The gamer looked confused for a second, but then his face brightened with remembrance and he fixed Jack with an expression of determination. "Yeah I like it. I like it a *lot*."

"Then go get it. It's yours."

Tadd disappeared inside the bedroom, and the thin door shut with authority. Rubbing his hands together, Jack turned around to find his way blocked by the indignant face of Bernice Fitzgibbons. She'd distracted Gary by handing him her coat, and now looked ready to do battle.

"Damn you, Jack." She said at a conversational volume, but she didn't seem to be kidding.

Still standing in her way, Jack leaned forward so that their eyes were on the same level. "Consider it payback for not giving me a head's up in Schenectady."

They stood there facing each other, motionless, for several seconds before Gary tried to make the peace. Stepping up behind Berni, he placed a large hand on her shoulder, fixed her with a winning smile, and asked if she wanted him to get her some coffee.

Berni's eyes narrowed, and she slowly rotated her head until her eyes were on the offending hand. Gary didn't move it, so she decided to speak. The words came out as an acid command. "Unless you wanna be pitched you off your own balcony, you better move that paw."

Gary yanked his arm back as if he'd touched something that was on fire, but Berni had already decided the fight was over and simply turned around and walked back into the living room. Jack gave a thoroughly cowed Gary a quick wink and followed her.

Barron's assistant had gone to the fire escape door and was looking out its window into the bright blue sky and the snow-kissed trees. Jack knew better than to push her, and instead went over to the couch and helped himself to a snack. Gary had shown the sense to go with him, but still stood uncertainly on the other side of the coffee table. He looked down at Jack, who gave him no encouragement at all, and back at Berni a couple of times before deciding to simply stand there. His mission had been accomplished, albeit by a curvaceous blonde with a good eye for fashion, and he seemed to recognize the victory.

"Hey. Boy toy." Berni's voice cracked across the room, and both men turned to see her facing them. "Where's that coffee I heard about?"

"Coming right up." Gary fairly hopped across the floor, but stopped just short of the hallway. "How do you like it? Cream and sugar?"

"Doesn't matter. I'll just keep sending you back until you get it right."

"Okay." With yet another confused look, Gary headed in the direction of the kitchen. A burst of laughter came from Tadd's room, but Jack resisted the urge to grin as Berni dropped onto the couch next to him.

Extending a hand, she spoke in the same tone she'd used on Gary. "We even?"

They shook. "Even."

"We on the same side again?"

"Always."

Berni sagged against the cushions, her head coming to rest on the sofa's back. Her eyes closed behind the glasses, and when she spoke again it was in a sleepy drone. "How many times do you think I can make your gigolo remix my coffee before he wises up and brings everything out with him?"

The door opened forty-five minutes later, but the continuous laughter from the bedroom told Jack that the two young people had made the sale long before then. Lynnie came out first, grinning from ear to ear, followed by a still-talking Barron and a Tadd Wilkinson that Jack had never seen before: The programmer was practically glowing with achievement, and he gave him a happy thumb's up from behind the Director's back.

Barron separated himself from the others and walked right up to Jack wearing a pleased smile. He raised a hand above his shoulder, with the fingers joined as if he were winding up to slap him, but then slowly swung it down to shake his writer's hand. "Excellent work, Jack. Excellent. Where'd you find these two?"

"The only place to find real talent: A bar."

"I'm gonna have to start looking there myself, then." He released Jack and turned to Berni, steering her away from the group. "Schedule some time when we come back in April—as *soon* as we come back—so they can show me the finished product." He began going into greater detail concerning the purchase of the game, but Jack was no longer listening. Lynnie and Tadd clearly wanted to celebrate, but it didn't seem right to do that with their new client standing in the room. Jack stepped up to both of them, taking Tadd's hand in his and accepting a quick, silent kiss on the cheek from Lynnie.

Gary took his place next, receiving much the same reception, and whispered to Tadd, "I knew you could do it, buddy. I *knew* it."

Barron's voice interrupted the subdued celebration, and the foursome turned to see that the Director and Berni had scooped up their coats. "Jack, Berni and I will meet you downstairs." He flashed a smile at the group. "I think some people here want to do a little shouting."

Jack cleared his throat before beginning his own presentation. It was just after lunch, and he'd returned to Barron's suite with the Director and Berni. A projection screen stood in front of the door that separated the sitting room from the bedroom, and there was just enough space for the projector, Berni's laptop, and seats for her and Barron. Every shade in the suite was drawn, and Berni had swept it for bugs. The static image of the corpse floating under the ice was on the screen, and Barron didn't know that there would be no others. Jack began to speak in a low voice.

"Ryan Betancourt had a way of concepting his plays that I never particularly liked." He began slowly, holding his hands close to his chest with the fingertips touching. "Ryan compared his technique to the receding of flood waters, where the first solid ground to appear was of course the highest. The peaks, if you will.

"As the water slipped further away, it revealed other, lower patches of ground. Once it had completely disappeared, it would have exposed the valleys and the ravines that connected the previously isolated peaks. Ryan always said that the high notes of a play—the peaks, the big moments of drama and conflict—were the most important parts. And that was why he always expected them to emerge first."

The three of them were less than five feet away from each other, and Jack was careful to shift eye contact between the Director and Berni. His heart was pumping strongly, goaded by the knowledge that

256

he was plumbing unfamiliar depths and that the failure of this approach might doom the first draft of his play to rejection. Barron was leaning forward in the reading chair which had been shifted to face the bedroom, and Berni was looking on patiently.

"Because the original idea for this play was Ryan's, I decided to try it his way—at least at first. And to my great surprise, his approach suggested something to me that we haven't tried before. In identifying the big moments—the peaks—of the play I hoped to write, I recognized that one of the biggest moments in the show Ryan envisioned . . . occurs in the preamble.

"In every play I've written for this troupe, the introduction has been where you'd expect it: The events which set up the murder are shown in the first minutes of the performance. As you both know, this has greatly simplified the inclusion of the local theater group. It's allowed us to use them in a film segment which completely separates them from our players, both in rehearsal and on the big night. A while back I suggested that we should make a silent movie for that segment, in homage to the many pictures that were shot in the Adirondacks before anybody knew where Hollywood even was.

"Here's what I now propose: Scratch the film introduction entirely. Begin the play in the current time, with the investigator seated in a busy bar asking questions about the region's bootlegging past. In my play he says he's writing a book about the gangsters, but in reality he's the descendant of the disgraced broker who allegedly lost the town's savings in the Crash and then killed himself.

"In just a few scenes, my play shows the audience that the investigator has landed in a town with many secrets. Some people are friendly and some are not. Almost no one tells him anything, but when this guy—" he pointed a thumb over his shoulder at the corpse floating behind him "—starts spilling his guts about the town's sordid past, we switch to the Crash itself, the discovery of the dead broker, the revelation that he was mixed up with the Seven Seas Gang, the countless pointing fingers that followed, and end it with the broker's wife leaving the town in shame. That's a *very* big moment in this play.

"So I suggest that we use the local theater troupe, in period costume, live, right in the middle of the first act, to carry off that big moment."

He stopped then, but let Barron believe it was merely a pause. For his part, the Director lifted one long leg over another and clasped his hands around his raised knee. A distant look appeared on his face, pensive and wishful at the same time. Jack let him process whatever was going on inside his head, catching the one quick, sideways flash of Berni's eyes that the Director completely missed.

After waiting a decent interval, Jack concluded his presentation while trying to sound as much like an undertaker as possible. "I've completed the first draft, and Berni has it for your review. I know this means a lot of extra work, but I think this is the way to go."

Barron swung his suspended foot back onto the floor and stood up. Studying his writer as if seeing him for the first time, he brought his hands together in a light applause that he usually reserved for his actors. "Bra-vo, Jack. Bra-vo."

He turned to Berni as if seeking her opinion, but his assistant merely looked up at the two of them with a look of sweet neutrality. Regardless of her opinion of Jack's idea, there was a competing script that was supposedly penned by the man who always received her first loyalty.

"I won't make a decision until I've read your draft through, but if I were you I'd go out and buy a lottery ticket. Your kids hit a home run this morning, and you may have done the same this afternoon. I have to admit I like your flashback idea. I like it a lot."

Barron was fighting to keep his face impassive, but it wasn't working and for a brief moment Jack feared that the Director had been playing with him. Barron continued, barely able to contain the laughter that was obviously brimming inside him. "The question is, do *you* like it?"

"What?"

"I'm sorry, I said that wrong. Here's the actual line: Ya *like* it?" Barron let a demented expression float onto his face as he said the last words, and Jack came to understand that at least part of the laughter in Tadd Wilkinson's bedroom had been at his expense.

"That little bastard."

"Actually, it was the girl who told me. I promised I'd only use it in an emergency."

Berni was utterly confused by the turn the conversation had taken, and slowly stood with an air of bewilderment. Though shocked at the minor betrayal by two people he'd just given a major professional break, Jack was relieved to see that Barron's earlier compliments had been genuine.

"No cause for concern, Berni. I'm just being mocked by a coffee wrangler and a computer programmer."

That didn't make anything clear for her, but Barron waved her into silence while regaining his composure. "Great job, Jack. Really great job. Now get out of here so I can start reading this monstrosity you've created."

"Do I get to see yours?"

"I'm gonna hold off on that, for now." Barron gave him a friendly pat on the shoulder that nonetheless suggested that he move in the direction of the hallway. "Go on, get outta here. Don't get lost in the woods."

Jack emerged from the hotel with the qualified elation that he'd once associated with the completion of a tough exam at college. It was just as impossible to know what Barron would do with the script as it had been to guess the grade he would receive back in school, but in both cases the feeling was one of relief.

A work crew was busy stringing lights on the trees which rimmed the common, and for a moment Jack believed he was seeing things when one of the ice sculptures appeared to move. It was a just a flash, but then it appeared again between two more of the art pieces, and he finally recognized it as a skater. He didn't think it possible to skate on the snow where he had learned to cross-country ski, and so he moved back up onto the hotel's front steps to get a better look.

From there, he saw that a solid wall of snow had been plowed up all around the square, except for a single open path that crossed its midsection. The path itself looked like a trench, and the two large squares formed on either side of it shone where the afternoon's sun reflected off several inches of ice. He decided that the Mayor had dreamt this up at the last moment, and had flooded the town common to create an impromptu rink.

The individual coursing around the ice was female, clad in a set of pink tights that showed taught, slender muscles beneath the fabric even from a distance. A white coat with a fur-lined hood and a cinched waist complimented the girl's figure, and she moved with the light abandonment of a child. A simple twist of her hips sent her skating backward in a wide circle, and when she extended her arms the movement flowed all the way to fingers that turned upward like the unfurling of wings. She tilted her head back and looked directly up at the sky, her mouth open in unadulterated enjoyment.

The hood fell away just then, and the chestnut brown hair of Kelly Sykes spilled out with it. She began pumping her legs again, crouching down just a bit with her hair framing her face as she skated in reverse.

Jack might have stood there for many minutes, transfixed, were it not for the men stringing the lights. One of them noticed his trance and bumped the one next to him before tossing his head toward the hotel. Getting caught like that normally embarrassed him no end, but his recent successes and the beauty of the scene before him left Jack

259

in too good a mood to be bothered. He gave the workers a guilty smirk, just to show he was a good sport, before bouncing down the stairs and crunching off up the road.

"Ophelia's a *tramp*." Barron's words carried far in the Playhouse auditorium, and Jack heard them clearly from his shadowy spot near the back. Barron had made his first encounter with the community theater group open to the public, and there were roughly fifty people scattered in the seats closer to the stage. Barron was no fan of open rehearsal, but had told Jack earlier that this was a one-time thing more closely associated with Mystery Weekend than the upcoming show. Somewhat hidden in the balcony's overhang, Jack watched as the Director familiarized himself with the people his writer wanted to insert as live performers in the middle of his show.

"Ophelia's *not* a tramp." Glenda Riley, also on stage and just feet from Barron, protested evenly. "Everything Polonius and Laertes say to her is a *warning*, that's all. She hasn't done anything with Hamlet."

Barron placed his hands on his hips and asked sweetly, "Now why would they be giving her a warning if they didn't think she was easy?"

Jack stifled a laugh, knowing that Barron was testing the young actor. He'd re-read the *Hamlet* scenes involving Ophelia, and had come away with the same interpretation as Glenda. He wondered if she had the nerve to stick to her guns, and noted that a low level of tension had descended on the people watching. He recognized a few of them as relatives of the players, but didn't see Glenda's husband Curt and assumed he was at home watching the kids.

Glenda's red hair was pulled back with a barrette, and she wore a long dress that Jack felt was quite evocative of Ophelia. The skirt portion was dark brown, but the top was a cream fabric threaded with the vines of a rosebush and sleeves that puffed out around her arms as if she were already taking the fall that would kill her character. Mimicking Barron, she placed both fists on her waist.

"That's not what they're saying. They're saying that Hamlet is a prince and that no matter what he may promise, he's going to be told who he'll marry at the proper time—and that it isn't going to be her. *That's* the warning."

The audience tittered slightly, and Barron turned a speculative gaze in their direction. They'd been surprisingly well behaved during the Director's run-through of the *Macbeth* scenes with the Griffins, and had only reacted when something amusing had been said onstage. After winking at the residents, Barron turned back to Glenda.

"If that's true, then why does Polonius tell the king later on that Hamlet's gone head-over-heels for his daughter? To get her banished from the court? Of course not. He's angling to get his daughter married to the heir to the throne."

"No he's not." Instead of answering with frustration, Glenda took on the authoritative tone that she probably used to correct errant grade-schoolers. "He's trying to identify the source of Hamlet's strange behavior, as requested by the king. He thinks he's found the answer, and he's brought his boss to see proof when they eavesdrop on Hamlet and Ophelia."

The Lawtons were onstage as well, and they seemed to be drinking heavily from the cup of Jerome Barron. They'd spoken up a couple of times while the Griffins had been working, but seemed to be greatly enjoying the Director and, to Jack's surprise, not to fear him at all. He doubted they'd be able to stay out of this one, though, and waited for Barron to tip them over the edge.

"What . . . utterly . . . talentless . . . nitwit . . . told you *that*?"

"Nobody told me anything. I read the play. And that's what it says."

"Uh, Jerry?" The voice came from the front row, and Jack recognized the voice of Kelly Sykes. He'd sneaked in well after the rehearsal had begun that evening, and hadn't seen her until now.

"That's 'Mr. Barron', thank you." The Director threw this at her tartly, and then mugged at the people behind her in a quick double-take. The audience tittered again, and Kelly slowly stood.

"I'm sorry, *Mr. Barron*. It won't happen again."

"So whaddya want?"

"*I'm* the utterly talentless nitwit who told her that."

"She didn't tell me anything. We took the words apart as a group, and this is what they mean."

Barron turned to cock an eyebrow at the Lawtons, who both nodded with smiles of bovine contentment. The Director looked down at Kelly once more, and then out at the crowd. For a split second Jack thought he locked eyes with him, but it was a common illusion in theater and he couldn't be sure.

"Sounds like I'm the victim of a conspiracy."

"Well?" Kelly asked sweetly. "Are we right?"

"How should I know? The play's hundreds of years old." More giggling accompanied Barron as he walked over to a nearby stool and retrieved his water bottle. "All right, Miss Ophelia, pure and chaste as the driven snow and *completely* uninterested in the throne of all Denmark . . . let's do it again."

261

The knock came at the back door of Jack's cabin just after he got in. It was close to midnight, and he'd been busy. He'd stopped watching Barron put the locals through their paces around nine and gone over to the firehouse, where a modest—and pointedly unexplained—celebration was in progress. Earlier, he'd warned Tadd, Lynnie, and Gary that it was important to keep the videogame deal a secret. Otherwise Barron would be mobbed by every hustler for a hundred miles around, and there was also a chance that some residents might resent the way that Jack had promoted the three young people. They'd agreed to keep mum "as long as possible", and he'd accepted that with more than minor trepidation.

Fearing a repeat of the drunken excess at his first firehouse party, Jack had steered clear of the main celebration in the garage and used the side stairs. Both Lynnie and Tadd were strangely subdued, and he couldn't tell if they were working hard at keeping the secret or if the effort they'd put in that morning had simply exhausted them. He'd received more quiet thanks, and had left them chatting with a sedate group of partygoers.

Because of that, he knew that the visitor at the back door couldn't be Lynnie. He was relieved by that thought, not only because his latest encounters with Kelly had left him so obviously conflicted, but also because he hoped to see the face of Ryan Betancourt. His use of Ryan's words that afternoon had not been a bid for sympathy; the other writer's creative approach had given him the inspiration concerning the local players and he was in the man's debt.

Moreover, his last meeting with the other writer had left him concerned for his very sanity. Regardless of the harm Ryan had caused, Jack had once called him friend and believed that the same magnificent woman loved both of them. Ryan had invited him into his scheme in the name of protecting that woman, and in a way Jack felt he was doing something similar now. Whether complicit in Ryan's plot or ignorant of his continued existence, Allison would want him to try and talk some sense into him.

And so it was with great surprise that Jack pulled the door open to see the face of Wade Parker. He'd almost forgotten the advance man in the excitement of Barron's arrival and the success of the videogame demo, and he fairly jumped with shock.

"Expecting someone else, Jack?" Wade was wrapped in the same heavy trench coat he'd worn at the hospital weeks before, but had added a fedora to the getup. He was smiling pleasantly, but his eyes drilled into Jack from beneath the hat's wide brim.

"Ye-eah." Jack forced himself to sound concerned, knowing that an outright denial would only make the advance man suspicious. He looked over his shoulder at the gray, tree-covered slope behind him. "A lady friend, in fact."

Continuing the act, he looked down at Wade and aped annoyance. "You could have picked a better time. And why the back door?"

"I won't be long." Wade brushed past him, removing the hat and starting to unbutton the coat. Dropping into the rocking chair with the jacket flapping around him, he couldn't have known how much he resembled Ryan during his last visit. "So who's the lucky lady? That gal who did the graphics for the videogame?"

"Maybe."

"I hear she gets around."

"In the art world that's known as being a free spirit."

"In the real world it's known as being a tramp."

Ophelia's a tramp.

"Well no matter what world we're in, she's not a tramp. Those two violin ice sculptures? They were hers. She did all the graphics for the game from scratch, she works like a dog, and she's a good friend too."

Wade raised both hands as if in self defense, laughing. "Hey, I got no problem with that. You know I'm no prude. Besides, it's nice to hear you're at least considering other contestants instead of sticking on Allison."

Like every man in America, he's fallen for her.

Ryan's original accusation rang out in his mind as Jack walked to the desk and sat down. He admired the construction of Wade's last sentence, the way the advance man had suggested he was playing the field with an eye toward dumping Allison.

"So what brings you here, Wade?"

"I'm a little concerned by your new pals out at that firehouse."

"I'm supposed to get to know the people in the host town, and maybe even make friends with some of them. You got a problem with any of my other pals? Like the mayor, or the couple who own Maddy's Place and the diner, or the public relations officer . . . oh yeah, and the half of Schuyler Mills that turned out to save my ass a few weeks ago?"

Wade fixed him with a speculative stare, his face clouding over. "What's going on, Jack? What's got you so worked up?"

"All right. You want it, you got it. I can't help remembering how many times you've told me to dump Allison over the years. You know, something you said way back in Utica stuck with me: You said

Allison was faithful to Ryan the same way she'd been with me. That got me to wondering, how could you know something like that? How could anyone, even if they followed her around all day and night? It's not like she couldn't have found five minutes to slip into a closet with somebody."

"Wow. Five minutes in a closet. You're a fun date, Jack. No wonder you're so popular." Wade tried to smile, but it was a thin, bloodless line and he quickly removed it when he saw Jack wasn't mollified. "Okay, here it is: I won't tell you which, but one of Allison's lackeys used to work as a personal assistant to a business exec I know. The kid was too Hollywood for the job, but his boss liked him and wanted him to land right when he let him go. He knew I'd moved into the entertainment industry, so he asked me to find him a home.

"I got him on board with Allison because I wanted a way to track just how many times Ryan slipped away from work to go see her."

Jack didn't respond, instead just sitting there glaring, so Wade continued. "I'd forgotten I said that thing about her being monogamous, but I can always count on a writer's ear for dialogue, can't I?"

"Why's that? Because it helps us pick out the lines that sound wrong?"

"No. Because it turns you into fucking tape recorders." Wade leaned forward so that his forearms rested close to his knees. "But now that we've got that out of your system, I want to warn you about getting too close to that crew in the firehouse. I've checked them out, and they come up reasonably clean. If they didn't, I wouldn't have let you get them anywhere near the Barron.

"But I want you to remember what we're doing here, and how many people are working very hard to steal our secrets. One of your pals is a computer programmer who's done his share of hacking. The girl's been arrested for pot possession, although it was a few years ago. And the other one, the one who works for the cable company . . . well put 'em all together and I have to be concerned about somebody breaching the security in your laptop."

"That wouldn't happen."

Wade's mouth opened in an exasperated grin while he looked at the ceiling. "'That wouldn't happen.' You writers make me laugh. You think you've got such a handle on everything. Well listen to me, Jack: The only thing you control is what's on the page in front of you —and not even that, when the Barron gets his hands on it."

"What about you? What do you control? You didn't know Allison was cheating on me, when you were tracking Ryan's every move. And you didn't even know there was still a member of that family left alive in Red Bend."

"That's a low blow."

"And if I *do* control what's on the page, that puts me one up on everybody else on the planet. At least I've got one thing that does what I want it to do."

Wade's irritated look was replaced with a mix of concern and befuddlement, and he left it there for Jack to see. After a few moments he gave his eyebrows a quick flip up and down, as if resetting his features. He reached for the hat and stood up.

"I better get out of here before your lady friend shows up." Holding the fedora by its top, he pointed the hat at Jack. "Remember what I said. Keep your eyes open. Keep your ears open. And keep the laptop locked up—especially when that blonde's around."

He was gone a moment later, and Jack looked out the tiny window as the man's shadow morphed into the gloom and disappeared. His heart was pounding, and not from the heat of the discussion.

"That's not what he came here for." He whispered to the empty room.

Chapter Eighteen

Friday dawned into a crisp blue sky that seemed to summon people from all points of the compass. Cars and trucks with license plates from much of the northeast began trickling into the town center in the midmorning, and by mid-afternoon it was a steady stream. Campers and recreational vehicles found their way to frozen campsites around the town, and the parking area of the Great View Motel was soon filled to capacity.

Jack had gone trail skiing just before the new arrivals began appearing in force, and then spent a nerve-racking afternoon finalizing his class for the next day while doors slammed and engines revved outside his cabin. Barron had shanghaied the entire community theater group out to the Playhouse for the day, and intensive rehearsals for his symposium were reportedly in progress. Tillman and Kelly were both busy supervising Mystery Weekend events, and Wade's admonition concerning Lynnie, Tadd, and Gary provided sufficient impetus for Jack to stay at the motel.

His class was scheduled for the next morning, and would only run for two hours as opposed to Barron's all-day workshop at the Playhouse. Jack had never had trouble discussing his craft with anyone of a similar bent, but he was keenly aware that his entire experience with theater involved murder mysteries of one kind or another. He doubted he would hold up well against anyone who had studied it for more than a semester, and hoped he wouldn't have to resort to telling tales from Hollywood to stay ahead of the discussion.

Thoughts of Kelly kept returning to him, and for once they were simply pleasant. The town had lost interest in their alleged difficulties when the ice sculptures had started appearing, and with Mystery

Weekend in full swing they weren't likely to remember it. Recognizing his true attraction to the publicity officer helped him deal with the recurring images of her skating on the common and standing up to Barron, but he somehow knew that wasn't entirely it. She was certainly attractive physically, and they obviously had much in common, but there had to be some other reason why she kept coming to mind.

Their brief discussion in the Playhouse balcony on the night of Barron's arrival had rekindled his interest in her, partially because she'd shown a trace of jealousy over Lynnie. What had she said when he'd asked if she could keep a secret?

"You have no idea how good I am at that."

Had he missed something there? Intending to tell her about the next day's demo, and truly wanting to justify the time he was spending with Lynnie and her friends, he'd gone straight into his explanation without really considering her answer. Had she been trying to say something, using words that required interpretation? She'd brought up the subject, so had she been making a competing bid for his affections?

Jack shook his head and poured himself another cup of coffee. He'd almost finished making the background slides he would use for his class the next day, but they needed editing. Whatever was sticking in his mind regarding the Schuyler Mills publicity officer, it would either resolve itself or vanish. He'd had similar experiences in the past when writing passages that simply didn't seem to work, and had learned to wait for them to reveal themselves. They either came to him at an unguarded moment or they did not, and if they failed to appear he would eventually drop the entire segment that didn't seem to hang together.

Punching up the first slide, he admitted to himself that he did not want to drop the segment involving Kelly, the one that didn't currently seem to work.

He was at the elementary school an hour early the next morning, meeting Curt Riley to prepare the classroom. It was actually the school gymnasium, where several rows of folding tables had been set up facing a screen that rolled down from above. Curt set up the projector and loaded the slides for Jack's presentation onto a laptop provided by the school.

Bib Hatton arrived shortly after that, carrying a lock box which he would use to collect fees from anyone who hadn't already registered for one of the different Mystery Weekend event packages. Jack had already seen different colored badges hung from various attendees' necks, but was surprised to see Bib was assigned to his class. The big man didn't leave him wondering, coming straight across the basketball court while still wearing his jacket and with the lock box tucked under one arm. He was smiling broadly, and Jack feared the worst.

"You *dog* you!" Hatton whispered when they shook hands, mindful of the elementary school teacher nearby. "I had no idea you were chasin' Lynnie Eckart when I said all those nasty things at Maddy's! I had you figured for Kelly Sykes from the moment the two of you came into my shop, and the way she fought me over your half-dead carcass that night sealed the deal as far as I was concerned . . . as far as a lot of people were concerned, too."

"Uh, Bib, there's really nothing going on between me and Lynnie. We're just friends."

"Okay, tiger . . . it's just that there's plenty of guys in this town who wouldn't mind bein' 'friends' with that little lady." The big man gave him a playful swat on the shoulder before heading back to his station at the door.

Refreshments in the form of coffee, hot water, tea, and an assortment of breakfast rolls arrived then, and Curt supervised its setup on tables off to the side. Cars began rolling into the school parking lot shortly after that, and a respectable number of attendees were soon mixing beverages or catching a light breakfast before the class was due to start. Jack noted with pleasure that he had a good cross-section of ages and sexes, and was even more relieved when Lynnie, Tadd, and Gary appeared in the line at the door at the last minute.

His three co-conspirators gathered around him and wished him luck before taking their seats, and Jack would have enjoyed Lynnie's peck on the cheek were it not for the jubilant thumbs-up he received from Bib standing in the back. Taking a last sip of water and clearing his throat, he flipped the projector on to show the now-familiar image of the floating corpse under the ice. The play didn't have a title yet, so Jack had labeled the presentation with something innocuous about building plot and character in a mystery.

"Good morning, everybody. I'm Jack Glynn, the current writer for the Jerome Barron Players. Before I get started, I wanted to say how pleased I am to see so many of you turn out this early in the morning, and I want to encourage you to participate if you have anything to add to the discussion. So if at any point you've got something to say, just blurt it out. No need to raise your hand—"

It never failed. As soon as he offered that little piece of instruction, someone would raise a hand. Luckily this particular crowd had a good sense of humor, and several people began giggling. Putting an expression of helpless mirth on his face, Jack pointed at the bearded twenty-something who was the hand's owner.

"Here's our first comment. What's on your mind?"

"Mr. Glynn, how did you sell your screenplay in Hollywood?"

So much for the fall-back position. Maybe I can divert him and still save that for later . . .

"I'll be glad to talk about that, and I'm sure we'll have time toward the end, but I think most of the group would like to hear about the various ways we writers can build plot and develop characters—"

"Actually, I'd like to hear about the screenplay." This came from a woman with glasses and gray hair in the third row.

"Me too."

"Yeah, that's really why I came here."

Jack listened to the chorus of polite objection with a look of genuine surprise. Except for periodic updates from his agent, he'd largely forgotten *Beaten Ground* during his stay in Schuyler Mills. His focus had shifted to the play he was to write for Death Troupe, no matter how badly Wade, the Director, and Ryan had distracted him.

"Uh, can I get a show of hands, just to be fair? I can talk about this right now if you want, so who wants to hear some lies about Hollywood?"

Every one of the roughly twenty visitors raised a hand, including Bib at the back and Lynnie, Tadd, and Gary, who each raised two hands.

"Well all right then." He glanced at the screen behind him and decided to leave the image in place. The projector sat on one half of a sturdy wooden table, and Jack hopped up on the other half so that he was practically on top of the people in the first row. "Where would you like me to start?"

"Why's your movie called *Beaten Ground*?"

Jacks mind frantically reached back ten years for the memories. "Well, as you know it's a war picture, the Pacific part of World War Two, and while researching that theater of operations I came across a military term called a 'beaten zone'. It can refer to a lot of things, from the portion of ground being hit by machinegun fire to an entire area where everything from artillery to bullets is landing, but the upshot is that you didn't want to find yourself in a beaten zone.

"I was trying to capture the sensation of fear that would come with realizing you were in such a place, and I pictured the ground itself as being whipped into chopped-up pieces of dirt and sod and rocks . . ." There had been more to that idea, but it was escaping his attempts to recall. He paused for a moment, and was elated to see that most of the heads before him were bowed while the budding writers scribbled down his words. This calmed him, and he remembered the other reason.

"But I also wanted to relate the toughness and the resilience of the people who were fighting in those battles, too. While I was imagining the ground being whipped up by explosions and bullets, I had a strange idea . . . that no matter what you do to the ground, it doesn't make much difference. The ground's the ground. The dirt's the dirt. And that's where I got the name, *Beaten Ground*. It's supposed to symbolize the horror of what the weapons can do, as well as the strength of the human spirit . . . essentially saying that there are people on whom that kind of beating, or any beating for that matter, won't have any more effect than whipping the ground."

The pens and pencils continued to move, and he waited for them to catch up. Gary was nodding approvingly, Tadd seemed half asleep, and Lynnie wore the same expression she'd shown when contemplating the ice sculpture she'd been asked to make. Her mouth opened when she caught his gaze, and she mouthed the word "Wow" in a way that seemed genuine. Even Bib was nodding approvingly, and when Jack looked back at the others he could see they were waiting for him to continue.

"Next question."

It was just before lunch, and just after his seminar had ended, when Kelly walked up to Jack at the front of the impromptu classroom. Lynnie, Gary, and Tadd had left during the first break, but he hadn't been surprised by that. They weren't writers, and had explained that they were needed at an event that sounded like a potato sack race. Either this was some kind of wintertime variation on that old favorite (probably involving snowmobiles) or he'd been too distracted to hear them properly.

The second option was probably the reason, as Jack had experienced a huge revelation while discussing *Beaten Ground* with the class. Most of the attendees had turned out to be aspiring screenwriters who'd come from many miles around Schuyler Mills, and the conversation with them had resolved something he thought he'd forgotten.

"Great class, Jack!" Kelly spoke quietly when she approached, aware that he was writing steadily on a notepad and not wanting to startle him. Curt was dismantling the projector, and Bib was doing a final count of the money in the lockbox.

Jack looked up with a quick, birdlike shift of his head. His mouth looked like he'd just bitten into something sour, but he was actually trying to get his thoughts down on paper before losing them. His eyes were unfocused for just an instant, and then he smiled in obvious pleasure.

"Kelly!" He breathed this out as if he hadn't seen her in ages. "When did you get here?"

"I slipped in at the very end. I waved, but you were talking with the class and I don't think you saw me."

"I didn't. Sorry." He wasn't surprised by this. The attendees had been well versed in film, and had built a wide-ranging conversation around the title of the war picture he'd written in college. Although he'd participated whenever he felt it necessary, his explanation of *Beaten Ground's* title had stirred something in his mind regarding the film adaptation of *Wind in the Palms*. He now saw that he'd been much too focused on the differences between stage and screen when he'd attempted to write the adaptation, and that he should have been as attentive to the characters and their interaction as he'd been with the soldiers in *Beaten Ground*.

He'd felt like a split personality, guiding the classroom talk while mentally reviewing the characters of *Wind in the Palms* and beginning to see how their individual motivations should have morphed from the stage to the screen. He hadn't missed a beat with the seminar attendees, no matter what unusual observation they'd made, and had deftly steered them toward discussion of their own works and experiences while he sorted through the burgeoning re-write of his latest screenplay. It was no shock that he hadn't seen Kelly standing in the back.

"Somebody made an observation, right at the beginning, that jogged my mind about something I was writing. It really got me thinking."

"Is it about the play?"

"No, no, the play's pretty much written." He gestured at the pad before him. "This is about the screenplay for *Wind in the Palms*. Don't tell anybody, but I was never happy with the adaptation I wrote, and I think that this little seminar . . . these people . . . just jawing away . . . might have given me a breakthrough."

His voice was heavy with the tingling awe he sometimes felt when a part of a story that he'd thrown in on a whim later proved important in a way he'd never envisioned. At times like those he honestly wondered if the thing he called inspiration wasn't something else, something alive, speaking through his pen.

Kelly looked down at the small stack of papers already ripped from the pad, covered with notes and little sketches, the interest in her eyes matching his own. She smiled in appreciation, and spoke in a whisper. "Isn't that wonderful, when that happens?"

"It is. It really is."

They shared a smile for a moment longer, and then she placed a hand on his shoulder. She kneaded the muscle there once, twice, and then let go. "Then stay with it. These moments don't come 'round too often."

Jack pulled the metal door shut behind him as he left the school building. Curt and Bib had departed hours before, asking him to make sure the door was locked when he was finished. Lost in his plan to revise *Wind in the Palms*, Jack had been unwilling to uproot himself back to the possibly noisier Great View. He'd enjoyed the time spent in the near-silence of the gym with its slanting rays of sunlight and dancing dust motes.

His inspiration had proved itself while he first scratched out a rough outline and then rearranged it to see if it flowed. He knew the characters well, even as they had ultimately been changed for the stage, and through that analysis he'd discovered a possible reason for his earlier failure. Instead of adapting his original script to the screen, he'd tried to take the actual Death Troupe performance and translate it into a movie. As was always the case, he'd agreed with only some of the changes made by the Director and the actors. He now saw that he'd been bamboozled into keeping one particularly errant depiction of a major character because the audience had responded to it so heartily. Returning to the play that he'd written, digging down to the bedrock, had helped him sort through the problem areas that he remembered from the screenplay.

The slanting of the sun's rays had finally shaken him out of his creative trance, and he'd remembered with a dull kind of alarm that he was close to missing Barron's entire symposium. He'd seen the Director in action so many times before that his handling of the local theater troupe and an auditorium full of devotees hardly interested him, but he did hope that Barron had read through his rough draft. Various celebratory events were scheduled for that evening, and Jack didn't want to have to wait until the next morning to find out which way the Director was leaning.

His laptop was safely secured back at the Great View (and had nothing of value stored on it anyway) so he tossed his book bag onto the pickup's front seat and drove off down the tree-lined road that led to the Playhouse. The descending sun had turned the sky red, and the scene presented to him as he drove onto the theater parking lot was breathtaking. Round Pond was still a deeply frozen disc, but the sun had turned it into a rosy pink that reached right up to the commanding presence of the Playhouse. The new banner snapped merrily in the breeze from atop the cupola, and Jack stood there among the cars and trucks, alone, just to drink it all in.

Cleaning the soles of his boots on the upturned teeth of a pair of wire-brush contraptions at the door, he entered the Playhouse to find the lobby deserted. He smiled knowingly as he hung up his coat, having seen this effect before: Even the people minding the store had been sucked into Barron's orbit.

He opened one half of the auditorium's double doors without making a sound, and gingerly stepped inside. He'd somehow managed to time his entrance with a moment of total silence, and looked up at the distant stage over a sea of motionless heads.

Barron, dressed in a black turtleneck, was standing off to the side of the stage, staring at Glenda Riley and Al Griffin at its center. The two actors were dressed casually, and although they held pages in their hands they didn't seem to be using them. Jack recognized the pause when two performers were about to begin whatever Barron had requested, and he stood stock still at the back.

He shut his eyes as soon as he recognized the scene from the Rileys' kitchen, the one where Lady Macbeth is steeling her husband's nerves so that he will murder the king. Although Sarah Griffin had rehearsed this scene with Al, Glenda clearly had the whole thing prepared and flowed through it with ease. Keeping his eyes closed, Jack found it easy to imagine the two of them in costume, the stage cast in shadows as dark as the deed itself and the night that cloaked it.

Opening his eyes halfway through, he was impressed by Glenda's physical interpretation of the lady's words. It wasn't overdone, but it still transmitted the message that she was ready to take up the knife and do it herself if Macbeth wasn't man enough for the job. A microphone stood between them, allowing both Al and Glenda to utter the dread-filled lines in the tones one might expect from two conspirators standing just feet from the rooms that contained their intended victim.

The audience was silent as well, which helped, but Jack didn't notice this until the scene ended and they broke out in applause. They'd no doubt been clapping at various times throughout the day, and Jack found it highly interesting that they'd be so engrossed in an exercise late in the afternoon. Many of them were out-of-towners, which made him doubt that this was some kind of local support mechanism. Clearly Barron had captured their attention, and the players had risen to the occasion.

Barron raised a hand toward the two actors, and they were joined by Al's wife, the Lawtons, and much of the rest of their troupe. The applause rose as they assembled, and Barron asked the audience to thank them for all their hard work, both in preparing for the workshop and then performing throughout its length.

Standing in the back, unnoticed and unconcerned, Jack shut his eyes again. The clapping increased in volume, no doubt when the players took a bow, but he put a different picture in his mind. It was in the same location, and the applause was there as well. Instead of the local troupe, however, it was the Barron Players on stage. It was the end of the performance roughly two months away, and Jack Glynn imagined a thunderous ovation from the people of Schuyler Mills for the show they'd just enjoyed.

My show.

An unusual motion on stage caught his attention when he opened his eyes, and it took him a moment to identify it. Barron, still standing off to the side, had joined in the applause and was clapping his hands in the direction of the local troupe. This was out of character in many ways: First, he wasn't in the middle of the curtain call, second he was applauding someone else's actions in a symposium where he'd been the star, and finally he was paying respect to a group of amateurs.

Jack was still pondering this when Barron looked out over the crowd and saw him. The Director was already smiling, but he positively beamed when he made eye contact with his writer. He extended his right arm at shoulder level, aiming an index finger in a way that could not have been anything but congratulatory.

Once he was sure he'd gotten his attention, Barron exchanged the pointed finger for a thumb's up. The audience didn't seem aware of Jack's presence to their rear, and probably thought the Director was signaling to someone in their midst, but none of that mattered. Barron had accepted the draft of his script, and Jack found his heart thumping just a beat or two faster.

My show.

A little after nine that evening, Jack turned off his laptop and leaned back in his chair at the Great View. He'd intended to continue with the re-write of *Wind in the Palms,* but had been sidetracked at the Playhouse when he finally got to speak with Barron. The Director had been mobbed by people who had enjoyed his seminar, many of them asking questions but most of them seeking autographs. After that had subsided, the Lawtons and many of the local players had wanted to stop and thank him for what had obviously been a very rewarding experience. Berni had started moving people along after that, reminding them that the Director would be present at the cocktail party scheduled for that evening.

Barron had been riding a great high when he and Jack were finally able to catch a few minutes' conversation. His eyes were still glowing from the day's class, and Jack could see that the man's imagination had been fired by the players, the setting, and the crowd. Aware of the many eyes still in the auditorium, Barron had inclined his head while shaking Jack's hand when the writer mounted the stage.

"You really *should* get lost in the woods more often." He'd whispered. "That's one heck of a concept you've got there, and we're going with it. I've asked Berni to email you the script I put together, but only because I want to take one or two scenes from that and plug them into yours. Great job, Jack. You really saved us."

Berni had sent the encrypted file while he'd been driving back to the Great View, ecstatic at the day's developments. He was still soaring on the wings of his re-write idea for the screenplay, and even Barron's desire to incorporate some of his work hadn't worried him much. Barron always tinkered with a new play, and it happened all over again, on a more specific level, when the actors got the script in their hands.

He'd popped a celebratory beer, having stopped drinking altogether at some point in the writing of the new script, and sat down to peruse Barron's efforts. He hadn't been lying to Ryan when he'd said that he believed the Director could write a competent mystery play, and he was interested in how good it might be. He also wanted to see if he could identify the parts which Barron was likely to transfer onto the script he'd penned.

That was why he was so surprised by the quality of the play he then read. It was nothing he would have expected from Barron, and the writer in him began to admire what he was reading for its artistry as much as for its tricks. Though using a similar storyline that mixed the gangsters with the townspeople, the draft Barron had allegedly produced contained so many poignant moments and authentic characters that Jack could only read in awe. He might have felt a twinge of jealousy if he'd had the time to recognize the feeling, but the tale he was experiencing was so intriguing that he read it straight through in one sitting. The beer was warm and flat by the time he took his second sip, but he hardly noticed.

The play before him raised new questions even as it answered several old ones. Unless the Director had changed a lot over the previous two years, there was no way that he'd written anything like this. His touch was detectable at a few points, so it was likely that he'd assisted in its creation, but he hadn't been the sole, or even principal, author.

It wasn't Ryan Betancourt, either, so Jack was at least able to finally set aside the possibility that Barron and Ryan were conspiring together. There was a deftness to this piece that had never manifested itself in Ryan's headlong pursuit of the big moment. Jack had re-read several passages in the script because he felt he'd missed something in the first run-through, and had come to see that he'd missed more than he'd even suspected. The subtle telling of this tale had allowed a pair of heart-wrenching moments to slip by him in the same way that several major clues had sneaked under his radar.

The thing was amazing, and it left him with two new questions: Who had written it, and why had Barron rejected it?

He'd read it through a second time before shutting off the machine, but was no closer to an answer when a heavy hand had knocked on his front door. Mystery Weekend was in full swing and it was also a Saturday night, so he assumed that many cars had come and gone in the Great View's parking lot while he'd been immersed in the new play. Making sure that the laptop was indeed off, he rose and went to answer the knock.

The three people Wade had warned him about all shouted, "Surprise!" when he opened the door. The night air was bracingly cold, and they were all dressed for the elements in a variety of waist-length ski jackets and hats. Gary wore a billed hunting cap with earflaps that would have gone nicely with Tillman's favorite coat, Tadd's spikes were no doubt mashed flat by the red watch cap he wore, and Lynnie sported a pink beret with fabric flowers to one side.

"Get your boots on, Jack!" Gary commanded happily, and the three of them pushed by him into the small room.

"My boots?" Jack shut the door even as the cabin's heating unit kicked back on, almost in protest at the amount of cold that had been allowed inside. "Where are we going?"

"Skating!" Tadd practically shouted from near the back door. Lynnie had dropped onto the bed, and Gary had already found one of the boots he'd mentioned.

Raising a bent leg, he pressed the sole of Jack's boot against his own and seemed pleased at the result. "Told ya his feet are almost as big as mine. He can use my spares."

"You do know how to skate, don'tcha Jack?" Lynnie asked from the bed, her eyes practically dancing with excitement. Jack sat down next to her and began lacing up his boots.

"I can stay up." That was an understatement. He was a fair skater, but had to wonder why the three of them were so jazzed about a few spins around the common. "I saw that they flooded the town square to make a rink. That where we're going?"

They all laughed at that, but Tadd regained his sense of manners sooner than the others. "The kiddy rink? Naw, we leave that to the tourists."

Lynnie laid an affectionate hand on his shoulder. "We're gonna show you how North Country people *really* do it."

They'd piled into Tadd's car and fishtailed down the road in the direction of Newville before heading off into the hills. There were no lights out there, and the car's beams only managed to illuminate a small cone of packed snow directly in front of them as they went. The woods on either side were pitch black, and the weak headlights occasionally flashed on a mailbox here and a side road there. Tadd wasn't sparing the horses, and the light vehicle slewed around on the slick at just about every turn. Jack might have found that disconcerting were he not seated next to Lynnie, who slid into him even when the skid didn't force it.

After a few minutes they turned down a narrow passage flanked on both sides by a low stone wall that probably dated back to colonial times. Things brightened up when the car crested a slight rise which allowed Jack to see their destination. It was a frozen pond roughly two hundred yards wide by a hundred across, and the near bank was lined with dozens of cars, trucks, and snowmobiles. Several portable light towers had been erected in the snow or stood in the beds of different pickup trucks, so one half of the ice was illuminated brightly. The remaining half slowly shifted from a gray gloom to outright darkness, even though the trees which bordered the far side were just visible against the star-blanketed sky. Jack was astounded to see skaters zipping out of the darkened netherworld and straight into the human traffic on the floodlit side of the ice, but there seemed to be few collisions.

Once out of the car, he was able to see that several burn barrels had been put in place near the ice and that a few dedicated souls were tending the warming fires. There were no benches anywhere, so he wrestled his way out of his boots and into Gary's spare skates while sitting half-in and half-out of Tadd's car. The others were much more practiced in this maneuver, and had already slipped out onto the ice before he was finally ready. He tottered over to the edge and was relieved to find that it lapped right up onto dry land. With a quick look to his left, he slid a foot out onto the surface and gently skated away.

Gliding along, he was struck by how quiet it was out there. He was quickly overtaken and passed by several other skaters of varying ages, but with the exception of a few hoots and an occasional word the entire expanse was nearly silent. He held to the outside while getting reacquainted with the act of propelling himself across a nearly frictionless surface, and could hear the scraping of the blades on the frozen water beneath him. He was a good skater, and was soon transferring his weight from side to side with greater ease. He picked up the pace, and finally reached a comfort level where he could hang his arms by his sides and simply float along.

He'd made a circuit of the illuminated zone by then, passing so close to the trees on the far side that he could have reached out and touched their overhanging branches. Most of the others were doing the same thing, staying where they could actually see what they were doing, while a few would peel off and disappear into the shadows that covered the other half of the ice. His writer's eye compared them to meteors being sucked into a black hole, and when they emerged on the other side he likened them to particles being fired at a charged field of other particles inside an atom smasher.

The second comparison seemed to fit better, as long as the fired molecule was one that repelled the particles in its path. Lanes magically opened for the skaters rejoining the group, and yet he still didn't hear much in the way of words. The rhythmic scraping of the blades had a calming effect on his respiration, and he was warm in his jacket while the cold kissed his face. He floated along in the middle of the pack for a time, his legs gently pushing whenever he lost momentum, allowing his mind to surrender.

He caught sight of Gary at one point, skating side by side with a startlingly beautiful brunette, their arms around each other's waists and moving as one. A while later he was passed by Tadd and Lynnie, jokingly taunting him for skating like an old man, and was pleased to see them join hands once they were by. He'd long suspected the boy harbored feelings for the worldlier blonde, and now hoped the success of the previous Thursday had provided the spark that Tadd needed to make his move.

As if imitating that moment of decision, Jack failed to change course as he headed straight for the unlit part of the ice. Having gone by it so many times, he now knew that it was a larger, oval area not unlike the top of a mushroom on the stalk of the lake's illuminated portion, and that it wasn't quite as dark as it had at first seemed. Gliding into it, he passed through the first dim shadows feeling like a diver beginning to descend into ocean depths. His eyes had difficulty adjusting in time with the rapidly increasing darkness, but he was unconcerned because he could see the white boundary where the lake ended and the snow began.

Another skater flashed by him in the murk, a tall man dressed in dark clothing, and he was startled by the thought of the phantom who had accosted Ryan in Red Bend. Though the man was gone in an instant, Jack found his eyes seeking the shelter of the lights that now appeared to be miles away. His skates seemed to be making a huge racket now that he was alone, but even so he was aware of the wind sighing in the trees as he went by them. This reminded him of the sinister poster for the Schuyler Mills play, the one with the body under the ice, and he had to fight a genuine impulse to flee for the light. Another figure passed him, this one a blonde girl with long hair fluttering behind her, and he had to resist the urge to catch up to her. He was reaching the outermost part of the curve that would take him into the more populated zone, and was disgusted to register just how much he wanted to be back out there.

Ice crystals scattered in a wave when he turned both blades against his direction of travel, bringing himself to a sudden stop. The gloom enfolded him, but he simply stood there looking at the other end of the lake. One set of floodlights caught him just the wrong way, filling his vision with a retina burn, and he turned his gaze away until it cleared. Two other people went by in that moment, and he forced himself to stand there without even trying to see if they were male or female, tall or short.

His vision cleared, and he raised his eyes to see yet another skater, this one a teenaged boy totally oblivious to his presence, passing by within a few feet. That gave him an idea, and he tilted his head unconsciously as he mulled the similarity between his unobserved spot in the shadows and the view from a seat in a theater. He could clearly distinguish individual skaters in the illuminated part of the ice, and they looked surprisingly like actors on a floodlit stage.

His earlier bout of panic slowly evaporated with the realization that he was now the only one there who could see everyone else. Even the skaters braving the darkness couldn't detect him, their eyes barely adjusting to the decreasing light just before they turned to embrace it again. He waited for close to a minute until the tall skater in dark clothing came back around under the floods and then flashed into the audience.

The figure came within a few yards as he passed, and Jack experienced a delicious thrill at the idea that he was invisible to the man whom he had mistaken for Ryan's phantom. A flood of images, similes, and analogies rushed through his mind in a torrent, and he might have stood there for some time if a new participant hadn't zoomed into view.

Kelly Sykes wore the same white jacket he'd seen her skating in before, but the short skirt and tights were dark blue under the floodlights. She must have just arrived, or at least just taken to the ice, because he was sure he'd have noticed her before then. She appeared to be warming up, effortlessly swaying from side to side and staying in the light as she moved. The hood was down, and she wore a pink band around her head that partially covered her ears. She was soon immersed in the crowd, and he wondered if she would swing out into the shadows or stay in the light.

Stay in the light. Enter the darkness. Emerge from the shadows.

A memory came into his mind unbidden, a moment that should have received more of his attention when it happened. It was the rehearsal where Barron had been grilling Glenda Riley about her depiction of Ophelia.

"Uh, Jerry?"

The voice had been Kelly's, and she'd been literally rising to Glenda's defense. Another sentence, also spoken by Kelly, came back to him from their first conversation.

"He lets me call him Jerome."

Jack let out a slight snort of laughter when the puzzle finally began to fall into place. It was like the moment in the play when the culprit is identified, as the slowly building presentation of the crucial evidence points inexorably toward one character. He now saw that she'd even tried to give him a hint, when he'd asked if she could keep a secret:

"You have no idea how good I am at that."

More images and sounds came into his head. Kelly looking at the ice sculpture of the violin outside the fire station, seeming to know that it wasn't an authorized clue. Referring to the Seven Seas Gang as 'the Seven Gang' even though none of the troupe's hints had yet used the gangsters' pet name for themselves. Barron blurting out, "She *said* you were behind this!" when he'd confessed authorship of the violins. The photo supplied by Ryan, the one with Kelly and Barron standing together at the hotel in Schenectady.

She was always busy with something, right around the times when I went to visit Barron.

A broad smile crept onto his face, and he turned in a slow circle out in the darkness. A final image came and went, the scene he should have read for what it really was: Barron sitting in the booth at the hotel in Maine, with Kelly supposedly interviewing him. He'd started speaking louder when Jack approached, and had intentionally praised Ryan Betancourt even though Jack knew the Director never spoke well of writers—even dead ones—in public.

She even pretended to have another question for him. And Berni pretended to cut her off.

With a mild shake of his head he pushed off, slowly approaching the revolving mass of humanity that now looked like a display of wind-up Christmas toys in a store window. He timed his exit so that he was just a bit in front of her, and Kelly turned a pleasant face in his direction when he emerged.

"Jack!" She sounded happy, and reached out a mittened hand to snag his arm when he drew near. "I didn't know you skated!"

"I suppose I should have mentioned it . . . but you know Death Troupe; nothing's what it seems to be."

His response had been light, but even so she was having trouble keeping her smile from warping. "That's what they tell me."

"You seem happy about something." They skated along together, arm in arm, moving in unison while people passed them on either side.

"Of course. Mystery Weekend's as good as over. The town pulled in a lot of money, and people can't stop talking about Barron's seminar."

"You mean Jerry."

"I'm afraid he's still Jerome to me. Didn't you say he lets you call him Jerry?"

"I did. It's a strange thing, because there are even some actors he doesn't let do that. But the writers . . . well, me and Ryan . . . we always got away with it."

The smirk was threatening to overflow the banks of her self-control, and they turned toward the darkened section of the pond as she fought for an answer.

"I'll have to try that someday. Maybe toward the end of the engagement."

"I thought I heard you say it the other night. When Barron was giving fair Ophelia a ration of abuse."

"Really? As I recall, he made me call him Mr. Barron at the time."

"You recall correctly." Jack reached across with his right hand and took a firm grip on her arm, the one that was linked through his left. "Wanna brave the dark side?"

She twisted away easily, turning to face him while skating backward. The smirk was gone, exchanged for a grin that was both challenge and insult. She began opening the distance with long, sinuous back strides. "*Brave* it? I ain't afraid a nothing, mystery man."

He pushed off with greater strength, but she wasn't trying to lose him. After they were deep in the murk she twirled on one skate and then swung around in a tight circle that took her all the way around him as he moved.

"What's on your mind, Jack?" The darkness had turned her into a glowing, taunting wraith floating around him, and he cut across her path just to make her change it.

"I read a play tonight. A new one."

"Really?" He couldn't make out her features, but he imagined she was showing all her teeth and that her eyes were flashing in merry expectation. "I bet it sucked."

"It beats the one I wrote."

"You're just saying that to sound humble. You're a fraud, Jack Glynn."

They were almost at the spot where he'd been standing not five minutes earlier, and he stopped there again. That surprised her, and she reversed directions with a rasp of metal on ice. Kelly materialized next to him with a questioning look, and then resumed her lazy circles.

"No I'm not. I couldn't figure out who wrote the thing, but then I remembered this gal . . . somebody who'd been coaching the local community players, and how she slipped up just a tad. She called Barron 'Jerry', which was a little odd for the town publicity lady. And that reminded me of how she was never available for dinner in the days before or after one of my out-of-town meetings with the D. Claimed she was busy with work."

The shears-on-paper sound of an approaching skater silenced him, but not before Kelly pulled up and stopped directly behind him. He stood stock still, and the third party came up and then passed as if unaware of their presence. Even after the intruder was gone he still stood there, transfixed by the simplest of gestures. Kelly's left hand was holding his left elbow and squeezing it, and she stood close enough for him to feel her breath on his neck.

"Is that how they do it? The signal to watch your words? Berni tried to teach me, just for fun, but I'm not sure I got it right." Her opposite hand now squeezed his other arm, and she pressed up against him from behind. Her chin tilted up to rest on his shoulder, and he imagined her leaning forward on the blades as if on tiptoe. "I've been dying to let you in on the secret . . . but 'Jerry' wouldn't let me."

He turned, placing his hands on her hips. They kissed gently, hardly noticing when another skater went by. She broke it off first, allowing him to ask the question he'd been wanting answered for a long time. "So why'd you tell everybody in town that something had happened between us?"

She rubbed his shoulders briskly, and he could see that she was close to laughing. "Figured out I was behind that, did you? I really should apologize; it was all my fault to begin with. I forgot how small a place this is. I'd been spending so much time with you, picking your brains for how you dealt with Barron, that people began to talk. I needed an excuse to step away from you, so I'm afraid I made them think we'd had a little spat."

She pushed off just then, taking his hands in hers and pulling him along. Kicking forward in response, he replied without heat. "You know I took a lot of grief for that."

"I do. But hey, if you couldn't figure it out you shouldn't be writing for Death Troupe." She stopped after that, still in the concealing embrace of the shadows. He slid right up to her, and they kissed again, longer this time. "Besides, maybe that helped you write your version of the play . . . which is really very, very good. I'm not surprised Jerry picked it over mine."

"I am."

"Well that just goes to prove you've got no taste . . . except in women, of course."

Kelly turned so she was standing beside him. She took his arm again, and they slowly pushed off toward the light.

Underneath their blades, the ice gave off a low popping noise, and Jack could have sworn he felt it move. Kelly had sensed it too, and gave a small laugh.

"You feel that?"

"Yes! Are we in danger?"

"Not at all . . . but it *is* March. That was Mother Nature saying the thaw isn't far off." She squeezed his arm again in warning as they rejoined the others. "Spring's coming, Jack. Rebirth. Warmth. Fun. It's all on the way."

Part Three

The Show

Chapter Nineteen

The Mystery Weekend ended with a late brunch at Maddy's Place on Sunday. Mayor Tillman was thrilled by the event's success and exhausted from its demands, but he circulated among the tables and booths anyway. He had the sense to recognize that there were too many hangovers for formal closing remarks, and allowed everyone to enjoy the company they selected. Although a steady flow of cars heading out of town was visible through the front windows, the brunch was well attended and Barron wasn't able to get back to his room before one.

Berni had already packed most of their things, but the ongoing winter meant that no one was waiting for Barron's suite. He'd asked Jack to come up to the room for a final conference when they'd met at the brunch, and the writer had agreed with a pleasant nod.

So it was with some surprise and a little concern that the Director opened the door to see both Jack and Kelly standing in the hallway wearing smiles more fitting to a feline who had just dined on a small yellow bird. Jack blinked several times in quick succession, as if trying to charm the man at the door, while Kelly raised a hand to flutter her fingers in insolent greeting.

Barron's mouth puckered into an "O" shape, and he exhaled audibly while surveying the latest shock of the Schuyler Mills engagement. His two visitors didn't say a word, and he recovered his composure quickly enough.

"I assume there's a reason you're looking at me like that."

"Maybe we should talk about this inside." Jack replied brightly. "That is, as long as the room's been swept for bugs today."

"Oh it has!" Berni sang out helpfully from the bedroom. She came through the doorway into the sitting room with a suitcase in either hand, and stopped short when she saw Jack wasn't alone. An uncharacteristic look of consternation popped up onto her features and stayed there. Taking pity, Jack tossed a friendly wink her way before speaking in a chiding fashion.

"Shame on you, Berni. Not telling me."

Barron's assistant placed both suitcases on the carpet, and when she came back up it was to fix Jack with a look of amused superiority. "Hey Jack?"

"Yes?"

"*Now* we're even."

". . . so she showed me a few things she'd written, I liked them, and I decided to take her up on her offer." Barron, seated in the reading chair, finished the tale of how Kelly had talked her way into a secret and probationary role as Death Troupe's backup playwright. "God knows Ryan wasn't working out, you'd gone off to the desert to become a holy man, and I was looking around for a new writer anyway.

"Besides . . ." the Director allowed himself a private smile. "It's a great twist. Everybody's watching my main writer, trying to get him to spill something, when one of their own is penning an alternate script. Imagine their faces when they find out."

"Which raises an interesting question: When are they supposed to find out?" Jack inquired softly. Kelly hadn't been concerned with this detail when she'd told him essentially the same story the night before, but she still didn't know that the real writing hadn't even begun.

"Well, I was planning to keep it a secret until just after the show, and I'd like to stay with that if possible." Barron looked puzzled for a moment and turned his attention to Kelly, who was seated on the floor next to Jack in front of the shaded window. "I honestly didn't think he'd figure this out. Just how did he get you to admit it? What did he do?"

The man and woman on the floor both snorted in unison, trying to keep from laughing out loud. Jack dropped his hand onto Kelly's shoulder, the first time he'd touched her in Barron's presence, but this only served to confuse the Director further.

Kelly removed her hand from her mouth as soon as she thought she could reply with a straight face. She managed it, but her voice was strained with barely controlled mirth. "He's a very persuasive man, Jerry. I think I've seen a side of him you may not be acquainted with."

Berni, seated at the desk, fixed them with a knowing look of reproof until Jack made a kissing gesture in her direction. She looked away quickly, not sure if Barron had caught on yet.

"Persuasive, eh? That *is* a side of him I've never seen." Still puzzled, the Director looked over their three faces before giving his head a slight toss as if dismissing the whole quandary. "Well, the cat's out of the bag now, so we need to make sure that nobody else catches on. You two are going to be working together closely on this, so we need to come up with some kind of cover story. Some reason for the two of you to be seen spending time together. Any ideas?"

This question summoned a veritable tsunami of laughter, and even Berni was swept away. Jack and Kelly were collapsed against each other, and it was only when he noticed the way Kelly's forehead was nestled against Jack's neck that Barron understood.

"Oh." He whispered from deep in his throat. "Well . . ." he allowed himself a small laugh. "That certainly works as a cover. Very good. I approve."

Jack got back to his cabin a couple of hours later, to find a message waiting on his cell phone. He'd completely forgotten the device that morning, and accessed the message to find it was from Lynnie. Her voice fairly bubbled over the machine.

"Hey Jack, where'd ya go last night? We found Gary's skates in the car and your boots were gone so we figured you didn't fall through the ice." She gave off a happy laugh. "And *somebody* . . . told me they saw you gettin' friendly with Kelly Sykes. Remember to tell her your boss disapproves." She giggled again, and then took her voice down a notch. "Ah, it's just as well . . . Tadd and me are kinda together, after last night . . . thought you should know. Call me back. Lova ya, bye."

He put the phone back in its cradle, taking the message and its content to be a sign. He hadn't been sure of how he was going to break the news to Allison, but if a shameless spirit like Lynnie felt it was proper to provide notification the very next day, he figured he had to do the same. He sat down in the chair and mentally composed a few phrases that he knew he wouldn't retain once the conversation started, somehow feeling that Allison wouldn't be surprised. She might even be relieved.

Jack dialed the number and turned to look at the shambles of his bed. He wasn't sorry at all, but he did reach out and snake the bra off the bedpost where Kelly had hung it as if marking her territory. He pulled himself back to the job at hand just after sliding the garment out of sight under the covers.

He had steeled himself for a blunt argument with whichever lackey answered the phone, and so was unprepared when Allison's voice came at him.

"Hi, Jack. It's nice to hear from you."

"Hey there, Allison. I'm a little surprised to hear you answer the phone."

"Don't be." She gave a small chuckle. "I had to let my assistants go."

Momentarily derailed, Jack conjured up images of the annoying Mickey Parsons and Todd Lambert. One of them had been a spy for Wade, and he wondered if that was what had gotten both of them fired. "What happened? They forget to tell you someone called?"

"Oh, nothing, really. Just a pair of pushy boys who really like California and don't know enough about the stage. I'm sure they'll be fine. So what's going on?"

Her voice was calm and level, and he couldn't tell if someone (Berni, perhaps) had beaten him to the punch in order to protect the troupe's leading lady.

"I've got something to tell you . . . I would have preferred to do this face-to-face, but—"

"We haven't been face-to-face since Maine, Jack." The tone was soft and comforting, and made him more certain that she knew what was coming. He took a breath, but she beat him to it. "I think we both know this isn't really working out."

It sounded like a line from a relationship movie, but Jack was thrilled to hear it. He hadn't given her a thought at any point the previous night, and was shocked that he didn't feel guilty. He harbored no ill will against her for cheating on him with Ryan, and knew in his heart that he didn't mean to hurt her, but perhaps that was what was so strange. The woman he'd longed for all those months had become a nonentity even before she'd returned to him, and he hadn't known that until she'd been replaced.

"I'm afraid so. You know I'm not trying to get back at you, right?"

"I know that, sweetheart." She gave a frustrated chuckle, as if talking to the village idiot. "And I can't explain why, but being on the receiving end of one of these is a lot easier."

He briefly remembered the ugly confrontation when she and Ryan had revealed themselves to him, but pushed it away out of fear that it would somehow taint his honest intentions. "Maybe we've both reached an age where we need somebody who's going to be physically with us . . . ya think?"

"Oh, Jack." He could see her head shaking. "You were always that age. It's one of the things I love about you. You put up with the separation because you really wanted to be with me. I want you to know I did notice." There was a long pause. "If I had two lives, I would have given you one of them long ago. But maybe that's why it didn't work. I only have the one."

"A bright, beautiful life."

"You're trying to make me cry, aren't you?"

They both laughed gently, and he remembered one of the phrases he'd prepared. "I've finished the first draft of the play, but I'm going to punch up your part just a bit. A bright, beautiful role."

"Please don't. The parts you wrote for me were always perfect because you didn't try to do that. Make me a quiet little church mouse for this one, okay?"

"I will."

"Promise me that."

"I promise."

He heard her take a deep breath, not knowing how to end the call, so he gave her time. When she came back on, her voice was stronger. "So . . . is it still winter there?"

A feeling of intermission followed the conclusion of Mystery Weekend. The brief influx of tourists went out like the tide, the various monuments arranged around the town common were slowly removed, and everyone seemed to be catching their breath.

Jack, knowing Barron's inability to leave a script alone, put the time to good use by working on his re-write of *Wind in the Palms*. His agent was overjoyed that he was giving it another try, and he even received a couple of phone calls from the producers who were treading water on the project.

More importantly, he now had the opportunity to spend a lot of time with Kelly and didn't need to explain any of it. Word had spread quickly of their budding romance, and many a head had nodded that the predicted match had finally sorted itself out. They ate dinner together, went on long walks, and even took a day trip to the deserted mining town that so many Schuyler Mills residents had recommended. They both enjoyed the deception, largely because it was only half a lie, and also because Kelly was convinced that the townspeople would find her secret role to be one fine joke when it was revealed to them.

For his part, Jack had to remind Kelly more than once that Barron was almost guaranteed to tinker with the play right up until the night of the performance. The three weeks between the Mystery Weekend and the troupe's arrival in early April were not likely to be much of a hiatus, as he expected to start receiving Barron's first suggestions at any moment. They'd chosen the kitchen in her small house as the best place to work unobserved when the edits began rolling in, and it wasn't long before they heard from Barron again.

The new message from the Director was not pointed at them, and they heard about it in much the same fashion as they'd learned of the previous clues. Jack had forgotten that he'd once mentioned the abandoned billboard on the road leading out to the Playhouse, but apparently Barron had not. In yet another nocturnal strike, someone had ascended the thin aluminum ladder nailed to the structure's left-most upright and glued a larger-than-life advertisement in place.

"Those *are* the names of your characters, right?" Kelly asked him *sotto voce* as they admired the night stalker's handiwork alongside several other interested townsfolk.

Jack had given her a gentle nod, pleased to see that Barron had so much faith in a play he'd only just read a few days earlier. Against a white background with horizontal lines meant to establish height, six of the most prominent Death Troupe actors stood in a police lineup. Jack knew that the individual pictures had been taken wherever the players were currently performing, and that someone with computer skills had arranged them for the giant poster.

He also knew that the billboard's old floodlights didn't work, but Barron's operatives had managed to include them anyway. Hanging down like wilting tulips, they would have been aimed straight into the actors' eyes and so all six suspects were either squinting or glaring in reaction. It had a very noir feel to it, and so they were all dressed in outfits that could have come straight out of any detective film of that genre.

Each of them held a black signboard bearing their character's name, and Jack was delighted to see that Barron had assigned the roles the way he'd envisioned. A trench coat-clad Robert Hale had been cast as the investigator, and he looked sideways with a cocked eyebrow at a suit-wearing Puff Addersley. Puff had been chosen to play the patriarch of the most powerful of the Seven Seas Gang's familial descendants, and was staring ahead with disdain. Trask Saunders, dressed like a man down on his luck, had received the role of the doomed town resident who first tries to help the investigator and ends up under the ice for his troubles.

Barron's other casting decisions all met Jack's expectations, except he'd switched Allison Green and Sally Newsome. The role of the kindhearted town librarian who helps the investigator practically screamed for Allison, but he'd given that to Sally. She held her placard unevenly, looking out at the crowd in fear, and Jack shook his head that she couldn't even capture the character's essence in a publicity photo. As for Allison, she was now the guilt-ridden heiress of the Seven Seas Gang's most vicious family, and her pain practically flowed off the billboard.

"Make me a quiet little church mouse for this one, okay?"

As if anybody in the audience would ever believe you in a role like that.

Next to Allison, a hard-faced Paula Ninninger gave the impression of someone pretending to be tough because she knows she isn't, and Jack liked that a lot. She was the culprit in the rough draft, and although he would eventually write other endings where she was innocent, Jack hoped to stick with her as the murderess. She was playing it perfectly in the photo, with false self-confidence that seemed ready to collapse at any moment—which would neatly convince much of the audience she couldn't be the killer.

"Isn't Allison Green beautiful?"

The words interrupted his thoughts, and he turned to see an elderly lady in a full-length winter coat and a multicolored knit cap at his elbow. For an instant he'd thought Kelly had spoken the words, and hadn't known how to respond. He'd told her every detail of his relationship with Allison, including its end, although he suspected she'd already heard most of it from Barron or Berni long before.

Looking down at the hopeful, upturned face, he gave the woman a broad smile. "Just wait until you meet her in person. It's something you'll never forget."

The days had been getting noticeably longer, and the greater duration of the sun's presence had melted most of the snow on the roads by then. Jack had been hesitant to start jogging again, fearing a spill on unseen ice, but now there was no excuse and he decided to give it a try. Rising with the sun, he pulled on a full set of sweats over his running shorts and added the down vest from his cross-country skiing rig for good measure. Donning his wool hat and gloves, he'd stretched out on the porch while listening to birds chirping in the nearby trees.

Having taken care of the preliminaries, he slowly jogged out of the Great View's parking lot and began shuffling down the road in the direction of the Playhouse. He'd run on the treadmill at the volunteer fire department gym several times in the recent weeks, and had logged many miles skiing, but he knew that the muscles he'd built up in the desert would be badly atrophied and so he took it easy.

The road leading to the Playhouse was all woods, and he watched squirrels frolicking in the trees as he went along. Something larger went crashing off into the brush at another point, and he allowed himself to admit that the winter was finally easing its grip. His sneakers pounded small ridges of slush into nothing as he ran, and even this early in the day he could see snowmelt starting to flow down the road.

He'd planned to jog out to the Playhouse and back, but his arrival at the old billboard changed that. The thoroughfare had been almost empty of traffic until then, but when he came around the bend near the sign there were several cars and trucks parked just ahead of him. He recognized some of the faces in the group, standing near the snow bank piled up in front of the advertisement for the show.

Jack had seen vandalism on Death Troupe clues before, but it was usually a mindless variety that could be easily ascribed to the disaffected. This case was different, however, and he jogged in place for a few moments in order to take it in. Five of the six characters had been crossed off with broad X's that started at either shoulder and went to mid-thigh. The X marks were hand-painted in a bold red, and they were too wide to have been done with a spray can. There were no runnels of excess paint anywhere, and Jack took this as a sign that the perpetrator had been in no rush.

The X's didn't bother him quite as much as the single circle painted on the sign, an oval that neatly framed Paula Ninninger's face. The painter had finished that mark with a jaunty up-flip of the brush at its base, as if saying, "So there!" and the meaning could not have been more clear: Paula Ninninger's character was the culprit.

The mayor's truck came around the bend and joined the others at this point, so Jack jogged over as both Tillman and Kelly got out. The mayor's face was clean-shaven and he was wearing his red and black jacket, but Kelly looked like she'd come straight from bed. Loose hair hung out from under her hat, which suggested the rest of it had been stuffed up under there in a hurry. She wore the full-length olive drab coat, but still seemed cold as she regarded the defacement of the poster.

"Morning, Jack. Out for a jog?" Tillman asked, his face turned up toward the billboard.

"I was, until I got here and saw this."

"Is this a clue?" Kelly asked, also looking at the sign. "A clue on top of another one?"

"Not sure. If I had to guess, I'd say no. Those six actors are likely to be among the seven named suspects in the show, so we'd be taking a big chance with a visual like that."

"Look at those strokes. Whoever did this wasn't in a hurry." Kelly made this observation to Tillman. She was avoiding Jack's gaze, and he gave her credit for doing that. This was their first joint appearance involving the show, and it was fraught with danger that a careless word would reveal her hidden role.

"That's what I was thinking." Tillman said this judiciously, neither concerned nor dismissive. "I sure hope nobody's gone and vandalized this thing. What would you like to do if that's the case, Jack?"

"The Director's always encouraged outside involvement, so if it bites us on the butt once in a while I can't say I'm surprised. A clue like this one is just ripe for this kind of thing, and of course the original poster is still clearly depicted on the website . . . so I say no harm done." He was impressed at the way the words came out, as if he really meant them. Graffiti on the sign was nothing to get excited over, but he couldn't ignore the fact that the vandal had correctly picked the culprit in the current script. "Besides, I'm still not sure it might not be part of the act. I'll have to make a call."

"I appreciate your attitude, Jack." Tillman turned to Kelly. "If it's just the work of some wiseacre, is there any way to take that paint off?"

Jack started to protest, but Kelly cut him off. "Oh, I'd say that would be tough, without ruining the sign. But here's what I've been thinking, standing here: If it's a prank, how about we get some paint of our own and write in a caption? Something like, 'Don't Forget to Vote'."

The two men turned and studied the sign once again, obviously imagining it with the explanatory words painted under the suspects' feet. Tillman waited patiently for the sign's owner to provide an opinion, and Jack didn't take long.

"I like that. We get to leave the billboard up, and it actually promotes the show." He turned an admiring look at Kelly. "You must be one of those trained public relations people."

Tillman peeled back the sleeve of his jacket to look at his watch. "Oops. I've got a patient waiting for me, so I gotta run. Let us know if you want to add that caption." He started back toward the truck, and Kelly leaned over to give Jack a kiss on the cheek.

"How'd I handle that?" she asked, mindful of the people nearby.

"Perfectly. And that's a great idea, too. You should write for Death Troupe."

She gave his arm a swat with one of her mittened hands before following the mayor.

Jack brought flowers when he went over to Kelly's house that night, and anyone watching would have believed it a simple dinner date. They wouldn't have been wrong, as there was a meal involved and Jack was shortly pressed into service browning hamburger meat for the tacos Kelly was fixing.

Her place was very similar to the Riley house, and like that couple they'd decided the kitchen was the best place for work. Pull-down shades on the back door and the window above the sink would shield them from prying eyes once they got to the rewrite stage, but for now they could be left up.

Kelly had supervised a work detail that afternoon out at the defaced billboard. She'd gone one better on her original idea, adding an X across Paula Ninninger's torso and circles around the faces of the other five players on the sign. By marking all of the characters in the same way, she'd transformed the original vandalism into a reasonable facsimile of a ballot. The caption, "Don't Forget to Vote" now stood out in hand-painted red block letters across the bottom.

Jack had complimented her on the job, and she'd told him all about the project as they prepared the meal. She'd originally wanted to enlist the aid of the older elementary school children, feeling it would be a good exercise in civic responsibility, but the platform itself was so rickety that it was out of the question. Jack protested that he would have volunteered, but Kelly had been worried that such direct involvement by Death Troupe's writer might be misunderstood. The ladies' sewing club had come to her rescue upon learning of the predicament, pooh-poohing the instability of the painting platform and clambering up the ladder with gusto.

"Their only concern was about their clothing. They wanted to be warm, but they didn't want to get paint on their winter jackets." Kelly finished chopping an onion into small bits and then began seasoning the hamburger in the skillet Jack was minding.

"So what did you do?" Jack had only seen the end result of the sewing society's day on the scaffolding.

"Marv remembered we had a bunch of those cheap throw-away ponchos, the ones they sell at ball parks, in the back of the Visitor's Center. Left over from God knows what, but they did the job. You should have seen the ladies prancing around up there in those things."

"You weren't with them?"

"Somebody had to stand back and tell them if the X's were long enough or the circles were wide enough." She responded defensively, turning off the heat under the pan. "Beside, I'm not crazy. I thought that platform was gonna let go at any moment!"

They settled into chairs once the food was ready, and the conversation lagged for a bit while they ate. Jack began to speak after his overloaded taco shell loudly disintegrated onto his plate. "I talked to the D this afternoon. He's a little concerned about this, but not much." Pictures of the billboard were all over Rumor Control, but so far the phantom Scarlet hadn't added anything to the conversation in the chat room.

"I saw that Berni disowned the original marks. I guess that was the only thing to do."

"In this case, probably. But there's a catch to denying too many of these things, no matter where they come from: It can make the potential audience lose interest in the whole process. It can also rev up whoever's bothering us."

"How would that work?"

"If someone puts up a clue of their own, or pulls a prank like this one, rejecting it right away just gives them a reason to do something else. But if we let it run for awhile, that sometimes stretches out the time between incidents. And don't forget: We're not on the hook for anything that we don't positively identify as one of our clues. So if somebody in the audience gets led astray by a local nut job, it's not our fault."

"Is that what you think it is? Some kind of crazy person?"

Jack felt a twinge of guilt just then, knowing that he was keeping Ryan's existence from her and the rest of the troupe. He felt he had solid reasons for that, though; his new romance with Kelly, Barron's acceptance of his script, and the painless breakup with Allison had intensified his feelings of sympathy for Ryan. He'd always suspected the other writer's overstated confidence masked a deep insecurity, and he now believed that the incidents in Red Bend had brought that weakness to a head. He couldn't stop imagining a gaunt Ryan Betancourt in a small camper somewhere, wrestling with a mystery that was no more real than anything else the writer had ever imagined.

"Not this time, no. I'm more concerned that someone's gotten a look at the play. Someone who shouldn't have."

They both ate in silence for close to a minute, but the elephant in the room wouldn't be ignored. Kelly finally broached the topic on both their minds. "Is there a chance Barron's behind it? He's been doing unusual things on this engagement, starting with me, so maybe he's having some fun with this."

"I thought of that when I was talking to him. He didn't sound like he was up to something, but you don't spend your entire life around actors without picking up a few of their tricks." He took a sip from his water glass. "You know, in a way I hope that's what it is. 'cause if he's behind this, the script's still secure."

"And if not?"

He reached a hand across and squeezed one of hers with true warmth. "Then I guess we're lucky to have an excellent backup play, written by a very gifted writer."

She gave him a look that was part gratitude and part disbelief, but squeezed his hand in return. "You think we might have to do that? Switch plays?"

"Right now, probably not. But if there are any more indications that the first draft's been compromised we're going to have to get realistic. Of course we've got one thing that helps us in that arena: You and I were going to have to rewrite that version anyway, building different endings and adding the parts from your play that Barron liked best. So even if somebody's seen the whole thing, at this stage it's not an absolute killer."

"It might be."

"How's that?"

"Well, we're talking about my play as if it's locked up at Fort Knox when it isn't. It got emailed around almost as much as yours did." Jack's brow furrowed with this new wrinkle. He hadn't considered that, but now remembered the careless way that Kelly's script had been sent to him. The troupe's communications were encrypted and secure, but that morning's prank suggested they weren't inviolate. If that was the case, perhaps both versions of the play were tainted.

"You're thinking we might have two drafts that are suspect?"

Kelly raised both hands as if in defense. "I didn't want to be the one to say it."

Jack pushed his chair back and allowed himself to sag just a little. After a moment he directed a half smile at Kelly while squinting his eyes in accusation. "Anybody ever tell you that for a pretty girl you're a real downer?"

"I gotta call 'em like I see 'em. But it's not all lost just yet." Kelly reached over to the kitchen counter top and snagged a small manila envelope that had escaped Jack's eye. "Here. I got you a little present."

Jack took the envelope and lifted its unsealed flap. A plain wire ring holding two brass keys fell onto his place mat, and he looked up in sappy gratitude. "Darling. You shouldn't have."

Kelly pointed at the keys. "The big one's to the boom blocking the Campion Hill Road, and the little one's to the fence around the fire tower. Whoever put that mannequin up there did us a real favor. He created our own little *pied a terre*."

"Don't you think it's a little soon for us to move in together? Even if it's just our own little tree fort?"

"What a dope you are. You're lucky you're cute." She gestured at the keys again. "Marv doesn't know it, but he gave us our very own writing sanctuary when he fenced the place off. We can go up there whenever we want, and no one'll be the wiser."

She stood slowly, stepped across to him, and sat on his lap. "And even if they do catch on, they'll just assume it's two crazy kids looking for some privacy."

Although he couldn't be sure that the phantom Scarlet was connected to the billboard's defacement, Jack came to believe that was the case the next afternoon.

He'd been monitoring the comments on Rumor Control closely, believing Scarlet would be unable to ignore the new paint on the billboard, but he'd relocated to Wicked Wanda's when that had proved boring. Lynnie had been pleased to see him, and her budding romance with Tadd seemed to be making inroads on her façade as a jaded smart aleck. She'd given him his coffee for free, and thrown in a large cookie that he hadn't ordered. She fairly glowed behind the counter, and promised to come out and join him once she was on break.

He'd set up the laptop as usual, running the security software before punching up the Death Troupe website. Kelly had sent Berni a high resolution photo of the doctored billboard, and now the site's introductory picture was the lineup with all six characters crossed out and circled, complete with the admonition to vote. Rumor Control had reiterated its stance that the original markup had been the work of an overeager fan while at the same time praising the hooligan for artistic style. Berni's gossip columnist alter ego had gone on to say that the Barron Players were sure the unidentified painter had meant to create the ballot look that now graced the billboard, and had probably been interrupted before the work's completion.

That might have done it, or perhaps it was the modification of the original graffiti, but whatever the case, Scarlet now decided to provide a few comments. Munching away on the cookie, Jack almost choked when he read an entry that he recognized word for word.

"You know the number seven that he wrote on the floor in his own blood? It wasn't a seven at all. It was an upside-down letter L."

Jack took a hurried gulp of coffee that burned his throat as it washed the cookie bite down. He stared at the screen, bug-eyed, for close to a minute while the chat room's other participants questioned the meaning of the enigmatic entry. They had no way of knowing that it was taken from the very end of Jack's script, and that it was the clue that pointed toward Paula Ninninger's character as the killer.

He'd taken Delilah Emerson's joke about the first clue, the giant number seven near Long Lake that she'd said looked like an inverted L, and used it in the play. The hapless informant who ended up under the ice hadn't been drowned; he'd been shot in his home and had managed to draw a symbol on the floor before his killer had moved his body. The single digit message had been mistaken for a seven—and a reference to the Seven Seas Gang—but it was really supposed to be the letter L, the first letter of the killer's last name.

Whoever Scarlet was, he or she knew how to leave an audience wanting more. The people who had been posting comments about the billboard returned to their original topic when their queries went unanswered. They couldn't have known what Jack and Scarlet knew: For the first time in Death Troupe history the draft script for the show, the show they were to perform in a month and a half, was completely compromised.

Jack began to chuckle slowly, a deep, mournful sound that resembled choking more than mirth.

"Whatsamatter, Jack?" Lynnie called out from the counter, her face tight with the beginning of real concern. "Little trouble swallowing?"

He let an idiotic grin slide onto his face while he waved a restraining hand in her direction. Scarlet had made his or her point with stunning clarity, and was unlikely to add anything because it wasn't needed. Jack began shaking his head in slow, abbreviated arcs while the chuckling turned into the low giggle of a lunatic.

"Aw-w-w shhh-it." He stuttered before sliding down a bit in his chair and beginning to laugh like a man who has bet his entire future on a wager that just came up short.

Chapter Twenty

Jack and Kelly got to use their Campion Hill refuge a little sooner than either one of them had planned. Jack had called Berni shortly after reading the post containing the leaked words from his script, and she'd arranged for a conference call with both Barron and Wade that evening.

Jack and Kelly had traveled to the tower separately just after dark, hoping not to attract attention. Whoever was dogging their footsteps on the website might be right there in town, and they had no way of knowing if the phantom had guessed Kelly's secret role with the troupe. She was already there when Jack arrived, and he'd been pleasantly surprised to see a large space heater already glowing in the corner of the cab when he'd poked his head above the floorboards at the top of the steps. He'd then set up his secure phone on the cab's center table and they'd placed the call.

". . . I don't want anybody getting upset with my questions, but we've got to narrow down what we're looking at here." Wade was speaking, trying to be specific without mentioning the play by name. "Did anyone print out a copy of the item?"

Jack turned a questioning look at Kelly for the briefest moment, long enough to get an annoyed shake of her head, while Barron and Berni replied in the negative.

"No one on this end did, either." He answered quietly. Although they were using secure communications, the mystery of how someone had hacked into their systems had prompted them to be cautious with Kelly's identity. She wouldn't be mentioned by name, and wasn't supposed to talk.

"What about the papers you used for the earliest doodles, Jack?"

"Doodles?"

"You know—sketches, the earliest brainstorming. Where are those?"

"Locked up in the safe, as always. And they wouldn't have been the problem anyway. I didn't think of the upside down L until I was writing the end. The only way somebody saw that line was off of the item itself."

Kelly muted the phone and pouted at him with eyes full of sympathy. "I loved that part. I'm sorry, Jack."

He was leaning over to kiss her when Barron spoke. As usual, he didn't even attempt to encode his words. "It really doesn't matter how they did this. What matters is that both of our scripts are useless as they are right now. Jack?"

"Right here." He knew what was coming.

"This really isn't as bad as it may seem. First, we were going to do a lot of work on that draft and then create several different endings anyway. Second, I planned to modify your script with some elements of the other one. Third, we've already disseminated so many clues that we couldn't start from scratch even if we had the time.

"So here's what I want to do. Jack, you rough out a couple of different ways of combining the two scripts, and then start work on both of them right away. I'm going to have to revamp the clue distribution from here, making it more generic."

At this stage of the game live actors were supposed to start appearing in the host town, sometimes in the roles they would play in the show, but always giving out hints. Although the compromised script had rendered all of that moot, the townspeople would be looking forward to the live bits and so Barron would have to come up with something the actors could perform.

"You got it. It won't be hard."

Like hell it won't.

"I know that. You two . . . I know you'll get it done, Jack. Wade?"

"Yeah."

"How do we keep them from getting the new stuff? If they do this to us a second time, we're finished."

"You ain't gonna like this part of it."

"I don't like any of it. What do we do?"

"Go low-tech. Write it by hand. Keep it off the computers entirely."

Aw-w-w shhh-it.

"Why would that be more secure? Didn't you just ask whether or not anyone had printed a hard copy of the thing?"

"For someone to physically get hold of the paper that Jack will be writing on, they'd have to be in Schuyler Mills. From what I've seen, there's no reason to believe that's the case. I think they got the script by hacking one of the computers, which could have been done from anywhere. Ditto for their latest message—I don't think they're in Jack's vicinity."

"And why is that?"

"Because whoever posted that one line is letting us know they're smarter than we are. Think about it: They could have kept quiet, let us rehearse that script right up until just before the show, and *then* dropped this bomb on us. We'd've been completely screwed if they did that. And notice how they didn't let the people in town know they've got the script. They wanted to keep this message nice and focused, to show us they're in control. They're trying to rattle us, in other words. Which makes me think that if they were physically near Jack, I'd say they'd have let us know that too."

"Meaning?"

"Instead of a line on our website, they would have nailed a page from the script to the door of his cabin."

Jack felt a thrill of fear as he envisioned a hooded figure sneaking onto his porch in the dead of night, just feet away from where he lay sleeping.

"But that's just my read of this, and it might be wrong. There are some tricks that I've already taught Jack, things like keeping his notes scrambled so they can't figure them out even if they do get hold of them, that he should start using right now. He's also gonna have to disguise the work in progress, with fake pages and excess scribbling to confuse the meaning.

"And even then he's got to guard it with his life."

When Jack pushed the chair back, it was well past midnight. The laptop was open in front of him on his desk at the Great View, and he'd just reviewed every bit of brainstorming material committed to it over the previous weeks. Blowing air through his puckered lips, he reached up and began rubbing his temples in slow circles. His eyes burned and his head ached, but not from the long session staring at the screen.

"You really let the rules slip this time, didn't you?" he whispered, acknowledging that he'd committed far too much information to the machine. The protocols that he and Wade had evolved over the years, the same ones that Ryan had usually ignored, had required the writer to assume the laptop could be stolen at any time. Once gone, it would be just a matter of time before the right people—or wrong people, depending on the viewpoint—defeated the security software and accessed everything in the computer's guts.

Because of that, nothing important was ever supposed to reside on the laptop that everyone in town had seen with the writer. A second computer, little more than a word processor, was used to type the actual play. It was always kept hidden, separate from the laptop and the safe, and had no Internet capability of any kind. He'd written the play on that device, and downloaded it to Berni's laptop using a special cable that was the only way the secret word processor could transfer data. Unfortunately, the electronic versions of both scripts had then been emailed back and forth among the people on that night's phone call. Although that method of communication was supposed to be secure, clearly it was not.

Wanting to use his brainstorming notes to write the modified version of the play, Jack had first decided to review everything on his work laptop. Changing the script gave him some leeway regarding how much of that possibly compromised information might still be used, but he wanted to know when he was taking that chance. Having finished reviewing all of those notes, he reached out for the stack of dog-eared papers on which he'd done so much of the play's earliest musings.

Those papers had been secured in the laptop's safe, and he had little reason to suspect the lockbox had been cracked during his time in Schuyler Mills. Just as he lifted the stack in the air, a heavy object fell from its middle. Startled, he looked down as the leather-bound book which had been Ryan's Red Bend journal fell to the floor. It landed on its head, and he took on a pained expression when he saw that he'd damaged the binding.

He leaned over and picked it up, seeing that the back cover had almost completely separated from the bound pages. The aggrieved look remained as he flipped the loose portion and forth, because he'd meant to return the journal to Ryan at the next opportunity. He'd even rehearsed a small speech to go along with it, reminding his former partner of why he'd written the journal in the first place. Jack hoped to talk Ryan out of his quixotic sojourn in the wilds and convince him that his work, as represented in the journal, was a worthy reason for him to rejoin civilization—and give up his suspicions of a plot that didn't exist.

Toying with the flap revealed something he hadn't noticed before, which was that a long piece of white tape had been holding the book's back cover attached to the block of pages within. It initially appeared to have come from the factory that way, but when he inspected the front cover there was no corresponding tape there.

Returning to the back flap, he saw that someone had carefully cut the reinforced paper that had connected the cover to the body of the book. Pulling the severed edge of that page back, he now saw that the machine sewing which had bound all of the pages into a block had been removed. A precise double row of thread holes looked up at him, most of them empty.

That didn't mean the pages weren't attached, though. A strong black thread had been fed through some of the machined holes, obviously by hand. It looked like the hurried closure of a botched surgery, and Jack was struck by the idea that Ryan couldn't possibly have done it. The other writer edited his journals by cutting out whole pages, and there was evidence that he'd done the same with this book. Jack had never known him to go to this extent in that pursuit, and couldn't understand why he'd employ such a difficult means of doing it. Even the ugly mishmash of black thread suggested it wasn't Ryan; he'd been a sailor since an early age and Jack knew he had a meticulous hand with needle and thread.

"Now why would anybody have done something like that?" He asked out loud, turning it over and over in his hands.

The next two days and nights passed in a blur. To preserve the secret of Kelly's role in the play, Jack could only meet her after work. He brainstormed during the day, taking the clues that had already been made public and building several different options for the adjusted play from that. They'd spent an entire night at Kelly's place and another at the watch tower, poring over the new ideas and proposing new resolutions for each of them.

Kelly hadn't been inactive during that period, but scheduling the publicity for the upcoming show consumed much of her work day. She'd arrived at both meetings carrying alternatives that Jack felt were borderline genius, and although they still hadn't written a word of the new version, he was beginning to feel slightly optimistic about the process.

The excessive concentration was beginning to tell on him, though, and he'd been pleased to get a break when Berni had called with the cryptic message that he and Kelly should be near the town library the next day at lunch time.

The frigid temperatures that had gripped the town as long as he'd been in residence had lessened somewhat by then, and Jack was allowed to witness a phenomenon peculiar to cold climates. The townspeople, inured to the elements and primed for the better weather, took to the outdoors without their heavy winter clothing even though the temperature was barely fifty degrees. Although the snow still clung to much of the landscape, and a stiff breeze would quickly remind him that spring was not yet there, Jack found himself imitating the others. He'd emerged from his cabin that morning wearing his long coat and had quickly decided it was too warm out for that. He'd found a short leather jacket in the back of the truck, and headed out.

He and Kelly had eaten lunch at the S&M, and he'd decided to take a chance by warning the mayor that a spectacular clue was about to be dropped in Old Town. Word had spread like wild fire, and so when the hint arrived it had to nose through a considerable number of people ranged around the square.

It was almost impossible to miss when it rolled in, and expectant bystanders on the wrong side of the field quickly began to follow as it headed for the library. It was an old style car that would have fit into any Roaring Twenties gangster movie: Long, boxy, and black with a flat roof and front fenders that sloped up and over its white-walled tires like waves. Jack and Kelly had quietly put themselves in position to observe the front of the library, but they hadn't noticed anything different about the big stone building itself just yet.

The car slowed to a halt in the middle of the street so that it was framed perfectly by one of the town's oldest and most imposing structures. A man Jack recognized from the special effects crew, in a gray chauffeur's rig with a matching cap, sat stoically at the wheel while beige curtains prevented anyone from seeing inside the main compartment. The onlookers stayed a respectful distance away at first, but after a minute curiosity got the better of them.

Jack leaned over and whispered in Kelly's ear. "This is marvelous. Did you see the way they built suspense by just *sitting* in there? Takes nerves of steel."

As if summoned by his words, the door furthest from the library swung open. A man's black dress shoe slid out, topped by the cuff of a pair of dark trousers that sported a loud blue pinstripe. The shoe was joined by its mate, and a figure in a dark fedora emerged holding a Thompson machinegun. The gangster's face was obscured by the hat until he stood up, to reveal a tie but no coat, and a white shirt that was rolled up to hairless elbows.

A thin, unlit cigar was tucked into the corner of the gangster's mouth, and when Jack finally recognized the face he was shocked to see that it was Wendy Warner. Her blonde hair was braided into a single ponytail that hung halfway down her back, and her breasts stood out against the fabric of the shirt as if to let everyone know that this was not a female actor pretending to be a male gangster. She was playing the role of a female hoodlum, and a trigger-puller at that.

Jack studied the young girl's face, and honestly experienced a sensation of mild fear at what he beheld. Wendy had let her features go almost completely slack, the cigar tilted slightly toward the pavement, and the effect was one of power and disregard. Her eyes completed the image as they slowly, intentionally, sought out the irises of every individual near her. They were the focused headlights of a predator, and a frost of cold malice drifted off of them.

She held the Thompson gun by the pistol grip behind its disc-shaped drum magazine, casually pointed toward the ground. With great deliberation, she reached up a hand and took the cigar from her lips. She cleared her throat once, as if to get everyone's attention, and uttered two words at a volume that was just above conversational.

"Stand. Back."

It was perfect. Though not as close as many of the others, both Jack and Kelly joined them in a collective step to the rear that earned them no recognition from the menacing figure. The words were clearly the cue for the other actor in the car, as a bareheaded Kirk Tremaine unfolded from the door closest to the library.

He wore a pair of light gray trousers and the matching vest from a three-piece suit, as well as a red silk tie that stood out against his crisp white shirt like blood on new snow. His dark hair was parted in the middle, and though shining with mousse it still seemed to bounce as he stepped around the back of the vehicle.

His contrast with Wendy was nearly total. His eyes burned with anger, and he curled his lips into an evil smile that would have done justice to a skull. His shoulders rolled as he moved closer to the crowd, and they took an additional step backward even though he was unarmed and had said nothing.

"Awesome." murmured Kelly.

Tremaine stopped abruptly, and raised open hands as if imploring the audience.

"What?" he called out, only slightly louder than Sally. "We ain't friends no more? The Seven Gang got no friends in Schuyler Mills?"

He was answered with dead silence, and exchanged the smile for sad-eyed disappointment. He gave off a slow shrug and turned as if to go back in the car. Someone in the crowd coughed nervously, and Jack watched with interest as a childish grin worked its way up onto Wendy's face. She'd put the cigar back in the corner of her mouth, and now took the forward handle of the machinegun in her other hand. The barrel was still aimed at the ground, but she seemed expectant of action.

Kirk's voice yanked Jack's attention back to him when he roughly ordered the driver, loud this time, "Hand me the chopper."

Another Thompson gun, this one fitted with the smaller stick magazine, came out the window butt-first, and Kirk took it in both hands. Pulling it in close to his chest, with the barrel pointed skyward as if showing it off for the crowd, he took a deep breath and then bellowed, "How many times we gotta tell ya? The *Seven Seas Gang* runs Schuyler Mills!"

Like a robot, he turned toward the stone face of the library not ten yards away. He raised the weapon to his shoulder, and at the last second Jack finally saw that someone had affixed a thick board, painted to match the stone behind it, onto the library wall. It was the size of a desk top, and holes the size of silver dollars exploded from it as the imitation machinegun in Tremaine's hands gave off a rattle that was meant to sound fake. The actor swept the Thompson gun left to right horizontally, and then back again diagonally in a two-step movement.

Small, electrically-detonated charges known as 'squibs' blew out of the fake stone in sequence with the firing. Looking at the now-forgotten chauffeur, Jack saw the slightly inclined head as the special effects man worked the controls which remotely set off the minor explosions. It looked like Kirk had just fired a dozen slugs into the face of the library, and when he lowered the gun a large number seven was stitched there.

With the weapon still pointed at the ground, Tremaine looked over his shoulder as if expecting some kind of response. The people of Schuyler Mills didn't disappoint him, as his display was answered with a sprinkling of applause. Jack heard someone say the word "blanks" and was relieved to notice that no one seemed perturbed. That wasn't surprising, given that this was gun country and it was clearly a show, but Death Troupe clues had gone awry in the past and he didn't want to see that here. Not now.

Allowing himself a slight smile, Tremaine tossed the fake gun into the car. The angry look was back when he straightened up again, and he stormed around the rear of the vehicle to stand next to Wendy. For her part, the female gunslinger raised her Thompson across her chest so that she appeared ready to defend her loud partner at the first sign of trouble. Tremaine's fists were balled up, and he let loose again in a furious tirade.

"That's right! The *Seven Seas Gang* runs this town! We ain't goin' *nowhere*, no matter what the Feds might tell you, so button yer lips when they're around!" He raised his left hand and pointed behind him in the direction of the library while still glaring at the audience. "Anybody feels like gassing to outsiders, you tell 'em to come take a look at this mark! That's our brand—" he swung the finger back around, encompassing them all "—and it's on every one of you!"

This last outburst silenced the crowd, but that had been its intention. Lowering his hands as if defeated, Tremaine spoke to Wendy in a calm voice. "Ya know, I don't think they're ever gonna catch on." He shook his head, suddenly looking tired. "Let's get outta here."

Wendy obeyed slowly, backing toward the vehicle while he went around to the other side. She folded back into her seat while maintaining eye contact with the onlookers, and when she pulled the door shut the machinegun's barrel poked out the window.

Tremaine was almost back in the car when it happened. Out of nowhere, a voice in the crowd started shouting. For a moment Jack thought it was the "U-S-A!" chant from so many international sporting events, but then he heard it correctly. A man in the crowd he couldn't see was chanting, "Se-ven Seas! Se-ven Seas! Se-ven Seas!"

The others took it up almost immediately, and in a trice it was accompanied by three handclaps, one with each syllable. They were close enough to the big stone building to get an echo, and it began to sound like a much bigger throng was chanting the name of a bootlegger gang that had never existed. Wide smiles sprang up on the faces of the crowd, and the chant rose in volume.

"Se-ven Seas! Se-ven Seas! Se-ven Seas!"

Kirk was genuinely taken aback by this, and stopped at the side of the car. He looked over its flat roof in consternation for just a beat, and then shut the door without getting in. He stepped up on the wide running board, and the barrel of Wendy's weapon suddenly disappeared. Jack could only assume that Kirk had ad libbed this action, and he watched as Wendy's arm snaked out the window to wrap protectively around her partner's waist. The vintage car fell into gear with a sudden jerk forward.

Tremaine, transported in more ways than one, was holding the inside of the vehicle with his right arm while facing its rear. His left hand came up in a fist, and he began pumping it in time with the chant. The car slowly slid forward, and the crowd closed in on it, still clapping and shouting. Tremaine joined in with the chant, consumed by his role, looking like a man lost in the desert who has stumbled across an oasis.

The onlookers followed a short distance as the car headed out of Old Town, and Jack looked down to see that Kelly had taken his hand. She was squeezing his fingers hard, and her face bore the focus of the completely enthralled.

"—what we need now is a whole range of possible motives why each of the characters from the billboard might have committed the murder." Jack stirred sugar into a mug of coffee that he'd poured from a large thermos.

He and Kelly were back up in the Campion Hill watch tower, but now it was fitted out to suit their needs. Heavy fabric covered all four of the cab's wall-length windows, preventing the escape of any light. This was important, because they'd exchanged the low-wattage ceiling bulb for one that turned the small room bright as day. Jack had wandered around the base of the tower several times, talking to Kelly on his cell phone while she adjusted the blackout curtains.

In addition to the space heater that she'd moved up earlier, the tower now hosted two chairs that sat on either side of the central table. Jack had offered to bring up a folding cot, but had received a deathly stare in return for the idea. The gangster performance of the day before had fired Kelly's imagination, and she'd rededicated herself to solving their current predicament.

"Are we absolutely stuck with that? The billboard was an advertisement at best, not really a clue at all. And there were only six actors on it when we're allowed seven possible suspects."

"Yeah, but most of the time we don't use all seven. It makes the locals feel like we're being a little more sporting."

"I'm a local, and I guarantee I could figure out who the culprit was by Act Three, even with seven possibles."

"Really?" Jack tried not to sound too doubtful. "Maybe you could, but it has to be a majority vote. With a range of five or six identified suspects, you'd be surprised how many times they don't even reach a majority. And the few times they have . . . they've been wrong."

"That's because you guys cheated. You changed the ending once the votes were counted."

Jack came back from the observation counter where he'd set up the coffee. He sat down and blew on the mug, contemplating whether or not Barron would want him to spill the troupe's dearest secret. "We only changed the ending once in the six shows I worked on, and I can almost guarantee they didn't do it when Ryan was the writer."

Her eyes flashed in interest, and she put down the marker she'd been holding. "You're kidding me! That's half your reputation: Death Troupe can change the ending on a hand signal."

He laughed, enjoying the reaction. "Quite a shtick, isn't it? Our best trick isn't a trick at all—although it is our greatest diversion. And that one time we actually did change the ending? That was pretty much an accident."

"What?"

"I know, I know, it's a little embarrassing. It was our second show, it was out west, and we weren't too sure the story was gonna fool the audience. So Barron paid for an open bar—they had one in the lobby of the theater—and unfortunately the early attendees snagged a couple of our players as they were on their way in.

"It really was a nightmare. The stage managers were losing their minds looking for these guys, and I finally found them at the bar, doing shots with this gang of miners and ranchers. Neither one of 'em's with the troupe anymore." That was a justifiable lie, because there had been more than two of them and they weren't all gone. Puff had been among the offenders and Allison, anxious about her first Death Troupe performance, had almost assaulted him backstage. Jack had overcome his shyness toward the beautiful young actress while physically restraining her, and believed he owed Puff a great debt for his transgression. "I pried them away from the party, but of course they were still looped when they went out on stage.

"Amazing how well they did, though. They only got confused when one of the others, somebody who hadn't been in the bar, said a line from a different ending."

"Oh my God."

"Exactly. Barron was having a fit, but the troupe just went on as if that was the ending they were supposed to use. It wasn't a completely different third act, by the way, more like one scene that could pivot in two directions. They carried it off, and the audience didn't pick the right culprit anyway, so no harm, no foul."

"You mean the drunken miners and cowboys actually reached a majority?"

"Oh, worse than that. They were *organized*. Their vote was unanimous. Lucky for us they picked the wrong suspect. But they were good sports about it, and we emerged with this reputation for being theatrical wizards." He looked down at the table, his eyes taking on a sentimental glaze. "Man those guys could drink."

He stopped talking, seeing that Kelly eyes were roaming around the small room. He wondered how he'd lost her attention so quickly. "What is it, Kell?"

"This." She fluttered a hand at the ceiling, and brought her eyes back onto his. She smiled serenely, and he felt warmth spreading all over him. "I just thought of something. This . . . right here . . . this is our place. Every couple's got a spot that's special to them, something nobody else could understand. And that's right here. This is our place."

Jack cocked his head to one side, smiling at the notion. He and Allison had never had a "place" as such. They'd both been moving around too much and too fast for that. Giving it some thought, he found that he liked the suggestion.

"Having you here makes it our place."

"And this." She laid a flat hand on the papers spread between them. "This is going to be one of your stories someday, Jack. We're going to make something very special here."

Jack finished rolling up the last blackout curtain and tying it out of sight. He'd sent Kelly home an hour before, knowing she had to be at work early the next day. That was already upon them, as it was almost three in the morning, but he'd spent another hour scratching away at the ideas they'd been fleshing out. They were making progress, and he was beginning to believe they might actually pull it off.

There was almost a full moon out, and it transformed the black sky and the snow into the gray-blue color that he remembered from his trek through the woods on Groundhog Day. It seemed like ages before, and he hardly noticed the cold as he descended the tower's stairs. Kelly had left the fence gate open, and he had to put the thermos on the ground when he went to lock it behind him.

"Evenin', Mr. Glynn." He actually jumped at the gruff voice, and looked around in fear before spotting Charlie Fannon, the aged poacher who had reported the mannequin hanging from the tower weeks earlier. The grizzled character was wearing the full-body camouflage suit from the time before, and cradled a hunting bow in both arms. The bow looked huge to Jack, and he was appalled to see the razor-sharp arrows attached to it in a plastic carrier.

"Hey Charlie." He exhaled unevenly, laying a gloved hand across his chest and grinning. "Almost gave me a heart attack. Whatcha doin' out here?"

Fannon tilted a hooded head at the bow. "You ain't gonna tell the mayor, are you?"

"Now why would I do that?"

"Dunno. Can't say why anybody'd wanna get in my business. Jest know there's a lot of people who do."

The hunter could easily have avoided him and not run the risk of being reported, so Jack decided he had something to say. As they had only one common point of reference, he thought he'd start there. "So I've been meaning to ask you . . . what did you see up here that night, when that dummy was hanging from the tower?"

312

The gray stubble on Fannon's cheeks moved just a little, and in the darkness Jack thought he looked pleased. "Yer a sharp one, Mr. Glynn. I'll give ya that.

"Weren't much to see, actually. I was out huntin' down by the access road, and a car came by, goin' up the hill. I was followin' some tracks, so I didn't give it no mind. It came back down 'bout twenty minutes later, and I had to wonder what anybody'd be doin' up at the tower that late at night. Cold, too."

"I remember."

"So when the trace I was followin' took me up there, I looked around and sure 'nuff there it was, hangin' there like a real human being."

"Is that what you thought it was?"

"Nah. Was only the driver in that car, goin' up and comin' back, so 'less that hanged man was in the trunk I had to figure it wasn't real."

Jack took a step toward him without meaning to. "Did you get a good look at the driver? Or maybe recognize the car?"

Charlie shuffled his feet, lightly stamping his waterproof boots on the ground. "Weren't close enough to see behind the wheel, couldn't even say if it was man or woman. But it weren't anybody from around here."

"How could you tell?"

The old hunter lifted a gloved hand and pointed at his eyes. "Been in this town longer'n most. Weren't no local's car."

He turned his head as if hearing something, and sniffed the wind without making a sound. When he looked back, his eyes were already off on the new trail. "Nice talkin' to ya, Glynn. Take care of that Miss Kelly, ya hear? Good woman."

He turned as if in a trance and disappeared into the woods.

The night was far from over. Jack parked the truck in front of his cabin at the Great View, and took a moment to stand in the deserted parking lot. The stars overhead seemed to fill the night sky, and the only sound was the creaking of the trees behind the units. He was due to move out soon, to the campground near the theater, and fought the feeling of nostalgia.

Time was you upped stakes and moved to the next spot without noticing at all.

He kicked the toes of his boots against the steps as he mounted the porch, and then turned to look down on the sleeping roofs of Old Town. Kirk and Sally's bravura performance came back to him when he saw the library, and he felt yet another wave of reassurance.

313

Barron would come through with the show the same way he'd handled the change in the clue distribution. It was all going to work out. The worst was over.

He shut the door behind him quietly, and turned on the light to find a scowling Ryan Betancourt seated in the rocking chair. A brand-new ski parka, indigo blue, covered the back door window next to him. The blinds were firmly drawn, but he was now visible through the window in the front door. Without a word he tossed a towel through the air, and Jack dutifully blocked the aperture while looking over his shoulder.

Ryan had shed the bargain basement clothes of his other visit and was now attired in a sharp pair of brown snow boots that went halfway up his shin, factory-faded jeans, and a black turtleneck made up of some kind of insulating microfiber. He was still too thin, but Jack hardly noticed that once he studied the other man's face. His former partner looked ready to explode, and Jack kept his eyes on him as he took a seat at the desk.

"Hello, Ryan. Didn't know you were back."

"Why would you? I only left you a message at the drop two days ago."

Jack fought the impulse to respond with anger. He'd been hoping Ryan would resurface so he'd have a chance to talk some sense into him, but the rich man didn't look very receptive. He kept his face calm while answering. "Oh. I'm sorry. It's been a little busy around here."

"I know that. I saw. Just what are you and Sykes up to?"

This took him aback, as he'd momentarily thought Ryan was admitting he knew the original script had been leaked. Jack hadn't looked over at the safe when he entered because he knew there was nothing of value in it, but the question about Kelly was a true surprise. And a true revelation.

He really is *here alone. There's no way a PI in this town could have missed the news that Jack and Kelly finally got together.*

"Kelly and I are involved." He rephrased the question that almost got past his lips. "How'd you find out about that?"

"Saw her leaving here, the morning I was dropping the note that said I needed to see you." Ryan's eyes drilled into him, and it was more than reproach. His old partner was trying to read him. "So I gotta ask you, Jack: Are you playing me?"

"Playing you? Ryan, I'm your only friend here. I've been keeping your secret because most of what you've been telling me makes no sense. I'm worried about you."

"Makes no sense?" His voice rose on the last syllable, but he caught himself and resumed a tone that was more-or-less normal. "Somebody sabotaged your skis, switched the trail signs, and practically murdered you. They even took your equipment so that a search party wouldn't have a clue which way you went. Wake up, Jack. And tell me what's going on with Sykes."

Ryan's lips remained parted, and Jack could see the dark hollows under his eyes. As much as he wanted to tell the man who had stolen his girlfriend that his current relationship was none of his business, clearly Ryan was spooked by Kelly's presence. He remembered the look of triumph the rich man had displayed when showing him the photo of her meeting with Barron, and managed to keep himself in check.

"I'm not sure it's any business of yours, but I've spent these last months working with her and we hit it off. So yeah, we're together. And she's not conspiring with Barron or anybody else. She was doing publicity coordination when you—when your people—saw her in Schenectady."

Ryan's eyelids fluttered madly, and Jack braced himself for some kind of explosion. He was sure it almost happened, but somehow the rich man recovered his self-control at the last second. The thin opening between his lips widened as if he'd just solved a difficult puzzle, and he cleared his throat roughly when he saw that Jack had noticed.

"What's Allison think of that?"

Jack's mind jumped as if he'd just been hit with electricity. He'd linked Ryan's concern over Kelly to her supposed involvement with Barron, and he'd obviously been wrong.

"Allison? What's she got to do with Kelly?"

The rich man's face turned slightly, still trying to read him but now wearing a sly expression. "You mean you two didn't patch things up? Over my dead body maybe?"

He doesn't know about the night in Maine. Not for sure, anyway.

Jack reached for the right line, and the writer inside him supplied it. "That's a hell of a question, coming from you."

The head remained turned, but the solved-puzzle look had returned. "No offense, Jack. It's just that you're a big wheel out in Hollywood now, and she's been doing more movies . . . I figured the old flame might not have died out."

"I've got one script that sold well, that's all. And I'm with Kelly now."

Ryan looked down at the floor, as if trying to process the latest news. Jack's mind raced, trying to make sense of the conversation's effect on the other man. Ryan's entire plot had been based on the idea that whoever was dogging the troupe, Wade or Pauline, was doing it because of Allison. Clearly, whatever he'd known or suspected about her relationship to Jack had just taken a big jolt.

When Ryan looked up, his eyes showed a fearful glaze. It reminded Jack of the expression Charlie Fannon had adopted when he'd caught the scent of fresh game, with one difference. Where Charlie had looked hopeful, Ryan now looked scared.

He shook it off like rain a moment later, and regained the inquisitive stare. "So you think everything's fine, huh? That nobody's plotting against you?"

"Yes. We've had a few pranks, but I believe that's all there is to it."

"Like you're a good judge of that?" A smirk threatened to curl the ends of his mouth, and Jack found it was too much.

"You know, I still owe you a good solid ass-kicking. You want it now?"

"There's no time for that. You've got to see reason here, Jack. You've had the most important piece of evidence in front of you this whole time, and yet you can still tell me nothing's wrong." He pointed at the cell phone in its charging cradle. "Right there. The phone Wade gave you. The one that tells him where you are at all times. The one that broke down on you the night you were lost in the woods.

"Whoever messed with your skis knew exactly when you left here to go out on that trail. They switched that sign ahead of you, and then they switched it back. They blocked your calls for help, and they were following you so closely that they were able to *take your skis* right after you abandoned them." Ryan's voice was hot, but his expression was one of pleading.

"To do all that, they had to have a fix on your position the entire way. And they got that from the phone you were carrying, the one Wade said to keep on you at all times.

"He got rid of me because he wanted Allison, and when you took my place he had to start over. So he got you lost in the woods, and then he took your skis so that your friends couldn't find you and you'd die out there.

"It makes no difference that you're not with Allison right now; Wade has already done so many terrible things in this plot of his that he'll see it through to the end. Wake up, Jack. You're in a lot of danger."

316

Chapter Twenty-One

"Pardon me for saying so, Jack, but you look like hell." Tamara Madden's hand was on his shoulder, the other one holding an order pad. He hadn't slept at all after Ryan left, and had finally driven down to the S&M Diner for breakfast. "That Barron guy working you too hard?"

"You could say we're in a heavy re-write phase." He looked up at her affectionately, now wishing he'd taken the time to shave. Ryan's visit had disoriented him, and no matter how he tried to explain his accusations, he found they always led back to Wade.

"Well, re-write or no re-write, you need to take better care of yourself." Tammy began scribbling on one of the order slips without having asked what he wanted. "We're gonna whip you up an extra special omelet, one with all the things you need."

"Like what?" Even in his funk, Jack feared he was about to be handed a vegetarian nightmare.

"It's good. Tomato, onion, peppers, 'shrooms, ham . . . a few other things." She finished writing before bending over to whisper in his ear. "And maybe you and Kelly should take a night off, too. No reason to burn it at both ends, ya know what I mean?"

She kissed the top of his head and disappeared, and her solicitude almost brought tears to his eyes. As much as he'd hoped to see Ryan again, the man's visit hadn't ended the way he'd planned. Instead of talking the other writer back to the real world, his own grip on reality had been considerably loosened.

Jack still believed that he'd become lost in the woods due to his own negligence and a trail sign that might have been flipped in the wrong direction by a squirrel, the wind, or both. He had more trouble explaining the failed cell phone and the broken skis, and now he had to consider if both of those occurrences pointed at Wade. Ryan knew that the skis hadn't been found, but not that they'd ended up bashed to bits. His take on the night's events matched the story that everyone in town felt they knew, but only because Wade had kept his discovery quiet.

That idea led to another, and he let his mind rover over it no matter how much it hurt. Bib hadn't been able to find the skis the very next day, but Wade had gone out looking for them twice. Why would he do that when he and a local helper had failed to find them, and after Bib had looked as well? It was disturbingly logical—and neatly matched Ryan's suspicions—that Wade knew they weren't out there on the first trip. And the only way he'd know that would be if he hadn't been far away when Jack had been wandering the wasteland.

If all that were true, the last thing Wade would have done upon "arriving" in Schuyler Mills was hop on a snowmobile by himself and drive straight to the area where Jack had been lost. Instead he'd hired a guide, allowed himself to be shown the right trail, and then claimed to have finally found the fragments when he'd gone out a second time, alone. If Ryan was right, Wade had switched the trail sign, blocked the phone signal, and taken the skis—which would fit Gary Price's tale of having seen someone snowmobiling away with a set of cross-country skis on his back. Later, when Jack had miraculously survived, Wade had appeared with the broken ski and the suggestion that he quit the troupe.

Jack still hadn't figured out why the advance man had behaved so strangely during his last visit, appearing at the back door of the cabin late at night and far from friendly. His warning about the trio from the firehouse still seemed a flimsy excuse, and Jack remembered the way the investigator had appeared to be studying him that night. Had he been simply gauging his plot's effect on the psyche of its intended victim, with the replacement skis from Jack's trial in the woods just a few feet away?

Of course Ryan was equally a suspect for that, being an excellent sportsman and having skulked in the vicinity for many weeks before the mishap, but Jack couldn't see his motive. The rich man had triumphed over him in every way years before, and driven him from the troupe as well. Although Barron and Berni both maintained that Ryan had been a disaster as a solo writer, it hardly made sense for him to go to the absurd length of faking his own death just to get revenge on the Barron Players. He had riches, he had fame, and at the time of his disappearance he'd had Allison.

Jack's food arrived, along with a tall glass of orange juice, a tall glass of tomato juice, and a small sample pack of multivitamins that Tammy ordered him to take. He thanked her, and began to pick at the huge omelet before him.

No matter how much he wished it were otherwise, he'd come full circle just to face the fact that he was merely a playwright, not a private eye. And that the one professional investigator he could have consulted was possibly behind the whole thing.

That last observation turned out to be wrong, however. As if on cue, Bib Hatton loomed up over Jack's booth in his parka and overalls.

"Like a little company, Jack?"

"You're a mind reader, Bib. I was just thinking of you."

"Really? Gonna put me in your play?"

"Nah, I like you too much to do that." He waited while Tammy took the big man's order of eggs over easy, hashed browns, and chipped beef. Once she was gone, he lowered his voice and continued. "I was thinking about the night I was lost in the woods."

"You weren't lost. You knew where you were."

"Yeah—many miles from nowhere."

"Hey, fellah, this ain't nowhere." Bib chuckled at first, but then looked out the diner's window and seemed to reconsider. "But then again . . . what's wrong with nowhere?"

"Not a thing. A lot of people would say I live nowhere too, out in Arizona."

"Well of course they would—and they'd be right. It's the desert."

They both laughed some more, but Jack wasn't about to be dissuaded. "Sitting here thinking, it occurred to me that I don't know who took Wade Parker out on the trails after you found me."

"Oh, that was Sam Colvin." Bib's forehead furrowed. "You met him yet? Guy about my size, completely bald, probably woulda told you he's a retired hunting and fishing guide? Well, I'm not surprised you haven't bumped into him yet. Sam lives pretty far outside of town and doesn't come in too often. Not that he's weird or anything; he's just not much for towns."

"Sounds like a good temperament for a hunting and fishing guide."

"Exactly. Anyway, he took Wade around on his first visit last year, showed him all the back country scenes that he thought your

Mr. Barron might like. So it made sense that he'd call Sam when he got here that night."

"I see. You know this Colvin well enough to introduce me?"

"Sure thing. He and I go back a long way." His food arrived, a mountain of potato, meat, and gravy topped by two fried eggs, but he didn't touch it. "Can I know what you're digging at?"

"I'm still a little frowzy on how my skis could have disappeared from that trail. He and Wade went out there before you did, right?"

"Yeah." Bib picked up his utensils and began chopping up the pair of eggs and then mixing the result in with the potatoes and chipped beef. "I followed the ambulance to the hospital, but the docs said I wouldn't get to talk to you for a long time so I went back out.

"But Wade and Sam didn't find your skis either, Jack. So what are you gonna ask him?"

"I'm not sure why you're asking about this, Mr. Glynn." Sam Colvin sat with Jack and Bib at a large table in his living room. The Colvin place was a two-story log cabin fitted out with all the modern conveniences, and the spacious living room where they sat looked out on the forested valley below. Colvin lived far up in the hills, but Jack's original expectation that he'd be some kind of wild-eyed recluse had proven wrong. He'd come out onto the cabin's wide porch as they'd driven up, clean-shaven in a pair of khaki trousers with a knife-edged crease, brown shoes that were buffed to a high shine, and a collared wool shirt. He was completely bald and as tall as Bib, but where the outfitter carried many extra pounds he was lean. A long shed next to the cabin sheltered an assortment snowmobiles, all-terrain vehicles, a pickup truck, and a motorcycle, and he looked like he used all of them.

Jack cast a sideways glance at Bib, and then decided to plunge right in. "Bib doesn't know this, and maybe you don't either, but Wade Parker showed me a piece of one of my skis the day I left the hospital. He said he'd gone back out on that trail by himself, and that he'd found my equipment all mangled off to the side . . . like I'd gone nuts out there and smashed it against a tree."

Colvin's eyes were a dark brown, and he kept them on Jack's while he slowly nodded with a stone face. "I warned him that story about a second trip wouldn't hold up. He's a fair hand with a snowmobile, but he didn't find those pieces by himself. We came across them the first time we went out, but he made me promise to keep it quiet. He cooked up that lie about being on his own because he didn't want you worrying that people in town might find out."

Jack turned to Bib. "Sorry for keeping that from you. I didn't know he'd found them until the next day, or I damn sure wouldn't have let you waste your time."

"No worries, Jack. I get it. You lost your temper out there, and your buddy covered for you." He turned the corners of his mouth downward as if adjudicating something. "People get angry, and with less reason than you had. Man, if I had a dollar for every golf club I've chucked in a water hazard . . ."

But I didn't smash my skis. And the binding broke on its own.

He kept those protests to himself, and looked back at Colvin. "How did Wade explain this to you? Why he'd want you to keep quiet?"

"He's a sharp guy, and he sounds like he knows you pretty well. He said you work hard at establishing rapport with hicks like Bib here, and that you'd be mortified if they thought you were crazy."

"But we do think he's crazy. That's why he fits in with us hicks."

They all laughed at this, but Colvin could see Jack wasn't quite satisfied. "I wouldn't worry about it, Mr. Glynn. I've rescued a few people over the years, and some of them did some pretty strange things. All you did was express a whole lot of frustration. Granted it wasn't a very good idea to wreck your skis . . . but you already know that."

"Yes I do. So what did they look like? The skis, I mean."

"Like somebody really whacked them against a tree a few times. Those things are tough, so only one of them was actually broken. Some of the laminate was still holding it together, so I helped Wade cut that off when we got back here.

"He said he wanted to show it to you, and needed to fit it in a bag. I agreed to keep my mouth shut, but only when he promised he was going to speak to you about it. You have to be very careful not to lose your cool in emergencies, Mr. Glynn. Nine times out of ten, that's what actually kills people. Panicking when they need to think straight. Wasting their energy when they need to conserve it.

"But you already know that . . . now."

An immense weariness overtook Jack just after Bib dropped him at the Great View. The sun was shining brightly, and the remaining icicles across the complex were dripping a continuous stream. The bed beckoned, and he didn't bother shutting the blinds as he slipped under the covers.

He had no reason to believe Colvin was conspiring with anyone, and so he was now sure that Wade had not broken the skis. He had no idea who might have done it, but his flagging consciousness conjured up the excuse of a local wiseacre who had decided to tag along with the rescue party. Finding the skis by chance and deciding to play Brom Bones to Jack's Ichabod Crane, the man in his pre-sleep fantasy smashed the one ski to make the fancy playwright look like a panicky loon.

As he drifted off, Jack tried to remind himself to call Wade when he awoke. The troupe would be arriving soon, and it was time to let the now-exonerated security man in on Ryan Betancourt's little secret.

He slept through the afternoon, and at one point dreamed that he was back out on the trail where his broken skis had been found. It was high summer, and the forest had bloomed in a tumult of green. Various faces popped in and out as he walked, from Kelly's to Bib's to Tillman's, making no more sense than any other unconscious hallucination. In his dream he rounded a curve on the path and found Ryan standing there, dressed in Charlie Fannon's camouflage suit and aiming a hunting bow at him.

Just before he let the evil broad head fly, a huge black net dropped on the rich man, knocking him flat. In the dream Jack looked up to see Wade Parker standing on the bare limb of the dead tree that marked the beginning of the trail he'd taken on Groundhog Day. He was dressed like Robin Hood, and laughing heartily, when the ringing phone dragged Jack out of his slumber.

At first he believed he was still dreaming, because the voice on the other end of the line belonged to Wade.

"Hey Jack, did I wake you?" The words were spoken softly, and with concern.

"Uh, ye-ah." Jack sat up, looking around at the cabin's unexpected brightness. The sun was just dipping below the hills, and its rays shone straight into the small room. "Been some late nights. What's up?"

"I'll give you a second to come to. I'm flying up to your neck of the woods again, to Niagara Falls."

"You get married or something?"

"No, nothing like that." Wade let a small hint of levity come across the line. Satisfied that Jack was fully conscious, he resumed the more somber tone when he continued. "I've got good news and bad news, Jack. The good news is that I think we might finally know who's been dogging the troupe these past few months.

"The bad news is that the police in Niagara Falls found a car abandoned in a spot favored by the jumpers. They went through it, and they found Pauline Scott's driver's license."

"My God. Do you think . . .?"

"From what they're telling me, yes. I'm sorry to be the one to give you this news, but apparently there was another ID in the car, a fake one, along with some credit cards under the same name. The photo on the fake ID is Pauline, and there are some receipts from hotels and restaurants in this area.

"I can't be sure just yet, but it sounds like she was in the area for weeks. And it also looks like the poor girl decided to end the whole thing . . . whatever she was doing . . . the hard way."

"—yeah, it's sure not how anybody would want this to end, but at least now we know." Wade sat in the rocking chair late the next day, the same sunbeams streaming into the cabin. He'd driven down from Niagara Falls after conferring with the authorities there, and still wore the jacket and tie from that visit.

"Pauline disappeared just before the show in Red Bend, so she could have been behind the shenanigans up there—at least the ones directly involving Ryan. I've got people tracing the credit cards the police found in the car, but so far they don't lead to California. She might have been using different ones, or going straight cash for that part of this.

"Anyway, she only used them sporadically . . . she didn't stay in a lot of hotels, or at least didn't use the cards for that." He looked up at Jack, who was seated at the desk. "It seems to prove she was around here, and I have to believe she was watching you some of that time. You didn't see anybody who looked like her?"

"No. But you know how everybody was bundled up during the winter—" Jack marveled that he was already considering the winter finished even though the ground was still covered by snow "—she could have been right next to me on the street and I wouldn't have known."

"I suppose that's true. Heck, maybe that was what made her finally end it."

"Huh?"

"Think about it: No one was on the lookout for her up at Red Bend, so a hat and dark glasses would have worked there. Here she had the winter camouflage going for her, but now that's ending. She knew a lot of people would be looking for her by now, and of course you'd recognize her if she wasn't heavily disguised. Maybe that ended the game."

"Or maybe something else did."

Wade nodded ruefully. "I thought of that. You think she might have seen you with the new girlfriend?"

"I sure hope that's not it. But it makes sense if she was trying to help me. She never liked Ryan, so maybe she wanted to scare him off so I could come back. Maybe she thought she'd be able to surface at some point, tell me what she'd done for me . . . man I hope that's not what happened."

"Who knows, Jack? Mental illness isn't easy to spot sometimes, and you hadn't seen her in what? Two years? She also spent much of the last few months alone, under a lot of strain, afraid of being discovered the entire time. What I'm saying is it isn't your fault, if she did jump."

"One question here, Wade. I know I'm just a guy who scribbles mystery plays, but all we've got is a driver's license, a fake ID, and some receipts. How do we know it's not all a setup?"

Wade nodded judiciously. "That *would* be a bit of an assumption, except for one thing: The most recent receipt was a few nights ago, from a nice hotel about an hour's drive from where they found the car. I went by there with a couple of photos of Pauline and the guy working the counter remembered her. Not surprising; she was a pretty girl. I showed him the photos and he identified her. That proves it was her fake ID, those were her credit cards, and that was her car."

Wade looked out the window as the sun began to fade behind the trees. "Well I'm starving, and I think we've both earned a nice meal. So what do you say we call that girl of yours and go grab a bite at Maddy's?"

"Yeah, let's do that." Jack reached for his jacket, but stopped when he saw that Wade was standing motionless, as if waiting for something. "Wade?"

"I was a little rough on you recently, but it was because I didn't know what to think. Pauline's disappearance was just too much coincidence for me, you and she were close, you'd gone up to Red Bend, and when I found that broken ski . . . what I'm trying to say is I doubted you. That's why I jumped out at you last time I was here. I was trying to see if the Jack Glynn I thought I knew was really the Jack Glynn I knew." He bit his lower lip for an instant. "Sometimes I really hate my job."

"I was a little rough on you myself."

"You know you really were, you bastard. My last trip here . . . talk about hostile! I'm just a gumshoe trying to keep everybody safe, and look at all the grief I get."

They stepped out onto the porch, and Jack locked the door behind them. He straightened up and took a long, loud whiff at the air. Wade, halfway down the steps, stopped and looked back up as if waiting for him to speak.

"You smell that?"

"Snow doesn't have a smell, Jack."

"It's not the snow. It's spring—I can already smell it." He stepped down and clapped the other man on the shoulder, pointing him toward the truck. "Show time."

Chapter Twenty-Two

"Many people have asked a question about this . . . thing of ours." Jerome Barron stood center stage at the Schuyler Mills Playhouse, facing an audience composed of almost every actor and staff member in Death Troupe. They'd arrived in town over the previous three days, taking up sometimes-grudging residence in the camp cabins next to the theater or its more well-appointed dormitory. That morning was the first official day of rehearsal.

"Some of the actors who have been with us for a long time already know the answer to this question. Some of the newer faces out there haven't yet had the chance to ponder it. And the rest of you —the ones whom I will affectionately dub 'intellectually lazy'— never will." The deep voice flowed out over the seats, where the members had formed groupings based on friendship or work assignment. Most of them wore sweaters, warm-up jackets, or fleece tops, and Jack had mutely scoffed at their complaints about the cold.

Although it was early morning, every eye was open and fixed on the Director, who stood motionless in a pair of dark brown slacks and a black turtleneck. His jibe was answered with a small titter from the group, and he smiled in return.

"The question is simple: Why would a man my age, with so many successes and accolades, with an unassailable reputation in theater, with adoring fans all over the globe—" the tittering began again, and Barron quelled it with a fake glare "—get involved in something like this?

"You've heard the comments and read the reviews . . . the older ones, anyway . . . asking just what value could be derived from a script that isn't completed until the night of the show . . . roles that aren't defined until the curtain goes up . . . an audience that doesn't want the show to succeed . . . and a troupe of players that don't work together most of the year."

Spontaneous applause broke out, and Jack used the distraction to look around. He sat in the front row with Puff, and was discomfited by how many faces he didn't recognize. He'd taken pains to greet the members as they came into camp, but now saw that he'd missed a fair number of them.

"That's right. You've got it." Barron nodded with approval while the clapping died down. "Many answers to that question have been put forth over the years. My first writer—" he glared down at Jack, who raised both hands as if imploring forgiveness "—still believes it's because I'm some kind of a control freak. Jack believes I gave up directing Shakespeare because I can't tell the Bard what to do."

"Jack is right!" an anonymous voice shouted from the audience, the words so hurried that they came out as one word. Even Barron laughed.

"For the record, Jack is *never* right." More laughter followed this, but Barron pursed his lips in thought and then continued as if having changed direction. "But he sure can put the words together, can't he? I want to take a moment to acknowledge the herculean effort that Jack has made for us, from coming to our aid in a dark hour—" he skipped a beat "—to taking up residence here when it wasn't nearly as warm and sunny as it is right now—" boos and hisses erupted from the members who felt Schuyler Mills in April resembled the North Pole "—and writing a script that we as a group will rip to shreds and then reconstruct as something usable. Ladies and gentlemen, let's have a hand for our original playwright, Jack Glynn."

The applause broke out in a roar, and Barron motioned for him to stand. Taken aback by the unexpected praise, Jack rose and gave the thank-you gesture he'd learned from Puff, holding his clasped hands in front of him near his chest and pumping them a couple of times in the direction of the clapping. The recognition took a while to end, but he was already back in his seat by then.

"Okay, enough about him. Back to me. Back to why I do this." Barron frowned and scratched his head. "Why *do* I do this?

"Oh yes, I remember. It's because from man's earliest experiences in theater, there's been a conflict between the *exploration* of a story and the *telling* of that story. We have to learn our lines, but doesn't that memorization limit what we can do with that character? We have to rehearse our movements and actions, but once we've done that haven't we said, 'That's as much as we're going to develop that scene'?

"Some of the greatest names in theater have struggled with the idea that a play can get stale before it's ever performed. That individual actors can sometimes like their initial read of a character so much that they stop exploring that character right there. That the mechanics of set construction, costuming, music, and lighting can very much limit the room we have for interpretation."

He smiled again, looking out over the throng. "I see some nodding heads, and even a few looks of confusion. You ask, 'How do we end up with a show that's well-rehearsed *without* learning our lines, *without* setting our characters, *without* building a stage, *without* rehearsing everything until that it works together as a functioning whole?'" His voice rose in both pitch and volume as he finished the sentence, and he stopped with an expectant look aimed at the balcony.

"More to the point, how do we keep from getting stale when we *have to* decide how we're going to play a character and then rehearse all our movements so that we don't bump into each other?

"Two words: Death Troupe. Here we come as close to the never-ending rehearsal, with all its benefits, as we can without going full improv. Your characters can't become set because the culprit is different in every version of the play. Your lines can't become rote recitation because the execution of those lines has to leave you ready to believably shift your character in any number of different directions.

"And even if we reach the point where each and every one of you could perform every variant of the play *in your sleep*—" he bellowed this last, leaving the words hanging in the air "—there's an audience just feet away, working against you, trying to figure you out, trying to catch you slip *just once*."

The silence was glacial, and although Jack had heard Barron do First Day presentations before, he'd never heard one like this.

Barron folded his hands in front of him, regarding the group like a teacher who isn't sure his class is even awake.

"Anybody out there think a situation like that can *ever* get stale?"

The response was a roar, with some of the actors coming to their feet and everyone, including the film team, clapping loudly. Barron signaled for quiet, and his audience subsided with reluctance.

"So here it is. A month of ball-busting, heartbreaking, gut-wrenching work that, if we do it right, leads to no definite conclusion. Eighteen-hour days and eighteen-hour nights. For you new members, this will feel like some kind of an endurance race. We've got one month to break down this awful script, rebuild it, learn every one of its variations, and then rehearse the result until you *can* do it in your sleep.

"But even then we won't be finished, because there's a hostile crowd out there just dying to be the first ones to solve the mystery— which we will *not* let them do.

"Let's get to work."

The assemblage dispersed to different parts of the camp ground after that. The larger groups took advantage of the complex's more spacious meeting areas, such as the television room in the two-story dormitory that housed camp counselors during the summer, the conference room in the administration cabin, and the dining hall. Barron was going to conduct a technical meeting with the set design, costume, lights, film, and special effects people right there in the theater, but first he had a few comments for Jack.

The auditorium still rang with the footfalls and conversation of the departing troupe members when the Director took a seat on the stage facing his head writer. His face still held a glow from the presentation, and he looked toward the rear of the theater with open affection.

"Ah, I so look forward to rehearsal. It's where the script and the actors come together—"

"—like a ten-car pileup on the interstate."

"I've used that one before?"

"It's been awhile."

"Yes it has. Listen, I wanted to tell you how sorry I am about what happened to that girl up in Niagara. I never met her, but it's still a shame." He shook his head in regret. "You know what's crazy? Here we are, trying to capture people's imaginations, and yet when it actually happens, look how many times it ends badly. I mean, why did the poor thing have to kill herself?"

"She was a little attached to me. Wade thinks that might have done it."

Barron tipped his chin downward. "I've noticed you have that effect on a lot of women."

"Of course; I'm a writer. You actors and directors have no idea."

"Thank God for that. But it brings me to my point. Well, points, actually. I've got two of them. First, Allison's delayed and won't be with us for awhile. I knew about it in advance, and it won't be a problem. I was going to cast her in one of the supporting roles anyway."

Make me a quiet little church mouse for this one, okay?

"And of course the script's not finished, so it's not like she's missing anything." That wasn't quite true. Jack and Kelly had spent most of the previous evenings in the watch tower, writing the new play by hand. Jack and Berni had sorted through the results the night before, separating the real script from the phony scrawlings that disguised it, before feeding those pages into a secure scanner. The electronic file thus created was now under twenty-four hour guard right there in the theater, and Barron was going to go over it line by line sometime that afternoon.

"Second, I want you to spend as much time with Kelly and the local players as possible. I explained to her, right at the beginning, that my writers aren't a big part of the rehearsals and I thought she understood. She's pushing back on that now—a habit she no doubt picked up from you—and the only way to convince her is to kick you out of here as soon as possible."

"How convenient." It was an old argument, and not just for Jack and Barron.

"Don't start. Writers have no place in rehearsal after the first read-throughs. It's a distraction for the actors, and they've got enough on their minds already."

"It's a distraction to have the guy who wrote the play they're going to perform available to answer their questions?"

"Yes it is. You either gave them the right words or you didn't. Do I stand off to the side of the audience at showtime, explaining things to them during the performance? Of course not. Either I've done my job or I haven't, and the audience can tell if I've accomplished what I set out to do by what they see on the stage."

"I'd like to think the actors have something to do with that."

"Of course they do—the actors are the living manifestation of my will. Where would I be without them?"

"All alone with your giant ego, I suppose."

Barron dropped his feet onto the carpet, a proud expression on his face. "As long as I've got that, I'm never alone."

Jack drove into Newville shortly after that, hoping to find a quiet corner in a coffee shop there. The work he and Kelly had done was extensive, and had laid the groundwork for a great show, but now the real effort was about to begin. Barron would review the draft script that afternoon, and would no doubt have changes after that, but Jack knew the optional endings still weren't where they should be and wanted to work on them.

He wasn't overly concerned by this, having come to respect Kelly's talent for seeing the show through a radically different set of eyes than his own. She'd already furnished one alternative resolution that he considered brilliant, and their collaboration on the dialogue had lifted the script to a higher plane.

The only thing that bothered him just then was that he didn't believe they'd woven a story complex enough to guarantee they'd fool the crowd. The structure of each ending was sound, and he didn't think any of their possible culprits were terribly obvious, but he lived in fear of the unnoticed chink in the armor that would allow the crowd to spot the killer. The entire group would be searching for that single flaw until the curtain went up, but Jack had realized an ugly truth early in the troupe's existence: Sometimes the deadly defect is invisible.

And there was only one answer to that: Build enough obfuscation into the storyline that the viewers, even if they saw the critical fault, wouldn't be able to focus on it. This was by no means a simple solution: Audiences of all kinds dislike red herrings and useless filler. Jack felt that the solution to that lay less in the story than in the characters, and had already identified the qualities in each of the identified suspects that made them believable as the killer. Now he needed to fine-tune those characteristics by examining them with an eye toward their subtle manifestation on stage.

That could be as simple as changing a single word in a line of dialogue; the ability to build phrases with one denotation, but markedly different connotation, was part of the writer's toolkit. The actors and the Director practiced a similar dark art with movement, gestures, and expressions, but it was the writer's responsibility to bring them to the point where they could add those devices.

His concentration was interrupted when Gary Price slid into the booth opposite him. The cable company man was dressed in a tan overall that sported his employer's patch along with various dark smudges. He regarded Jack with an impish expression before speaking.

"Hey Jack. I thought I recognized your truck in the back parking lot. You hiding or something?"

"Sort of." Jack closed the notebook while giving his new companion a welcoming smile. He pointed at one of the newer stains on the coverall. "Tough day?"

"So far, not that bad. I like to leave a few smears on this thing. It makes my boss think I'm working hard."

"How's the game coming along?" Looking at Gary, Jack suddenly realized that the script emergency had pulled him away from the firehouse gang for more than two weeks.

"Which one?"

"I'm going to pretend there's only one. I meant the murder mystery video game that Tadd and Lynnie are working on."

"It's practically killed both of them. They've been putting in some seriously long hours on that thing . . . and on each other, if you get my meaning." His eyebrows lifted once and then came back down. "When this whole thing's finished, can you get Mr. Barron to send them on vacation? In two different countries?"

Jack couldn't help laughing at that, while at the same time trying not to compare the youngsters' situation to his own. "Must be a little tough, living in that apartment with those two going at it, huh?"

"Oh, I'm hardly there these days." He straightened up just a bit, looked over both sides of the booth, and then spoke in a whisper. "There's a lot of gambling going on, about the show. You have no idea how many different things there are to bet on. Which actors will get chosen to play the named suspects, whether or not the town picks the right one, heck, there's even a line on how the murder's going to be committed."

The troupe's wager with the host towns frequently generated side action like this, but even so Jack's stomach began to churn. Everything about the Schuyler Mills engagement had been unpredictably extreme, and there was no reason not to expect a similar intensity on this topic.

"Please tell me you're not organizing any of that." The connection between the two youngsters building the troupe's new video game and the bookie handling the bets on the show would not go over well with some people.

"Me? Of course not. It's a friend of a friend."

"So who does that make it? Lynnie or Tadd? I wouldn't have thought they'd have any time for that."

Gary waved a scoffing hand at him. "Don't worry, Jack. It won't come back on you. I just wanted to say that people are already getting excited about the show."

He stood up and confirmed that the booths on either side of them were indeed empty. He leaned in abruptly, almost knocking heads with the writer. "A lotta money says there's going to be a drowning, so if you can avoid that . . . it would be helpful."

"Most of you have been out and about the town by now, so I imagine you've formed an opinion of the people who live here. I'm hoping to incorporate that into our play somewhat—in a positive way of course." Barron sat on the edge of the stage in the dead center, his legs dangling like a schoolboy's. He'd already met with the managers of the various production teams, and was now sharing his general vision with the actual performers.

Jack sat in the back of the group, just a few rows up. The theater was empty except for the actors, the Director, and their playwright, and although it was just after dinner no one seemed ready to fall asleep.

"Our play is called *The Sins of the Seven* for a variety of reasons. We've invented a bootlegger ring called the Seven Seas Gang, and they figure prominently in the back story. The gangsters were all over this region during Prohibition, and many of the locals are alleged to have helped them smuggle the booze. Our Seven Seas Gang is made up of those locals, roughly seven families who were involved in the illegal trade to varying degrees.

"We've got a stockbroker character in the introduction, someone who was handling much of the town's money when the Stock Market crashed in 1929. He was found dead shortly after that, and was originally believed to have killed himself over losing the good citizens' nest eggs. After awhile, however, evidence surfaced that he'd actually moved a fair amount of the money out of the market before the Crash, and his suicide began to look more and more like a murder. The Seven Seas families were all suspected of having killed him, but even they weren't sure just who did it. That gets revealed as the play evolves, but all you need to know right now is that the Seven Seas Gang eventually got their cut from the stolen savings.

"Prohibition ended in 1933, and there was a scramble for control of the newly legal alcohol business. That fight became quite vicious because the Great Depression was in full swing. The members of our Seven Seas Gang fought each other for that business, and eventually the power ended up in the hands of just three families. They went more or less legitimate at that time, and with the money stolen from the stockbroker and the wealth they'd amassed from alcohol, they bought off many of the townspeople in the region to forget about their bootlegging past.

"That's the back story. I've only just read the latest version of the script—which is excellent, by the way—and so you'll be getting to look at parts of it in the next day or so. But in the meantime I want you to think in terms of the play's title. If you haven't guessed, *The Sins of the Seven* is a take-off on the phrase 'the sins of the fathers are the sins of the sons'. Which means we're going to be exploring the reactions of the bootleggers' modern-day descendants when an investigator shows up claiming he's researching the history of rum-running in the Adirondacks.

"As you can imagine, some families won't be happy about that, and might take extreme action to keep the truth from surfacing. Others might see their chance to avenge their forebears, the Seven Seas Gang families that lost out in the power struggle. And still others might be hard to gauge, the ones whose people weren't actual gang members but still profited from the misdeeds of the bootlegger families."

Jack watched as some of the heads began nodding in agreement. Most of these belonged to seasoned troupe members, people who had worked with Barron long enough to have gleaned a modest understanding of his methods. The ends of Barron's mouth curled up, and he went on.

"I have to tell you, this one really leaves a lot of room for character interpretation. I love it. You can go straight forward, you can mix the emotions, or you can go completely in an unexpected direction. Some of these families have a lot to lose if the truth comes out. Some of them feel enough time's gone by and that no one will care. Some of them are ashamed of their roots, and others are proud of them. Some believe that the same violence and avarice exemplified by the bootleggers runs in their veins as well." He cleared his throat. "Still others might believe they don't carry that gene at all—and they might be in for one heck of a surprise."

"So start kicking it around in your heads. Let it go wherever it wants. Without tipping them off, talk to the locals about why they like it up here. Take a walk or a drive—" he glanced at Jack "—but don't get lost doing it. Try to get in contact with this place. Was it a backwater, or a paradise? Were these people fleeing society or shunning it? Was the bootlegging mere criminality, or was this the last flowering of American rugged individualism?

"Don't point it anywhere just yet. Let it flow. If it gets hung up somewhere, leave it there for awhile and then kick it back into motion. Somewhere along the way, imagine just how a place like this might respond to an outsider asking uncomfortable questions. And then surprise yourself with the answers."

"Hey Jack." Wade took a seat in the row behind him just as the last actors left the auditorium.

"Say hey, Wade. I wondered where you'd gotten off to."

"Security never sleeps. You know that." Wade handed him the set of keys to the Campion Hill watch tower. "I checked out your little penthouse. Not a bad retreat, and you're right—nobody's bugged the place."

"I've swept it every time we've been up there. Same with Kelly's kitchen."

"Make sure you keep doing that. Both of you are looking a little rough around the edges, and you'll be tempted to cut corners as the changes start piling up." Wade made a clicking noise in his throat, as if resetting his thoughts. "I finally got a chance to talk to that Charlie Fannon friend of yours."

"More of a bow hunting acquaintance."

"Don't I know it. You should see the shack where he lives. Daniel Boone would've felt right at home. Anyway, I showed him a couple photos of the Niagara Falls car, the one Pauline was probably driving, and he said it wasn't the one he saw that night at the fire tower."

"Really? It would have been dark out; how can he be sure?"

"He's one of those eyes-and-ears people I keep trying to turn you into. Very observant guy. But you're right about the darkness, so I brought him a silhouette photo as well. He says the lines don't match, and I believe him."

"So what's that mean? I would have sworn that anybody hanging that mannequin, with it wearing that robe, was making a connection to Red Bend."

"Well, a different car doesn't prove Pauline wasn't at the wheel. She went to a lot of trouble getting that fake ID and those credit cards, so why wouldn't she have more than one vehicle?"

"I guess."

"Don't worry about it—she was behind the whole thing. There haven't been any new pranks, Scarlet hasn't been in the chat room . . . a damned shame, but at least we know."

Kelly Sykes came down the aisle at that moment, dressed in jeans and a light sweater top. She dropped into the seat next to Jack as if ready to collapse.

"I am *bushed.* How long is this gonna go on for?" She was only half-serious, but the strain of the long hours, combined with fooling the townspeople and most of the troupe, was beginning to show. "Hi Wade. Catch anybody drilling peepholes in the walls?"

"Found a couple in the ladies' changing room, but I don't think it's somebody trying to steal the show's ending."

"Don't forget this is a summer acting camp for horny teenagers. Those holes are probably a little old."

"I thought some of them were a little close to the floor." Wade gave her shoulder a squeeze before heading off.

As soon as he was gone, Jack put an arm around Kelly. She snuggled in against him as if they were waiting for a double-feature to start, and he resisted the urge to tell her that Barron had requested major changes to the latest version of the script.

"Wake me when the players start getting here." She mumbled, already nodding off.

The community theater group would be rehearsing in the Playhouse for the next several nights under the watchful eyes of Wade's security people. The building was swept for bugs almost continuously, but Barron needed to work with them and it made no sense to do it anywhere else. Ideally their portion of the show would quickly reach a level of competence that would allow the Lawtons to polish the act somewhere else. Once the Barron Players had received the script and gone over it in collaborative rehearsal, they would start putting it all together on stage—and then they'd need the Playhouse night and day.

Kelly's breathing had already moved into the easy rhythm of sleep, and Jack gently nuzzled her hair with his nose. He slowly pulled away from that movement when Barron and the Lawtons unexpectedly came out on stage. The lights in the auditorium were all on, and he and Kelly were clearly visible though many rows back.

"Allison Green won't be joining the troupe for at least another week, so I need someone with talent to take her place in my rehearsals until she gets here. I'd like to use one of my own people, but I've got a bit of a casting problem with my other female players and I want them to focus on the parts I'm considering for them.

"I don't know if this is even possible, what with her work schedule and her family, but I think that Glenda Riley would do very well in this capacity if you—and she—are willing to have her on double duty."

Both Lawtons began to speak at once. Jack could tell they were thrilled by the opportunity for one of their players, but Barron cut them off.

"I want to make a few things clear before we even mention this to Glenda. My people will make her feel right at home, and the experience alone should be worth the minor interruption in her routine. We won't do anything crass like asking her to step outside when we're discussing an important clue, but there are some things to which she won't be privy. She absolutely will not be performing with my people on the big night, and she'll be expected to step aside with good grace when Allison arrives.

"That, of course, means she can decide not to participate in the show's introduction—which is a choice I hope she won't make—or to learn two roles. Although her part in the back story scenes are of course limited by its brief duration, the role she'll be . . . oh, I'm going to just call it an understudy role and be done with it. The understudy role will not be a place-filler, though. She'll be working just as hard as if she were Allison herself.

"So. What do you think she'll say?"

"She'll be overjoyed, Jerome. Overjoyed."

"And we'll do whatever needs doing to make it all happen. I'm sure the school will be willing to rearrange some of her schedule . . . after all, it's only for a week."

"Let's hope it's only a week. But if it's much more than that I'll be forced to make Sleeping Beauty out there"—he pointed at Jack and Kelly, taking a dangerous chance that the Lawtons might wonder who he was pointing at—"re-write the play to remove that role entirely."

"Oh, don't do that!" Patrice Lawton was horrified at the very notion. "I'm sure Glenda can give you as much time as you need, even the entire month."

"Less than a month now." Dennis Lawton chimed in optimistically. "And people are going to be so excited that a member of our troupe is actually working with the Barron Players!"

"I was hoping you'd say that." Barron threw an evil glance at Jack, who had known all along that the Director was manipulating the Lawtons. As if on cue, Barron began walking off the stage with the other two trailing behind him. "So when Glenda gets here we'll take her aside and see what she thinks—"

They disappeared from sight, and Kelly stirred against him. He turned and absently kissed her head. Allison's part was a supporting role that she could learn in her sleep, so there was little need to involve Glenda in the troupe's rehearsals. Although he accepted Barron's reasons why he couldn't use one of the other female players, bringing in a local was going to complicate things greatly. The troupe had never done anything even remotely similar to this.

What the heck is he up to?

The next days and nights ran together until Jack couldn't accurately guess the date. Barron's script changes sent him and Kelly scrambling back to her place after the first night's rehearsal with the local players, and it didn't slow down after that. During the day, when Kelly was performing her duties as the town's publicity agent, Jack was typing away at a laptop in a back room of the Playhouse. Enough of the script had been okayed by Barron for a partial distribution to the actors, and that of course brought its own flood of adjustments.

In an odd role reversal, the newly arrived members of Death Troupe now began to befriend the residents of Schuyler Mills while Jack dropped almost completely out of sight. By the time Kelly got to the Playhouse each night, he was usually stretched out on a battered couch that had probably been used as a piece of stage furniture at some point. Once he'd been shaken awake, they would review the day's changes together until the community players had all assembled.

Those rehearsals also produced new ideas, and Barron took an almost demonic delight in encouraging the Lawtons, the Griffins, the ecstatic Glenda Riley, and the rest of the local troupe to let their imaginations run wild. After two nights of this, Jack had convinced Barron to spin a cover story about an emergency publicity meeting with Kelly which had allowed the two of them to retire to the back room and work on the laptop there for the evening.

All printed pages of the approved segments were kept inside the Playhouse, and it wasn't unusual to see veteran theater actors hunched over in the auditorium's seats, scratching notes on their copies like school kids. Alternatively, individuals could be seen walking back and forth in the backstage passages, up in the balcony, or even in the lobby, mouthing or even speaking the lines they were dissecting for the first time.

Once real rehearsal began, small groups of players would be allowed to take serial-numbered copies of the script to the administrative cabin or the mess hall, under the close supervision of Wade's security people. Barron's days were equally full, meeting with the design teams, the lighting and sound technicians, and the film crew among many others. To Jack, these conferences seemed intended to generate fiendishly different ways of telling his story—or to ruin it entirely. He frequently ended up in long conferences with Barron, explaining the finer points of the plot or the mystery itself, and how the latest bright idea from the film crew would blow the whole thing out of the water.

And yet it was as exhilarating as it was exhausting. Barron frequently rejected his head writer's protests, forcing him to incorporate the latest innovations while granting him leeway in how that was accomplished. Jack had a good ear for dialogue, but his true strength lay in his understanding of what an audience could follow and what they couldn't. He used that skill to modify the input he was receiving, and soon learned that Kelly had a knack for finding the solution whenever he reached a complete impasse.

In the past he would have sought out Berni or Puff for the answer that eluded him, but now he didn't have to do that. Ryan had never been good counsel for such things and, now that Jack thought of it, neither had Allison. Looking across the desk at Kelly one late night backstage, he'd been forced to stop typing just to watch her at work on a large piece of drafting paper tacked to the wall. She was diagramming the interplay of clues and misinformation, and he looked on in admiration as she distilled the chaos into a simple series of phrases and arrows.

In all the time we were together, Allison and I never talked about the mechanics of writing one of these things. I honestly don't think we could have.

Chapter Twenty-Three

"—no offense, Bob, but I just don't think this role has any pop to it."
Kirk Tremaine stood center stage, right next to Robert Hale. This put
them directly in front of Jack, who was seated in the first row with
Barron. Hale had been selected to play the role of the historian who
comes to town asking embarrassing questions, and Kirk had been
tentatively assigned the part of a wealthy descendant of the Seven
Seas families.

"Why would I be offended?" Hale asked easily. Like Kirk, he
was wearing a sweater over slacks and holding the first few pages of
the script. Standing there together, they looked like brothers. "Jack
wrote the part, so if it sucks it's his fault."

Jack didn't take offense, knowing Hale well and obeying
Barron's request that he should keep his comments to a minimum that
day. This was one of the unusual moments when he agreed with the
Director regarding his role in rehearsal: The actors were taking their
first cracks at the script and it was important to let them run with it.

"What are you trying to say, Kirk? What's your suggestion?"
Barron asked quietly, slouched inside a khaki turtleneck. He had a
black-and-olive striped scarf draped around his shoulders, but Jack
knew this was a sop to those actors who still felt Schuyler Mills was
an Antarctic weather station.

"I'm saying that this is a major role, and it's got no life to it. The
character might as well be an accountant asking how many barrels of
hooch passed through the area during Prohibition. He's supposed to
be a disturbing element for the whole town and he comes across like a
census taker."

It wasn't a surprising observation, and it wasn't necessarily wrong. Jack had built the investigator into a low-key individual who justified his inquiries with the story that he was writing a history of Adirondack bootlegging. He'd based the character on Glenda Riley's unassuming husband, and had only allowed it to evolve in later scenes. As a descendant of the murdered stock broker who had allegedly ruined the town, the historian would eventually reveal that link and his reasons for pursuing such an old family stain. In the beginning, however, Jack had written him as a mirror-like individual who could only incite extreme feelings from those townsfolk who were already harboring them.

Hale answered, as if reading his mind. "I get that too. I think this character probably has a little more fire to it later on, either when he gets the locals all worked up or when he lets them know why he's really here."

"And I can see that." Kirk answered in a mild voice, knowing that he was commenting on another player's role. "But in the meantime I've—we've—got a lot of scenes with this character where I don't see him inciting anything. He asks his questions like he's some kind of bank examiner and couldn't care less what the answer is. I just think it's not going to have any life to it, and that's no good, this early in the play."

Puff Addersley was also on stage, seated on a stool behind the two actors and off to the side. He was dressed in staid gray trousers and a white dress shirt, topped off with a black brimmed hat. As was his custom, he tried to start dressing for his part early on. By the time he was finished, Puff would be showing up at rehearsal wearing the full suit and pompous air of his character.

"I gotta agree with Kirk on that." He spoke up in a neutral tone, dropping his script onto the stool before joining the other two actors. "I like what Jack is trying to do here, keeping the role low-key so that it can build into something bigger later on . . . whatever that is."

One of the advantages of Barron's early rehearsals was that the actors weren't given any of the play's many possible endings. It left them guessing at how their roles could change in the course of the story, and the Director felt it allowed them to fully explore those characters as a result. It probably wouldn't have worked with an established script, but this kind of discovery had been built into Death Troupe's process early on, and usually yielded a good result.

Puff continued. "But I am concerned that we've got a major character who's going to put people to sleep. He's in a lot of the early scenes, and although we see the effect he's having on various townspeople—some good, some bad—that's all the drama the audience gets for quite a while."

"They do get the back story up front, remember; the gangsters turning on each other as well as the tale of the dead stockbroker." Sally Newsome spoke up from a few seats to Jack's right. Among his many major adjustments, Barron had finally dropped the idea of embedding the local theater group's performance inside the play. The back story would be presented as a filmed introduction after all. "If those scenes connect, it's going to be a nice piece of drama right at the start."

"But just how long is it between the arrival of the investigator and when they see my bloated, floating corpse?" Trask Saunders sat behind Sally, and had already grown a nice field of gray stubble on his chin. He would play the informant who ends up under the ice, and as a quasi-Method actor had taken on the doomed persona of the play's first actual murder victim.

Jack caught a look from Puff that was meant for Berni, and then saw the gesture that he'd only heard about until then. The veteran pinched the tip of his nose between thumb and forefinger, and then lowered the same hand to his stroke his throat exactly once. Barron's assistant, seated next to him on the side opposite Jack, lifted the screen of her cell phone as if looking at a text message and then nudged the Director. He inclined his head, and nodded sagely after she'd whispered a few words.

"Sorry, I've got to answer this." He stood up slowly, giving a slight groan as he stretched his legs. Berni rose with him, and started up the aisle before he spoke again. "Keep kicking this around among you. I like the discussion. Jack, can you come with us?"

It wouldn't be the first time that he'd been politely removed from the mix, but Jack knew Puff's intervention wasn't aimed at him and wondered why Barron was taking him along. He found the debate so far to be only slightly uncomfortable because he had the same doubts himself. What had started as a fine inspiration at the Riley house had ended as something only half as striking as he'd hoped, and he found legitimacy in what the actors were saying.

Out in the lobby, Barron walked over to the concession counter where a large bullet of coffee was sited with all the fixings. With the exception of Wade's man guarding the door, the atrium was empty. Berni stayed with them, and Barron spoke over a shoulder while mixing coffee in a Styrofoam cup.

"What are your thoughts, Jack?"

The writer turned to Berni, who was dressed in her usual business rig of a jacket and skirt, glasses, and pulled-back hair. She pulled a face of amazement at him, and he returned it honestly. At this stage of the production, Barron habitually wrenched the power from the writer and handed it to the actors and designers.

"As much as it pains me to say so, I have to agree with Kirk. The character I wrote for Bob is a little flat at first."

Barron turned, the steaming cup in his hand. He smiled at Berni and pointed a finger in Jack's direction. "You hear that phrasing? 'The character I wrote for Bob'. That's what I love about you, Jack. You're a stand-up guy. Even in accepting criticism of your play, you still word your answer so everybody knows you take responsibility."

"I wouldn't go *that* far. There was this crazy director who kept changing most of the things I wrote . . ."

"I'm contrasting you with Ryan, so take it with good grace. He would have suggested that Hale isn't interpreting the character correctly, or that a solid actor could find subtle ways of improving the role without changing the words." He took a sip of the coffee, leaving Jack to realize that he hadn't spared Ryan more than a passing thought since discovering the truth about Pauline. "So here's the real question: Kirk identified this flaw, and you said he really hit his stride with that gangster bit in the town square—"

"Both him and Wendy."

"Don't interrupt. I'm still trying to compliment you. Kirk recognized that the historian needs to be strengthened, and you said he did very well with that gangster role." He sipped again. "I'm considering making a casting change."

He stopped there and turned back to the counter. Opening another sugar packet, he took his time pouring the contents into the coffee. It took him a moment, but Jack realized with a start that the Director was suggesting more than switching out the lead actor. Now so closely attuned to the latest version of the script that he could see the entire thing in his mind, he rapidly calculated how he might execute Barron's transformational new idea.

"If you put Kirk in the part of the historian, it's going to have to be a *much* stronger role."

Barron granted him a meaningful look before sipping the coffee again. Appearing pleased, he cast his eyes downward into his latest creation.

"Exactly right."

"So how is Glenda holding up?" Kelly asked Jack as he drove them toward the Campion Hill watch tower. The community theater group wasn't rehearsing that evening, and the sky was still light. They had major work to do, and had opted to use the tower again because of its isolation and because the floor was too hard for sleeping.

"She's doing a great job. Barron must have noticed something over Mystery Weekend, because she's easily keeping up."

"It is a minor role . . . so far, anyway." That last comment wasn't lost on Jack. Barron's latest inspiration regarding the historian character carried a huge amount of work with it. Although substituting Kirk Tremaine for Robert Hale didn't require much adjustment of the script by itself, Barron's newest innovation for the historian's role certainly did.

That was ironic, because the theft of the original play hadn't required a full-scale rewrite. Because so many of that story's clues had already been made public, Jack and Kelly had been able to keep most of the existing first act and much of the second. The various third acts, already different because of their separate culprits, had always been fair game for modification almost right up to the night of the show. Strengthening the historian's role so that he could be named as one of the potential suspects in the murder was a very different matter, however; it required Jack and Kelly to go back and rewrite his part from the beginning.

Jack's original concept of an unassuming, incisive historian was now morphing into someone who was either hiding a dark secret or keeping his volatile nature in check. Jack had returned to Ryan's earliest notes once the decision to alter the character had been made, knowing he'd wanted to make the investigator a figure of depth and intrigue right from the first scenes.

Jack pulled up at the base of the tower in a spray of gravel. A warming trend had finally arrived, and the hard-packed ice of the winter was slowly disappearing all across the region. Most of the snow was already gone, and buds were beginning to sprout on the trees.

They climbed out of the truck carrying their writing equipment in bags. They were still banned from using electronic devices except at the Playhouse, and had resolved early on not to leave anything incriminating in the tower. The new lights, the heater, and the blackout curtains could stay, but all writing materials had to be carried up and back down each time they visited. Despite this extra chore, they had both found the location inspiring, and had taken to simply texting each other with the message 'our place' whenever one of them felt a tug in that direction.

Jack unlocked the chain on the fence gate, and the section wobbled as he held it open for Kelly. The barrier was purely temporary, like the chain link around some construction sites, with the poles attached to heavy cement blocks that a single individual could move only with great difficulty. The fence, the boom at the road entrance, and a sign on the boom indicating that the tower was off limits had combined to keep the curious away.

The metal stairs rang out with their footsteps as they ascended, and the cables stretched across the tower's frame sang like tuning forks. The air was cool but moist, and the promise of spring was heavy on it. Reaching the cab, Kelly went to turn on the heater while Jack began rolling the curtains down into place. In no time at all the small space began to warm up under the bright lights that glowed over the center table.

Kelly had already opened a large sketch pad in front of her when Jack walked by and raised the curtain on the side facing away from the town. The light was just fading, and the sky on the horizon was a mix of pink and red. The smaller hills rolled around the tower like green waves, and he could see for miles.

The overhead light turned off with a slight snap, and then Kelly was beside him, tucked up close. He wrapped an arm around her and then the two of them simply stood there, motionless, taking in the scene of rebirth as if waiting for a message to flicker at them from across the peaks.

"The crowd's kinda thin here tonight, isn't it?" Puff Addersley asked Tamara Madden as the group of actors followed her to a long table set up in the middle of the dining area. Although the troupe had spread its patronage around the entire town, its major actors had adopted Maddy's Place. The film team had found a spot they liked in Newville, the design team ordered takeout (delivered to their non-stop set construction at the Playhouse) more often than not, and the costume team drifted from place to place.

"Missing your audience, Puff?" Tammy shot back at him as she motioned the others to the table.

"Oh no; I'm thrilled that we have you all to ourselves." He made a half-hearted attempt to circle her waist with his arm and she swatted it away with a loud slap.

"Owwww." Puff moaned in fake pain. "And here I figured your husband would be the one to be hitting me."

"He just might." Tammy took several menus from the server who had approached to handle the table. She kissed Jack on the top of his head when she handed him one and then murmured, "He's been getting to the gym a lot lately."

"Really?" Jack looked up, always interested in physical fitness. His own attempt to get back into running shape had been sidetracked by the non-stop script revisions. He hoped to resume the regimen once the script was finalized—but not until after getting ten straight hours of sleep. "Swimsuit season coming up?"

"Worse—tuxedo season."

Jack flipped a devilish grin at Robert Hale, seated across from him, before looking up in mock surprise. "No! They're not actually going to go through with that, are they?"

Tammy Madden was having a hard time keeping her mirth in check. "Oh yes they are! They all convoyed over to Glens Falls the other day and you never saw more thunderstruck faces than when they came back! The next day the whole group—the mayor, Bib, Maddy, a few others—were all at the gym at sunup!"

She finished handing menus to Paula Ninninger and Sally Newsome, giving Sally's shoulder a light squeeze. Early on, Tammy had sensed the fragility in the actress and practically adopted her. As much as Sally had lusted after the play's female lead, the absence of Allison Green had left her without a valued support mechanism.

Tammy had just turned toward the kitchen when she seemed to remember something. Jack was seated at one of the corners, and Kirk Tremaine had taken the spot to his left, at the head of the table. Wendy Warner sat on Jack's right, and Tammy looked at the empty seat on Wendy's right with true disdain.

"Jack Glynn, are you actually crazy or are you just stupid?" She pulled out the empty chair on Wendy's right as if waiting for him to occupy it, and the entire table gave off an expectant "woooooo" sound.

"What? What did I do?" The writer was truly ignorant of his transgression, but he obediently rose anyway.

"Wendy, be a dear and sit next to Kirk." Wendy smiled before rising gracefully and sliding over one seat. "Now you sit here, Jack."

Still perplexed, he sat in the chair Wendy had just vacated. The men in the group all shook their heads as if finally giving up on him, but his expression was so genuine that Tammy had to give him a hint.

"Kelly's going to be joining the group for dinner, Jack. You knew that." She bounced her index finger in the air as she indicated Kirk, then Wendy, then Jack, and then the empty chair to his right. "Boy girl boy girl, just like in elementary school."

She disappeared in the direction of the kitchen while the others laughed. Although they were still unaware of Kelly's role in writing the play, they'd all gotten to know her through Jack and accepted her as part of the group. As much of their public conversation—among themselves or with the townsfolk—naturally involved the play, Death Troupe hands were adept at using many words to say nothing at all and that was what they did around Kelly. At times like those she had taken to squeezing Jack's elbow as a joke, and he thought he'd caught Puff noticing this once. After he'd warned her of this, she'd switched the movement to a more intimate squeeze under the table and dubbed it their own little warning against outsiders.

For his part, Jack looked forward to revealing Kelly's special relationship to the players. He didn't like misleading fellow members of the troupe, and it galled him that he couldn't bring Kelly into the fold just yet. He knew the players would be properly impressed when they learned the truth, but half the fun of Death Troupe was its mystic solidarity and he wanted that feeling for his girlfriend.

Puff had been right in observing that Maddy's Place was only half-full, but Barron had called an early dinner break and so it was likely that the place would fill up in short order. The unexpected end of the afternoon rehearsal had put the actors in a good mood, and Jack looked up and down the table, taking in the scene. Puff was telling Wendy about the performance where he'd mispronounced the name of the host town (to deafening boos) while Paula Ninninger and Sally Newsome were regaling Trask Saunders with an off-color version of Abbot & Costello's "Who's on First".

They'd performed this bit during a break earlier in the day and Jack had only caught the second half, so he turned to his right to listen. He was so engrossed in the licentious wordplay that he didn't detect the approach of the woman who dropped a hand on his left shoulder and whispered straight into his ear, "Hey sexy, is this seat taken?"

He was so startled that he didn't have the chance to realize that the voice he recognized was not Kelly's. He turned with a jerk, and almost smacked his cheek against the beaming face of Allison Green. She was leaning over close enough to have kissed him—and may have been about to do that—when he'd moved. He was so astounded by her presence that he was taken completely unawares by another female hand, landing on his right shoulder.

"Yes, that seat *is* taken. It's mine. And so is he."

The new voice was Kelly's, and it rang with iron authority. Jerking his head back to his right, he looked up to see his girlfriend glaring at a now-erect Allison. The blonde hadn't removed her hand from his shoulder, and when he attempted to rise both woman firmly pressed him back into his seat.

"Siddown, Jack. I'm about to give your hick girlfriend here a good old-fashioned ass-kicking."

"Hick? *You'll* be the one who looks like a hick—once I've knocked a few of your teeth out."

Jack had just planted his feet when Kelly lost her composure. Her lips pressed together until they disappeared, and her entire face began to tremble as she tried to control her laughter. For her part, Allison switched from animosity to pity, the emerald eyes widening and the lashes beating sweetly.

"Aw, Kelly, we really had him going there until you lost it."

The entire table erupted in laughter, as did most of the other diners. Looking about him in shock, Jack now saw that Tammy Madden and much of the kitchen staff were watching off to the side. Recognition that he'd been set up flowed through his body even as Allison and Kelly both wrapped their arms around him and kissed him on either cheek. Several cell phone cameras flashed, but that seemed to be the signal for the Allison Green fans in the restaurant. Her continuing absence had been a source of endless speculation, and she was quickly surrounded by early diners seeking autographs.

Kelly kept her arms around Jack's neck even as Allison stepped away toward the seat at the head of the table that Kirk had graciously vacated. She didn't remove them as she settled into the chair next to his.

"You've been hanging around this bunch of wiseacres too long." He muttered to her, and she squeezed him even harder.

"It was all her idea. She said she wanted to meet me before anyone knew she was in town. Then Puff had this great suggestion for a practical joke . . . hey, don't act like it *hurt* or anything! For a moment there, you had two sexy ladies fighting over you."

"You two were fighting over me a lot longer than that. More than either of you knew."

"I know it now. She's beautiful, Jack." Kelly's face became serious for a moment, and she eased her grip without breaking it. She planted a long kiss directly on his ear. "But I won."

The arrival of Allison Green marked the beginning of the end of the writing phase, and Jack wasn't sorry to see it finish. Death Troupe had always been unique in its approach to the script, and that distinctiveness extended to the very night of the show. He knew other playwrights who were integral parts of the rehearsal process the whole way through, but he knew far more who were not. It made sense to him that the actors reached a point where they were reacting to the words on their own, under the guiding hand of the director, and that too many voices could interfere with that interpretation.

And even though every production adjusts the script to some extent, he knew that no matter what they did, they couldn't actually change what he'd written. That had a life separate from the stage show, in his creative conscious, and what he'd handed over to the troupe was on its own journey now. They would find things in it that he had not put there, add things to it that he had never imagined, and then bring it to life in a way that he simply could not.

He'd spent many hours preparing Kelly for this moment, and she accepted it with great equanimity as a result. She was also physically exhausted from the long effort, so it was with considerable relief that she looked up to see Barron entering the backstage room where she and Jack were working late. The changes had grown smaller and smaller in the previous nights, shifting from broad strokes to hairline corrections, and like the final rumbles of a departing thunderstorm they were their own indication that the process was drawing to a close.

Barron had changed into a bright orange turtleneck for the occasion, and he was alone. Jack was making modest edits on a printed page, and Kelly was reflecting those changes on the schematic she'd drawn so long before. The Director walked in with a somber look and silently crossed the room to where she stood.

Reaching out, he took the marker and capped it. He then grasped her hand and led her back to the table where Jack was seated. He placed a palm on Jack's upper back, and the veteran writer stood without a sound. Turning the couple toward the open door, Barron walked them to the hallway that waited outside. The rest of the troupe had departed an hour earlier, and even the set designers had stopped work for the night by then, so the corridor was empty.

Barron released Kelly's hand and rested his fingers on her shoulder. Standing between and behind them, he intoned the words like a benediction. "Outstanding job, you two. We'll take it from here. We're going to find a way to sneak you both into the balcony for the dress rehearsal, but until then . . . you're banned from my theater."

They walked across the empty street hand in hand once the security man had let them out. There was no moon in sight, but the stars shone over them like a chorus. The thawed water of Round Pond gently lapped against its banks, and there wasn't another sound as they walked to the two-story dormitory where Jack was staying. The cabins around them appeared to be deserted, but they knew that most of them were filled with the actors and support personnel of the troupe. They passed under scented pine trees and then mounted the open staircase to the second floor, where a railed walkway held the entire building in its embrace.

Jack didn't even turn on the light as they passed into his room, and they only bothered to remove their shoes before climbing onto his bed. He managed to pull a blanket over them before both of their bodies, having operated at maximum capacity for far too long, shut down as if they had both quietly expired.

"—caught up on my sleep, my laundry, even some of the friends I made here in the town." Jack held a mug of steaming coffee in both palms while leaning his forearms on the dormitory's second-floor railing. It was early morning, two days after he'd been ordered out of the Playhouse, and he was greeting the new day with Puff.

Although it was late April, the nights were still cold and so both men wore fleece tops over their clothes. Jack had on a set of sweat pants and running shoes caked with new mud, having run all the way around the pond just as the sun was rising. Puff was holding his own mug of coffee, but he was also munching away on a breakfast burrito in preparation for work. Jack didn't envy him; one of the good things about having Barron take control of the script was the long break this gave the troupe's exhausted writers.

"That's one of the things I like most about the theater biz—the people I've met all over the world. I swear there isn't a major city left where there isn't somebody I know." Puff finished the burrito and washed it down while Jack took in the pine trees around the dormitory. Light green shoots were already furring the tips of the branches, and he heard a woodpecker hard at work somewhere nearby. "Of course, all the travel means there's more people to catch up with, but that really can't be helped, can it?"

"Afraid not. At least not with Death Troupe." Jack found he didn't like the direction the early morning banter was taking, having suddenly realized how little time he had left in Schuyler Mills. He'd only signed on for one show with Barron, and had no idea what the Director might have promised Kelly, but one way or another his time there was coming to an end.

As if conjured up by his very thoughts, Kelly appeared below them. They heard her approach at least a minute before her arrival, when they'd noticed a low growling somewhere in the forested hills beyond the campground. The sound didn't get much louder, but as it got closer it resolved itself into something mechanical. The camp was just getting in motion at that time, with various clusters of technicians, designers, and actors shuffling toward the Playhouse, and many of them stopped to try and identify the source of the noise.

Their curiosity was finally satisfied when Kelly came out of the woods at the handlebars of a camouflage-painted four-wheeled all-

350

terrain vehicle. It was impossible to identify her at first, as she was hidden inside a set of knee-high boots, mud-spattered canvas trousers, and a long-sleeved tan work shirt. She had a camouflage rag tied bank robber-style over her nose, mud-flecked goggles, and a black bicycle helmet on top of that when she pulled up outside the dorm directly beneath Jack and Puff. She switched off the engine and began removing the protective layers while the rest of the camp resumed its meandering toward work.

The helmet came off to show that she'd tied her hair back, and when she pulled the goggles and the rag down around her neck two brown ovals marked her eyes. She proudly raised both of these in their direction, and Puff turned to Jack with an expression of horror.

"Does she look like that *every* morning?"

"Nah. She usually takes the boots off." Jack turned a pleasant look toward Kelly and raised his voice. "Right, honey?"

"Whatever you say, sweetheart!"

"Are you taking me on a hunting trip, darling?"

"Nothing good is in season. Come on, get dressed. I want to show you some of the sights."

"All right." Jack sounded doubtful but obedient. "Uh, exactly what am I supposed to wear?

"Remember those hiking boots you wore on the first day? Those would be a good start."

"Do I have time for breakfast?"

She turned and patted a compartment behind her with a gloved hand. "Got everything you need right here."

"Okay . . . give me a minute." He disappeared inside his room, and Puff descended the stairs carrying a small bag. He walked over to Kelly and surveyed her with mock distaste.

"So you really *are* a hillbilly, after all."

"Gives you a thrill, doesn't it?"

"Actually, it does. Can I come along?"

"Noooo." Kelly deepened her voice in imitation. "This is just for the grownups."

"Grownups?"

"As in, 'You kids study hard at school while we enjoy a day off'."

"My God, this is a side of you I hadn't seen before." The older man looked around him, determining that no one else was in earshot. "This must be the persona that helped Jack write the play."

"Shhhhh." Kelly raised a finger to her lips, fixing him with a hard smile.

"No worries. I only guessed it recently, and nobody else seems to have caught on. But I do have one request: If you're planning to come with the troupe, please bring Jack along." He kissed her cheek and then walked off toward the Playhouse, making a slight spitting sound as he went. "Lord I hope that was mud."

The ATV slewed around in the places where the sun had already melted the trail, but there was still enough shadow in the forest to keep most of the ground dry. Jack hung onto Kelly from behind, and couldn't help being reminded of his snowmobile evacuation from those same woods in February. Back then he'd been only semi-conscious and strapped to the woman in front of him, and he found this ride much more enjoyable.

She took him up a dirt trail at first, leaving the Playhouse and the campground behind as they climbed. Snow still lay in piles inside the tree line, like doomed refugees waiting to be hunted down by an implacable foe, but all around them were the signs of spring. Buds now studded most of the tree branches, colored leaves had sprung up on many of the bushes, and a carpet of green shoots bordered much of the trail. Jack guessed they were headed north based on the still-climbing sun, and he believed Kelly was taking him somewhere he'd never been.

He was correct in the general direction, but wrong in the assumption. The trail banked around a curve where industrious beavers had walled off a small lake, and from the ATV's height Jack could see that the water was above the level of the road. They ducked under a low-hanging branch just after that, and then Kelly turned east on a trail that Jack easily recognized.

As if to check, she reached back with one hand and squeezed his thigh. He was wearing her spare bike helmet along with a pair of sunglasses and a colored handkerchief that covered his mouth and nose, but the similarity ended there. She'd sent him back up to his room twice, first to add his down vest to the sweat top he'd chosen, and then to get a pair of gloves. His hiking boots, now caked with mud, poked out from under a set of dungaree trousers that had seen better days.

Pressing his mouth to her ear, he shouted, "Are we going where I think we're going?"

"You got it! Thought you'd like to see your hill in the good weather!"

She accelerated just then, taking them down the trail which he'd first seen on Groundhog Day, when he'd started on his disastrous cross-country ski trek. They'd joined it at a spot after the fork where he'd taken the wrong turn, so it could only end in one place.

He'd skied along that route many times since the mishap, but never all the way to the end as he'd (almost) done the night he'd been rescued. Somehow he'd expected the route to be much shorter once he'd done parts of it at his leisure and gotten to know them, but every time he'd been daunted by just how much distance he'd mistakenly covered that evening. Even now, astride the mechanical beast that was doing all the work for him, he was surprised at how long it took them to navigate the passing terrain, the hills closing in on the trail and the trees getting thicker as they neared its end.

He found he easily recognized the downhill slope which presaged the pile of rocks and what was essentially a box canyon where the trail terminated. Instead of a white carpet beneath them, he now saw a slowly dissolving path that had once been made of tiny pieces of shale and other gravel. Much of this had worn away, but not from use, and he saw large segments of loose dirt as they traveled. The cliffs on either side, which had been rendered almost featureless by the snow in February, now revealed horizontal striations and violent vertical cracks. The reviving vegetation was already vying for position on the terraces formed by the rock, and even among the pile of huge boulders that sat at the path's terminus.

Kelly stopped the ATV there, shutting off the engine and unfastening her helmet. Jack left his on until she motioned for him to remove it, and she took it from him when this was done.

"There's a small path leading up the hill off to the left—" she motioned with a gloved hand "—you wouldn't have been able to see it that night in the snow. It won't be much of a hike to the top if you use it."

He dismounted slowly, feeling a pins-and-needles sensation in one leg from how he'd been forced to sit. The strange journey smacked of ritual, and he remarked to himself that this would be the point in a movie where he'd be murdered or given a chance to run for his life. Seeing that Kelly had no intention of getting off the ATV, he canted his head.

"You're not coming?"

"No. I'll be here when you come back down, but take your time. It's a tremendous view from up there and I wanted you to see it when it was green."

"Come with me."

"No." She removed a glove and reached out a hand to squeeze his arm. "This is your place, Jack. You saved your own life here, and you were alone when you did that. You should be alone when you see it again."

"I wasn't alone. You were out here too, looking for me. So this is as much your place as it is mine."

She smiled at that, and for an instant he thought he detected a hint of tears in her eyes. "Campion Hill is our place. When you come back I'm going to show you some other spots, really pretty ones. We'll picnic, and just enjoy ourselves. And maybe we'll decide one of those is ours too."

He sensed it was time to broach the subject, and he spoke in a rush. "I've been thinking, there's a little place in Arizona—"

The tips of her fingers touched his lips, and he stopped obediently. She raised the fingers once, then twice, as if keeping time, before taking the hand away. "Go on up and see it. We'll talk when you get back."

The 'path' Kelly had mentioned was little more than a washed-out line of dirt zigzagging its way to the top, but it was infinitely preferable to going over the boulders on either side. Sometimes climbing hand-over-hand, and even once grabbing hold of an exposed tree root to keep from tumbling back down, Jack labored up the hill with a steadily increasing sense of anticipation.

In February he'd made his painful crawl over the rocks wearing the wrong kind of boots and unable to see what was beneath the snow, and now he experienced a giddy feeling of revenge over the inanimate obstacles. Reaching a relatively level stretch of dirt, Jack stopped to catch his breath and flipped a middle finger at the boulders that had tortured him months before. Looking about him, he was finally able to identify the sensation aroused by this ground which he knew so well and yet not at all: With the snow gone, it was like the unwrapping of a present. That was it, and in a way every spring was like that too; the snow had hidden marvelous gifts beneath its wrappings, and the sun slowly removed that covering to reveal what lay beneath.

Although tall trees marched alongside him as he ascended, he saw now that his grove of pines lived only at the very top. Emerging from the rock field onto a sodden mash of their dead needles, he found that he'd expected the summit to be still encased in snow. Looking up, he saw that the sun was penetrating the grove deeply and so he stopped and raised closed eyes to soak up its warmth. He stood that way for at least a minute, hearing the call of birds and smelling a mossy rankness that suggested the riotous growth to come.

The drop-off where he'd stood when spotting the power lines was easy to detect, as the trees went to its edge and simply vanished after that. He moved along the exposed rocks in an attempt to find the spot where he'd emerged the first time, but in full daylight and with all his faculties it was impossible to know for sure. Walking forward on legs still brimming with strength, he reached out a hand to gently stroke the hard bark of the pines as he passed them. Arriving at the cliff edge, he selected one of the trees to act as surrogate and leaned his cheek against it, this time receiving a wet kiss that smudged his face with black.

The valley spread out before him for miles, and he noted the dark blue of the lakes that had been frozen the first time he'd stood there. The trees, which he'd last seen stripped of foliage and heavy with snow, were now wrapped in the green of new growth. The sun shone brightly in a cloudless sky, and he saw it glint off of the trickle of water in the pass he'd taken to reach the power lines.

His head moved slowly as he took in the vista, and his nostrils gently expanded and contracted as he breathed it all in. Over and over again, under his breath he repeated two words, but not the words from the first trip.

"Thank you. Thank you. Thank you."

Chapter Twenty-Four

Jack's running shoes were soaked through as he ran on the muddy path that circled Round Pond. It was early morning a few days before the performance, and water vapor hung suspended over the lake and at the bases of the surrounding trees. This was now his morning ritual, and he'd recently taken to stopping on the side furthest from the Playhouse and the campsite, just to soak up the sights and the smells. Winter's grip was finally broken with the end of April, and Jack often heard small animals racing off through the underbrush whenever he ran this route.

He and Kelly were still heavily involved with the community players, whose work had actually increased instead of going in the opposite direction. The film team had already compiled several scenes-worth of back story with them, but Barron wasn't satisfied with the results. As much as he enjoyed watching the film team squirm under the Director's demands, Jack had to question Barron's never-ending demands for more footage.

To confuse matters even more, the Director had decided to keep Glenda Riley as Allison Green's understudy. Although her part in the introduction was minimal, and she was clearly having the time of her life with the professional actors, Jack could not imagine why an outsider was being used in such a position. Death Troupe didn't need understudies because the main cast performed the show exactly once. Including a non-member stretched the boundaries of security to an unhealthy extent, and he knew Wade had raised that objection more than once. Barron was certain that Glenda was enjoying the experience far too much to divulge any secrets, but Jack still couldn't fathom the decision.

He was pondering that exact question when he rounded a bend that opened into a slight clearing. A large rock sat in the middle of the glade, and on other mornings his writer's mind had conjured up images of faeries and sprites dancing around it. He didn't need any imagination that trip, however, as a very real Ryan Betancourt was seated on the rock when he drew up.

Jack stopped in momentary fright, and not just because he'd unexpectedly encountered a human being out there. Weeks had passed since he'd last seen Ryan, and the rich man had made no attempt to contact him. Jack had come to believe that Ryan had heard the news about Pauline Scott, and that he'd cleared out of the area in embarrassment. Pauline's activities amply disproved his accusations about Wade, and Jack suspected the rich man now feared his faked death would make him an object of professional ridicule. With that in mind, he'd remained silent about Ryan's existence—in the hope of letting his fellow writer choose the circumstances of his return from the dead.

Ryan was just as emaciated as he'd been all winter, but he seemed almost happy as he regarded the approaching jogger. He wore a brown set of hiking boots, black jeans, and a camouflage-patterned coat made of a light, almost rubbery fabric. His hands were tucked into the jacket's pockets, and the lower part of the coat was pressed between him and the rock. His face was clean shaven, and his hair was neatly combed.

"Hello, Ryan."

"Good morning, Jack. I see you're getting back into running shape."

"Why not? The script's all done, showtime's almost here, and in a week I'll be back in Arizona." He casually looked around him. "So what brings you here?"

"Same as always. How is Allison?"

"Same as always. And perfectly safe." Jack decided to take the bull by the horns. "Want to go say hello?"

"I don't think Wade would like that."

"I don't think Wade would care."

"Oh, I'd have to disagree with that." Ryan murmured this last while slowly rising and reaching inside the coat. He pulled out a small nickel-colored box, and when he lifted the lid Jack saw that it was a portable movie player. His heart began beating faster as the screen warmed up, and he felt strangely drained of strength when Ryan put it on the stone and hit a button.

The screen faded into life with a green-and-black image that looked like it might have been filmed underwater. It took Jack a moment to make out what was happening, but he soon recognized it as some kind of sex tape. Two figures wrestled on the bed, the man silent while the girl moaned happily, and Jack started in alarm when he recognized his own hands peeling away the sheer leotard that Pauline Scott had been wearing under her dress.

The tape was more than two years old, made on the night when he'd learned about Allison and Ryan. That was the night when he'd gotten so blindly drunk that he'd bedded the sultry Pauline. The camera didn't move, telling him it must have been placed somewhere near the ceiling, and he vaguely remembered seeing an old-styled fan over the bed, just as they'd entered the room.

"Oh, my God." He whispered.

"It gets worse." Ryan obviously didn't understand that Jack's revulsion came from the knowledge that the girl he was watching was now dead by her own hand. "One of my guys traced this to a storage site on the Web, several times removed but still traceable to Wade. Amazing, the lengths that guy will go to."

Jack stepped forward as the man and the woman began writhing together. He reached down and found the button to make it stop, knowing that it had ended with her cries of joy and his tears of sorrow and not willing to see it. He stared at the blank screen as if it was still in motion, and wasn't aware Ryan had moved until he folded the machine closed and placed it inside the coat.

"I'm sorry I had to do that, Jack, but I only recently got this. I can't prove Wade was behind it, but who else would plant a camera in some groupie's room, in the hope that *somebody* might give in to temptation?" Ryan took a few steps away, to the other side of the rock. "That storage site hadn't been visited in over a year, and my guys think he might have forgotten all about it. You see, Wade didn't care what happened to this clip because he never had to use it. You can bet he planned to have Allison see this at the time, but then you quit the show and there was no need.

"You see what we're up against here?"

Jack pushed the feeling of shame away, sorting quickly through what he knew and what Ryan apparently did not. His memory flashed to another bedroom, this one in Schuyler Mills, where he'd turned down the advances of a girl very much like Pauline—and for that very reason. It focused his thoughts into brutal clarity.

"Ryan, Pauline's dead."

The rich man's head jerked once, as if trying to shake off an insect. His eyes widened, and he took a step backward as if about to fall. His neck looked impossibly skinny inside the folds of the jacket, and the taut skin along his jaw line tightened just a little bit more.

"What?" he barely got the word out, and it sounded like it came from a one hundred year-old man.

"That's right. It was her all along. Just after our last conversation the police found a car up at Niagara Falls, abandoned where the jumpers go. Her driver's license was in the car, with a fake ID, fake credit cards, and the receipt from a hotel where the clerk remembered her checking in. It's not Wade. It never was."

Ryan's mouth worked once, then twice, like a fish tossed up on a riverbank. He raised his left hand, index finger poised, but only got it to waist level. "But . . . how do you know that? Wade told you, right?"

"Stop it, Ryan." Jack let an edge enter his voice, knowing that it was time to shake his former partner back into reality. "I was interviewed by the police right after that, and I spoke with Pauline's parents on the phone later. Couldn't tell them anything of substance, but I wanted to say that I'd known their daughter and that I was sorry to hear what had happened."

"But . . . that doesn't mean anything. What if she and Wade were working together?" He tapped the device inside his jacket, as if for reassurance. "That makes sense! He put her up to it, she filmed you two, and she gave the tape to Wade. And what about the fake ID and credit cards you mentioned? Who better to help her get those?"

"Cut it out, Ryan. You know that's all nonsense."

"How? How would I know?"

"Because if Wade wanted Allison for himself like you've been saying, why hasn't he made his move yet? I've been with Kelly for weeks, everybody knows it, so the way's clear. For a guy who's done all the crazy things you say Wade has, he sure is taking his time popping the question, isn't he?"

The words had the same effect as if Jack had punched Ryan hard in the diaphragm. The other writer swayed on his feet, then leaned over to touch the rock in front of him, and finally sat down on it. His mouth hung open, his hand remained on the stone, and he stared off down the trail as if seeing something horrible approaching.

He's in shock. He's actually in shock.

Jack stepped closer, squatting down so he could look into Ryan's eyes. He gently placed a hand on his knee, and waited until the touch registered on the man's shattered face. Ryan's eyes finally regained their focus, and he craned his neck forward as if seeing Jack for the first time.

"My God . . . is that it?"

"Yes. She was up here, she was probably in Red Bend too, and I'm afraid it all got to be too much for her so she ended it." He didn't mention his fear that Pauline had learned about Kelly and killed herself in despair. It was impossible to know if she'd had anything to do with the old man in Red Bend, but if her intention had been to frighten Ryan off so that Jack could rejoin the troupe, it must have been an unbearable jolt to see him with a new girlfriend.

"I went through all this . . . for nothing?" Ryan's eyes were taking on a crazy glint, and he placed a weak hand on Jack's shoulder like a drowning man reaching for a matchstick.

"Not for nothing, Ryan. Who knows what she might have done if you'd stayed with the troupe?" He'd come up with this angle of reasoning many days earlier, on the off chance that Ryan would reappear. "If you ask me, by pretending to be dead . . . you saved your life."

"But I'm ruined . . . ruined. Can you imagine what people are going to say?"

"About what? That Death Troupe's writer decided to go on sabbatical and spiced things up with a scary story about his own demise? Anybody who knows us is going to think it was a publicity stunt. And you must have at least *thought* about how you were going to come back to life, right?"

"Every day of this." The hand fell off his shoulder, and Ryan looked at the ground again. "You have no idea what it's been like. I've been living in a fucking trailer most of this time. I haven't even been able to call Emily, for fear that Wade . . . you're sure it's not him?"

"I'm sure. I have to admit I doubted him there for awhile myself, but that's all done now. We have to go forward from where we are. From here. Right?"

Ryan's expression brightened just a bit at the suggestion that the long ordeal was over, and he returned his gaze to the man who had been his writing partner. "You're a good friend, Jack. A better friend than I deserved."

"I'd say we were looking out for each other this time. Wouldn't you?"

He actually smiled at that, and his hand came up. "I'm so sorry for what I did to you and Allison. Forgive me?"

He took the hand, and they shook. "Nothing to forgive. Now let's talk about getting you back home to Emily so you two can plan the back-from-the-dead party you're gonna throw."

The next day, Jack sat by himself in the balcony of the Schuyler Mills Playhouse. The house lights were still up, but the balcony was cloaked in shadow. It was the full-dress rehearsal, and Kelly was to be joining him at any moment.

He'd spent the previous day feeling good about the way he'd resolved Ryan's crisis, and the sensation hadn't left yet. As much as he'd been hoping Ryan had simply left the area on his own, Jack now saw that it was far better to know that he'd settled things with the other writer. Ryan's clumsy attempts to see Pauline's demise as one more twist in Wade's bizarre quest for Allison's affections was proof that he'd needed a mental course correction—and Jack had supplied that.

Sitting there in the darkness, watching the final preparations for the dress rehearsal, he congratulated himself on dispatching the troubled writer back to his sister and the family lawyers. He had no idea if a fake suicide was going to cause lasting problems, but Emily was unlikely to allow that to happen. Although Jack had always found the woman to be as charming as her brother, he'd also detected signs that she went to great lengths to suppress the wild artist gene that so obviously ran in the family. Jack had felt that was a shame when he'd known her, but now he hoped that same strictness would help Ryan find the resolution he needed.

A shaft of light stretched across the empty seats as the balcony door opened and then closed, and he watched Kelly as she came down the side aisle. His eyes having adjusted to the darkness, he now saw with delight that she wore a sleeveless cocktail dress and that her hair was made up. He'd put on a jacket and tie for the occasion, and complimented himself for his foresight.

"Nice to see some people still dress for the theater." He whispered as they kissed. She settled into the seat next to his, reminding him of their conversations in that very balcony and the many times they'd sat together in rehearsal.

"A lot of good it did me. Wade brought me here in the back of a moving van, and I came in through the loading dock."

"Did they carry you in rolled up in a carpet?"

"If they did, does that make you Julius Caesar?"

"Hope not. Things didn't end too well for him."

The mewing of stringed instruments rose up to them, as if an orchestra was tuning up. The Playhouse sound system was so good that Jack almost looked for the musicians before remembering that there weren't any. The lights and the sound effects were all controlled remotely, and he'd sat through the earliest technical rehearsals to act as a sounding board for their effect.

The seats below were dotted with those members of the troupe who had no responsibilities on opening night, from the film team to the designers. On the night of the show every one of those chairs would be reserved for a local, and the Director had arranged for Tadd, Lynnie, and Gary to get three of those coveted spots so that his game team could see a live performance. The rest of the seating had been handled by the town in a lottery, and large video screens had already been erected in the fields outside for anyone who wasn't lucky enough to get a spot inside. Jack had heard that the lottery had been heavily influenced by Tillman in an effort to pack the voting part of the audience, and that most of the townsfolk had gone along with him.

Watch this guy, Jack.

The sound of the stringed instruments slowly subsided, and the house lights dimmed while Jack smiled. The plot of this play was good, and he doubted very much that even a concerted effort by the locals would identify the culprit. He'd seen such voting schemes fall flat before, and also knew that a fair number of the bar-coded ballots never seemed to make it into the box. This was attributed to audience members who were so enthralled by the first two acts that they honestly didn't want to ruin the experience by picking the right suspect. The rules required a majority vote for a single suspect, and that majority was calculated against the available ballots—not the number of votes cast.

Barron marched out on stage to polite applause, issued a brief welcome, and then walked off. He insisted that dress rehearsal be run like the actual performance in every way, and so Jack already knew that the local players were not present. Barron had finally accepted the filmed introduction, dousing any hope that the community theater group would be performing live. Jack understood the many reasons for that decision, but he accepted it with true remorse.

A bouncy ragtime song, joined in mid-number, gradually wafted from the building speakers as the curtain separated. Three large projection screens materialized from the blackness beyond, and a montage of black-and-white scenes from the Roaring Twenties rolled across them like cascading waves. A man wearing a shirt with rounded collars and a straw boater spoke silently into an absurdly large microphone before being washed away by archival footage of a horserace attended by a madly exulting crowd. A massive grain harvester churned a field of tall wheat before surrendering to an assembly line of Model T's. A steamboat churned the waters of some Adirondack river, festooned with bunting that was clearly red, white, and blue even though the image was not in color.

Next, a Prohibition raid stormed into an illegal distillery while exuberant agents smashed foaming kegs of beer with axes. A close-up of a chattering Thompson gun lit the stage with bright flashes, and for a brief instant the wild-eyed face of Kirk Tremaine, partially shielded by a fedora, appeared above it. Two large automobiles raced down a country road at night, exchanging gunfire until they were replaced with a still image, the hoodlum lineup Jack had used in his first briefing to Barron. The sullen gangsters took up the middle screen while large freighters on either side of them offloaded barrels onto fast boats that then sped up inland streams in the dead of night. The separated pictures then merged into a formal dinner party where tuxedo-clad gentlemen whirled gowned ladies across a huge ballroom floor and champagne corks flew through the air.

The ragtime song came to an abrupt stop, and a dramatic ruffle of trumpets replaced it. Newspapers began spinning on all three screens, coming to a halt with the dire news of the Stock Market Crash.

A strident radio announcer's grainy voice took over, declaring that "Washington fears a grave crisis is at hand."

The newspapers dissolved into scenes of terrified crowds outside banks whose doors were shuttered and locked, and Jack felt Kelly's hand reaching for his in the darkness.

"A run on several regional banks has caused many financial institutions to temporarily close their doors . . . the governor is appealing for calm and threatening to call the National Guard into service to quell any rioting."

Familiar faces, still shot in black and white, began to weave their way into the archival footage. Al Griffin, clad in a dark homburg and long overcoat and angrily puffing on a cigar, pushed his way past a group of people in vintage clothing who were trying to get him to stop. A clutch of the local troupe's younger players sprang up on one screen, wearing the clothes of working men and their wives, shaking their fists and shouting even though nothing they said could be heard.

"Even the racketeers are feeling the pinch. The dreaded Seven Seas Gang of the Adirondack waterways has split into rival factions in a battle for the flow of illegal alcohol . . ."

Briefly, Kirk and Sally reappeared in their gangster outfits, standing back-to-back and blazing away with their machineguns. Jack found his eyebrows contracting as he viewed the momentary scene, struck by the deadly focus displayed by the two young actors. As in the town square, they were thoroughly believable as lethal soldiers in a doomed battle, and he asked himself just when the two people he'd first known as child actors had grown up.

The chaos on the stage slowly resolved into a panoramic shot across all three screens, a view of Schuyler Mills as it had existed circa 1929. Large factories stood next to smoke-belching mills, and Jack was just able to make out the Civil War monument in the town center. The picture stayed up for half a minute while the announcer droned on:

"In Schuyler Mills, New York, the financial advisor hired to manage the town's money is found dead at his desk, believed to have killed himself after losing the life savings of so many who now exist in desperate need . . ."

The film started after that, a black and white production featuring the local players as the townsfolk at the time of the Great Depression. Jack was familiar with most of it, but so much excess footage had been shot that he leaned forward to see which scenes would actually be used. A hand lightly landed on his shoulder, and he felt Kelly pushing him back against his seat as if he were in the way.

"Enjoy it, Jack." She whispered without looking at him. "Lay back and take it all in."

Chapter Twenty-Five

And then the big night was finally there. Jack moved all of his possessions out of the dormitory while many of the other players could be seen all over the campground, getting their things together as well. The sharp scent of pollen and the bright green of new vegetation filled his senses with memories of springs past, and the bustle reminded him of the end of many school years from his youth.

The town's wood sculptors had been working overtime in preparation, and the common was now ringed with new works. These were almost all mystery-themed, and in addition to the monuments honoring the mythical Seven Seas Gang there was even a pair of wooden violins resembling the ice sculptures of months before. The sewing club had outdone itself, transforming the Mystery Weekend banner into twin "Sins of the Seven" greetings that now stretched across the main road at both ends of town. The red seven overlooking Long Lake (which was now full of bright blue water and frequently dotted with boats) had been electrified so it was visible at night, and a new Death Troupe flag snapped gaily from the cupola of the Schuyler Mills Playhouse.

To Jack, the night of the show always felt like watching a movie that was missing major scenes. The exhilaration seemed to speed everything up, and the sensation was intensified by the relentless countdown to the opening curtain. When he looked back on a show night he was often at a loss to remember most of the connecting moments.

Not that he minded. Yet another characteristic of show night was the feeling of being carried along by something enormous and alive, something yearning to break free, like a beast that has outgrown its cage. There was almost a party atmosphere to the whole thing, and to Jack the hours before the curtain went up flashed by as if recorded in disjointed snapshots.

Just after the actors had all arrived at the theater, Barron had the cast in a tight circle on stage. The curtain was drawn and no one would be allowed into the auditorium for some time, but Jack still felt his pulse quicken as the players assembled. This was a common ritual in theater, the director giving a short pep talk, and Jack had already found himself a shadowy spot in the wings so he could hear it.

"I've never liked the term 'actor'." Barron spoke slowly, holding hands with Paula Ninninger to his left and Allison Green to his right. The rest of the cast joined hands as well, and he continued. "Seriously now, is anyone here 'acting'? Is anyone here pretending?

"Me, I'm a theater director. One hundred percent, all the time. I'm not pretending, or acting, or trying to fool anyone. This is what I do, and I give it my all—just like you. I look around me, and I don't see a single phony. I see people who give their hearts, their minds, and their very lives to being serious performers on the stage. In the last weeks I've watched every one of you give up the easy life to come here and bust a gut to make this show a reality.

"And that's why I call you performers. Not actors. Performers. Because when it's time to prepare, you prepare every nuance of a role. When it's time to step in front of the crowd, you reach out and pull them in with both hands. When it's time to say your lines, you deliver them with skill and meaning. That's performance. And there's nothing phony about that. There's nothing pretend about that. There's no acting that will take the place of that.

"And so that's my wish for you tonight: Have a great performance. You've done the work, you're ready, and now it's time to show off. Have fun out there, gang. Perform."

The next moment he and Barron were standing outside at the top of the stairs leading into the Playhouse, the light just beginning to fade. The nearby fields were already full of picnickers eating an early dinner before watching the show on the big screens before them, and a healthy part of the Playhouse audience was walking down the road from the parking areas. Suits and tuxedos mixed with gowns and cocktail dresses, and the cloudless sky gave the whole scene an air of approval.

A black limousine pulled right up to the steps, and Barron pointed at the vehicle's unusual hood ornament.

"Is that what I think it is?" he asked gruffly.

"It is indeed. I told you it was making the rounds."

Proudly perched on the hood of the limousine, like the naked carvings that had once decorated the bows of sailing ships, was the plastic head that had first been discovered by a local ice fisherman months before. The limousine was a long one, and its rearmost door opened as Mayor Tillman, impressive in a black tuxedo, emerged. He helped his gown-clad wife get out, but then gave an impish tilt of his head toward the car's hood.

"I couldn't resist!" he shouted as Bib Hatton, almost unrecognizable without his overalls, followed his wife out of the car. The enormous man was also dressed in a tuxedo, and Jack could only marvel at how much material it required. The Maddens emerged next, and the group approached the stairs like foreign dignitaries at an international summit.

Many of the other partygoers had reached the building by the time Tillman and his wife touched the step just below Barron, and so the mayor intoned his question for their benefit.

"Do you have the envelope, Mr. Barron?"

"I do, Mr. Mayor." Barron held aloft a large gold envelope for all to see. A red ribbon held it closed, and a plastic seal had been affixed to the flap. "Please follow me as we place it in the hands of the witnesses."

The doors opened behind them, and the entire group began filtering into the building. The envelope contained the identity of the culprit, and had become standard practice once the troupe had been accused of changing the play's ending after the votes were cast. A trusted delegation from the town would watch the play on closed circuit television alongside one of Wade's security people as they jointly stood guard over the envelope (and enjoyed a sumptuous catered meal). The envelope would be opened after the show was over, revealing whether or not the townspeople had guessed the play's murderer.

Jack and Barron left the early arrivals in the lobby for a pre-show reception, and a security man let them into the empty auditorium. They both stopped just after that, looking down the central aisle past the rows of mute seats toward the curtained stage. To Jack, the aisle's slight downward grade looked like the precipitous drop at the top of a ski jump, but he was interrupted in that thought by Barron's quiet comment.

"I love an empty theater."

"Why—all the boundless possibilities?"

367

"No. It's because an empty theater means I'm in control. Right now I'm in control. During rehearsal I'm in control. But when those seats are filled . . . anything can happen."

They were backstage after that, where Jack got caught up in the quiet maelstrom of activity. The peculiar nature of their show granted him access there, as the seats in the host town theaters were at such a premium that there was no way a troupe member could actually sit and watch the play. He didn't feel cheated, having seen the dress rehearsal, and planned to sneak Kelly inside after the voting was completed. He believed it was simply wrong for her to miss the experience of the final act, with a real audience, after how much she'd put into the show. She was outside somewhere, helping the guests who would watch the performance on the big screens in the field.

One instant he was surrounded by people he knew, dressed in everyday clothing and appearing quite relaxed, and then things changed. The actors started appearing in makeup, production managers began hustling about, and then the players transformed entirely as they got into costume and character. Puff appeared before him, resplendent in a tuxedo with pointed lapels, and they shook hands while speaking in utter doggerel. It was an old ritual for them, their way to wish the entire troupe luck without actually saying the forbidden words.

The audience buzzed just beyond the curtains, and as always Jack was struck with awe at the idea that the crowd was finally there, just outside the fabric barricade. The time warnings piled on top of each other: Production managers quietly moving through the group to whisper "half-hour", "fifteen minutes", and then "places". Trying not to get in the way, he failed to notice just how many of the actors were costumed as if for a formal occasion and not in the outfits he'd seen in the rehearsals. Instead, he found his face lighting up in much the same way as most of the players around him. They smiled in a buoyant mix of excitement and expectation, like the bridesmaids at the wedding of two very popular people.

And suddenly Barron was at his elbow, looking uncertain for the first time in the many years Jack had known him. He wore a black turtleneck with a dark gray suit and appeared ready to greet the crowd as he always did, but something in his demeanor caused the writer's antennae to twitch. As if responding to that impulse, the gray-bearded man turned watery eyes to him as they stood in the wings just in front of the curtain.

"What's wrong?"

"Ahhhh." The Director reached up with his thumb and forefinger, as if to squeeze the tears away. "I thought I was going to be able to do this. I really did. But I can't."

Barron raised his free hand and extended an index card in the small space between them. Jack took it without comprehension, but before he could look down a motion across the stage drew his attention. Allison Green appeared in the opposite wing, her hair done up in high swirls. She wore a sleeveless silver dress that shimmered even in the dim light, and blew him a soft, soulful kiss with a hand that slowly turned until it looked like she was waving goodbye.

"She's leaving us, Jack. Leaving the troupe." The older man's voice broke on the last syllable. "That's why this one was moved up to the spring. Her career's taking off, and now we have to let her go."

Jack read the brief message on the card and saw it was an announcement that Barron had been planning to make as part of his welcome to the audience. His heart started beating faster with the full implication of the words, but Barron didn't wait for it to sink in.

"I want you to go out to the microphone and say those words." He flipped a vacant finger at the card. "It's fitting, in a way. She was always more yours than ours."

Jack opened his moth to protest, and then shut it when a single tear rolled down the Director's face. He put his hand on Barron's shoulder and simply nodded before straightening his tie and clearing his throat in preparation.

He'd taken the first step, now exposed to the audience in the front seats on the far side but not yet recognized, when the Director spoke from behind him.

"Jack."

He turned easily, surprised that he didn't fear being seen. "Yes?"

"These people love you. They're gonna go ape when you walk out there, so let 'em. You deserve it. Wait until they quiet down, say the words, and then walk across the stage to Allison."

"Got it."

Pulling down on the sleeves of his suit jacket, he marched out toward the single mike stand in the center of the stage. He didn't get three steps before a voice that he didn't recognize as Bib Hatton's bellowed, "Hey, it's Jack! Jack's in the show!"

The uproar was immediate, and he felt like he'd walked out into a gale force wind. The house lights were all blazing away in front of him, and the audience was a sea of color. Tuxedos and jewelry, gowns and dresses of every description, and they all came to their feet as if he'd just finished the greatest one-man show in history. Jack kept his eyes fixed on Allison, who beamed at him in an expression of intense joy while giving him the Puff Addersely clasped-hand salute. He stopped at the mike, but stayed facing her for a few more moments before turning to look at the crowd.

The applause and the cheering passed over him in a warm wave, but that wasn't all. Someone began chanting his name over and over, and soon the others had picked it up. The entire theater trembled as they began stamping their feet with every shouted "Jack!" and he was reminded of the time he'd sat in the cheap seats at a baseball game many years before. That particular group of fans had been equally boisterous and very intoxicated, and there had been moments in the game when he thought they were going to boil out onto the field.

He smiled weakly at them, still unable to enjoy the moment because of Barron's latest surprise. He now knew what Allison had told the Director at least a year earlier, when she'd saved Ryan's job: She was planning to leave, and it made sense that Barron would hang onto her writer-boyfriend as long as she was with the troupe.

The cheering finally subsided, and the citizens of Schuyler Mills slowly seated themselves again. The microphone was disguised to look like one of the star-shaped devices used in the Twenties, and he didn't get the significance of it at first. Still stunned by the news and overpowered by the applause, he cleared his throat again and lifted the index card.

"In tonight's show, the role scheduled to be played by Allison Green . . . will be performed by Glenda Riley."

There was a long moment of total silence, and he feared that the microphone hadn't been turned on. The sea of faces before him started to change just after that, however, and he watched as smiles began to creep up all over the auditorium. If the crowd's reaction to his appearance had been a storm of approval, the response to his announcement was an outright hurricane. They leapt to their feet again, the din threatened to shake the building's foundations, jumping up and down and hugging each other.

He stayed there long enough to see Mayor Tillman, standing in the front row, turn and make an unusual hand gesture several times. Holding his fingers together in a knife edge, he passed his palms over each other again and again in an exaggerated pantomime of washing his hands. The meaning couldn't have been more clear: Whatever plot he'd hatched to control the vote, he was freeing every member of the audience from their obligation.

This one's already in the bag. Barron, you're a stone genius.

Dazed, Jack turned and started across the hard wood of the stage in Allison's direction. Instead of waiting for him in the wings, she stepped out and began walking toward him with a broad smile. Carefully directed lights caught her dress, and people all over the crowd began pointing. The hubbub subsided almost immediately, and Jack knew why.

God *is she beautiful.*

He meant to walk past her stoically, his moment on the stage ended, but she wasn't having it. Allison stepped directly in his path, grasped his upper arms, and kissed him firmly on the lips. It lasted just a second, and then she was gone, headed for the microphone in front of the still-closed curtains. His eyes were so full that he barely made it to the wings, and Berni materialized out of the darkness to steady him. After giving him a brief, silent hug, she took his arm and turned him to face the stage again.

The house lights faded, and a single large spotlight illuminated Allison and the microphone. Jack was slightly aware of people moving past him behind the curtain, and then a slow piano tune began drifting from the speakers in the rear. The music grew from back to front, and Allison took the microphone stand in delicate fingertips and began to sing.

It started out as a happy song about good times and young love, and she ran through the first stanza alone in front of the closed curtain, mesmerizing the crowd in the darkness. The first verse ended on a rising note, and the piano was then joined by the muted melody of a brass orchestra. The curtain parted silently, and the actors who had moved into position behind it were revealed in their tuxedos and gowns, dancing formally in time with the song. A rotating silver ball had descended over the stage, and it twinkled with reflected light that moved in shimmering waves across the dancers while Allison sang.

The words of the song began to change after that stanza, hinting at the intrusion of harsh reality on good times and young love, and slowly moved into the pain of lost innocence and life's hard road. Allison maintained the expression of blissful joy throughout, even as the dancers slowed in their movements and the couples closest to the wings passed from view. The light on the rotating ball dimmed, and shadows began obscuring the remaining dancers even while the spotlight stayed on the singer.

By the time she reached the end, crooning a lament about how foolish they'd been in the good days and how tough they were going to have to be in the bad, she was the only illuminated figure on the darkened stage. The song slowly reached its dénouement, and as her voice softened into the last note, the spotlight abruptly shut off.

There was a moment's silence, and then the applause started, heartfelt and loud. Jack watched the three projection screens descend in the darkness as they prepared to tell the tale of the Stock Market Crash and its effect on Schuyler Mills, the Seven Seas Gang, and an unlucky money manager.

He put his arm around Berni, and whispered into her ear. "The old man just keeps getting better."

"I know." She wrapped her arms around his middle and pressed her face into his chest, and Jack felt the tears on his shirt as he gently caressed her hair.

He watched the first two acts from the same spot, hidden in the wings, alone. The film had set up the story perfectly, and Kirk had proved an excellent choice for the outsider with all the questions. Right from the start he'd appeared to be a man on a mission instead of a humble historian trying to write a chronicle of the bootlegging years in the Adirondacks. The audience reacted to him on a visceral level, knowing he was a possible suspect and yet not seeing how he could have been involved in the killing of the only local willing to speak to him.

As for that, Trask had brought his role to life as an aging drunkard with a chip on his shoulder about how his ancestors had been edged out by the other Seven Seas Gang families. He'd hinted at a string of dark deeds, continuing down through the generations to the present day, as the descendants of the original gangsters had struggled to maintain their primacy in the region. His request for money in exchange for that information had been his final scene, and he'd left Kirk sitting on a cold park bench under a weak streetlight to think it over.

Eerie music had flowed from the speaker system just after that, and the three screens had come together as one just as a light blue background had risen up on them. The effect was of cold water slowly filling an empty space, and the background had shifted around minutely until the image of Trask's corpse floated up into view. Filmed from below, it ascended spread-eagled toward the top of the screens and then stopped with a slight bump, as if arrested by an invisible barrier.

The camera had retreated from the close-up to show tiny bits of debris frozen in the lake ice over the dead man, and a chill had swept across the audience. They were so fixated on the corpse that they didn't notice the two shadowy lines above it until the boots of whoever stood on the ice, looking down at Trask, casually turned and walked away. It was so well done that more than one of the ladies in attendance gave out a minor shriek.

That had ended the first act, which had been filled with characters burdened in some way by the sins of their gangster forebears. Glenda had held her own with the professionals, playing a guilt-ridden descendant of the most vicious Seven Seas family. Though a genuinely good person, and not one of the show's named suspects, her character was still unsettled by the intruder digging up the past. Wendy Warner had consumed the role of the local librarian, supposedly not related to the gangsters, who was so attracted to the handsome young writer in their midst.

Puff had been spot-on in a minor role that was nonetheless a named suspect and a likely culprit in the silencing of Kirk's only informant. Big and important, he played the richest man in town like a king trooping over his domain. It wasn't hard to see that he treasured the blood of the criminals that flowed in his veins—or to envision him acting like the hoodlums he considered virtuous and courageous men of action. He had little use for Kirk's character, but attempted at one point to explain the nature of Adirondack bootlegging to him:

"No one in the area was *afraid* to speak out. They just thought it was a wrong thing to do. Unsportsmanlike, if you will. This whole rum running thing was a game of cops 'n robbers for so long that going to the authorities was like asking the referee to put more time on the clock. Didn't your parents teach you to be a good sport?"

"Good sports are just good losers." Kirk had replied darkly. "And I'm not a good loser."

That scene appeared to set Kirk and Puff on a collision course, and Jack had smirked in the darkness at how artfully he'd placed such a major clue. Much of the audience was looking for the dead stock broker's yet-unidentified descendant—the widow of the slain investor had sworn they would someday return—and many of them naturally suspected Kirk was that character. In the earlier version of the play he'd been just that, come home to wreak havoc on the people who had gotten rich through the murder of his forebear.

The next scene, closing the second act and ushering in the intermission when the vote would take place, had shattered those assumptions. Wendy, now lovestruck by the writer, revealed to him in a moment of passion that she was actually the great-granddaughter of the disgraced stock broker, having quietly returned to the area years before under a different name. The two of them had agreed to work together from that point on, and the curtain closed the second act to a shocked silence that then burst into applause once the audience recognized that they had no idea who the killer was.

Jack emerged from the building only after being accosted by numerous townsfolk in the lobby. Wade's security people were guarding the other entrances with great determination, and so he'd been forced to brave the foyer. He'd hardly recognized Gary, Lynnie, and Tadd when they'd jumped out of the crowd at him. The two men sported jackets and ties, and Lynnie wore a strapless black dress with a string of imitation pearls around her neck. Both Tadd and Lynnie were ready, then and there, to start work on the "Sins of the Seven" game, but he'd urged them to watch the final act instead.

He extricated himself from that conversation with some difficulty, only to become ensnared by the Lawtons and the Griffins. It was important not to slight them on the night of their big performance, but he had a limited amount of time before the intermission ended and needed to meet up with Kelly outside. He'd switched his cell phone back on as he'd entered the atrium, and it vibrated urgently in his pocket as if trying to save him.

"I'm sorry, I really have to take this." He interrupted the ebullient voices, taking out the phone and opening it. It was a text message, but he put the device to his ear and pushed his way out the door before anyone else got a crack at him.

Once outside, he took the nearest ramp and headed toward the cabins. Kelly was supposed to meet him there, but when he finally got to view the text message he saw that the earlier plan had been scrapped. It was fully dark by then, but floodlights lit up the area and many people milled around near the outdoor viewing screens. The closest screen showed a mute countdown for the end of intermission, and Jack shook his head when he saw how little time he had.

The text was simple, but confusing. It was from Kelly, and it invited him to "our place" as it had so many times in the past weeks. For an instant he wondered if they'd forgotten to move something out of the watch tower when they'd dismantled their writing area days before, but he rejected that as silly. He looked about him nervously, not wanting to miss the third act, until a new explanation came to mind.

Come to our place.

They'd both seen the end of the show in rehearsal, so was it possible that Kelly had something romantic in mind? His male vanity imagined a champagne bottle and a blow-up mattress, but he dismissed that as unlikely. Kelly had a wild side, but she'd chafed at not being allowed into rehearsals and wouldn't frivolously give up the chance to view the final act from backstage.

Our place.

The champagne bottle came back into his mind, alongside the sudden notion that Kelly might be planning something that wasn't frivolous—like a proposal. They'd already discussed taking a long trip together after the show, so it wasn't that big a stretch. Besides, what else could it be? What else could be more important than seeing the audience reaction when they learned the identity of the culprit?

Well you better get up there, whatever it is. Maybe you can get back in time for the very end.

He ran down the alley between the nearest cabins and hopped into the truck, trying to remember the trail that Kelly had used during their ATV trip. It would bypass the main road leading back into town and allow him to reach the Campion Hill Road turnoff, and so he stomped on the gas and went roaring off in a shower of small rocks.

The boom was in place and locked when he reached the base of Campion Hill, but that made sense if Kelly wanted privacy. The town had many visitors for the show, and the watch tower would be an inviting diversion if the road was left open. He hopped out, opened the lock and swung the gate out of the way before driving the truck through and reversing the process. The trees on either side of the road were now lush with greenery, and he marveled at the difference made by a few weeks.

Kelly's car was parked just outside the chain link barrier surrounding the tower's base, and he detected the weak glow of the cab's original lights in the night air above him. He doubted there would be much of a view, and hoped that Kelly wouldn't be too disappointed that her romantic moment would be robbed of scenery.

Glancing at his watch and seeing that the show had already resumed, he took the steps two at a time. The night was warm for early May but still just a little brisk, and he felt the cool air pumping into his lungs as he moved. He wasn't in quite the running shape he'd brought to the town in January, but he still reached the top without losing his breath.

That is, until his head rose above the cab's floor and allowed him to see Kelly sitting in the far corner wearing a look of consuming hatred, and Ryan Betancourt squatting across from her holding a large and evil-looking pistol.

Ryan nodded in greeting, the weapon pointed at Kelly. "Well hello, Jack. Glad you got my message."

Chapter Twenty-Six

Jack's head and shoulders were up above the level of the floor, but the rest of him was still on the stairs leading into the cab. He knew his cell phone was still on, and even in his panicked state he tried to reach for its buttons.

"Oh, don't bother with the cell." Ryan was still wearing the camouflage jacket and dark jeans, and he smiled with contentment. He motioned toward the center table, where Jack now saw a large satchel. "See that? Inside it there's a jammer specially tuned to your phone. You could take it out and dial anyone you wanted, and you'd get nowhere."

"That's how he kept you from calling for help that night in the woods." Kelly almost spat the words, and Jack's head jerked in her direction. He knew the black dress she was wearing, and saw that she'd managed to get out of her shoes. She sounded mad enough to lunge at Ryan, but from a seated position that would be suicide. "He says he's been around here for months, waiting his chance."

"Don't rush it." Ryan cooed at her. "Come on up and sit next to your lady fair, Jack. I don't think she understands what an event this is. I'm going to tell you both a story."

Jack put his hands on the cold planking and took the last steps into the small room. In response, Ryan pushed his back into the corner and aimed the gun straight at him. Without a word, Jack walked across the floor that he'd paced on so many other nights and sat down next to Kelly.

"Now put your legs out straight in front of you so I can tell my story without having to wonder if you're going to try something stupid. But before I start, why don't you tell your girlfriend that I wasn't lying? That I was here all along, and that you knew it."

Kelly hadn't looked at him or made a move in his direction even though he was close enough to touch her, and Jack's worst fears were confirmed: She was looking for the slightest opportunity to lunge at Ryan. He considered this for an instant before seeing its cause.

She's sure he's going to kill us. Maybe she's right.

"Come on, Jack. Tell her."

"Tell her what? That I shielded you from Wade, like a fool? That I thought I was helping a delusional old pal, and the whole time he was playing me for a sucker?"

Ryan's face contorted with a soundless snicker, his eyes dancing on the ceiling for an instant. "I never get tired of hearing you say things like that. As many times as I've tricked you, you always see it as your fault. Man do I wish I'd brought a video camera along that night out in the woods. I was laughing my ass off, skiing circles around you while you stumbled up that trail like a blind man."

"He came out of it alive, which is more than I'd expect from you in the same situation." The venom dripped from Kelly's lips, and Jack tried to catch her eye to warn her off that particular course.

"I'll say this for your girlfriend, Jack: She's really very well spoken."

Kelly didn't give him a chance to answer. "I ought to be. I'm your replacement."

Ryan gave her a quizzical look. "What did you just say?"

"Think you're pretty sharp, don't you? Big Broadway playwright." Kelly leaned forward, raising her knees under the dress so that the soles of her feet were flat on the deck. "I got news for you: Jerry was fed up with your ass, and he hired *me* to write a backup play just in case you completely melted down on him."

The gun seemed forgotten in Ryan's hand. His eyes blinked rapidly, and his mouth opened long before he spoke. "What?"

"That's right, numb nuts. Your own director hired the host town *publicity girl* to do your job. That's what he thinks of you."

Ryan's mouth hung open after that, and another revelation came to Jack at that instant.

If she keeps pushing him, he's gonna skip the story and do it right now.

Back at the Playhouse, the final act was fully in progress. The projection screens had descended behind a long table where Kirk sat with Wendy, the librarian descendant of the disgraced stock broker. She was showing him various documents related to the business enterprises of the Seven Seas families, and a parade of maps, bonds, and titles slowly materialized and then vanished on the screens behind them.

"You see, my great-grandfather had transferred most of the town's investments out of the stock market prior to the Crash. He'd actually saved their money, but no one knew it and his assistant saw his chance." A black-and-white close-up of a revolver appeared on the middle screen, held by a gloved hand in the darkness. It fired a single, silent bullet in a cloud of white smoke before vanishing. "He was tired of playing second fiddle to my great-grandfather—" several rapid images flashed across the panels, various still photos of the violin ice sculptures Jack had commissioned, to an accompanying chorus of "ooh" and "second fiddle; so *that's* what that was about" from the crowd "—and so he made it look like a suicide.

"He thought he'd be able to just keep all that money, but he underestimated the Seven Seas Gang."

Kirk, wearing a white dress shirt rolled up to his elbows and a loosened tie, leaned back in his chair. He seemed impressed by her research, and gently stroked her arm. "Tell me more."

"Shut up." Ryan had regained his composure, and Jack could tell he'd simply dismissed Kelly's accusations. As was his habit, if he didn't like the truth he simply ignored it. "And put your legs out straight in front of you the way I said when you first came up here. I won't tell you again.

"So Jack. You knew I was alive all along, you could have told Wade or Barron or the skirt here, and yet you didn't. Know what that tells me? You had no idea you were my target right from the very start."

"I still don't. Why are you doing this, Ryan? Why have you done any of this?"

The other man's face finally showed annoyance, and he pushed off of the wall. "Why am I doing this? How many times do I have to tell you? For Allison!"

"That's what you told me at the beginning, but you said you were protecting her from Wade."

"And you believed me. At least enough to keep quiet, anyway. Hey, I bet you came close to telling him a couple of times, didn't you? That's why I made sure to keep feeding you reasons not to— like the smashed-up ski. Did you like that? I bet you thought Wade did it."

"I did, at first. But one of the other rescuers saw a snowmobiler with a set of skis strapped to his back. It was you, wasn't it?"

"Yeah." The buoyant look returned to his face, and Ryan walked around the cab's table. "This is one strange town, Jack. They don't react to *anything* the way they should. I thought I'd have you all to myself out there in the woods. I tracked you using your own phone from the moment you went out, and right when things were getting interesting I heard the snowmobiles and had to get out of there. But I did manage to take your skis, and after everybody had gone home I went back and broke them against a tree.

"But as I said, nobody around here reacts the way they should. They took the head I put in the fishing hole and turned it into a joke. They spotted the mannequin hanging up here—" a wave at the window where the headless effigy had been hung, which Jack now saw was open "—and just took it down. And then that madness with the ice sculptures and the wood carvings all over the place . . . I had so many great clues I was going to drop for you, just like a real Death Troupe show, but I had to forget all of them because they would've been lost in all the other noise."

'Just like a real Death Troupe show'. Remind him he was once part of the family.

"If it's any consolation, we had the same experience. We had to forget the clue distribution because of all those sculptures."

"And you had to rewrite the script too, didn't you?"

"Yeah, we did." Jack let a tone of disappointment into his voice, hoping to keep the other man talking. No one knew where they were, and no one was likely to come up there with the boom in place, so talking Ryan down was their only hope. "How'd you manage to steal it?"

"Same way I tracked your position and blocked your calls that night—I know every piece of equipment Wade ever gave you. He gave me the same phone, so it was a simple thing to get the right gear to mess with you. He gave me the same laptop with the same security software, so it was pretty easy for me to hack you. I am able to pay for that kind of help, you know."

"But you didn't bring any of that help here, did you?"

Ryan shook his head slowly, smugly. "That's right. There never were any private investigators. I didn't think it would be wise to involve anybody else in this. And you didn't take the bait on that one, anyway: I was hoping you'd start asking people if they'd seen any suspicious strangers in town, but you didn't. It sure would have helped prove that you've lost your marbles."

"I knew you were alone."

"Did you? And how so?"

"Because you didn't know who Kelly was. She and I have been an item of gossip ever since I got here, and yet you had no idea. You really blew up when you saw she was with me. So what was that about?"

"I told you. Allison."

"I'm gonna need a little more than that."

"All right. Here it is. Allison gets a little confused when she listens to the wrong people, and for awhile there every member of that godforsaken troupe was talking trash about me. Oh, you should have heard it, all that shit about how they never should have let you go. And her two lackeys were even worse, always trying to keep us apart. So all of a sudden, out of nowhere, she gets this idea that she's going to pursue a film career."

Kelly, unable to restrain herself any longer, broke in. "Maybe she outgrew you."

Ryan's face tightened in anger. His eyes flashed at Kelly as he extended his gun hand, and his teeth were visible when he hissed his response. "That's *exactly* the kind of talk that split us up."

The stage was transformed into a wintertime forest. The three screens had descended to floor level, with a still scene of the woods near the town broadcast across them. Three prop trees stood out on the stage, their snow-dipped boughs disappearing into the rigging. A carefully directed lighting array made the floor appear white, and Kirk and Robert Hale emerged in front of the crowd.

Hale came from stage right, wearing a heavy blue parka, and Kirk stepped in from stage left wearing a red and black jacket like Mayor Tillman's. Both men had their hands in their pockets and seemed wary of each other. Hale was already known to the audience as the slippery local politician with his eyes on higher office, and Kirk had recently been told that Hale's ancestors had acted as the front for the surviving Seven Seas families when they'd gone more-or-less legitimate.

"Thanks for meeting me here." Hale spoke with warmth, but the crowd was on edge. They already knew he was a deceitful backstabber and that it was unwise for Kirk to be in the woods alone with him.

"Someone knows where I am."

"That's fine. How many times do I have to tell you? There's bad people in these parts, but I'm not one of them. I wanted to try one last time to get you to pack up and leave, before anybody else gets hurt."

"That sounds like a threat."

"Oh, the time for threats has come and gone. What do you think that body under the ice was? You should be smart enough to figure that out—"

The audience jumped with the rifle shot, and someone in the front row gave out a brief cry when the explosive squib embedded in one of the fake trees went off. Bits of bark burst out of the side facing stage right, and a ghostly mist of snow drifted downward as both actors turned in alarm.

"Are there hunters out here?" Kirk blurted out, squinting into the distance.

"Hunters?" Hale scoffed as he drew a pistol from the pocket of his jacket. He was already behind a tree and facing stage right, and when he saw Kirk simply standing there he bellowed, "Find some cover, kid!"

Kirk obeyed in obvious fear, just as a second shot rang out and another squib, this one in the tree Hale was using for protection, went off. More bark flew and more snow descended, and Hale loosed off two bullets in the direction of the shooter. Turning to Kirk, he shouted, "See what you've done? I told you: It's in the blood around here, and you went and woke it up! Now will you get out of here before anybody else gets killed?"

He looked back in the direction of the shooter, and Kirk did the same, peeking around the tree that was offering him shelter. Seeing this, Hale yelled in a voice of command, "Run, I said!"

Dancing uncertainly, Kirk was on the verge of flight when a third gunshot exploded another squib in his tree. Touching the trunk with his left hand as if tagging up, he took off running and disappeared stage left before the last of the shaken snow settled on the floor.

Hale watched him go, appearing unconcerned as he made a show of putting the pistol back on safe and returning it to his pocket. Stepping out into the line of fire, he waved a hand and then confidently walked in the direction from which the rifle shots had come.

"Split you up?" Jack's forehead wrinkled. "You and Allison? When did that happen?"

Ryan slowly turned his attention from Kelly, and leaned back against the cab's center table. He was still out of reach, and the gun was ready in his hand. "Just after I went to Red Bend—as if you didn't know. That was a really bad location for Allison. Hollywood was just a little too close, and so was Saint Jack, wandering out of the desert in his camel hair jacket and clutching that ridiculous movie script."

Jack's mind raced with the missing piece of the puzzle. Until then, he'd believed Allison and Ryan were still together when the other writer pretended to kill himself. It was one of the main reasons he'd never truly seen him as a suspect: No man in his right mind would separate himself from Allison Green voluntarily—unless he believed he was protecting her. Jack numbly questioned why she hadn't told him they'd broken up, but the answer came quickly.

That's *why she didn't want to talk about him. She believed he killed himself because of their breakup. She thinks he did it over her.*

Ryan motioned with the pistol, as if to regain his attention. "But I do have to hand it to you. I never would have believed you'd be able to take her back from me. You almost did, too, and pretty much the same way I took her from you. She dumped you for me because I was connected on Broadway, and she was gonna go back to you because you know people in Hollywood."

Hiding the real fear that now gripped him, Jack kept his words level and neutral. "That's not Allison at all. Did she actually say any of this?"

"Of course not. You know how she is. I sometimes wonder if even *she* knows when she's acting."

Jack then remembered an odd phrase Allison had used during the phone call just after Mystery Weekend, when he'd been breaking up with her: *And I can't explain why, but being on the receiving end of one of these is a lot easier.* He'd thought she was referring to the ugly night when she'd confessed her hidden love for Ryan, but that wasn't it. She'd been talking about what must have been an even uglier scene, telling the rich man that it was over.

"And so you went on this rampage . . . based on your best guess of what someone else was thinking?"

"Rampage? What rampage? I planned out a brilliant mystery, and you fell for every bit of it."

"You think pushing that old man off that roof was brilliance?" A worse thought came to mind. "And I bet you killed Pauline too. I'd call that a rampage."

Ryan straightened up, a tiny grin appearing on his lips. "That old man was so spaced out he never knew what hit him . . . even when it was the ground. Heck, I probably did him a favor, and besides I needed something to get this whole thing rolling. Thought I got spotted going down the fire escape afterward, but it seems the staff there wanted to cover it up more than they wanted to figure it out. And as for dear Pauline, I didn't make her suffer, Jack. It was quick, and she didn't even know I was there . . . you really should thank me."

"And why's that?"

"Because you're going to get blamed for it, and it would be nice if people thought you weren't a complete and total monster."

"Me? How am I going to get the blame for any of this?"

"That was the easy part. As I said, Arizona's close to Red Bend. Close enough for you to drive up undetected—which I'm told you did, on the night of the show. But I needed something more solid than that, something I could rely on, and so poor Pauline had to vanish. She disappeared just before all those spooky things began happening to me . . . rendering your Arizona alibis moot. Everybody knew you were close to her, and my little videotape, the one I said belonged to Wade, proves she would have done anything for you. It won't take the police long to see she was your helper in California, that you brought her to New York after the two of you scared me into killing myself, and that when you took up with sweet Kelly here you decided you didn't need poor Pauline anymore. And so up to Niagara Falls you went."

"But she was never here."

"That's right. I buried her at sea—one of the perks of having my own boat—after grabbing her license and a few other items that would let me bring her back to life if necessary. Kept my options open, like a real Death Trouper, just in case I had to do a minor rewrite."

The horror of the words seemed to constrict his heart as Jack listened to them, and he felt physically ill at the thought of the innocent girl. A dull anger crawled along with that sensation, but he knew better than to listen to it. What had Sam Colvin, Wade's wilderness guide, said about that?

You have to be very careful not to lose your cool in emergencies, Mr. Glynn.

Kelly seemed on the verge of saying something, and he gave her the slightest shake of his head. Antagonizing the murderer before them was only going to speed up the scene's ghastly conclusion.

I've got to keep him talking.

"So what points the police at me now?"

"Just a few things, but that's all they'll need. You know my journal, the one Emily sent after you took the job here?" In his mind, Jack saw the book's broken binding and the haphazard sewing job it had concealed. "She made a copy before she mailed it, and when they compare that to the original they're going to discover you removed a

383

few pages once you saw what was written inside. Innocent commentary about me spotting Pauline in Red Bend."

"Along with your double."

"Wasn't that inspired? *I* was the guy yelling in the street that night, and do you know not one of those yokels thought I looked like me? Must have overdone it on the makeup . . . but it was important because I needed an alibi for my visit to the old folks' home. An unavoidable trip, but so easily blamed on my evil twin." He beamed, as if enjoying a private joke. "They'll assume you hired someone who looked like me for that one. The same way I hired a girl who looked like Pauline to rent that hotel room near Niagara . . . a beautiful young stripper from Montreal, and believe me we didn't let that room go to waste."

"You kill her too?"

"Of course not. The story didn't need it."

"It needs something. I'm still not seeing how this all comes back to me."

"I'm not surprised. You never were any good at this. Don't you get it? You took out the pages of my journal that said Pauline was in Red Bend! Why would you do that if you weren't working together? The two of you wanted to scare me off so that you could get your old job—and your old girlfriend—back."

"No audience would ever buy that. And neither will the cops."

"It *is* a bit sketchy, isn't it? But what else are they likely to think when they find your new girlfriend shot to death right here, and you wearing gloves coated with the gunpowder residue?" He raised his free hand to show it was covered.

He then pointed that same hand out the open window, where Jack now saw that the supply pole had been extended into the darkness. "And swinging from a noose just like the mannequin that you hung here a few weeks ago?"

"Right here." Wendy led Kirk through a field of short grave markers in the dead of night. The stage had been transformed into the town's old cemetery, and the screens behind and above them showed a dark blue field of stars. A light wind, rattling frozen tree branches, breathed from the auditorium speakers. She stopped in front of a small, thin headstone that was tilted as if someone had kicked it. "This is my great-grandfather's spot. I can only come here at night, and I can't even complain when one of the locals messes with it."

She squatted down and gently lifted the prop, shifting it around until it fell back into place. While she was doing this, Kirk took a step or two backward and looked around as if fearing they would be seen.

Standing up, Wendy wiped her hands noisily before noticing that Kirk had moved away. "Don't be worried; nobody comes here this late at night."

"I know. In fact, I'm counting on that." Kirk's tone took on an edge, and he pulled a pistol out of the black-and-red jacket. He held it with his elbow tucked into his side, pointed at Wendy, and they simply stood there to give the audience a moment to react.

The two actors weren't disappointed. There was an audible inhalation as different members of the crowd realized that Kirk, the writer-historian outsider who'd been threatened by so many people in the town, was actually the murderer of Trask Saunders. The revelation was so stunning that the silence was broken by more than one breathless "No!" from the audience.

"What?" Wendy's voice broke on the single syllable, and she stepped backward in fear. "What are you doing? Why do you have a gun?"

"Oh, it's pretty standard equipment in my line of work. I've been carrying it the entire time I was here." A rapid-fire succession of film clips went across the starry screens behind them, showing that Kirk's right hand had been inside his pocket every time he'd been threatened throughout the show. Moans flowed from the crowd as they watched Kirk being confronted by Puff's henchmen, then being shot at in the woods, and a few other instances when they'd failed to note his defensive posture. "You see, sweetheart, I'm not here to write the history of the bootlegging days. I'm here to make sure that ugly stories—you know, the crooked land deals and all those other things you told me about—don't ruin a certain someone's bid for higher office.

"That silly old man—" a picture of Trask Saunders flashed on the left-most screen among the stars "—just couldn't keep his mouth shut, so he had to go." Two more scenes rolled across the remaining screens so that the crowd saw them left-to-right, one of Trask conspiring with Kirk and the other showing him floating under the ice.

"But you, angel . . . you're the jackpot. You're not just the only other individual in this whole town who was willing to speak up, but you've actually got evidence of recent crimes, things that could end someone's political future. *And* you're that patsy stockbroker's great-granddaughter too!"

"But . . . but . . . the two of us . . . that was all an *act*?"

Kirk gave off a short laugh. "Oh, not that it wasn't fun, but yeah it was all in the name of finishing the job. And you want to know the best part? We're practically related. My family was part of the Seven

Seas Gang—the only ones whose last name didn't start with C. My people didn't like it when things around here got so peaceful, so they went to the big city looking for work. We've been with a certain well-known family down there ever since, handling jobs like this one. A nice little clean-up crew, if you will."

He extended the pistol as if preparing to shoot. "Amazing how three generations later everything's the same. I'm the one holding the gun and you're the sap who didn't see it coming."

"Stop! Don't do it!" The voice was male, emanating from stage left. Robert Hale, the politician who had tried to scare Kirk away, stepped out onstage dressed in the same blue parka and holding a pistol aimed at the assassin.

"What are you doing here?" Kirk shouted, turning his back on Wendy so he could face the new threat. "You can't be here! They told me to keep you out of this!"

"They? Who's they?"

"Just some people that want to see you in high places. Now you're not supposed to be involved in this, so just walk away—"

"Not a chance! I'm sick of this Seven Seas nonsense! Sick! Do y'hear? I don't care what my grandfather might have done eighty years ago! It all stops here! Put the gun down!"

"Put the gun down?" Kirk motioned behind him with his free hand, without actually looking at Wendy. "Do you have any idea what she's got on your people? And not just your grandfather, either —your dad, your brother, even your father-in-law! It'll *bury* you!"

Wendy moved with desperate speed, bending over and wrenching her forebear's headstone out of the frozen ground. Raising it high, she slammed it down on the back of Kirk's head. He collapsed as if actually knocked unconscious, and a primitive roar of approval burst from the crowd. Wendy let the moment land, standing there clutching the stone while pretending to be fighting for breath. Hale lowered the gun and took an uncertain step forward, giving the applause a chance to go silent.

Approaching the prostrate form, he put the gun back inside his coat and stood there looking down. "I'd say *you're* the one who's gonna get buried, buster."

The crowd erupted as the curtain closed.

Kelly's hand slowly slipped into Jack's, and he tried to see her out of the corner of his eye. She was staring fixedly at Ryan, but her insistent squeezing was trying to tell him something. The rich man, who'd been looking out into the darkness as if enjoying the image of Jack twisting in the wind, now looked back at them. His gaze was so distant that Jack feared he'd already reached a terrible decision point, and so he tried to get him talking again.

"So why go to all this trouble? You had me out in the woods, and we've been alone together since then. It would have been easy. Why wait until now?"

The dull glow of the overhead bulb silhouetted Ryan's head as he moved closer. "Oh, I had no intention of killing you in the woods, Jack. I sabotaged your ski as a prank, just one more indication that somebody was out to harm you, and then it all played out so perfectly that I just couldn't resist torturing you for a while.

"In fact, I turned off the jammer when your friends started crashing around out there. If you'd kept your head and tried calling for help after that, you'd've been picked up in no time."

Kelly's hand tugged at Jack's ever so slightly, as if urging him to come with her somewhere. He couldn't fathom the message, but Ryan kept talking anyway.

"You see, this is the part you never understood. The high point. Even if I made it look like you killed yourself out there, it wouldn't have had the *impact* that I was always trying to teach you. Your stuff was always so understated that when the big moments in your plays came and went, almost nobody noticed."

"It's called subtlety. It's called giving the audience a little credit."

"It's dull, is what it is. And it doesn't get the message across. Like if I'd just offed you one night—how would that have served my purpose? Sure, the cops would have linked you to the old man and Pauline and it probably would have destroyed the troupe . . . lousy bunch of backstabbers that they are . . . but I needed to show Allison that she was right about picking me and wrong about picking you."

The hand was actually pulling him closer, and Jack realized with a shock what Kelly was suggesting. A moment earlier he wouldn't have believed it possible to be more scared, but just the thought of what she wanted to do proved that wrong.

"And so that's why it has to be this way. You almost saved yourself when you took up with this bimbo—" Kelly's hand practically crushed Jack's at that moment "—but then I saw that it really didn't change anything. Even if you dropped Allison, she'd still chase after you in Hollywood. No, she has to see what a wrong turn you really were, Jack.

"And besides, I've already murdered two people and I need to point the cops somewhere."

Kelly made her move just then, and it was everything Jack had feared. It really wasn't much of a feat, and she'd done it many times in the past, but the movement had never frightened him before now. In two simple actions, she reached across him and levered herself into his lap.

Ryan looked down at them with a disappointed sneer. "Oh, this is just too darling. Shielding the man you love. Taking the bullet for him. I'm touched."

"You're also wrong." The same spite was in Kelly's voice, and Jack slid his arms around her waist out of fear that she meant to use him as a launch pad. "You shoot me right now, there's no way the police will believe Jack did it."

Ryan canted his head to one side, considering her words. He didn't look worried, but it was clear he was reviewing the angles. Kelly didn't give him a chance to finish.

"That's right, shithead. Any bullet you fire will go through both of us. How you going to explain that one?"

"I'm not." Ryan pointed the pistol at one of her knees. "Turns out you are quite the monster after all, Jack. Tearing up your girlfriend this way before you killed her—"

"Ryan."

The voice was low, but it still seemed to ring out in the cold air. Both Jack and Kelly, focused on their tormentor until then, turned their heads toward the sound at the same time. Ryan didn't turn, but he did raise the pistol so it pointed toward the ceiling.

At the stairway entrance, the head and shoulders of Wade Parker were visible. He was wearing a dark jacket over the shirt and tie rig he'd been sporting at the Playhouse, and was balancing a large pistol against the floorboards.

Ryan shifted his feet slowly, making a gradual turn with the gun still pointed skyward. His face wore a pained expression, and his shoulders slumped just a bit when he saw the head at the stairs.

"Hello, Wade." His voice was almost a whisper. "I knew I should have sidelined you at the very beginning."

"Listen to me, Ryan. I've wanted to kill you as long as I've known you. Don't make it easy for me. Walk over to the open window and throw the gun out."

As if serving a tennis lob ball, Ryan dropped his gun hand and gently swung it in the direction of the yawning blackness. The heavy pistol disappeared through the opening as if it were nothing more than a wadded up piece of paper.

"Thank you, Ryan. Now move over to the window like I told you. Jack, you and Kelly stay put."

Ryan lowered his arms and meekly walked to the opening. He looked out into the darkness as if admiring its beauty, and then turned to face Wade. "So tell me, Advance Man: Where'd I go wrong?"

"Right at the start." Wade came up into the cab, keeping as much distance between him and Ryan as possible. "Vain guys like you don't do it with a shotgun."

"Ah."

"You also blew it with that newspaper article in Red Bend. Took me awhile, but I traced the payment you made to that reporter."

"Unavoidable. I had to connect the old man to the troupe."

"And then, of course, there was this." Wade pointed his free hand at the cell jammer on the center table. "I took Jack's phone all over that ski trail the day he was rescued, and it worked just fine. So somebody . . . somebody who knew the equipment . . . had to have blocked his signal that night.

"That's why I didn't give him a different phone when I got back."

Ryan's face pinched up in discomfort. "I wondered about that."

"You should have. Funny thing about jammers: They have their own electronic signature, and they can be traced just like the phone they're blocking. I've had a tracker set up in this area for weeks, but I didn't get a hit until tonight. You had to test it, didn't you?"

"I hadn't used it in so long. I wanted to be sure."

"I got a signal from the tracker earlier, told me a jammer like yours had briefly activated nearby. I figured you'd try something during the show, so I was ready to move when Jack pushed his way out of the theater. Rode here in the back of his truck, hidden by all that camping gear he carries. He drove me right up here."

"So you heard everything."

"I heard enough."

Ryan glanced behind him at the darkness again, and Jack knew what his old partner was thinking. He pushed Kelly off and started to rise from the floor.

"Stop right there, Jack. He's still dangerous." Wade's eyes didn't move from Ryan.

The rich man smiled weakly, looking down at the floorboards and then back over at the advance man. "Not going to let them put me in a cage, Wade."

"Neither would I."

"Don't do it, Ryan." Jack called out, ignoring Wade's order and coming to his feet. "You've got money, Emily will get you the best lawyers . . . you don't know what's going to happen."

"Yes he does."

"Yes I do."

Kelly stood up behind him, but Jack was hardly aware of her. In his mind he saw an old man plummeting through the air and a brunette girl sinking beneath the waves. "Not like this, Ryan! Come on, don't end it this way!"

The other writer backed toward the window ledge, his eyes on Jack. "It's like I always told you: Actors are all about entrances, but we writers are all about exits. Pay attention; this'll be a good one."

He hopped up onto the ledge in a sitting position, and then kicked himself over backward. He was gone in an instant, but not before Kelly's arms wrapped around Jack's waist like iron bands, rooting him to the spot just as he was about to leap.

Wade crossed the space quickly, looking out and down with squinted eyes. Apparently satisfied by what he saw, he turned to the others. "Wait here until I call for you."

And then he went down the stairs.

Wade dropped them off near the Playhouse. He was at the wheel of Kelly's car, which he planned to exchange for his own before heading back to the watch tower. Fireworks were exploding over Round Pond, and both of the outdoor screens that had broadcast the play were now playing music videos. There was a carnival atmosphere to it all, with people dancing on the camp basketball courts while others celebrated in the open fields.

The doors to the Playhouse were wide open, and a party raging inside had spilled out onto the veranda. Jack and Kelly sat in the back of the car, clutching each other in silence.

"I know this is rough, but you have to do it." Wade had talked to them briefly after covering Ryan's body and locking the fence around the tower. "Think of it as the biggest acting job of your lives. Tell yourselves this never happened . . . because as far as you're concerned, it didn't."

"But what about the body? And Pauline? And the old man in Red Bend?" Jack stammered, the true shock of the night's events finally coming home. Kelly had her arm around him, and had taken on a serene, almost satisfied mien.

"Don't worry about any of that. I'll bring the cops in later tonight, and talk to them myself. Just remember: You weren't there. You know nothing. As far as you're concerned, Ryan killed himself in January and that's that."

"But what are you going to tell them?"

"As much as they need to know. Ryan called me to the tower, I was astounded he was alive, and he confessed to the killings before jumping off." Wade leaned over the front seat, a look of sympathy on his face. "I'm going to try to convince the authorities to keep this quiet. Ryan was already officially dead, and Emily is a very rich, very connected woman who isn't going to like seeing any of this in public."

"But what do we tell everybody here, right now?"

Wade looked out at the dancing lights around the Playhouse. "About what? You two sneaked off to the dorms at the end of the second act and lost track of time. That's all."

He reached over to open the door. Kelly put a hand on Wade's shoulder, leaned across the seat, and kissed him on the cheek before sliding out of the car. Jack followed her as if sleepwalking, but the mystery writer in him was already running over Wade's story. Holding the door open, he leaned back into the car.

"Wade."

"Yeah."

"Make sure you find his gun."

"That's why I'm going back right now. The gun, the jammer, the noose . . . it'll all be gone before I make the call." He held up Jack's key ring. "This'll be in the rear wheel well of your truck once I move it down the road. *Don't* forget to go get it."

They nodded at each other gravely, and Jack shut the door. The car slowly pulled away, and Kelly took his arm. They were already being recognized, and Jack heard Puff yelling his name from a distance. Looking up, he saw that the principal cast had taken control of the cupola on the Playhouse roof. He recognized Kirk and Sally in the front, still wearing parts of their costumes, waving to the crowd and holding champagne bottles. Allison came up next to the two young actors just then, catching his eye and blowing him a kiss. He waved back while fighting off a sudden attack of tears.

Kelly clutched his arm tightly, looking at him with real concern, until he pointed up at the players on the roof. Adopting a happy expression, she waved at the cupola while carefully propelling him toward the stairs. They passed through a raucous gauntlet of shoulder slaps and shouted congratulations, and halfway along Jack realized that Kelly's authorship of the play had been revealed during their absence. Above them, the banner of Death Troupe snapped gaily in the night sky. The masked Janus faces came together as the fabric billowed, and came apart again, over and over, to reveal the death's head between them.

The symbol jolted him into a realization that should have come much earlier, when Wade had first mentioned the preposterous notion that he could contact the authorities and convince them to keep mum.

He leaned over and spoke directly into Kelly's ear, somehow sure she already knew.

"Wade's not going to call the police."

In his racing mind, Jack saw the advance man bundling up Ryan's body and driving off with it. Concealing it somewhere far from the town so that Emily's helpers could retrieve it, possibly for a secret burial in an empty grave in Maine. Or unrolling the bundle over a deep ravine so that the body would appear to be that of a man who had jumped to his death—if the remains were ever discovered at all.

Kelly's hand came up behind his head, and she touched her temple to his. "I know. I know. But I'm not sorry. It's the only way to protect the town . . . and the troupe."

Jack shook his head as if to clear it, reliving the horror of what had almost happened. Ryan's insane eyes in the tower's dim light. Kelly's bravery and Wade's coldness. A set of boots disappearing into the night air.

He pulled her in close before whispering a truth he had not known until that instant.

"I'm not sorry either."

I'm glad he's gone. Finally.

They got up the stairs and into the lobby, where a succession of familiar faces began coming out of the crowd. Tillman sweeping Kelly up in his arms, laughing and calling her a deceitful little thing while swinging her in a circle. Bib pounding Jack on the shoulder, shouting that they'd never had a chance in hell of figuring this one out, now did they? Gary whispering in his ear that he'd made a small fortune on the betting, thanking him for not including a drowning. And then Barron himself, stepping between Jack and Kelly, one arm around each of them, his mere presence silencing the crowd as if parting the waters.

"Ladies and gentlemen, as promised: I give you Jack Glynn and Kelly Sykes, the playwrights of tonight's show!"

The applause was mixed with hoarse cheers, but the crowd was already too inebriated to stay focused for long. The Lawtons took hold of Kelly at that point, and a mob of Schuyler Mills residents gathered around the three of them. Barron kept his arm around Jack, and easily maneuvered him off to the side.

"Look at her. She's a natural. I knew it from the moment I met her. And you two are going to write some great plays for the troupe."

Jack turned shocked eyes to the Director, but the older man mistook the emotion.

392

"I mean it, Jack. Tonight was the best one yet. Sure, I take credit for blowing their concentration with Glenda—not that she didn't do a marvelous job—but you two wrote an outstanding play. I thought the crowd was going to tear the place apart when Wendy brained poor Kirk with that headstone. What symbolism!

"So what do you say? The next one's not for a year, so there's plenty of time for you two to take a little vacation." The Director was behind him now, a hand lightly resting on his shoulder while Jack watched the throng around Kelly.

Barron's voice was barely audible above the crowd when he finished his pitch. "I always thought you two were a better couple."

THE END

About the Author

Vincent H. O'Neil brings a wealth of life experience to his writing. After graduating from West Point, he served as an infantry platoon leader in the 10th Mountain Division at Fort Drum, New York—just outside the Adirondack region. Following that assignment, he traveled to the Republic of Panama and commanded a paratroop company in the 1-508th Airborne.

He is a graduate of the Defense Language Institute's Mandarin Chinese program, and holds a Master of Arts in International Affairs from The Fletcher School of Law and Diplomacy. Among his many different experiences, he has provided consulting services to a software development firm, managed risk in a major corporation, created marketing campaigns, and worked as an apprentice librarian.

After writing in his spare time for many years, he finally got published by winning the St. Martin's Press "Malice Domestic" Writing Competition in 2005.

His critically-acclaimed debut novel *Murder in Exile* was followed by three more books in the Frank Cole / Exile series: *Reduced Circumstances*, *Exile Trust,* and *Contest of Wills*.

www.vincenthoneil.com